EVERYMAN'S LIBRARY

EVERYMAN,
I WILL GO WITH THEE,
AND BE THY GUIDE,
IN THY MOST NEED
TO GO BY THY SIDE

JULIAN BARNES

FLAUBERT'S PARROT

A HISTORY OF THE WORLD IN 10½ CHAPTERS

WITH AN INTRODUCTION
BY SARAH CHURCHWELL

EVERYMAN'S LIBRARY
Alfred A. Knopf New York London Toronto

348

THIS IS A BORZOI BOOK
PUBLISHED BY ALFRED A. KNOPF

US website: www.randomhouse.com/everymans

ISBN: 978-0-307-96143-3 (US)
978-1-84159-348-7 (UK)

A CIP catalogue reference for this book is available from the British Library

Library of Congress Cataloging-in-Publication Data
Barnes, Julian.
Flaubert's parrot; A history of the world in 10½ chapters / by Julian Barnes;
with an introduction by Sarah Churchwell.
p.   cm.—(Everyman's library)
"This is a Borzoi book."
Includes bibliographical references.
ISBN 978-0-307-96143-3
I. Barnes, Julian. A history of the world in 10½ chapters   II. Title.
PR6052.A6657F56   2012   2012020823
823'.914—dc23   CIP

Book design by Barbara de Wilde and Carol Devine Carson
Typeset in the UK by AccComputing, North Barrow, Somerset
Printed and bound in Germany by GGP Media GmbH, Pössneck

GENERAL CONTENTS

————

INTRODUCTION

Musing on the 'object of poetry', Pascal suggested in his *Pensées* that 'As we speak of poetical beauty, so ought we to speak of mathematical beauty and medical beauty. But we do not do so; and the reason is that we know well what is the object of mathematics, and that it consists in proofs, and what is the object of medicine, and that it consists in healing. But we do not know in what grace consists, which is the object of poetry.' If grace is the object of poetry, is truth the object of history – and if it is, do we know in what truth consists? Or should history seek something less grandiose, more human and more marvellous than the truth?

For more than thirty years, Julian Barnes has been asking these (and other) questions in beautiful novels that approach weighty matters with a light touch, novels that feature poetical grace, historical objects, resistance to proofs, searches for truth, a confirmed Francophilia, and even the occasional doctor. Barnes challenges received categorical distinctions and received ideas, while proving to us all that poetry, philosophy, biography, history and fiction need not – indeed, should not – be cleanly divided from each other. And he suggests that beauty can be found in the most unexpected places, if we have the wit to look for it. Mostly we don't, but evidently he has not yet despaired of us.

It was clear from the start of Barnes's career that here was a writer of talent – his first book, *Metroland* (1980), won the Somerset Maugham award for a first novel. But it was Barnes's third novel, *Flaubert's Parrot* (1984), that established his reputation at home and abroad, and that for many readers remains his masterpiece. When he won the Man Booker prize in 2011 for *The Sense of an Ending*, Barnes was asked the inevitable question about his favourite of his books; he was quoted saying that he remains 'very attached' to *Flaubert's Parrot*. It seems an apt metaphor for a book about fixations.

Early reviewers of Barnes were prone to comment on his disquieting tendency to write 'essays' as much as 'novels', his persistent habit of jumping out of the boxes into which they were busily trying to shove him. (His first job was as a lexicographer, working for the *Oxford English Dictionary,* so Barnes would presumably have been unimpressed by efforts to draw rigid, or even useful, distinctions between a word meaning 'attempt' and a word meaning 'new'.) Their dogged efforts at categorizing a writer who was cheerfully demolishing their categories now seem rather touching: the word 'postmodern', in particular, was cited with fervent regularity, a totemic charm to ward off the gods of misrule. The truth, etymologically speaking, is that even the distinction between fact and fiction is nugatory: both terms originated in the Renaissance, when a fact meant a thing done or performed, and fiction meant the act of fashioning or imitating. Julian Barnes's novels do both, with panache; *Flaubert's Parrot* is a fusion of fact and fiction, a novel and an essay, an unconventional biography, a fictional autobiography, an autobiographical fiction, a fiction about biography and a biography of fictions. One of the things that Flaubert teaches us, it suggests, is 'to dissect out the constituent parts of reality, and to observe that Nature is always a mixture of genres'. *Flaubert's Parrot* is also a mixture of genres and it is *sui generis,* which is to say it is in a class by itself.

In my own literary history, I arrived at *Flaubert's Parrot* working backwards, so to speak, from Barnes's fifth novel, *A History of the World in 10½ Chapters,* published in 1989, when I was studying literature as an undergraduate. Someone gave me a copy, to whom I should be eternally grateful if only I could remember who it was. I had never read anything like it; *A History* transformed my ideas of what literature could do, of what fiction could be. For starters, it appeared that it could be non-fiction. And art history, geopolitical history, religious history, a meditation on love, faith, death and other catastrophes, including art and cannibalism. It could be funny, and dispense with unity of character, setting, or plot; it could have a full-colour fold-out of Géricault's *The Raft of the Medusa* stuck right in its middle; it could do anything it pleased. I was dazzled and delighted: the book coloured my mind, as Emily Brontë once said, like wine colouring water. It is a novel that insists on the priority of ideas, even as it recognizes the world as a place with little time for and

viii

less interest in them. It is a series of interlocked essays, which understand that just because a writer is thinking hard doesn't mean he has permission to bore his reader to death; it uses fiction and imagination to explore ideas with drama and wit. I adored it. My voyage of discovery took me next to the inimitable, brilliant *Flaubert's Parrot*, the book that taught me in no uncertain terms that critical writing could be creative and that creative writing could be critical, forever changing my approach to my own writing and thinking. Barnes is what they call a writer's writer: his verbal finesse sometimes borders on legerdemain, it is so inventive, surprising, and playful. He opens up words, even as he opens our eyes and our minds.

Its American publisher called *Flaubert's Parrot* 'a novel in disguise'. One of its disguises is the detective story; it is also literary criticism in camouflage. Virginia Woolf famously once told a roomful of undergraduates at Cambridge, 'Don't begin by being a critic; begin by being a writer.' Geoffrey Braithwaite, the narrator of *Flaubert's Parrot*, may remark that he's 'saving Virginia Woolf for when I'm dead' (he also announces, 'Let me tell you why I hate critics'), but surely this is one statement of hers with which he would concur. Braithwaite objects to contemporary writers, each of whom, he says, 'seem to do one thing well enough, but fail to realise that literature depends on doing several things well at the same time.' This can be no less true for the critic of literature than for its author: they all need to realize that literature must do several things well at once. At one point, Braithwaite shares some of the laws he would pass if he were a 'dictator of fiction', including a total ban on novels about other novels, on plots depending on incest or coincidence, and a partial ban on novels set on university campuses. If I were a dictator of literary criticism, I would force all aspiring critics to begin as writers, and then to read *Flaubert's Parrot* repeatedly until they begin to appreciate its artfulness and dexterity, its intricate machinery; until it reminds them that they are supposed to begin, and end, with a love of words and some kind of lingering faith in their meaning. They must then find a way to reconcile this faith with a cold-eyed admission of the foolish inadequacy of language. 'Mystification is simple,' Braithwaite rightly declares. 'Clarity is the hardest thing of all.'

Flaubert's Parrot tells the story of an eccentric and erratic quest for a peculiar poetic object, one that essays in the etymological sense of putting to the proof, the testing of excellence. Geoffrey Braithwaite, retired doctor, widower, and amateur Flaubert enthusiast, stumbles across a parrot that purports to be the original stuffed parrot that inspired – and irritated – Flaubert as he composed *Un coeur simple*. But then Braithwaite finds another stuffed parrot that also claims to be Flaubert's inspiration. The discovery triggers a series of ruminations on the search for origins and inspirations, and on the relationship between writers and words, between the literal and the figurative, between literature and life, between reader and writer. 'Who needs whom more?' Braithwaite asks at the end of his 'Dictionary of Accepted Ideas', which offers an ironic version of Flaubert's *Dictionnaire des idées reçues*. 'Discuss without concluding.'

Most great books resist summary (if their ideas can be articulated so briefly, then those ideas probably do not require a book to elaborate them), but *Flaubert's Parrot* is especially intransigent; indeed Braithwaite forestalls any attempt at summary by pointing out the inadequacy of précis in cases such as personal advertisements, which 'aren't lying – indeed, they're all trying to be utterly sincere – but they aren't telling the truth'. Braithwaite is such a sprightly, amusing guide to the difficulty in accessing the truth that we may not realize for some time that the novel he inhabits has almost entirely dispensed with a plot. But if very little happens, in the traditional sense, that doesn't mean that nothing is going on; instead of action, we get ideas (received and original), variations, versions, claims and counter-claims, quotations, *aperçus* and aphorisms. Barnes offers two chronologies of Flaubert's life: both are true, and yet they seem mutually incompatible. Put crudely, one is the 'happy' version of Flaubert's life, the other the 'sad' version; one focuses on success, the other on death and despair. We see Flaubert's mistress, Louise Colet, long dismissed as little more than a pest, the whining distraction who kept intruding on the great man's art ('tedious, importunate, promiscuous woman'). And then in a virtuosic flourish, Barnes gives us Louise Colet's perspective, the story as she might have seen it ('brave, passionate, deeply misunderstood woman'), in which

Flaubert becomes the parrot, rather than the wild beast he fancied himself. We get dictionary entries, quotations, taxonomies, chronologies, lists, catalogues, bestiaries: fragments to shore against the ruins of our certainty. 'Demand violently: how can we know anybody?'

Looked at from one angle, *Flaubert's Parrot* is a novel about devotion, a celebration of literary obsession and a display of mastery. It catches the gaps in biography, showing the impossibility of ever reconstructing a life, especially the life of a great writer resistant to being written about. A refusal of the biographical enterprise and a recherché celebration of it, *Flaubert's Parrot* is a treasure hunt, a scavenger hunt, and a confrontation, amused and melancholic, with the detritus of history. In fact, the novel elegantly laces together Pascal's three beauties: the poetic, the mathematical and the medical. The poetic is embodied by the great bear, Gustave Flaubert, the subject and object of most of the novel's ruminations (it is also embodied, more comically, in the decaying, multiplying parrot); the mathematical is implied by the book's proliferation of enumerations and lists, its interest in figures and symbols ('poetry is a subject as precise as geometry,' Flaubert declares at one point); and the medical is the profession of both Geoffrey Braithwaite and Flaubert's father. One of the book's motifs is the rebuke it offers to the notion that the purpose of literature is spiritual uplift, or 'healing': 'Do you want art to be a healer?' Braithwaite demands. 'Send for the AMBULANCE GEORGE SAND. Do you want art to tell the truth? Send for the AMBULANCE FLAUBERT: though don't be surprised, when it arrives, if it runs over your leg.'

In an interview celebrating the twentieth anniversary of the publication of *Flaubert's Parrot,* Julian Barnes explained that the genesis of his novel was a trip he'd taken to Normandy during which he encountered the two parrots, both of which claimed to be the original: 'What if someone – clearly not me, but someone sufficiently interested in Flaubert, someone whose life might have parallels and points of bouncing contact with Flaubert's work and perhaps life – were to have the same experience? It could be the opening – or perhaps clinching – moment in a story about life and art, about France and

England, about the pursuit of the writer by the reader, and that moment of contact – practical yet mystical – between the two of them.' Bouncing contact is the method: Barnes puts his finger on the scale, and up another part of the story bounces, like quicksilver.

Braithwaite's profession is one way he bounces against Flaubert, an author who was famously caricatured bending over the dissected body of Emma Bovary and triumphantly flourishing aloft her heart; Flaubert was accused for years of being too scientific, too heartless, too diagnostic in his fiction. Moreover, by focusing our attention on Braithwaite Barnes reminds us, obliquely, that *Madame Bovary* is not a story framed around Emma, but around Charles Bovary; it opens with his youth, not hers, and ends with his death; there are two Madame Bovarys, Braithwaite points out. Charles Bovary is also, by no coincidence, a doctor, and it turns out that Braithwaite's late wife Ellen shares more with Emma Bovary than just the same initials. *Flaubert's Parrot* emerges, through a version of what it calls 'the Mauriac game' – defining people or stories not directly, but indirectly, through other stories, perspectives, reflections and refractions – as a kind of reframing of *Madame Bovary*, a fact that considerably undermines Braithwaite's dismissal of 'novels about other novels'. *Flaubert's Parrot* is about parroting Flaubert.

Julian Barnes seems perfectly prepared to admit that he, too, is Flaubert's parrot. At one point Braithwaite criticizes a writer for getting his facts wrong in 'a well-praised first novel in which the narrator – who is both sexually inexperienced and an amateur of French literature – comically rehearses to himself the best way to kiss a girl without being rebuffed: "With a slow, sensual, irresistible strength, draw her gradually towards you while gazing into her eyes as if you had just been given a copy of the first, suppressed edition of *Madame Bovary*." I thought this was quite neatly put,' Braithwaite remarks, 'indeed rather amusing. The only trouble is,' he adds, 'there's no such thing as a "first, suppressed edition of *Madame Bovary*" ... I expect the young novelist (it seems unfair to give his name) was thinking of the "first, suppressed edition" of *Les Fleurs du mal*. No doubt he'll get it right it in time for his second edition; if there is one.' Naming the young novelist may have been unfair, but it would also have been unwise: his name was Julian Barnes, and the novel was *Metroland*.

If, as I said a moment ago, looked at from one angle *Flaubert's Parrot* is a story of devotion, from a more straightforward perspective it is a story of adultery. This means it is also, necessarily, about fidelity: to another person, to a writer, to the past, to an idea, to a belief. Flaubert's fidelity to his art is a constant theme; Braithwaite's fidelity to the truth over the facts is another. 'Books are where things are explained to you,' Braithwaite remarks; 'life is where things aren't.' Flaubert teaches him about loneliness, and provides a perverse solace. Braithwaite is trying to come to terms with his wife's actions, and he is trying to avoid thinking about them all together; his interest in Flaubert both reveals and conceals his deeper, more painful preoccupations. Both fixations involve trying to understand the past, an impossible proposition.

'I'm not sure what I believe about the past,' Braithwaite admits: 'The past is a distant, receding coastline, and we are all in the same boat ... But this is an illusion.' It is an illusion not least because it is a metaphor – the same metaphor that famously closes another remarkably economical novel featuring an unreliable narrator trying (and failing) to understand the people around him. The famous closing of *The Great Gatsby*, narrated by the self-deceiving Nick Carraway, puts us all in the same boat as well, beating against the current of history. As it happens, adultery is also the engine that drives the plot in *Gatsby*, but there is nothing so active as Nick Carraway's nostalgia at work in Barnes's novel; no worries about some broken promise called the American Dream, just a constant irony that sees disappointment as no less inevitable, but considerably less surprising.

The metaphor of the voyage, with its attendant discoveries, shipwrecks, our tendency to be marooned, adrift, boats swamped by history, is the leitmotif that links the more symphonic *A History of the World in 10½ Chapters*. Another novel that rejects novelistic conventions and is impossible to summarize, it ranges widely, even promiscuously, across eras, nations, characters and subjects. It rejects Marx's famous reworking of Hegel: 'History repeats itself, the first time as tragedy, the second time as farce'; and it demonstrates the proposition that history can repeat itself as fiction.

A History offers ten variations on the theme of survival; a meditation on what makes such survival worthwhile; and a rejection of the dogmatic human systems that lead to artificial, and lethal, division and categorization. If *Flaubert's Parrot* was about adultery, *A History* is about adulteration, the impossibility of separating the pure from the impure, the clean from the unclean. This, presumably, is why we get a 'half-chapter': because the world does not divide neatly into decimal categories. There will always be something left over, an excess, a ghost – in this case, a 'Parenthesis'.

The notion of survival is meaningless without death to define it, and so it should be no surprise to find death and decay lurking from the novel's opening pages, the history of humanity as a vessel forever carrying within it the seeds of its own destruction. Nor should it be a surprise to find religion loitering with intent, as it represents humankind's persistent effort to imagine a survival that might be absolute, rather than just relative: the ultimate survival is immortality. Which belief systems might prove adequate for navigating the voyage of life, or surviving the shipwreck of history? 'Myth will become reality, however sceptical we might be,' the narrator tells us, and proceeds to show us the truth of this postulate.

Sailing in an erratic way from ancient history to the present day, *A History* opens not with history but with myth, in a comic revision of Genesis and the Flood, told from the perspective of a stowaway woodworm on Noah's Ark. Lest anyone mistake this myth for fact, the opening sentence firmly plants the fantastic among the realistic: 'They put the behemoths in the hold along with the rhinos, the hippos and the elephants.' After Noah – drunken, incompetent, bigoted – fails to pilot mankind to safety, the next chapter rewrites the 1985 hijacking of the *Achille Lauro*, a cruise ship taken over by terrorists, to offer an ironic parable as a self-satisfied historian is forced to deliver a lecture retelling modern history from the perspective of the hijackers, who hijack his good intentions as well as history. Woodworms return in a hilarious send-up of an ecclesiastical trial in sixteenth-century France, as the Church attempts to excommunicate the woodworm for making a bishop lose his mind (Barnes slyly suggests that this was not very difficult). A woman thinks she is the survivor of nuclear fallout after Chernobyl, but may only have been hijacked by her own mind as her relationship falls apart. The *Medusa* is wrecked in 1816, and its survivors resort to cannibalism; Géricault's great painting of the raft is reproduced – resurrected – and prompts a meditation on the relationship between art and catastrophe. A devout Victorian woman is overcome by literalism in her belief that the real Noah's Ark must have survived history, and is waiting to be found on Mount Ararat, suggesting the destructiveness of our search for the real thing, our rampant faith that if we believe in it, there must be a sacred relic somewhere that will confirm our faith. (They are all materialists, or, as Braithwaite describes himself in *Flaubert's Parrot*, 'randy for relics'.)

'Three Simple Stories' follow, each a parable of survival and metaphorical shipwreck: first the *Titanic;* then the *St Louis,* the boat with Jewish refugees from Hitler that was left adrift as a raft of governments refused its passengers entry in 1939; finally a real-life Jonah and the whale, which becomes a kind of prototype for the refugee, for anyone shipwrecked by history. In 'Upstream!' an actor travels down – or is it up – the Amazon while making a film that reconstructs an historical trip down (or up) the river; both history and fiction end in death. An American astronaut has a conversion experience on a voyage to the moon, and goes on his own search for Noah's Ark on Mount Ararat, where, unlike the Victorian woman before him, he finds a sacred relic that confirms the belief he already held; the reader knows, as the astronaut does not, the true origins of the relic he finds. Finally we are offered 'The Dream', a version of Revelation that offers a vision – suitably ironic – of heaven. We move from genesis to afterlife, from Flood to Paradise. And two-thirds along the way comes the half-chapter, 'Parenthesis', a brief meditation on love that offers what might be the novel's *ars poetica:* 'The history of the world? Just voices echoing in the dark; images that burn for a few centuries and then fade; stories, old stories that sometimes seem to overlap; strange links, impertinent connections.' It is a wonderful use of 'impertinent', harking back to its archaic, literal meaning of inapt, not-pertinent. But the past is also officious, intrusive, presumptuous: it doesn't know its place. As one woman – 'the survivor' – tells us, 'Everything *is* connected, even the parts we don't like, especially the parts we don't like.' History is repetition; but it is also recapitulation, permutation; it is protean. 'Time dissolves the story into form, colour, emotion.'

Along the way, *A History* constantly questions humanity's invidious categorical divisions between clean and unclean, faithful and infidel, even human and animal. Those questions are answered by the book's symmetrical refusal to respect categorical artistic distinctions, between fiction and non-fiction, novel and essay, creative and critical, story and philosophy, history and art. Thus one chapter offers art history as the history of art: 'Shipwreck' is the section in *A History* that is closest in form to the method of *Flaubert's Parrot*. Its first half offers a factual chronicle of the wreck of the *Medusa* in 1816; its second an account of Géricault's 1819 *Scene of Shipwreck*, known ever since as *The Raft of the Medusa*. It is the transformation of catastrophe into art that fascinates the narrator; it tempts him into the extreme, and extremely tendentious, claim that 'what catastrophe is *for*' is to become art. (Demand violently: art may depend upon catastrophe but does it necessarily follow that catastrophe is there to provide art with inspiration? Discuss without concluding.) But it then becomes an account of the process of creation, the 'excitements' that can distract the artist from successful ideas, the artist's need to be prepared to distort or fictionalize the facts, to choose 'truth to art' over 'truth to life'. *A History* ends with a refusal of even the neat distinction between life and death, and reality and dreams; and it rejects the neat divisions of chapters, tossing in a half-chapter about love for good measure.

'If we look at the history of the world, it seems surprising that love is included. It's an excrescence, a monstrosity, some tardy addition to the agenda. It reminds me of those half-houses which according to normal criteria of map reading shouldn't exist,' says the narrator of 'Parenthesis', who identifies himself as someone named Julian Barnes, but will not cop to being precisely the same person as the author of the book we are reading. People will not survive the ruin of history; the narrator of

'Parenthesis' wants to believe that love might survive, but has serious doubts. Art survives longer than people, but it, too, rots eventually; history outlives us all, but it is transformed into myth and consolatory fable. It is certainly not truth, merely fabulation: 'We make up a story to cover the facts we don't know or can't accept; we keep a few true facts and spin a new story around them. Our panic and our pain are eased by soothing fabulation; we call it history.'

Reviewing a 2010 translation of *Madame Bovary* in the *London Review of Books*, Julian Barnes noted 'the Flaubertian virtues of compression, irony and an extreme sense of control'. Both *Flaubert's Parrot* and *A History of the World in 10½ Chapters* show how well Barnes has learned the lessons of the master. But to the virtues of compression, irony and control, Barnes also brings flair, fun, and an endless curiosity about the transformative processes of memory and history. These two novels showcase Barnes's range, but they share a binding interest in the importance of alternative, competing versions, of writers playing variations on themes. *Flaubert's Parrot* and *A History of the World in 10½ Chapters* accept that we can never find a definitive truth, but realize that we also cannot stop looking for one. The more we seek the definitive version, the more the alternative versions proliferate. 'We all know objective truth is not obtainable,' the narrator writes in 'Parenthesis', 'that when some event occurs we shall have a multiplicity of subjective truths which we assess and then fabulate into history, into some God-eyed version of what "really"' happened. This God-eyed version is a fake – a charming impossible fake ... But while we know this, we must still believe that objective truth is obtainable; or we must believe that it is 99 per cent obtainable; or if we can't believe this we must believe that 43 per cent objective truth is better than 41 per cent ... If we don't we're lost, we fall into beguiling relativity, we value one liar's version as much as another liar's version.'

Demand violently: how can we know anything? And yet how can we fail not to know something?

Discuss without concluding.

Sarah Churchwell

SELECT BIBLIOGRAPHY

BOOKS BY JULIAN BARNES

FICTION

Metroland, Jonathan Cape, London; St Martin's Press, New York, 1980.

Before She Met Me, Jonathan Cape, London, 1982; McGraw-Hill, New York, 1986.

Flaubert's Parrot, Jonathan Cape, London, 1984; Alfred A. Knopf, New York, 1985.

Staring at the Sun, Jonathan Cape, London, 1986; Alfred A. Knopf, New York, 1987.

A History of the World in 10½ Chapters, Jonathan Cape, London; Alfred A. Knopf, New York, 1989.

Talking it Over, Jonathan Cape, London; Alfred A. Knopf, New York, 1991.

The Porcupine, Jonathan Cape, London; Alfred A. Knopf, New York, 1992.

Cross Channel, Jonathan Cape, London; Alfred A. Knopf, New York, 1996.

England, England, Jonathan Cape, London, 1998; Alfred A. Knopf, New York, 1999.

Love, etc, Jonathan Cape, London, 2000; Alfred A. Knopf, New York, 2001.

The Lemon Table, Jonathan Cape, London; Alfred A. Knopf, New York, 2004.

Arthur & George, Jonathan Cape, London, 2004; Alfred A. Knopf, New York, 2005.

Pulse, Jonathan Cape, London; Alfred A. Knopf, New York, 2011.

The Sense of an Ending, Jonathan Cape, London; Alfred A. Knopf, New York, 2011.

NON-FICTION

Letters from London 1990–1995, Picador, London; Vintage, New York, 1995.

Something to Declare, Picador, London; Alfred A. Knopf, New York, 2002.

The Pedant in the Kitchen, Atlantic Books, London, 2003.

Nothing to be Frightened of, Jonathan Cape, London; Alfred A. Knopf, New York, 2008.

TRANSLATION

In the Land of Pain by Alphonse Daudet, Jonathan Cape, London; Alfred A. Knopf, New York, 2002.

BOOKS ABOUT JULIAN BARNES

CHILDS, PETER, *Julian Barnes (Contemporary British Novelists)*, Manchester University Press, Manchester, 2011.

GROES, SEBASTIAN and CHILDS, PETER (eds): *Julian Barnes (Contemporary Critical Perspectives)*, Continuum, London and New York, 2011.

GUIGNERY, VANESSA, *The Fiction of Julian Barnes: A Reader's Guide to Essential Criticism*, Palgrave Macmillan, Houndmills, Basingstoke and New York, 2006.

GUIGNERY, VANESSA and ROBERTS, RYAN, *Conversations with Julian Barnes*, University Press of Mississippi, Jackson, MS, 2009.

PATEMAN, MATTHEW, *Julian Barnes: Writers and Their Work* Northcote House, Tavistock, Devon, 2002.

CHRONOLOGY

DATE	AUTHOR'S LIFE	LITERARY CONTEXT
1946	Birth of Julian Barnes in Leicester, England (19 January).	Faulkner: *Portable Faulkner*. Auerbach: *Mimesis*.
1949		De Beauvoir: *The Second Sex*. Orwell: *Nineteen Eighty-Four*. Bowen: *The Heat of the Day*. Miller: *Death of a Salesman*.
1952		Waugh: *Sword of Honour Trilogy* (to 1961). Pym: *Excellent Women*. Dylan Thomas: *Collected Poems*.
1954		Golding: *Lord of the Flies*. Amis: *Lucky Jim*.
1955		Nabokov: *Lolita*. Highsmith: *The Talented Mr Ripley*.
1957	Attends City of London School.	Pasternak: *Doctor Zhivago*. Pinter: *The Birthday Party*. Waugh: *The Ordeal of Gilbert Pinfold*.
1959		
1961		Naipaul: *A House for Mr Biswas*. Heller: *Catch-22*.
1962		Nabokov: *Pale Fire*. Burgess: *A Clockwork Orange*. Lessing: *The Golden Notebook*. Solzhenitsyn: *One Day in the Life of Ivan Denisovich*. Bassani: *The Garden of the Finzi-Contini*.
1964	Reads Modern Languages at Magdalen College, Oxford.	Bellow: *Herzog*. Barthes: *Critical Essays*.
1966		Rhys: *Wide Sargasso Sea*.
1967		Márquez: *One Hundred Years of Solitude*.
1968	Graduates from Oxford, with Honours, and begins working as a lexicographer at the *Oxford English Dictionary*.	Solzhenitsyn: *Cancer Ward*.

Nuremberg trials. 'Iron Curtain' speech by Churchill.

Federal Republic of Germany established. Communist revolution in China.

Accession of Elizabeth II. Eisenhower is elected US President. Britain produces its first atomic bomb.

Vietnam War begins. Nasser gains power in Egypt.

Albert Einstein dies.

Macmillan becomes Prime Minister. Treaty of Rome: Common Market established.

Fidel Castro forms new government in Cuba. Conservative party wins UK general election with increased majority. The nation is told by Macmillan 'most of our people have never had it so good'.
John F. Kennedy elected President in the US. Erection of Berlin Wall.
Yuri Gagarin becomes first man in space.
Cuban missile crisis.

Khrushchev deposed in USSR and replaced by Brezhnev. Mandela imprisoned in South Africa (until 1990).
Mao launches Cultural Revolution in China.
Arab–Israeli Six Day War. Nigerian Civil War.

Student unrest throughout Europe and the US. Soviet-led invasion of Czechoslovakia. Assassination of Martin Luther King. Nixon US President.

DATE	AUTHOR'S LIFE	LITERARY CONTEXT
1969		First Booker Prize for fiction awarded in Britain.
1972		Stoppard: *Jumpers.*
1973		Murdoch: *The Black Prince.* Greene: *The Honorary Consul.*
1974		Stoppard: *Travesties.*
1975		Levi: *The Periodic Table.*
1976		
1977	Begins working at the *New Statesman* and *New Review.*	Vargas Llosa: *Aunt Julia and the Scriptwriter.* Morrison: *Song of Solomon.*
1978		Greene: *The Human Factor.* Murdoch: *The Sea, The Sea.*
1979	Begins work as a television reviewer for the *New Statesman* and then for the *Observer.*	Calvino: *If on a winter's night a traveller.* Kundera: *The Book of Laughter and Forgetting.* Penelope Fitzgerald: *Offshore.*
1980	*Metroland.*	Burgess: *Earthly Powers.* Golding: *Rites of Passage.*
1981	Receives the Somerset Maugham Award for *Metroland.*	Rushdie: *Midnight's Children.* Yourcenar: *Anna, Soror.*
1982	*Before She Met Me.*	Levi: *If Not Now, When?* Márquez: *Chronicle of a Death Foretold.*
1984	*Flaubert's Parrot* is published, and shortlisted for the Booker Prize.	Brookner: *Hotel du Lac.*
1985	Receives the Geoffrey Faber Memorial Prize for *Flaubert's Parrot.*	Márquez: *Love in the Time of Cholera.* Winterson: *Oranges are not the only Fruit.* Murdoch: *The Good Apprentice.*
1986	*Staring at the Sun.* Awarded the Prix Médicis for *Flaubert's Parrot,* and the E. M. Forster Award by the American Academy and Institute of Arts and Letters.	
1987	Receives the Gutenberg Prize.	Atwood: *The Handmaid's Tale.* Winterson: *Sexing the Cherry.* Morrison: *Beloved.*
1988	Receives the Grinzane Cavour Prize in Italy. He is made a Chevalier de l'Ordre des Arts et des Lettres.	Rushdie: *The Satanic Verses.* Carey: *Oscar and Lucinda.* Wolfe: *The Bonfire of the Vanities.* Larkin: *Collected Poems.*

CHRONOLOGY

HISTORICAL EVENTS

Americans land first man on the moon. British troops assume responsibility for security in Northern Ireland.
Bloody Sunday in Northern Ireland. Direct rule imposed by Britain.
Miners' strike. Energy crisis prompts state of emergency in Britain.

Resignation of Nixon following Watergate scandal.
End of Vietnam War. USSR and Western powers sign Helsinki Agreement.
Death of Mao Tse-Tung. Saddam Hussein becomes President of Iraq. Carter elected US President. Soweto massacre in South Africa.

Camp David Agreement between Carter (USA), Begin (Israel) and Sadat (Egypt).
Winter of Discontent in Britain. Strike of public sector workers, including dustmen and grave-diggers. Margaret Thatcher becomes first woman Prime Minister in UK. British rule in Zimbabwe (former Rhodesia) formally ends.
Soviet forces invade Afghanistan. Iran hostage crisis (to 1981). Carter and Brezhnev sign SALT-2.
Over 2 million people are unemployed in Britain, a level not reached since the 1930s. Many thousands of these are teenagers or young people. Lech Walesa leads strikes in Gdansk, Poland. Iran–Iraq war (to 1988).
Race riots in Liverpool and London. Reagan becomes US President.
President Sadat assassinated.
Falklands War between Britain and Argentina.

Famine in Ethiopia. British miners strike in March, and do not return to work for another year.

Gorbachev–Reagan summit. Nuclear explosion at Chernobyl.

Margaret Thatcher defeats Labour's Neil Kinnock, winning her third successive general election.

George Bush elected US President. Gorbechev announces big troop reductions suggesting end of Cold War. Benazir Bhutto is elected Prime Minister of Pakistan. Terrorist bomb destroys Pan Am flight 103 over Lockerbie.

DATE	AUTHOR'S LIFE	LITERARY CONTEXT
1989	*A History of the World in 10½* Chapters.	Ishiguro: *The Remains of the Day.* Martin Amis: *London Fields.*
1990		Byatt: *Possession.* Penelope Fitzgerald: *The Gate of Angels.* Updike: *Rabbit at Rest.*
1991	*Talking it Over,* for which he received the Prix Femina.	Márquez: *The General in his Labyrinth.* Okri: *The Famished Road.*
1992	*The Porcupine.*	Ondaatje: *The English Patient.*
1993	Awarded the Shakespeare Prize by the FVS Foundation.	
1994		Trevor: *Felicia's Journey.*
1995	*Letters from London.* He is made an Officier de l'Ordre des Arts et des Lettres.	Martin Amis: *The Information.* Murdoch: *Jackson's Dilemma.* Atkinson: *Behind the Scenes at the Museum.* Penelope Fitzgerald: *The Blue Flower.*
1996	*Cross Channel.*	
1997		McEwan: *Enduring Love.* Arundhati Roy: *The God of Small Things.*
1998	*England, England,* shortlisted for the Booker Prize.	Iris Murdoch and Ted Hughes die. Hughes: *Birthday Letters.* McEwan: *Amsterdam.*
1999		
2000	*Love, etc* (sequel to *Talking it Over*).	Atwood: *The Blind Assassin.* Ishiguro: *When We Were Orphans.* Martin Amis: *Experience.* Roth: *The Human Stain.*
2001		Lessing: *The Sweetest Dream.* McEwan: *Atonement.*
2002	*Something to Declare.*	
2003	*The Pedant in the Kitchen.*	

CHRONOLOGY

Collapse of Communist Empire in Eastern Europe. Fall of the Berlin Wall.
First democratic elections in USSR. Tienanmen Square massacre in China.
De Klerk becomes President of South Africa.
Margaret Thatcher ousted: John Major becomes Prime Minister in UK.
Iraq invades Kuwait. Nelson Mandela released from gaol after 27 years'
imprisonment. Yeltsin elected first leader of Russian Federation.

Gulf War. Central government in USSR suspended. War begins in former
Yugoslavia.

Bill Clinton elected US President. Britain forced to drop out of the
European Exchange Rate Mechanism on Black Wednesday.
Palestinian leader Arafat and Israeli Prime Minister Rabin sign peace
agreement in the US. Maastricht Treaty (creating European Union) ratified.
Mandela and ANC sweep to victory in South African elections. Civil war in
Rwanda. Russian military action against Chechen Republic. IRA ceasefire
announced. The Channel Tunnel is opened. Tony Blair succeeds the late
John Smith as leader of the Labour Party, hailing the advent of 'New Labour'.
Rabin is assassinated.

A huge bomb blast in Canary Wharf, London, brings to an end the uneasy
truce in Northern Ireland. President Clinton re-elected.
Tony Blair elected Prime Minister (first Labour government since 1979).
Princess Diana is killed in a car accident in Paris.

The *Washington Post* discloses a sexual liaison between President Clinton
and a White House intern. Northern Ireland Referendum accepts the Good
Friday Agreement; an assembly is elected. Omagh Bomb in August kills
29 people. Clinton orders air strikes against Iraq.
Serbs attack ethnic Albanians in Kosovo; US leads NATO in bombing of
Belgrade.
Milosevic's regime in the former Yugoslavia collapses. George W. Bush is
elected President of the US, although there is some controversy surrounding
the election results.

Al-Qaeda terrorist attacks of 9/11. US and allied military action against the
Taliban in Afghanistan.
US troops invade Afghanistan. Jacques Chirac re-elected as President of
France.
Iraq weapons crisis. American and British troops invade Iraq.

DATE	AUTHOR'S LIFE	LITERARY CONTEXT
2004	*The Lemon Table*. Barnes is made a Commandeur de l'Ordre des Arts et des Lettres. He also wins the Austrian State Prize for European Literature.	
2005	*Arthur & George*, shortlisted for the Booker Prize.	Banville: *The Sea*. Smith: *On Beauty*.
2007		
2008	*Nothing to be Frightened of.*	Philip Roth: *Indignation*.
2010		
2011	*Pulse.* *The Sense of an Ending,* winner of the Booker Prize. Awarded the David Cohen Prize for Literature, honouring a lifetime's achievement.	

CHRONOLOGY

HISTORICAL EVENTS

Terrorist bombings in Madrid. Beslan school hostage crisis. George W. Bush re-elected. Indian Ocean tsunami.

Blair re-elected as Prime Minister in Britain. Terrorist bombings in London. Provisional IRA formally orders end to its armed campaign (since 1969). First forced evacuation of settlers under Israel Unilateral Disengagement Plan. First parliamentary elections in Iraq since US-led invasion; Shia-led United Iraqi Alliance wins but does not obtain an absolute majority.

Nicolas Sarkozy becomes President of the French Republic. Blair resigns; succeeded by Gordon Brown as British Prime Minister. ANC elects new party leader, Jacob Zuma. Turkey targets Kurdish rebels in northern Iraq. Benazir Bhutto, leader of Pakistan People's Party, killed in a suicide bomb attack. Controversial presidential elections in Kenya see Kibaki claim a second term of office, triggering a wave of violent unrest.

Largest global recession since the Great Depression begins. Barack Obama becomes the first African-American to be elected US President.

British general election returns a hung parliament. Conservative leader David Cameron forms a coalition government with the Liberal Democrats. Osama Bin Laden is ambushed and killed by American forces in a house in Pakistan, and his body is dropped into the sea. French Government imposes a ban on headscarves in public life.

FLAUBERT'S
PARROT

To Pat

When you write the biography of a friend,
you must do it as if you were taking *revenge* for him.

FLAUBERT, *letter to Ernest Feydeau*, 1872

NOTE

I am grateful to James Fenton and the Salamander Press for permission to reprint the lines from 'A German Requiem' on page 100. The translations in this book are by Geoffrey Braithwaite; though he would have been lost without the impeccable example of Francis Steegmuller.

J.B.

CONTENTS

FLAUBERT'S PARROT

SIX NORTH AFRICANS were playing boule beneath Flaubert's statue. Clean cracks sounded over the grumble of jammed traffic. With a final, ironic caress from the fingertips, a brown hand dispatched a silver globe. It landed, hopped heavily, and curved in a slow scatter of hard dust. The thrower remained a stylish, temporary statue: knees not quite unbent, and the right hand ecstatically spread. I noticed a furled white shirt, a bare forearm and a blob on the back of the wrist. Not a watch, as I first thought, or a tattoo, but a coloured transfer: the face of a political sage much admired in the desert.

Let me start with the statue: the one above, the permanent, unstylish one, the one crying cupreous tears, the floppy-tied, square-waistcoated, baggy-trousered, straggle-moustached, wary, aloof bequeathed image of the man. Flaubert doesn't return the gaze. He stares south from the place des Carmes towards the Cathedral, out over the city he despised, and which in turn has largely ignored him. The head is defensively high: only the pigeons can see the full extent of the writer's baldness.

This statue isn't the original one. The Germans took the first Flaubert away in 1941, along with the railings and door-knockers. Perhaps he was processed into cap-badges. For a decade or so, the pedestal was empty. Then a Mayor of Rouen who was keen on statues rediscovered the original plaster cast – made by a Russian called Leopold Bernstamm – and the city council approved the making of a new image. Rouen bought itself a proper metal statue in 93 per cent copper and 7 per cent tin: the founders, Rudier of Châtillon-sous-Bagneux, assert that such an alloy is guarantee against corrosion. Two other towns, Trouville and Barentin, contributed to the project and received stone statues. These have worn less well. At Trouville Flaubert's upper thigh has had to be patched, and bits of his moustache have fallen off: structural wires poke out like twigs from a concrete stub on his upper lip.

Perhaps the foundry's assurances can be believed; perhaps this second-impression statue will last. But I see no particular grounds for confidence. Nothing much else to do with Flaubert has ever lasted. He died little more than a hundred years ago, and all that remains of him is paper. Paper, ideas, phrases, metaphors, structured prose which turns into sound. This, as it happens, is precisely what he would have wanted; it's only his admirers who sentimentally complain. The writer's house at Croisset was knocked down shortly after his death and replaced by a factory for extracting alcohol from damaged wheat. It wouldn't take much to get rid of his effigy either: if one statue-loving Mayor can put it up, another – perhaps a bookish party-liner who has half-read Sartre on Flaubert – might zealously take it down.

I begin with the statue, because that's where I began the whole project. Why does the writing make us chase the writer? Why can't we leave well alone? Why aren't the books enough? Flaubert wanted them to be: few writers believed more in the objectivity of the written text and the insignificance of the writer's personality; yet still we disobediently pursue. The image, the face, the signature; the 93 per cent copper statue and the Nadar photograph; the scrap of clothing and the lock of hair. What makes us randy for relics? Don't we believe the words enough? Do we think the leavings of a life contain some ancillary truth? When Robert Louis Stevenson died, his business-minded Scottish nanny quietly began selling hair which she claimed to have cut from the writer's head forty years earlier. The believers, the seekers, the pursuers bought enough of it to stuff a sofa.

I decided to save Croisset until later. I had five days in Rouen, and childhood instinct still makes me keep the best until last. Does the same impulse sometimes operate with writers? Hold off, hold off, the best is yet to come? If so, then how tantalising are the unfinished books. A pair of them come at once to mind: *Bouvard et Pécuchet*, where Flaubert sought to enclose and subdue the whole world, the whole of human striving and human failing; and *L'Idiot de la famille*, where Sartre sought to enclose the whole of Flaubert: enclose and subdue the master writer, the master bourgeois, the terror, the enemy, the sage. A stroke terminated the first project; blindness abbreviated the second.

I thought of writing books myself once. I had the ideas; I even made notes. But I was a doctor, married with children. You can only do one thing well: Flaubert knew that. Being a doctor was what I did well. My wife . . . died. My children are scattered now; they write whenever guilt impels. They have their own lives, naturally. 'Life! Life! To have erections!' I was reading that Flaubertian exclamation the other day. It made me feel like a stone statue with a patched upper thigh.

The unwritten books? They aren't a cause for resentment. There are too many books already. Besides, I remember the end of *L'Education sentimentale*. Frédéric and his companion Deslauriers are looking back over their lives. Their final, favourite memory is of a visit to a brothel years before, when they were still schoolboys. They had planned the trip in detail, had their hair specially curled for the occasion, and had even stolen flowers for the girls. But when they got to the brothel, Frédéric lost his nerve, and they both ran away. Such was the best day of their lives. Isn't the most reliable form of pleasure, Flaubert implies, the pleasure of anticipation? Who needs to burst into fulfilment's desolate attic?

I spent my first day wandering about Rouen, trying to recognise parts of it from when I'd come through in 1944. Large areas were bombed and shelled, of course; after forty years they're still patching up the Cathedral. I didn't find much to colour in the monochrome memories. Next day I drove west to Caen and then north to the beaches. You follow a series of weathered tin signs, erected by the Ministère des Travaux Publics et des Transports. This way for the Circuit des Plages de Débarquement: a tourist route of the landings. East of Arromanches lie the British and Canadian beaches – Gold, Juno, Sword. Not an imaginative choice of words; so much less memorable than Omaha and Utah. Unless, of course, it's the actions that make the words memorable, and not the other way round.

Graye-sur-Mer, Courseulles-sur-Mer, Ver-sur-Mer, Asnelles, Arromanches. Down tiny sidestreets you suddenly come across a place des Royal Engineers or a place W. Churchill. Rusting tanks stand guard over beach huts; slab monuments like ships' funnels announce in English and French: 'Here on the 6th June 1944 Europe was liberated by the heroism of the Allied Forces.' It is very quiet, and not at all sinister. At Arromanches I put two one-franc pieces into the Telescope Panoramique (Très Puissant 15/60 Longue Durée) and traced the curving morse of the Mulberry Harbour far out to sea. Dot, dash, dash, dash went the concrete caissons, with the unhurried water between them. Shags had colonised these square boulders of wartime junk.

I lunched at the Hôtel de la Marine overlooking the bay. I was close to where friends had died – the sudden friends those years produced – and yet I felt unmoved. 50th Armoured Division, Second British Army. Memories came out of hiding, but not emotions; not even the memories of emotions. After lunch I went to the museum and watched a film about the landings, then drove ten kilometres to Bayeux to examine that other cross-Channel invasion of nine centuries earlier. Queen Matilda's tapestry is like horizontal cinema, the frames joined edge to edge. Both events seemed equally strange: one too distant to be true, the other too familiar to be true. How do we seize the past? Can we ever do so? When I was a medical student some pranksters at an end-of-term dance released into the hail a piglet which had been smeared with grease. It squirmed between legs, evaded capture, squealed a lot. People fell over trying to grasp it, and were made to look ridiculous in the process. The past often seems to behave like that piglet.

On my third day in Rouen I walked to the Hôtel-Dieu, the hospital where Gustave's father had been head surgeon, and where the writer spent his childhood. Along the avenue Gustave Flaubert, past the Imprimerie Flaubert and a snack-bar called Le Flaubert: you certainly feel you're going in the right direction. Parked near the hospital was a large white Peugeot hatchback: it was painted with blue stars, a telephone number and the words AMBULANCE FLAUBERT. The writer as healer? Unlikely. I remembered George Sand's matronly rebuke to her younger colleague. 'You produce desolation,' she wrote, 'and I produce consolation.' The Peugeot should have read AMBULANCE GEORGE SAND.

At the Hôtel-Dieu I was admitted by a gaunt, fidgety *gardien* whose white coat puzzled me. He wasn't a doctor, a *pharmacien* or a cricket umpire. White coats imply antisepsis and clean judgment. Why should a museum caretaker wear one – to protect Gustave's childhood from germs? He explained that the museum was devoted partly to Flaubert and partly to medical history, then hurried me round, locking the doors behind us with noisy efficiency. I was shown the room where Gustave was born, his eau-de-Cologne pot, tobacco jar and first magazine article. Various images of the writer confirmed the dire early shift he underwent from handsome youth to paunchy, balding burgher. Syphilis, some conclude. Normal nineteenth-century ageing, others reply. Perhaps it was merely that his body had a sense of decorum: when the mind inside declared itself prematurely old, the flesh did its best to conform. I kept reminding myself that he had fair hair. It's hard to remember: photographs make everyone seem dark.

The other rooms contained medical instruments of the eighteenth and nineteenth centuries: heavy metal relics coming to sharp points, and enema pumps of a calibre which surprised even me. Medicine then must have been such an exciting, desperate, violent business; nowadays it is all pills and bureaucracy. Or is it just that the past seems to contain more local colour than the present? I studied the doctoral thesis of Gustave's brother Achille: it was called 'Some Considerations on the Moment of Operation on the Strangulated Hernia'. A fraternal parallel: Achille's thesis later became Gustave's metaphor. 'I feel, against the stupidity of my time, floods of hatred which choke me. Shit rises to my mouth as in the case of a strangulated hernia. But I want to keep it, fix it, harden it; I want to concoct a paste with which I shall cover the nineteenth century, in the same way as they paint Indian pagodas with cow dung.'

The conjunction of these two museums seemed odd at first. It made sense when I remembered Lemot's famous cartoon of Flaubert dissecting Emma Bovary. It shows the novelist flourishing on the end of a large fork the dripping heart he has triumphantly torn from his heroine's body. He brandishes the organ aloft like a prize surgical exhibit, while on the left of the drawing the feet of the recumbent, violated Emma are just visible. The writer as butcher, the writer as sensitive brute.

Then I saw the parrot. It sat in a small alcove, bright green and perky-eyed, with its head at an inquiring angle. '*Psittacus*', ran the inscription on the end of its perch: 'Parrot borrowed by G. Flaubert from the Museum of Rouen and placed on his work-table during the writing of *Un cœur simple*, where it is called Loulou, the parrot of Félicité, the principal character in the tale.' A Xeroxed letter from Flaubert confirmed the fact: the parrot, he wrote, had been on his desk for three weeks, and the sight of it was beginning to irritate him.

Loulou was in fine condition, the feathers as crisp and the eye as irritating as they must have been a hundred years earlier.

I gazed at the bird, and to my surprise felt ardently in touch with this writer who disdainfully forbade posterity to take any personal interest in him. His statue was a retread; his house had been knocked down; his books naturally had their own life – responses to them weren't responses to him. But here, in this unexceptional green parrot, preserved in a routine yet mysterious fashion, was something which made me feel I had almost known the writer. I was both moved and cheered.

On the way back to my hotel I bought a student text of *Un cœur simple*. Perhaps you know the story. It's about a poor, uneducated servant-woman called Félicité, who serves the same mistress for half a century, unresentfully sacrificing her own life to those of others. She becomes attached, in turn, to a rough fiancé, to her mistress's children, to her nephew, and to an old man with a cancerous arm. All of them are casually taken from her: they die, or depart, or simply forget her. It is an existence in which, not surprisingly, the consolations of religion come to make up for the desolations of life.

The final object in Félicité's ever-diminishing chain of attachments is Loulou, the parrot. When, in due course, he too dies, Félicité has him stuffed. She keeps the adored relic beside her, and even takes to saying her prayers while kneeling before him. A doctrinal confusion develops in her simple mind: she wonders whether the Holy Ghost, conventionally represented as a dove, would not be better portrayed as a parrot. Logic is certainly on her side: parrots and Holy Ghosts can speak, whereas doves cannot. At the end of the story, Félicité herself dies. 'There was a smile on her lips. The movements of her heart slowed down beat by beat, each time more distant, like a fountain running dry or an echo disappearing; and as she breathed her final breath she thought she saw, as the heavens opened for her, a gigantic parrot hovering above her head.'

The control of tone is vital. Imagine the technical difficulty of writing a story in which a badly-stuffed bird with a ridiculous name ends up standing in for one third of the Trinity, and in which the intention is neither satirical, sentimental, nor blasphemous. Imagine further telling such a story from the point of view of an ignorant old woman without making it sound derogatory or coy. But then the aim of *Un cœur simple* is quite elsewhere: the parrot is a perfect and controlled example of the Flaubertian grotesque.

We can, if we wish (and if we disobey Flaubert), submit the bird to additional interpretation. For instance, there are submerged parallels between the life of the prematurely aged novelist and the maturely aged Félicité. Critics have sent in the ferrets. Both of them were solitary; both of them had lives stained with loss; both of them, though full of grief, were persevering. Those keen to push things further suggest that the incident in which Félicité is struck down by a mail-coach on the road to Honfleur is a submerged reference to Gustave's first epileptic fit, when he was struck down on the road outside Bourg-Achard. I don't know. How submerged does a reference have to be before it drowns?

In one cardinal way, of course, Félicité is the complete opposite of Flaubert: she is virtually inarticulate. But you could argue that this is where Loulou comes in. The parrot, the articulate beast, a rare creature that makes human sounds. Not for nothing does Félicité confuse Loulou with the Holy Ghost, the giver of tongues.

Félicité + Loulou = Flaubert? Not exactly; but you could claim that he is present in both of them. Félicité encloses his character; Loulou encloses his voice. You could say that the parrot, representing clever vocalisation without much brain power, was Pure Word. If you were a French academic, you might say that he was *un symbole de Logos*. Being English, I hasten back to the corporeal: to that svelte, perky creature I had seen at the Hôtel-Dieu. I imagined Loulou sitting on the other side of Flaubert's desk and staring back at him like some taunting reflection from a funfair mirror. No wonder three weeks of its parodic presence caused irritation. Is the writer much more than a sophisticated parrot?

We should perhaps note at this point the four principal encounters between the novelist and a member of the parrot family. In the 1830s, during their annual holiday at Trouville, the Flaubert household regularly used to visit a retired sea-captain called Pierre Barbey; his ménage, we are told, included a magnificent parrot. In 1845 Gustave was travelling through Antibes, on his way to Italy, when he came across a sick parakeet which merited an entry in his diary; the bird used to perch carefully on the mudguard of its owner's light cart, and at dinnertime would be brought in and placed on the mantelpiece. The diarist notes the 'strange love' clearly evident between man and pet. In 1851, returning from the Orient via Venice, Flaubert heard a parrot in a gilt cage calling out over the Grand Canal its imitation of a gondolier: '*Fà eh, capo die.*' In 1853 he was again in Trouville; lodging with a *pharmacien*, he found himself constantly irritated by a parrot which screamed, '*As-tu déjeuné, Jako?*' and '*Cocu, mon petit coco.*' It also whistled '*J'ai du bon tabac.*' Was any of these four birds, in whole or in part, the inspiration behind Loulou? And did Flaubert see another living parrot between 1853 and 1876, when he borrowed a stuffed one from the Museum of Rouen? I leave such matters to the professionals.

I sat on my hotel bed; from a neighbouring room a telephone imitated the cry of other telephones. I thought about the parrot in its alcove barely half a mile away. A cheeky bird, inducing affection, even reverence. What had Flaubert done with it after finishing *Un cœur simple*? Did he put it away in a cupboard and forget about its irritating existence until he was searching for an extra blanket? And what happened, four years later, when an apoplectic stroke left him dying on his sofa? Did he perhaps imagine, hovering above him, a gigantic parrot – this time not a welcome from the Holy Ghost but a farewell from the Word?

'I am bothered by my tendency to metaphor, decidedly excessive. I am devoured by comparisons as one is by lice, and I spend my time doing nothing but squashing them.' Words came easily to Flaubert; but he also saw the underlying inadequacy of the Word. Remember his sad definition from *Madame Bovary*: 'Language is like a cracked kettle on which we beat out tunes for bears to dance to, while all the time we long to move the stars to pity.' So you can take the novelist either way: as a pertinacious and finished stylist; or as one who considered language tragically insufficient. Sartreans prefer the second option: for them Loulou's inability to do more than repeat at second hand the phrases he hears is an indirect confession of the novelist's own failure. The parrot/writer feebly accepts language as something received, imitative and inert. Sartre himself rebuked Flaubert for passivity, for belief (or collusion in the belief) that *on est parlé* – one is spoken.

Did that burst of bubbles announce the gurgling death of another submerged reference? The point at which you suspect too much is being read into a story is when you feel most vulnerable, isolated, and perhaps stupid. Is a critic wrong to read Loulou as a symbol of the Word? Is a reader wrong – worse, sentimental

– to think of that parrot at the Hôtel-Dieu as an emblem of the writer's voice? That's what I did. Perhaps this makes me as simple-minded as Félicité.

But whether you call it a tale or a text, *Un cœur simple* echoes on in the brain. Allow me to cite David Hockney, benign if unspecific, in his autobiography: 'The story really affected me, and I felt it was a subject I could get into and really use.' In 1974 Mr Hockney produced a pair of etchings: a burlesque version of Félicité's view of Abroad (a monkey stealing away with a woman over its shoulder), and a tranquil scene of Félicité asleep with Loulou. Perhaps he will do some more in due course.

On my last day in Rouen I drove out to Croisset. Normandy rain was falling, soft and dense. What was formerly a remote village on the banks of the Seine, backdropped by green hills, has now become engulfed by thumping dockland. Pile-drivers echo; gantries hang over you, and the river is thickly commercial. Passing lorries rattle the windows of the inevitable Bar le Flaubert.

Gustave noted and approved the Oriental habit of knocking down the houses of the dead; so perhaps he would have been less hurt than his readers, his pursuers, by the destruction of his own house. The factory for extracting alcohol from damaged wheat was pulled down in its turn; and on the site there now stands, more appropriately, a large paper-mill. All that remains of Flaubert's residence is a small one-storey pavilion a few hundred yards down the road: a summer house to which the writer would retire when needing even more solitude than usual. It now looks shabby and pointless, but at least it's something. On the terrace outside, a stump of fluted column, dug up at Carthage, has been erected to commemorate the author of *Salammbô*. I pushed the gate; an Alsatian began barking, and a white-haired *gardienne* approached. No white coat for her, but a well-cut blue uniform. As I cranked up my French I remembered the trademark of the Carthaginian interpreters in *Salammbô*: each, as a symbol of his profession, has a parrot tattooed on his chest. Today the brown wrist of the African boule-player wears a Mao transfer.

The pavilion contains a single room, square with a tented ceiling. I was reminded of Félicité's room: 'It had the simultaneous air of a chapel and a bazaar.' Here too were the ironic conjunctions – trivial knick-knack beside solemn relic – of the Flaubertian grotesque. The items on display were so poorly arranged that I frequently had to get down on my knees to squint into the cabinets: the posture of the devout, but also of the junk-shop treasure-hunter.

Félicité found consolation in her assembly of stray objects, united only by their owner's affection. Flaubert did the same, preserving trivia fragrant with memories. Years after his mother's death he would still sometimes ask for her old shawl and hat, then sit down with them to dream a little. The visitor to the Croisset pavilion can almost do the same: the exhibits, carelessly laid out, catch your heart at random. Portraits, photographs, a clay bust; pipes, a tobacco jar, a letter opener; a toad-inkwell with a gaping mouth; the gold Buddha which stood on the writer's desk and never irritated him; a lock of hair, blonder, naturally, than in the photographs.

Two exhibits in a side cabinet are easy to miss: a small tumbler from which Flaubert took his last drink of water a few moments before he died; and a crumpled pad of white handkerchief with which he mopped his brow in perhaps the last gesture of his life. Such ordinary props, which seemed to forbid wailing and melo-drama, made me feel I had been present at the death of a friend. I was almost embarrassed: three days before I had stood unmoved on a beach where close companions had been killed. Perhaps this is the advantage of making friends with those already dead: your feelings towards them never cool.

Then I saw it. Crouched on top of a high cupboard was another parrot. Also bright green. Also, according to both the *gardienne* and the label on its perch, the very parrot which Flaubert had borrowed from the Museum of Rouen for the writing of *Un cœur simple*. I asked permission to take the second Loulou down, set him carefully on the corner of a display cabinet, and removed his glass dome.

How do you compare two parrots, one already idealised by memory and metaphor, the other a squawking intruder? My initial response was that the second seemed less authentic than the first, mainly because it had a more benign air. The head was set straighter on the body, and its expression was less irritating than that of the bird at the Hôtel-Dieu. Then I realised the fallacy in this: Flaubert, after all, hadn't been given a choice of parrots; and even this second one, which looked the calmer company, might well get on your nerves after a couple of weeks.

I mentioned the question of authenticity to the *gardienne*. She was, understandably, on the side of her own parrot, and confidently discounted the claims of the Hôtel-Dieu. I wondered if somebody knew the answer. I wondered if it mattered to anyone except me, who had rashly invested significance in the first parrot. The writer's voice – what makes you think it can be located that easily? Such was the rebuke offered by the second parrot. As I stood looking at the possibly inauthentic Loulou, the sun lit up that corner of the room and turned his plumage more sharply yellow. I replaced the bird and thought: I am now older than Flaubert ever was. It seemed a presumptuous thing to be; sad and unmerited.

Is it ever the right time to die? It wasn't for Flaubert; or for George Sand, who didn't live to read *Un cœur simple*. 'I had begun it solely on account of her, only to please her. She died while I was in the midst of this work. So it is with all our dreams.' Is it better not to have the dreams, the work, and then the desolation of uncompleted work? Perhaps, like Frédéric and Deslauriers, we should prefer the consolation of non-fulfilment: the planned visit to the brothel, the pleasure of anticipation, and then, years later, not the memory of deeds but the memory of past anticipations? Wouldn't that keep it all cleaner and less painful?

After I got home the duplicate parrots continued to flutter in my mind: one of them amiable and straightforward, the other cocky and interrogatory. I wrote letters to various academics who might know if either of the parrots had been properly authenticated. I wrote to the French Embassy and to the editor of the Michelin guide-books. I also wrote to Mr Hockney. I told him about my trip and asked if he'd ever been to Rouen; I wondered if he'd had one or other of the parrots in mind when etching his portrait of the sleeping Félicité. If not, then perhaps he in his turn had borrowed a parrot from a museum and used it as a model. I warned him of the dangerous tendency in this species to posthumous parthenogenesis.

I hoped to get my replies quite soon.

2

CHRONOLOGY

I

1821   Birth of Gustave Flaubert, second son of Achille-Cléophas Flaubert, head surgeon at the Hôtel-Dieu, Rouen, and of Anne-Justine-Caroline Flaubert, née Fleuriot. The family belongs to the successful professional middle class, and owns several properties in the vicinity of Rouen. A stable, enlightened, encouraging and normally ambitious background.

1825   Entry into service with the Flaubert family of Julie, Gustave's nurse, who remains with them until the writer's death fifty-five years later. Few servant problems will trouble his life.

*c.*1830   Meets Ernest Chevalier, his first close friend. A succession of intense, loyal and fertile friendships will sustain Flaubert throughout his life: of particular note are those with Alfred le Poittevin, Maxime du Camp, Louis Bouilhet and George Sand. Gustave inspires friendship easily, and fosters it with a teasing, affectionate manner.

1831–2   Enters the Collège de Rouen and proves an impressive student, strong in history and literature. His earliest piece of writing to come down to us, an essay on Corneille, dates from 1832. Throughout his adolescence he composes abundantly, both drama and fiction.

1836   Meets Elisa Schlesinger, wife of a German music publisher, in Trouville and conceives an 'enormous' passion for her. This passion illuminates the rest of his adolescence. She treats him with great kindness and affection; they remain in touch for the next forty years. Looking back, he is relieved she didn't return his passion: 'Happiness is like the pox. Catch it too soon, and it wrecks your constitution.'

*c.*1836   Gustave's sexual initiation with one of his mother's maids. This is the start of an active and colourful erotic career, veering from brothel to salon, from Cairo bathhouse boy to Parisian poetess. In early manhood he is extremely attractive to women and his speed of sexual recuperation is, by his own account, very impressive; but even in later life his courtly manner, intelligence and fame ensure that he is not unattended.

1837   His first published work appears in the Rouen magazine *Le Colibri*.

1840   Passes his *baccalauréat*. Travels to the Pyrenees with a family friend, Dr Jules Cloquet. Though often considered an unbudgeable hermit, Flaubert in fact travels extensively: to Italy and Switzerland (1845), Brittany (1847), Egypt, Palestine, Syria, Turkey, Greece and Italy (1849–51), England (1851, 1865, 1866, 1871), Algeria and Tunisia (1858), Germany (1865), Belgium (1871) and Switzerland (1874). Compare the case of his *alter ego* Louis Bouilhet, who dreamed of China and never got to England.

1843   As a law student in Paris, he meets Victor Hugo.

1844   Gustave's first epileptic attack puts an end to his legal studies in Paris and confines him to the new family house at Croisset. Abandoning the law, however, causes little pain, and since his confinement brings both the solitude and the stable base needed for a life of writing, the attack proves beneficial in the long run.

1846   Meets Louise Colet, 'the Muse', and begins his most celebrated affair: a prolonged, passionate, fighting two-parter (1846–8, 1851–4). Though ill-matched in temperament and incompatible in aesthetics, Gustave and Louise nevertheless last together far longer than most would have predicted. Should we regret the end of their affair? Only because it means the end of Gustave's resplendent letters to her.

1851–7 The writing, publication, trial and triumphant acquittal
of *Madame Bovary*. A *succès de scandale*, praised by authors
as diverse as Lamartine, Sainte-Beuve and Baudelaire. In
1846, doubting his ability ever to write anything worth
publishing, Gustave had announced, 'If I do make an
appearance, one day, it will be in full armour.' Now
his breastplate dazzles and his lance is everywhere. The
curé of Canteleu, the next village to Croisset, forbids
his parishioners to read the novel. After 1857, literary
success leads naturally to social success: Flaubert is
seen more in Paris. He meets the Goncourts, Renan,
Gautier, Baudelaire and Sainte-Beuve. In 1862 the series
of literary dinners at Magny's are instituted: Flaubert is
a regular from December of that year.

1862 Publication of *Salammbô*. *Succès fou*. Sainte-Beuve writes
to Matthew Arnold: '*Salammbô* is our great event!' The
novel provides the theme for several costume balls in
Paris. It even provides the name for a new brand of
petit four.

1863 Flaubert begins to frequent the salon of Princesse
Mathilde, niece of Napoleon I. The bear of Croisset
eases into the pelt of the social lion. He himself receives
on Sunday afternoons. The year also contains his first
exchange of letters with George Sand, and his meeting
with Turgenev. His friendship with the Russian novelist
marks the beginning of a wider European fame.

1864 Presentation to the Emperor Napoleon III at Com-
piegne. The peak of Gustave's social success. He sends
camellias to the Empress.

1866 Created *chevalier de la Légion d'honneur*.

1869 Publication of *L'Education sentimentale*: Flaubert always
claims it as *un chef-d'œuvre*. Despite the legend of heroic
struggle (which he himself initiates), writing comes
easily to Flaubert. He complains a lot, but such complaints are always couched in letters of astonishing
fluency. For a quarter of a century he produces one

large, solid book, requiring considerable research, every five to seven years. He might agonise over the word, the phrase, the assonance, but he never endures a writer's block.

1874 Publication of *La Tentation de saint Antoine*. Despite its strangeness, a gratifying commercial success.

1877 Publication of *Trois Contes*. A critical and popular success: for the first time Flaubert receives a favourable review from *Le Figaro*; the book goes through five editions in three years. Flaubert begins work on *Bouvard et Pécuchet*. During these final years, his pre-eminence among French novelists is admitted by the next generation. He is fêted and revered. His Sunday afternoons become famous events in literary society; Henry James calls on the Master. In 1879 Gustave's friends institute the annual Saint Polycarpe dinners in his honour. In 1880 the five co-authors of *Les Soirées de Medan*, including Zola and Maupassant, present him with an inscribed copy: the gift can be seen as a symbolic salute to Realism from Naturalism.

1880 Full of honour, widely loved, and still working hard to the end, Gustave Flaubert dies at Croisset.

II

1817 Death of Caroline Flaubert (aged twenty months), the second child of Achille-Cléophas Flaubert and Anne-Justine-Caroline Flaubert.

1819 Death of Emile-Cléophas Flaubert (aged eight months), their third child.

1821 Birth of Gustave Flaubert, their fifth child.

1822 Death of Jules Alfred Flaubert (aged three years and five months), their fourth child. His brother Gustave, born *entre deux morts*, is delicate and not expected to live long. Dr Flaubert buys a family plot at the Cimetière Monumental and has a small grave dug in preparation for

Gustave. Surprisingly, he survives. He proves a slow child, content to sit for hours with his finger in his mouth and an 'almost stupid' expression on his face. For Sartre, he is 'the family idiot'.

1836   The start of a hopeless, obsessive passion for Elisa Schlesinger which cauterises his heart and renders him incapable of ever fully loving another woman. Looking back, he records: 'Each of us possesses in his heart a royal chamber. I have bricked mine up.'

1839   Expelled from the Collège de Rouen for rowdyism and disobedience.

1843   The Faculty of Law at Paris announces its first-year examination results. The examiners declare their views by means of red or black balls. Gustave receives two red and two black, and is therefore failed.

1844   Shattering first attack of epilepsy; others are to follow. 'Each attack', Gustave writes later, 'was like a haemorrhage of the nervous system . . . It was a snatching of the soul from the body, excruciating.' He is bled, given pills and infusions, put on a special diet, forbidden alcohol and tobacco; a regime of strict confinement and maternal care is necessary if he is not to claim his place at the cemetery. Without having entered the world, Gustave now retires from it. 'So, you are guarded like a young girl?' Louise Colet later taunts, accurately. For all but the last eight years of his life, Mme Flaubert watches suffocatingly over his welfare and censors his travel plans. Gradually, over the decades, her frailty overtakes his: by the time he has almost ceased to be a worry to her, she has become a burden to him.

1846   Death of Gustave's father, quickly followed by that of his beloved sister Caroline (aged twenty-one), which thrusts on to him proxy fatherhood of his niece. Throughout his life, he is constantly bruised by the deaths of those close to him. And there are other ways for friends to die: in June Alfred le Poittevin marries.

Gustave feels it is his third bereavement of the year: 'You are doing something abnormal,' he complains. To Maxime du Camp that year he writes, 'Tears are to the heart what water is to a fish.' Is it a consolation that in the same year he meets Louise Colet? Pedantry and recalcitrance are mismatched with immoderation and possessiveness. A mere six days after she becomes his mistress, the pattern of their relationship is set: 'Moderate your cries!' he complains to her. 'They are torturing me. What do you want me to do? Am I to leave everything and live in Paris? Impossible.' This impossible relationship drags on nevertheless for eight years; Louise is puzzlingly unable to grasp that Gustave can love her without ever wanting to see her. 'If I were a woman,' he writes after six years, 'I wouldn't want myself for a lover. A one-night stand, yes; but an intimate relationship, no.'

1848   Death of Alfred le Poittevin, aged thirty-two. 'I see that I've never loved anyone – man or woman – as I loved him.' Twenty-five years later: 'Not a day passes that I don't think of him.'

1849   Gustave reads his first full-length adult work, *La Tentation de saint Antoine*, to his two closest friends, Bouilhet and Du Camp. The reading takes four days, at the rate of eight hours per day. After embarrassed consultation, the listeners tell him to throw it on the fire.

1850   In Egypt, Gustave catches syphilis. Much of his hair falls out; he grows stout. Mme Flaubert, meeting him in Rome the following year, scarcely recognises her son, and finds that he has become very coarse. Middle age begins here. 'Scarcely are you born before you begin rotting.' Over the years all but one of his teeth will fall out; his saliva will be permanently blackened by mercury treatment.

1851–7 *Madame Bovary*. The composition is painful – 'Writing this book I am like a man playing the piano with lead balls attached to his knuckles' – and the prosecution frightening. In later years Flaubert comes to resent the insistent fame of his masterpiece, which makes others see him as a one-book author. He tells Du Camp that if ever he had a stroke of good luck on the Bourse he would buy up 'at any cost' all copies of *Madame Bovary* in circulation: 'I should throw them into the fire, and never hear of them again.'

1862   Elisa Schlesinger is interned in a mental hospital; she is diagnosed as suffering from 'acute melancholia'. After the publication of *Salammbô*, Flaubert begins to run with rich friends. But he remains childlike in financial matters: his mother has to sell property to pay his debts. In 1867 he secretly hands over control of his financial affairs to his niece's husband, Ernest Commanville. Over the next thirteen years, through extravagance, incompetent management and bad luck, Flaubert loses all his money.

1869   Death of Louis Bouilhet, whom he had once called 'the Seltzer water which helped me digest life'. 'In losing my Bouilhet, I had lost my midwife, the man who saw more deeply into my thought than I did myself.' Death also of Sainte-Beuve. 'Another one gone! The little band is diminishing! Who is there to talk about literature with now?' Publication of *L'Education sentimentale*; a critical and commercial flop. Of the hundred and fifty complimentary copies sent to friends and acquaintants, barely thirty are even acknowledged.

1870   Death of Jules de Goncourt: only three of the seven friends who started the Magny dinners in 1862 are now left. During the Franco-Prussian war, the enemy occupies Croisset. Ashamed of being French, Flaubert stops wearing his *Legion d'honneur*, and resolves to ask Turgenev what he has to do to take Russian citizenship.

1872   Death of Mme Flaubert: 'I have realised during the last fortnight that my poor dear old mother was the person I loved the most. It's as if part of my entrails had been torn out.' Death also of Gautier. 'With him, the last of my intimate friends is gone. The list is closed.'

1874   Flaubert makes his theatrical début with *Le Candidat*.
        It is a complete flop; actors leave the stage with tears in
        their eyes. The play is taken off after four performances.
        Publication of *La Tentation de saint Antoine*. 'Torn to
        pieces,' Flaubert notes, 'by everything from the *Figaro*
        to the *Revue des deux mondes* . . . What comes as a surprise
        is the hatred underlying much of this criticism – hatred
        for me, for my person – deliberate denigration . . . This
        avalanche of abuse does depress me.'

1875   The financial ruin of Ernest Commanville drags Flau-
        bert down too. He sells his farm at Deauville; he has
        to plead with his niece not to turn him out of Croisset.
        She and Commanville nickname him 'the consumer'.
        In 1879 he is reduced to accepting a state pension
        arranged for him by friends.

1876   Death of Louise Colet. Death of George Sand. 'My
        heart is becoming a necropolis.' Gustave's last years are
        arid and solitary. He tells his niece he regrets not having
        married.

1880   Impoverished, lonely and exhausted, Gustave Flaubert
        dies. Zola, in his obituary notice, comments that he was
        unknown to four-fifths of Rouen, and detested by the
        other fifth. He leaves *Bouvard et Pécuchet* unfinished.
        Some say the labour of the novel killed him; Turgenev
        told him before he started that it would be better as a
        short story. After the funeral a group of mourners,
        including the poets François Coppée and Théodore de
        Banville, have dinner in Rouen to honour the departed
        writer. They discover, on sitting down to table, that they
        are thirteen. The superstitious Banville insists that
        another guest be found, and Gautier's son-in-law Émile
        Bergerat is sent to scour the streets. After several rebuffs
        he returns with a private on leave. The soldier has never
        heard of Flaubert, but is longing to meet Coppée.

III

1842   Me and my books, in the same apartment: like a gherkin in its vinegar.

1846   When I was still quite young I had a complete presentiment of life. It was like the nauseating smell of cooking escaping from a ventilator: you don't have to have eaten it to know that it would make you throw up.

1846   I did with you what I have done before with those I loved best: I showed them the bottom of the bag, and the acrid dust that rose from it made them choke.

1846   My life is riveted to that of another [Mme Flaubert], and will be so as long as that other life endures. A piece of seaweed blowing in the wind, I am held to the rock by a single hardy thread. If it broke, where would this poor useless plant fly off to?

1846   You want to prune the tree. Its unruly branches, thick with leaves, push out in all directions to sniff the air and the sun. But you want to make me into a charming espalier, stretched against a wall, bearing fine fruit that a child could pick without even using a ladder.

1846   Don't think that I belong to that vulgar race of men who feel disgust after pleasure, and for whom love exists only as lust. No: in me, what rises doesn't subside so quickly. Moss grows on the castles of my heart as soon as they are built; but it takes some time for them to fall into ruin, if they ever completely do.

1846   I am like a cigar: you have to suck on the end to get me going.

1846   Amongst those who go to sea there are the navigators who discover new worlds, adding continents to the earth and stars to the heavens: they are the masters, the great, the eternally splendid. Then there are those who spit terror from their gun-ports, who pillage, who grow rich and fat. Others go off in search of gold and silk under foreign skies. Still others catch salmon for the gourmet or cod for the poor. I am the obscure and patient pearl-fisherman who dives into the deepest waters and comes up with empty hands and a blue face. Some fatal attraction draws me down into the abysses of thought, down into those innermost recesses which never cease to fascinate the strong. I shall spend my life gazing at the ocean of art, where others voyage or fight; and from time to time I'll entertain myself by diving for those green and yellow shells that nobody will want. So I shall keep them for myself and cover the walls of my hut with them.

1846   I am only a literary lizard basking the day away beneath the great sun of Beauty. That's all.

1846   Deep within me there is a radical, intimate, bitter and incessant *boredom* which prevents me from enjoying anything and which smothers my soul. It reappears at any excuse, just as the swollen corpses of drowned dogs pop to the surface despite the stones that have been tied round their necks.

1847   People are like food. There are lots of bourgeois who seem to me like boiled beef: all steam, no juice, and no taste (it fills you up straight away and is much eaten by bumpkins). Other people are like white meat, fresh-water fish, slender eels from the muddy river-bed, oysters (of varying degrees of saltiness), calves' heads, and sugared porridge. Me? I'm like a runny, stinking macaroni cheese, which you have to eat a lot of times before you develop a taste for it. You do finally get to like it, but only after it has made your stomach heave on countless occasions.

1847   Some people have a tender heart and a tough mind. I'm the opposite: I have a tender mind but a rough heart. I'm like a coconut which keeps its milk locked away beneath several layers of wood. You need an axe to open it, and then what do you find as often as not? A sort of sour cream.

1847   You had hoped to find in me a fire which scorched and blazed and illuminated everything; which shed a cheerful light, dried out damp wainscoting, made the air healthier and rekindled life. Alas! I'm only a poor night-light, whose red wick splutters in a lake of bad oil full of water and bits of dust.

1851   With me, friendship is like the camel: once started, there is no way of stopping it.

1852   As you get older, the heart sheds its leaves like a tree. You cannot hold out against certain winds. Each day tears away a few more leaves; and then there are the storms which break off several branches at one go. And while nature's greenery grows back again in the spring, that of the heart never grows back.

1852   What an awful thing life is, isn't it? It's like soup with lots of hairs floating on the surface. You have to eat it nevertheless.

1852   I laugh at everything, even at that which I love the most. There is no fact, thing, feeling or person over which I have not blithely run my clownishness, like an iron roller imparting sheen to cloth.

1852   I love my work with a frantic and perverted love, as an ascetic loves the hair-shirt which scratches his belly.

1852   All of us Normans have a little cider in our veins: it's a bitter, fermented drink which sometimes bursts the bung.

1853   As for this business of my moving at once to Paris, we'll have to put it off, or rather settle it here and now. This is *impossible* for me now ... I know myself well enough, and it would mean losing a whole winter, and perhaps the whole book. Bouilhet can talk: he's happy writing anywhere; he's been working away for a dozen years despite continual disturbances ... But I am like a row of milk-pans: if you want the cream to form, you have to leave them exactly where they are.

1853   I'm dazzled by your facility. In ten days you'll have
        written six stories! I don't understand it . . . I'm like one
        of those old aqueducts: there's so much rubbish clog-
        ging up the banks of my thought that it flows slowly, and
        only spills from the end of my pen drop by drop.

1854   I pigeon-hole my life, and keep everything in its place;
        I'm as full of drawers and compartments as an old travel-
        ling trunk, all roped up and fastened with three big
        leather straps.

1854   You ask for love, you complain that I don't send you
        flowers? Flowers, indeed! If that's what you want, find
        yourself some wet-eared boy stuffed with fine manners
        and all the right ideas. I'm like the tiger, which has
        bristles of hair at the end of its cock, with which it
        lacerates the female.

1857   Books aren't made in the way that babies are: they
        are made like pyramids. There's some long-pondered
        plan, and then great blocks of stone are placed one on
        top of the other, and it's back-breaking, sweaty, time-
        consuming work. And all to no purpose! It just stands
        like that in the desert! But it towers over it prodigiously.
        Jackals piss at the base of it, and bourgeois clamber to
        the top of it, etc. Continue this comparison.

1857   There is a Latin phrase which means roughly, 'To pick
        up a farthing from the shit with your teeth.' It was a
        rhetorical figure applied to the miserly. I am like them:
        I will stop at nothing to find gold.

1867   It's true that many things infuriate me. The day I stop
        being indignant I shall fall flat on my face, like a doll
        when you take away its prop.

1872   My heart remains intact, but my feelings are sharpened
        on the one hand and dulled on the other, like an old
        knife that has been too often sharpened, which has
        notches, and breaks easily.

1872   Never have things of the spirit counted for so little.
        Never has hatred for everything great been so manifest –
        disdain for Beauty, execration of literature. I have always
        tried to live in an ivory tower, but a tide of shit is beating
        at its walls, threatening to undermine it.

1873   I still carry on turning out my sentences, like a bourgeois
        turning out napkin rings on a lathe in his attic. It gives
        me something to do, and it affords me some private
        pleasure.

1875   Despite your advice, I can't manage to 'harden myself'
        . . . My sensitivities are all aquiver – my nerves and my
        brain are sick, very sick; I feel them to be so. But there
        I go, complaining again, and I don't want to distress you.
        I'll confine myself to your mention of a 'rock'. Know,
        then, that very old granite sometimes turns into layers
        of clay.

1875   I feel uprooted, like a mass of dead seaweed tossed here
        and there in the waves.

1880   When will the book be finished? That's the question.
        If it is to appear next winter, I haven't a minute to lose
        between now and then. But there are moments when
        I'm so tired that I feel I'm liquefying like an old
        Camembert.

3

FINDERS KEEPERS

YOU CAN DEFINE a net in one of two ways, depending on your point of view. Normally, you would say that it is a meshed instrument designed to catch fish. But you could, with no great injury to logic, reverse the image and define a net as a jocular lexicographer once did: he called it a collection of holes tied together with string.

You can do the same with a biography. The trawling net fills, then the biographer hauls it in, sorts, throws back, stores, fillets and sells. Yet consider what he doesn't catch: there is always far more of that. The biography stands, fat and worthy-burgherish on the shelf, boastful and sedate: a shilling life will give you all the facts, a ten pound one all the hypotheses as well. But think of everything that got away, that fled with the last deathbed exhalation of the biographee. What chance would the craftiest biographer stand against the subject who saw him coming and decided to amuse himself?

I first met Ed Winterton when he put his hand on mine in the Europa Hotel. Just my little joke; though true as well. It was at a provincial booksellers' fair and I had reached a little more quickly than he for the same copy of Turgenev's *Literary Reminiscences*. The conjunction induced immediate apologies, as embarrassed on his side as they were on mine. When we each realised that bibliophilic lust was the only emotion which had produced this laying on of hands, Ed murmured,

'Step outside and let's discuss it.'

Over an indifferent pot of tea we revealed our separate paths to the same book. I explained about Flaubert; he announced his interest in Gosse and in English literary society towards the end of the last century. I meet few American academics, and was pleasantly surprised that this one was bored by Bloomsbury, and happy to leave the modern movement to his younger and more ambitious colleagues. But then Ed Winterton liked to present himself as a failure. He was in his early forties, balding, with a

pinky glabrous complexion and square rimless spectacles: the
banker type of academic, circumspect and moral. He bought
English clothes without looking at all English. He remained the
sort of American who always wears a mackintosh in London
because he knows that in this city rain falls out of a clear sky.
He was even wearing his mackintosh in the lounge of the Europa
Hotel.

His air of failure had nothing desperate about it; rather, it
seemed to stem from an unresented realisation that he was not
cut out for success, and his duty was therefore to ensure only that
he failed in a correct and acceptable fashion. At one point, when
discussing the improbability of his Gosse biography ever being
finished, let alone published, he paused and dropped his voice:

'But in any case I sometimes wonder if Mr Gosse would have
approved of what I'm doing.'

'You mean . . .' I knew little of Gosse, and my widened eyes
hinted perhaps too clearly at naked laundresses, illegitimate half-
castes and dismembered bodies.

'Oh no, no, no. Just the thought of *writing* about him. He
might think it was a bit of a . . . low blow.'

I let him have the Turgenev, of course, if only to escape a discussion about the morality of possession. I didn't see where ethics
came into the ownership of a second-hand book; but Ed did.
He promised to be in touch if ever he ran down another copy.
Then we briefly discussed the rights and wrongs of my paying
for his tea.

I didn't expect to hear from him again, let alone on the subject
which provoked his letter to me about a year later. 'Are you
interested at all in Juliet Herbert? It sounds a fascinating relationship, judging by the material. I'll be in London in August, if you
will. Ever, Ed (Winterton).'

What does the fiancée feel when she snaps open the box and
sees the ring set in purple velvet? I never asked my wife; and it's
too late now. Or what did Flaubert feel as he waited for the dawn
on top of the Great Pyramid and finally saw that crack of gold
shine from the purple velvet of the night? Astonishment, awe and
a fierce glee came into my heart as I read those two words in Ed's
letter. No, not 'Juliet Herbert', the other two: first 'fascinating'
and then 'material'. And beyond glee, beyond hard work as well,
was there something else? A shameful thought of an honorary
degree somewhere?

Juliet Herbert is a great hole tied together with string. She became governess to Flaubert's niece Caroline at some time in the mid-1850s, and remained at Croisset for a few undetermined years; then she returned to London. Flaubert wrote to her, and she to him; they visited one another every so often. Beyond this, we know nothing. Not a single letter to or from her has survived. We know almost nothing about her family. We do not even know what she looked like. No description of her survives, and none of Flaubert's friends thought to mention her after his death, when most other women of importance in his life were being memorialised.

Biographers disagree about Juliet Herbert. For some, the shortage of evidence indicates that she was of small significance in Flaubert's life; others conclude from this absence precisely the opposite, and assert that the tantalising governess was certainly one of the writer's mistresses, possibly the Great Unknown Passion of his life, and perhaps even his fiancée. Hypothesis is spun directly from the temperament of the biographer. Can we deduce love for Juliet Herbert from the fact that Gustave called his greyhound Julio? Some can. It seems a little tendentious to me. And if we do, what do we then deduce from the fact that in various letters Gustave addresses his niece as 'Loulou', the name he later transfers to Félicité's parrot? Or from the fact that George Sand had a ram called Gustave?

Flaubert's one overt reference to Juliet Herbert comes in a letter to Bouilhet, written after the latter had visited Croisset:

> Since I saw you excited by the governess, I too have become excited. At table, my eyes willingly followed the gentle slope of her breast. I believe she notices this for, five or six times per meal, she looks as if she had caught the sun. What a pretty comparison one could make between the slope of the breast and the glacis of a fortress. The cupids tumble about on it, as they storm the citadel. (To be said in our Sheikh's voice) 'Well, I certainly know what piece of artillery I'd be pointing in that direction.'

Should we jump to conclusions? Frankly, this is the kind of boastful, nudging stuff that Flaubert was always writing to his male friends. I find it unconvincing myself: true desire isn't so easily diverted into metaphor. But then, all biographers secretly

want to annex and channel the sex-lives of their subjects; you
must make your judgment on me as well as on Flaubert.

Had Ed really discovered some Juliet Herbert material? I admit
I began feeling possessive in advance. I imagined myself presenting it in one of the more important literary journals; perhaps
I might let the *TLS* have it. 'Juliet Herbert: A Mystery Solved,
by Geoffrey Braithwaite', illustrated with one of those photographs in which you can't quite read the handwriting. I also
began to worry at the thought of Ed blurting out his discovery on
campus and guilelessly yielding up his cache to some ambitious
Gallicist with an astronaut's haircut.

But these were unworthy and, I hope, untypical feelings.
Mostly, I was thrilled at the idea of discovering the secret of
Gustave and Juliet's relationship (what else could the word 'fascinating' mean in Ed's letter?). I was also thrilled that the material
might help me imagine even more exactly what Flaubert was
like. The net was being pulled tighter. Would we find out, for
instance, how the writer behaved in London?

This was of particular interest. Cultural exchange between
England and France in the nineteenth century was at best pragmatic. French writers didn't cross the Channel to discuss aesthetics with their English counterparts; they were either running
from prosecution or looking for a job. Hugo and Zola came
over as exiles; Verlaine and Mallarmé came over as schoolmasters.
Villiers de l'Isle-Adam, chronically poor yet crazily practical,
came over in search of an heiress. A Parisian marriage-broker had
kitted him out for the expedition with a fur overcoat, a repeating
alarm watch and a new set of false teeth, all to be paid for when
the writer landed the heiress's dowry. But Villiers, tirelessly
accident-prone, botched the wooing. The heiress rejected him,
the broker turned up to reclaim the coat and watch, and the discarded suitor was left adrift in London, full of teeth but penniless.

So what of Flaubert? We know little about his four trips to
England. We know that the Great Exhibition of 1851 secured his
unexpected approval – 'a very fine thing, despite being admired
by everyone' – but his notes on this first visit amount to a mere
seven pages: two on the British Museum, plus five on the
Chinese and Indian sections at Crystal Palace. What were his first
impressions of us? He must have told Juliet. Did we live up to our
entries in his *Dictionnaire des idées reçues* (ENGLISHMEN: *All rich.*
ENGLISHWOMEN: *Express surprise that they produce pretty children*)?

And what of subsequent visits, when he had become author of the notorious *Madame Bovary*? Did he search out English writers? Did he search out English brothels? Did he cosily stay at home with Juliet, staring at her over dinner and then storming her fortress? Were they perhaps (I half-hoped so) merely friends? Was Flaubert's English as hit-and-miss as it seems from his letters? Did he talk only Shakespearean? And did he complain much about the fog?

When I met Ed at the restaurant, he was looking even less successful than before. He told me about budget cuts, a cruel world, and his own lack of publications. I deduced, rather than heard, that he had been sacked. He explained the irony of his dismissal: it sprang from his devotion to his work, his unwillingness to do Gosse anything less than justice when presenting him to the world. Academic superiors had suggested that he cut corners. Well, he wouldn't do so. He respected writing and writers too much for that. 'I mean, don't we owe these fellers something in return?' he concluded.

Perhaps I offered slightly less than the expected sympathy. But then, can you alter the way luck flows? Just for once, it was flowing for me. I had ordered my dinner quickly, scarcely caring what I ate; Ed had pondered the menu as if he were Verlaine being bought his first square meal in months. Listening to Ed's tedious lament for himself and watching him slowly consume whitebait at the same time had used up my patience; though it had not diminished my excitement.

'Right,' I said, as we started our main course, 'Juliet Herbert.'

'Oh,' he said, 'yes.' I could see he might need prodding. 'It's an odd story.'

'It would be.'

'Yes.' Ed seemed a little pained, almost embarrassed. 'Well, I was over here about six months ago, tracking down one of Mr Gosse's distant descendants. Not that I expected to find anything. It was just that, as far as I knew, nobody had ever talked to the lady in question, and I thought it was my ... duty to see her. Perhaps some family legend I hadn't accounted for had come down to her.'

'And?'

'And? Oh, it hadn't. No, she wasn't really of any help. It was a nice day, though. Kent.' He looked pained again; he seemed to miss the mackintosh which the waiter had ruthlessly deprived him of. 'Ah, but I see what you mean. What *had* come down to her was the letters. Now let me get this right; you'll correct me, I hope. Juliet Herbert died 1909 or so? Yes. She had a cousin, woman cousin. Yes. Now, this woman found the letters and took them to Mr Gosse, asked him his opinion of their value. Mr Gosse thought he was being touched for money, so he said they were interesting but not worth anything. Whereupon this cousin apparently just handed them over to him and said, If they're not worth anything, you take them. Which he did.'

'How do you know all this?'

'There was a letter attached in Mr Gosse's hand.'

'And so?'

'And so they came down to this lady. Kent. I'm afraid she asked me the same question. Were they worth anything? I regret I behaved in a rather immoral fashion. I told her they had been valuable when Gosse had examined them, but they weren't any more. I said they were still quite interesting, but they weren't worth much because half of them were written in French. Then I bought them off her for fifty pounds.'

'Good God.' No wonder he looked shifty.

'Yes, it was rather bad, wasn't it? I can't really excuse myself; though the fact that Mr Gosse himself had lied when obtaining them did seem to blur the issue. It raises an interesting ethical point, don't you think? The fact is, I was rather depressed at losing my job, and I thought I'd take them home and sell them and then be able to carry on with my book.'

'How many letters are there?'

'About seventy-five. Three dozen or so on each side. That's how we settled on the price – a pound apiece for the ones in English, fifty pence for the ones in French.'

'Good God.' I wondered what they might be worth. Perhaps a thousand times what he paid for them. Or more.

'Yes.'

'Well, go on, tell me about them.'

'Ah.' He paused, and gave me a look which might have been roguish if he hadn't been such a meek, pedantic fellow. Probably he was enjoying my excitement. 'Well, fire away. What do you want to know?'

'You have read them?'

'Oh yes.'

'And, and ...' I didn't know what to ask. Ed was definitely

enjoying this now. 'And – did they have an affair? They did, didn't they?'

'Oh yes, certainly.'

'And when did it start? Soon after she got to Croisset?'

'Oh yes, quite soon.'

Well, that unravelled the letter to Bouilhet: Flaubert was playing the tease, pretending he had just as much, or just as little, chance as his friend with the governess; whereas in fact . . .

'And it continued all the time she was there?'

'Oh yes.'

'And when he came to England?'

'Yes, that too.'

'And was she his fiancée?'

'It's hard to say. Pretty nearly, I'd guess. There are some references in both their letters, mostly jocular. Remarks about the little English governess trapping the famous French man of letters; what would she do if he were imprisoned for another outrage against public morals; that sort of thing.'

'Well, well, well. And do we find out what she was like?'

'What she was like? Oh, you mean to look at?'

'Yes. There wasn't . . . there wasn't . . .' He sensed my hope. '. . . a photograph?'

'A photograph? Yes, several, as a matter of fact; from some Chelsea studio, printed on heavy card. He must have asked her to send him some. Is that of interest?'

'It's incredible. What did she look like?'

'Pretty nice in an unmemorable sort of way. Dark hair, strong jaw, good nose. I didn't look too closely; not really my type.'

'And did they get on well together?' I hardly knew what I wanted to ask any more. *Flaubert's English fiancée*, I was thinking to myself. By Geoffrey Braithwaite.

'Oh yes, they seemed to. They seemed very fond. He'd mastered quite a range of English endearments by the end.'

'So he could manage the language?'

'Oh yes, there are several long passages of English in his letters.'

'And did he like London?'

'He liked it. How could he not? It was his fiancée's city of residence.'

Dear old Gustave, I murmured to myself; I felt quite tender towards him. Here, in this city, a century and a few years ago, with a compatriot of mine who had captured his heart. 'Did he complain about the fog?'

'Of course. He wrote something like, How do you manage to live with such fog? By the time a gentleman has recognised a lady as she comes at him out of the fog, it is already too late to raise his hat. I'm surprised the race doesn't die out when such conditions make difficult the natural courtesies.'

Oh yes, that was the tone – elegant, teasing, slightly lubricious. 'And what about the Great Exhibition? Does he go into detail about that? I bet he rather liked it.'

'He did. Of course, that was a few years before they first met, but he does mention it in a sentimental fashion – wonders if he might unknowingly have passed her in the crowds. He thought it was a bit awful, but also really rather splendid. He seems to have looked at all the exhibits as if they were an enormous display of source material for him.'

'And. Hmm.' Well, why not. 'I suppose he didn't go to any brothels?'

Ed looked at me rather crossly. 'Well, he was writing to his girl-friend, wasn't he? He'd hardly be boasting about that.'

'No, of course not.' I felt chastened. I also felt exhilarated. My letters. *My* letters. Winterton was planning to let me publish them, wasn't he?

'So when can I see them? You did bring them with you?'

'Oh no.'

'You didn't?' Well, no doubt it was sensible to keep them all in a safe place. Travel has its dangers. Unless . . . unless there was something I hadn't understood. Perhaps . . . did he want money? I suddenly realised I knew absolutely nothing about Ed Winterton, except that he was the owner of my copy of Turgenev's *Literary Reminiscences*. 'You didn't even bring a single one with you?'

'No. You see, I burnt them.'

'You what?'

'Yes, well, that's what I mean by it being an odd story.'

'It sounds like a criminal story at the moment.'

'I was sure you'd understand,' he said, much to my surprise; then smiled broadly. 'I mean, you of all people. In fact, at first I decided not to tell anyone at all, but then I remembered you. I thought that one person in the business ought to be told. Just for the record.'

FINDERS KEEPERS

39

'Go on.' The man was a maniac, that much was plain. No wonder they'd kicked him out of his university. If only they'd done it years earlier.

'Well, you see, they were full of fascinating stuff, the letters. Very long, a lot of them, full of reflections about other writers, public life, and so on. They were even more unbuttoned than his normal letters. Perhaps it was because he was sending them out of the country that he allowed himself such freedom.' Did this criminal, this sham, this failure, this murderer, this bald pyromaniac know what he was doing to me? Very probably he did. 'And her letters were really quite fine in their way too. Told her whole life story. Very revealing about Flaubert. Full of nostalgic descriptions of home life at Croisset. She obviously had a very good eye. Noticed things I shouldn't think anyone else would have done.'

'Go on.' I waved grimly at the waiter. I wasn't sure I could stay there much longer. I wanted to tell Winterton how really pleased I was that the British had burnt the White House to the ground.

'No doubt you're wondering why I destroyed the letters. I can see you're kind of edgy about something. Well, in the very last communication between the two of them, he says that in the event of his death, her letters will be sent back to her, and she is to burn both sides of the correspondence.'

'Did he give any reasons?'

'No.'

This seemed strange, assuming that the maniac was telling the truth. But then Gustave did burn much of his correspondence with Du Camp. Perhaps some temporary pride in his family origins had asserted itself and he didn't want the world to know that he had nearly married an English governess. Or perhaps he didn't want us to know that his famous devotion to solitude and art had nearly been overthrown. But the world would know. I would tell it, one way or another.

'So you see, of course, I didn't have any alternative. I mean, if your business is writers, you have to behave towards them with integrity, don't you? You have to do what they say, even if other people don't.' What a smug, moralising bastard he was. He wore ethics the way tarts wear make-up. And then he managed to mix into the same expression both the earlier shiftiness and the later smugness. 'There was also something else in this last letter of his.

A rather strange instruction on top of asking Miss Herbert to burn the correspondence. He said, If anyone ever asks you what my letters contained, or what my life was like, please lie to them. Or rather, since I cannot ask you of all people to lie, just tell them what it is you think they want to hear.'

I felt like Villiers de l'Isle-Adam: someone had lent me a fur overcoat and a repeating watch for a few days, then cruelly snatched them back. It was lucky that the waiter returned at that point. Besides, Winterton was not as stupid as all that: he had pushed his chair well back from the table and was playing with his fingernails. 'The pity of it is,' he said, as I tucked away my credit card, 'that I probably now won't be able to finance Mr Gosse. But I'm sure you'll agree it's been an interesting moral decision.'

I think the remark I then made was deeply unfair to Mr Gosse both as a writer and as a sexual being; but I do not see how I could have avoided it.

4

THE FLAUBERT BESTIARY

I attract mad people and animals.
Letter to Alfred le Poittevin, 26 May 1845

THE BEAR

GUSTAVE WAS THE BEAR. His sister Caroline was the Rat – 'your dear rat', 'your faithful rat' she signs herself; 'little rat', 'Ah, rat, good rat, old rat', 'old rat, naughty old rat, good rat, poor old rat' he addresses her – but Gustave was the Bear. When he was only twenty, people found him 'an odd fellow, a bear, a young man out of the ordinary'; and even before his epileptic seizure and confinement at Croisset, the image had established itself: 'I am a bear and I want to stay a bear in my den, in my lair, in my skin, in my old bear's skin; I want to live quietly, far away from the bourgeois and the bourgeoises.' After his attack, the beast confirmed itself: 'I live alone, like a bear.' (The word 'alone' in this sentence is best glossed as: 'alone except for my parents, my sister, the servants, our dog, Caroline's goat, and my regular visits from Alfred le Poittevin'.)

He recovered, he was allowed to travel; in December 1850 he wrote to his mother from Constantinople, expanding the image of the Bear. It now explained not just his character, but also his literary strategy:

> If you participate in life, you don't see it clearly: you suffer from it too much or enjoy it too much. The artist, to my way of thinking, is a monstrosity, something outside nature. All the misfortunes Providence inflicts on him come from his stubbornness in denying that maxim ... So (and this is my conclusion) I am resigned to living as I have lived: alone, with my throng of great men as my only cronies – a bear, with my bear-rug for company.

The 'throng of cronies', needless to say, aren't house-guests but companions picked from his library shelves. As for the bear-rug, he was always concerned about it: he wrote twice from the East (Constantinople, April 1850; Benisouëf, June 1850), asking his mother to take care of it. His niece Caroline also remembered this central feature of his study. She would be taken there for her lessons at one o'clock: the shutters would be closed to keep out the heat, and the darkened room filled with the smell of joss-sticks and tobacco. 'With one bound I would throw myself on the large white bearskin, which I adored, and cover its great head with kisses.'

Once you catch your bear, says the Macedonian proverb, *it will dance for you.* Gustave didn't dance; Flaubear was nobody's bear. (How would you fiddle that into French? *Gourstave*, perhaps.)

BEAR: Generally called Martin. Quote the story of the old soldier who saw that a watch had fallen into a bear-pit, climbed down into it, and was eaten.

Dictionnaire des idées reçues

Gustave is other animals as well. In his youth he is clusters of beasts: hungry to see Ernest Chevalier, he is 'a lion, a tiger – a tiger from India, a boa constrictor' (1841); feeling a rare pleni-tude of strength, he is 'an ox, sphinx, bittern, elephant, whale' (1841). Subsequently, he takes them one at a time. He is an oyster in its shell (1845); a snail in its shell (1851); a hedgehog rolling up to protect itself (1853, 1857). He is a literary lizard basking in the sun of Beauty (1846), and a warbler with a shrill cry which hides in the depths of the woods and is heard only by itself (also 1846). He becomes as soft and nervous as a cow (1867); he feels as worn out as a donkey (1867); yet still he splashes in the Seine like a porpoise (1870). He works like a mule (1852); he lives a life which would kill three rhinos (1872); he works 'like XV oxen' (1878); though he advises Louise Colet to burrow away at her work like a mole (1853). To Louise he resembles 'a wild buffalo of the American prairie' (1846). To George Sand, however, he seems 'gentle as a lamb' (1866) – which he denies (1869) – and the pair of them chatter away like magpies (1866); ten years later, at her funeral, he weeps like a calf (1876). Alone in his study, he finishes the story he wrote especially for her, the story about the parrot; he bellows it out 'like a gorilla' (1876).

He flirts occasionally with the rhinoceros and the camel as self-images, but mainly, secretly, essentially, he is the Bear: a stub-born bear (1852), a bear thrust deeper into bearishness by the stupidity of his age (1853), a mangy bear (1854), even a stuffed bear (1869); and so on down to the very last year of his life, when he is still 'roaring as loudly as any bear in its cave' (1880). Note that in *Hérodias*, Flaubert's last completed work, the imprisoned prophet Iaokanann, when ordered to stop howling his denunciations against a corrupt world, replies that he too will continue crying out 'like a bear'.

> 'Language is like a cracked kettle on which we beat out tunes for bears to dance to, while all the time we long to move the stars to pity.'
>
> *Madame Bovary*

There were still bears around in Gourstave's time: brown bears in the Alps, reddish bears in Savoy. Bear hams were available from superior dealers in salted provisions. Alexandre Dumas ate bear steak at the Hôtel de la Poste, Marigny, in 1832; later, in his *Grand Dictionnaire de cuisine* (1870), he noted that 'Bear meat is now eaten by all the peoples of Europe'. From the chef to Their Majesties of Prussia Dumas obtained a recipe for bear's paws, Moscow style. Buy the paws skinned. Wash, salt, and marinade for three days. Casserole with bacon and vegetables for seven or eight hours; drain, wipe, sprinkle with pepper and turn in melted lard. Roll in breadcrumbs and grill for half an hour. Serve with a piquant sauce and two spoonfuls of redcurrant jelly.

It is not known whether Flaubear ever ate his namesake. He ate dromedary in Damascus in 1850. It seems a reasonable guess that if he had eaten bear he would have commented on such ipsophagy.

Exactly what species of bear was Flaubear? We can track his spoor through the Letters. At first he is just an unspecified *ours*, a bear (1841). He's still unspecified – though owner of a den – in 1843, in January 1845, and in May 1845 (by now he boasts a triple layer of fur). In June 1845 he wants to buy a painting of a bear for his room and entitle it 'Portrait of Gustave Flaubert' – 'to indicate my moral disposition and my social temperament'. So far we (and he too, perhaps) have been imagining a dark animal: an American brown bear, a Russian black bear, a reddish bear from Savoy. But in September 1845 Gustave firmly announces himself to be 'a white bear'.

Why? Is it because he's a bear who is also a white European? Is it perhaps an identity taken from the white bearskin rug on his study floor (which he first mentions in a letter to Louise Colet of August 1846, telling her that he likes to stretch out on it during the day. Maybe he chose his species so that he could lie on his rug, punning and camouflaged)? Or is this coloration indicative of a further shift away from humanity, a progression to the extremes of ursinity? The brown, the black, the reddish bear are not that far from man, from man's cities, man's friendship even. The coloured bears can mostly be tamed. But the white, the polar bear? It doesn't dance for man's pleasure; it doesn't eat berries; it can't be trapped by a weakness for honey.

Other bears are used. The Romans imported bears from Britain for their games. The Kamchatkans, a people of eastern Siberia, used to employ the intestines of bears as face-masks to protect them from the glare of the sun; and they used the sharpened shoulder-blade for cutting grass. But the white bear, *thalassarctos maritimus*, is the aristocrat of bears. Aloof, distant, stylishly diving for fish, roughly ambushing seals when they come up for air. The maritime bear. They travel great distances, carried along on floating pack-ice. One winter in the last century twelve great white bears got as far south as Iceland by this method; imagine them riding down on their melting thrones to make a terrifying, godlike landfall. William Scoresby, the Arctic explorer, noted that the liver of the bear is poisonous – the only part of any quadruped known to be so. Among zoo-keepers there is no known test for pregnancy in the polar bear. Strange facts that Flaubert might not have found strange.

> When the Yakuts, a Siberian people, meet a bear, they doff their caps, greet him, call him master, old man or grandfather, and promise not to attack him or even speak ill of him. But if he looks as though he may pounce on them, they shoot at him, and if they kill him, they cut him in pieces and roast him and regale themselves, repeating all the while, 'It is the Russians who are eating you, not us.'
> A.-F. Aulagnier, *Dictionnaire des Aliments et Boissons*

Were there other reasons why he chose to be a bear? The figurative sense of *ours* is much the same as in English: a rough, wild fellow. *Ours* is slang for a police cell. *Avoir ses ours*, to have one's bears, means 'to have the curse' (presumably because at such times a woman is supposed to behave like a bear with a sore head).

Etymologists trace this colloquialism to the turn of the century (Flaubert doesn't use it; he prefers *the redcoats have landed*, and other humorous variations thereon. On one occasion, having worried over Louise Colet's irregularity, he finally notes with relief that Lord Palmerston has arrived). *Un ours mal léché*, a badly licked bear, is someone uncouth and misanthropic. More apt for Flaubert, *un ours* was nineteenth-century slang for a play which had been frequently submitted and turned down, but eventually accepted.

No doubt Flaubert knew La Fontaine's fable of the Bear and the Man Who Delighted in Gardens. There once was a bear, an ugly and deformed creature, who hid from the world and lived all alone in a wood. After a while he became melancholy and frantic – 'for indeed, Reason seldom resides long among Anchorites'. So he set off and met a gardener, who had also lived a hermetic life, and also longed for company. The bear moved into the gardener's hovel. The gardener had become a hermit because he could not abide fools; but since the bear spoke scarcely three words in the course of the day, he was able to get on with his work without disturbance. The bear used to go hunting, and bring home game for both of them. When the gardener went to sleep, the bear would sit beside him devotedly and chase away the flies that tried to settle on his face. One day, a fly landed on the tip of the man's nose, and declined to be driven away. The bear became extremely angry with the fly, and eventually seized a huge stone and succeeded in killing it. Unfortunately, in the process he beat the gardener's brains out.

Perhaps Louise Colet knew the story too.

THE CAMEL

If Gustave hadn't been the Bear, he might have been the Camel. In January 1852 he writes to Louise and explains, yet again, his incorrigibility: he is as he is, he cannot change, he does not have a say in the matter, he is subject to the gravity of things, that gravity 'which makes the polar bear inhabit the icy regions and the camel walk upon the sand'. Why the camel? Perhaps because it is a fine example of the Flaubertian grotesque: it cannot help being serious and comic at the same time. He reports from Cairo: 'One of the finest things is the camel. I never tire of watching this

strange beast that lurches like a turkey and sways its neck like a
swan. Its cry is something I wear myself out trying to imitate –
I hope to bring it back with me – but it's hard to reproduce – a
rattle with a kind of tremendous gargling as an accompaniment.'

   The species also exhibited a character trait which was familiar
to Gustave: 'I am, in both my physical and my mental activity,
like the dromedary, which it is very hard to get going and very
hard, once it is going, to stop; continuity is what I need, whether
of rest or of motion.' This 1853 analogy, once it has got going,
also proves hard to stop: it is still running in a letter to George
Sand of 1868.

   Chameau, camel, was slang for an old courtesan. I do not think
this association would have put Flaubert off.

THE SHEEP

Flaubert loved fairs: the tumblers, the giantesses, the freaks, the
dancing bears. In Marseilles he visited a quayside booth advertis-
ing 'sheep-women', who ran around while sailors tugged at their
fleeces to see if they were real. This was not a high-class show:
'nothing could be stupider or filthier', he reported. He was far
more impressed at the fair in Guérande, an old fortified town
north-west of St Nazaire, which he visited during his walking
tour of Brittany with Du Camp in 1847. A booth run by a sly
peasant with a Picardy accent advertised 'a young phenomenon':
it turned out to be a five-legged sheep with a tail in the shape of
a trumpet. Flaubert was delighted, both with the freak and with
its owner. He admired the beast rapturously; he took the owner
out to dinner, assured him he would make a fortune, and advised
him to write to King Louis Philippe on the matter. By the end
of the evening, to Du Camp's clear disapproval, they were calling
one another *tu*.

   'The young phenomenon' fascinated Flaubert, and became
part of his teasing vocabulary. As he and Du Camp tramped
along, he would introduce his friend to the trees and the bushes
with mock gravity: 'May I present the young phenomenon?' At
Brest, Gustave fell in with the sly Picard and his freak once again,
dined and got drunk with him, and further praised the magnifi-
cence of his animal. He was often thus overcome by frivolous
manias; Du Camp waited for this one to run its course like a fever.

The following year, in Paris, Du Camp was ill, and confined to bed in his apartment. At four o'clock one afternoon he heard a commotion on the landing outside, and his door was flung open. Gustave strode in, followed by the five-legged sheep and the showman in the blue blouse. Some fair at the Invalides or the Champs-Elysées had disgorged them, and Flaubert was eager to share their rediscovery with his friend. Du Camp drily notes that the sheep 'did not conduct itself well'. Nor did Gustave – shouting for wine, leading the animal round the room and bellowing its virtues: 'The young phenomenon is three years old, has passed the Académie de Médecine, and has been honoured by visits from several crowned heads, etc.' After a quarter of an hour the sick Du Camp had had enough. 'I dismissed the sheep and its proprietor, and had my room swept.'

But the sheep had left its droppings in Flaubert's memory as well. A year before his death he was still reminding Du Camp about his surprise arrival with the young phenomenon, and still laughing as much as the day it had happened.

THE MONKEY, THE DONKEY, THE OSTRICH, THE SECOND DONKEY, AND MAXIME DU CAMP

A week ago I saw a monkey in the street jump on a donkey and try to wank him off – the donkey brayed and kicked, the monkey's owner shouted, the monkey itself squealed – apart from two or three children who laughed and me who found it very funny, no one paid any attention. When I described this to M. Bellin, the secretary at the consulate, he told me of having seen an ostrich trying to rape a donkey. Max had himself wanked off the other day in a deserted section among some ruins and said it was very good.

Letter to Louis Bouilhet, Cairo, January 15th, 1850

THE PARROT

Parrots are human to begin with; etymologically, that is. *Perroquet* is a diminutive of *Pierrot*; *parrot* comes from *Pierre*; Spanish *perico* derives from *Pedro*. For the Greeks, their ability to speak was an

item in the philosophical debate over the differences between
man and the animals. Aelian reports that 'the Brahmins honour
them above all other birds. And they add that it is only reasonable
to do so; for the parrot alone can give a good imitation of the
human voice.' Aristotle and Pliny note that the bird is extremely
lecherous when drunk. More pertinently, Buffon observes that
it is prone to epilepsy. Flaubert knew of this fraternal weakness:
the notes he took on parrots when researching *Un cœur simple*
include a list of their maladies – gout, epilepsy, aphtha and throat
ulcers.

To recapitulate. First there is Loulou, Félicité's parrot. Then
there are the two contending stuffed parrots, one at the Hôtel-
Dieu and one at Croisset. Then there are the three live parrots,
two at Trouville and one at Venice; plus the sick parakeet at
Antibes. As a possible source for Loulou we can, I think, elimi-
nate the mother of a 'hideous' English family encountered by
Gustave on the boat from Alexandria to Cairo: with a green eye-
shade attached to her bonnet, she looked 'like a sick old parrot'.

Caroline, in her *Souvenirs intimes*, remarks that 'Félicité and
her parrot really lived' and directs us towards the first Trouville
parrot, that of Captain Barbey, as the true ancestor of Loulou.
But this doesn't answer the more important question: how, and
when, did a simple (if magnificent) living bird of the 1830s get
turned into a complicated, transcendent parrot of the 1870s? We
probably shan't ever find out; but we can suggest a point at which
the transformation might have begun.

The second, uncompleted part of *Bouvard et Pécuchet* was to
consist mainly of '*La Copie*', an enormous dossier of oddities, idi-
ocies and self-condemning quotations, which the two clerks
were solemnly to copy out for their own edification, and which
Flaubert would reproduce with a more sardonic intent. Among
the thousands of press cuttings he collected for possible inclusion
in the dossier is the following story, clipped from *L'Opinion
nationale* of June 20th, 1863:

'In Gérouville, near Arlon, there lived a man who owned
a magnificent parrot. It was his sole love. As a young man, he
had been the victim of an ill-starred passion; the experience had
made him misanthropic, and now he lived alone with his parrot.
He had taught the bird to pronounce the name of his lost love,
and this name was repeated a hundred times a day. This was the
bird's only talent, but in the eyes of its owner, the unfortunate

Henri K—, it was a talent worth all the others. Every time he heard the sacred name pronounced by this strange voice, Henri thrilled with joy; it seemed to him like a voice from beyond the grave, something mysterious and superhuman.

'Solitude enflamed the imagination of Henri K—, and gradually the parrot began to take on a rare significance in his mind. For him it became a kind of holy bird: he would handle it with deep respect, and spend hours in rapt contemplation of it. Then the parrot, returning its master's gaze with an unflinching eye, would murmur the cabbalistic word, and Henri's soul would be filled with the memory of his lost happiness. This strange life lasted several years. One day, however, people noticed that Henri K— was looking gloomier than usual; and there was a strange, wild light in his eye. The parrot had died.

'Henri K— continued to live alone, now completely so. He had no link with the outside world. He became more and more wrapped up in himself. Sometimes he would not leave his room for days on end. He would eat whatever food was brought him, but took no notice of anyone. Gradually he began to believe that he himself had turned into a parrot. As if in imitation of the dead bird, he would squawk out the name he loved to hear; he would try walking like a parrot, perching on things, and extending his arms as if he had wings to beat.

'Sometimes, he would lose his temper and start breaking the furniture; and his family decided to send him to the *maison de santé* at Gheel. On the journey there, however, he escaped during the night. The next morning they found him perched in a tree. Persuading him to come down proved very difficult, until someone had the idea of placing at the foot of his tree an enormous parrot-cage. On seeing this, the unfortunate monomaniac climbed down and was recaptured. He is now in the *maison de santé* at Gheel.'

We know that Flaubert was struck by this newspaper story. After the line, 'gradually the parrot began to take on a rare significance in his mind', he made the following annotation: 'Change the animal: make it a dog instead of a parrot.' Some brief plan for a future work, no doubt. But when, finally, the story of Loulou and Félicité came to be written, it was the parrot which stayed in place, and the owner who was changed.

Before *Un cœur simple*, parrots flit briefly through Flaubert's work, and through his letters. Explaining to Louise the pull of foreign lands (December 11th, 1846), Gustave writes: 'When we are children, we all want to live in the country of parrots and candied dates.' Comforting a sad and discouraged Louise (March 27th, 1853), he reminds her that we are all caged birds, and that life weighs the heaviest on those with the largest wings: 'We are all to a greater or lesser degree eagles or canaries, parrots or vultures.' Denying to Louise that he is vain (December 9th, 1852), he distinguishes between Pride and Vanity: 'Pride is a wild beast which lives in caves and roams the desert; Vanity, on the other hand, is a parrot which hops from branch to branch and chatters away in full view.' Describing to Louise the heroic quest for style that *Madame Bovary* represents (April 19th, 1852), he explains: 'How many times have I fallen flat on my face, just when I thought I had it within my grasp. Still, I feel that I mustn't die without making sure that the style I can hear inside my head comes roaring out and drowns the cries of parrots and cicadas.'

In *Salammbô*, as I have already mentioned, the Carthaginian translators have parrots tattooed on their chests (a detail perhaps more apt than authentic?); in the same novel, some of the Barbarians have 'sunshades in their hands or parrots on their shoulders'; while the furnishings of Salammbô's terrace include a small ivory bed whose cushions are stuffed with parrot feathers – 'for this was a prophetic bird, consecrated to the gods'.

There are no parrots in *Madame Bovary* or *Bouvard et Pecuchet*; no entry for PERROQUET in the *Dictionnaire des idées reçues*; and only a couple of brief mentions in *La Tentation de saint Antoine*. In *Saint Julien l'hospitalier* few animal species avoid slaughter during Julien's first hunt – roosting grouse have their legs cut off, and low-flying cranes are snapped out of the sky by the huntsman's whip – but the parrot remains unmentioned and unharmed. In the second hunt, however, when Julien's ability to kill evaporates, when the animals become elusive, threatening observers of their stumbling pursuer, the parrot makes an appearance. Flashes of light in the forest, which Julien assumed to be stars low in the sky, prove to be the eyes of witching beasts: wild cats, squirrels, owls, parrots and monkeys.

And let's not forget the parrot that wasn't there. In *L'Education sentimentale* Frédéric wanders through an area of Paris wrecked by the 1848 uprising. He walks past barricades which have been torn down; he sees black pools that must be blood; houses have their blinds hanging like rags from a single nail. Here and there amid the chaos, delicate things have survived by chance. Frédéric peers in at a window. He sees a clock, some prints – and a parrot's perch.

It isn't so different, the way we wander through the past. Lost, disordered, fearful, we follow what signs there remain; we read the street names, but cannot be confident where we are. All around is wreckage. These people never stopped fighting. Then we see a house; a writer's house, perhaps. There is a plaque on the front wall. 'Gustave Flaubert, French writer, 1821–1880, lived here while –' but then the letters shrink impossibly, as if on some optician's chart. We walk closer. We look in at a window. Yes, it's true; despite the carnage some delicate things have survived. A clock still ticks. Prints on the wall remind us that art was once appreciated here. A parrot's perch catches the eye. We look for the parrot. Where is the parrot? We still hear its voice; but all we can see is a bare wooden perch. The bird has flown.

DOGS

1 *The Dog Romantic.* This was a large Newfoundland, the property of Elisa Schlesinger. If we believe Du Camp, he was called Nero; if we believe Goncourt, he was called Thabor. Gustave met Mme Schlesinger at Trouville: he was fourteen and a half, she twenty-six. She was beautiful, her husband was rich; she wore an immense straw hat, and her well-modelled shoulders could be glimpsed through her muslin dress. Nero, or Thabor, went everywhere with her. Gustave often followed at a discreet distance. Once, on the dunes, she opened her dress and suckled her baby. He was lost, helpless, tortured, fallen. Ever afterwards he would maintain that the brief summer of 1836 had cauterised his heart. (We are at liberty, of course, to disbelieve him. What did the Goncourts say? 'Though perfectly frank by nature, he is never wholly sincere in what he says he feels and suffers and loves.') And whom did he first tell of this passion? His schoolfriends? His mother? Mme Schlesinger herself? No: he told Nero (or Thabor). He would take the Newfoundland for walks across the Trouville sands, and in the soft secrecy of a dune he would drop down on his knees and wrap his arms around the dog. Then he would kiss it where he knew its mistress's lips had been not long before (the location of the kiss remains a matter of debate:

some say on the muzzle, some say on the top of the head); he would whisper in the shaggy ear of Nero (or Thabor) the secrets he longed to whisper in the ear that lay between the muslin dress and the straw hat; and he would burst into tears.

The memory of Mme Schlesinger, and her presence too, pursued Flaubert for the rest of his life. What happened to the dog is not recorded.

2 *The Dog Practical*. Not sufficient study, to my mind, has been made of the pets which were kept at Croisset. They flicker into brief existence, sometimes with a name attached, sometimes not; we rarely know when or how they were acquired, and when or how they died. Let us assemble them:

> In 1840 Gustave's sister Caroline had a goat called Souvit.
> In 1840 the family had a black Newfoundland bitch called Néo (perhaps this name influenced Du Camp's memory of Mme Schlesinger's Newfoundland).
> In 1853 Gustave dines alone at Croisset with an unnamed dog.
> In 1854 Gustave dines with a dog named Dakno; probably the same animal as above.
> In 1856–7 his niece Caroline has a pet rabbit.
> In 1856 he exhibits on his lawn a stuffed crocodile he has brought back from the East: enabling it to bask in the sun again for the first time in 3,000 years.
> In 1858 a wild rabbit takes up residence in the garden; Gustave forbids its slaughter.
> In 1866 Gustave dines alone with a bowl of goldfish.
> In 1867 the pet dog (no name, no breed) is killed by poison which has been laid down for rats.
> In 1872 Gustave acquires Julio, a greyhound.
> *Note*: If we are to complete the list of known domestic creatures to which Gustave played host, we must record that in October 1842 he suffered an infestation of crab-lice.

Of the pets listed above, the only one about which we have proper information is Julio. In April 1872 Mme Flaubert died; Gustave was left alone in the big house, having meals at a large table 'tête-à-tête with myself'. In September his friend Edmond Laporte offered him a greyhound. Flaubert hesitated, being frightened of rabies; but eventually accepted it. He named the dog Julio (in honour of Juliet Herbert? – if you wish) and quickly grew fond of it. By the end of the month he was writing to his niece that his sole distraction (thirty-six years after casting his arms round Mme Schlesinger's Newfoundland) was to embrace his '*pauvre chien*'. 'His calm and his beauty make one jealous.'

The greyhound became his final companion at Croisset. An unlikely couple: the stout, sedentary novelist and the sleek racing dog. Julio's own private life began to feature in Flaubert's correspondence: he announced that the dog had become 'morganatically united' with 'a young person' of the neighbourhood. Owner and pet even got ill together: in the spring of 1879 Flaubert had rheumatism and a swollen foot, while Julio had an unspecified canine disease. 'He is exactly like a person,' Gustave wrote. 'He makes little gestures that are profoundly human.' Both of them recovered, and staggered on through the year. The winter of 1879–80 was exceptionally cold. Flaubert's housekeeper made Julio a coat out of an old pair of trousers. They got through the winter together. Flaubert died in the spring.

What happened to the dog is not recorded.

3 *The Dog Figurative.* Madame Bovary has a dog, given to her by a game-keeper whose chest infection has been cured by her husband. It is *une petite levrette d'Italie*: a small Italian greyhound bitch. Nabokov, who is exceedingly peremptory with all translators of Flaubert, renders this as whippet. Whether he is zoologically correct or not, he certainly loses the sex of the animal, which seems to me important. This dog is given a passing significance as . . . less than a symbol, not exactly a metaphor; call it a figure. Emma acquires the greyhound while she and Charles are still living at Tostes: the time of early, inchoate stirrings of dissatisfaction within her; the time of boredom and discontent, but not yet of corruption. She takes her greyhound for walks, and the animal becomes, tactfully, briefly, for half a paragraph or so, something more than just a dog. 'At first her thoughts would wander aimlessly, like her greyhound, which ran in circles, yapping after yellow butterflies, chasing field-mice and nibbling at poppies on the edge of a cornfield. Then, gradually, her ideas would come together until, sitting on a stretch of grass and stabbing at it with the end of her parasol, she would repeat to herself, "Oh God, why did I get married?"'

That is the first appearance of the dog, a delicate insertion; afterwards, Emma holds its head and kisses it (as Gustave had done to Nero/Thabor): the dog has a melancholy expression, and she talks to it as if to someone in need of consolation. She is talking, in other words (and in both senses), to herself. The dog's second appearance is also its last. Charles and Emma move from Tostes to Yonville – a journey which marks Emma's shift from dreams and fantasies to reality and corruption. Note also the traveller who shares the coach with them: the ironically named Monsieur Lheureux, the fancy-goods dealer and part-time usurer who finally ensnares Emma (financial corruption marks her fall as much as sexual corruption). On the journey, Emma's greyhound escapes. They spend a good quarter of an hour whistling for it, and then give up. M. Lheureux plies Emma with a foretaste of false comfort: he tells her consoling stories of lost dogs which have returned to their masters despite great distances; why, there was even one that made it all the way back to Paris from Constantinople. Emma's reaction to these stories is not recorded.

What happened to the dog is also not recorded.

4 *The Dog Drowned and the Dog Fantastical.* In January 1851 Flaubert and Du Camp were in Greece. They visited Marathón, Eleusis and Salamís. They met General Morandi, a soldier of fortune who had fought at Missolonghi, and who indignantly denied to them the calumny put about by the British aristocracy that Byron had deteriorated morally while in Greece: 'He was magnificent,' the General told them. 'He looked like Achilles.' Du Camp records how they visited Thermopylae and re-read their Plutarch on the battlefield. On January 12th they were heading towards Eleuthera – the two friends, a dragoman, and an armed policeman they employed as a guard – when the weather worsened. Rain fell heavily; the plain they were crossing became inundated; the policeman's Scotch terrier was suddenly carried away and drowned in a swollen torrent. The rain turned to snow, and darkness closed in. Clouds shut out the stars; their solitude was complete.

An hour passed, then another; snow gathered thickly in the folds of their clothes; they missed their road. The policeman fired some pistol shots in the air, but there was no answer. Saturated, and very cold, they faced the prospect of a night in the saddle amid inhospitable terrain. The policeman was grieving for his Scotch terrier, while the dragoman – a fellow with big, prominent eyes like a lobster's – had proved singularly incompetent throughout the trip; even his cooking had been a failure. They were riding cautiously, straining their eyes for a distant light, when the policeman shouted, 'Halt!' A dog was barking somewhere in the far distance. It was then that the dragoman displayed his sole talent: the ability to bark like a dog. He began to do so with a desperate vigour. When he stopped, they listened, and heard answering barks. The dragoman howled again. Slowly they advanced, stopping every so often to bark and be barked back at, then reorienting themselves. After half an hour of marching towards the ever-loudening village dog, they eventually found shelter for the night.

What happened to the dragoman is not recorded.

Note: Is it fair to add that Gustave's journal offers a different version of the story? He agrees about the weather; he agrees about the date; he agrees that the dragoman couldn't cook (a constant offering of lamb and hard-boiled eggs drove him to lunch on dry bread). Strangely, though, he doesn't mention reading Plutarch on the battlefield. The policeman's dog (breed unidentified in Flaubert's version) wasn't carried away by a torrent; it just drowned in deep water. As for the barking dragoman, Gustave merely records that when they heard the village dog in the distance, he ordered the policeman to fire his pistol in the air. The dog barked its reply; the policeman fired again; and by this more ordinary means they progressed towards shelter.

What happened to the truth is not recorded.

5

SNAP!

IN THE MORE BOOKISH areas of English middle-class society, whenever a coincidence occurs there is usually someone at hand to comment, 'It's just like Anthony Powell.' Often the coincidence turns out, on the shortest examination, to be unremarkable: typically, it might consist of two acquaintances from school or university running into one another after a gap of several years. But the name of Powell is invoked to give legitimacy to the event; it's rather like getting the priest to bless your car.

I don't much care for coincidences. There's something spooky about them: you sense momentarily what it must be like to live in an ordered, God-run universe, with Himself looking over your shoulder and helpfully dropping coarse hints about a cosmic plan. I prefer to feel that things are chaotic, free-wheeling, permanently as well as temporarily crazy – to feel the certainty of human ignorance, brutality and folly. 'Whatever else happens,' Flaubert wrote when the Franco-Prussian war broke out, 'we shall remain stupid.' Mere boastful pessimism? Or a necessary razing of expectation before anything can be properly thought, or done, or written?

I don't even care for harmless, comic coincidences. I once went out to dinner and discovered that the seven other people present had all just finished reading *A Dance to the Music of Time*. I didn't relish this: not least because it meant that I didn't break my silence until the cheese course.

And as for coincidences in books – there's something cheap and sentimental about the device; it can't help always seeming aesthetically gimcrack. That troubadour who passes by just in time to rescue the girl from a hedgerow scuffle; the sudden but convenient Dickensian benefactors; the neat shipwreck on a foreign shore which reunites siblings and lovers. I once disparaged this lazy stratagem to a poet I met, a man presumably skilled in the coincidences of rhyme. 'Perhaps,' he replied with a genial loftiness, 'you have too prosaic a mind?'

'But surely,' I came back, rather pleased with myself, 'a prosaic mind is the best judge of prose?'

I'd ban coincidences, if I were a dictator of fiction. Well, perhaps not entirely. Coincidences would be permitted in the picaresque; that's where they belong. Go on, take them: let the pilot whose parachute has failed to open land in the haystack, let the virtuous pauper with the gangrenous foot discover the buried treasure – it's all right, it doesn't really matter . . .

One way of legitimising coincidences, of course, is to call them ironies. That's what smart people do. Irony is, after all, the modern mode, a drinking companion for resonance and wit. Who could be against it? And yet sometimes I wonder if the wittiest, most resonant irony isn't just a well-brushed, well-educated coincidence.

I don't know what Flaubert thought about coincidence. I had hoped for some characteristic entry in his unflaggingly ironic *Dictionnaire des idées reçues*; but it jumps pointedly from *cognac* to *coitus*. Still, his love of irony is plain; it's one of the most modern things about him. In Egypt he was delighted to discover that *almeh*, the word for 'bluestocking', had gradually lost this original meaning and come to signify 'whore'.

Do ironies accrete around the ironist? Flaubert certainly thought so. The celebrations for the centenary of Voltaire's death in 1878 were stage-managed by the chocolate firm of Ménier. 'That poor old genius,' Gustave commented, 'how irony never quits him.' It badgered Gustave too. When he wrote of himself, 'I attract mad people and animals', perhaps he should have added 'and ironies'.

Take *Madame Bovary*. It was prosecuted for obscenity by Ernest Pinard, the advocate who also enjoys the shabby fame of leading the case against *Les Fleurs du mal*. Some years after *Bovary* had been cleared, Pinard was discovered to be the anonymous author of a collection of priapic verses. The novelist was much amused.

And then, take the book itself. Two of the best-remembered things in it are Emma's adulterous drive in the curtained cab (a passage found especially scandalous by right-thinkers), and the very last line of the novel – 'He has just received the Legion of Honour' – which confirms the bourgeois apotheosis of the pharmacist Homais. Now, the idea for the curtained cab appears to have come to Flaubert as a result of his own eccentric conduct in Paris when anxious to avoid running into Louise Colet.

To avoid being recognised, he took to driving everywhere in a closed cab. Thus, he maintained his chastity by using a device he would later employ to facilitate his heroine's sexual indulgence.

With Homais's *Légion d'honneur*, it's the other way round: life imitates and ironises art. Barely ten years after that final line of *Madame Bovary* was written, Flaubert, arch anti-bourgeois and virile hater of governments, allowed himself to be created a *chevalier* of the *Légion d'honneur*. Consequently, the last line of his life parroted the last line of his masterpiece: at his funeral a picket of soldiers turned up to fire a volley over the coffin, and thus bid the state's traditional farewell to one of its most improbable and sardonic *chevaliers*.

And if you don't like these ironies, I have others.

1 DAWN AT THE PYRAMIDS

In December 1849 Flaubert and Du Camp climbed the Great Pyramid of Cheops. They had slept beside it the previous night, and rose at five to make sure of reaching the top by sunrise. Gustave washed his face in a canvas pail; a jackal howled; he smoked a pipe. Then, with two Arabs pushing him and two pulling, he was bundled slowly up the high stones of the Pyramid to the summit. Du Camp – the first man to photograph the Sphinx – was there already. Ahead of them lay the Nile, bathed in mist, like a white sea; behind them lay the dark desert, like a petrified purple ocean. At last, a streak of orange light appeared to the east; and gradually the white sea in front of them became an immense expanse of fertile green, while the purple ocean behind turned shimmering white. The rising sun lit up the topmost stones of the Pyramid, and Flaubert, looking down at his feet, noticed a small business-card pinned in place. 'Humbert, Frotteur', it read, and gave a Rouen address.

What a moment of perfectly targeted irony. A modernist moment, too: this is the sort of exchange, in which the everyday tampers with the sublime, that we like to think of proprietorially as typical of our own wry and unfoolable age. We thank Flaubert for picking it up; in a sense, the irony wasn't there until he observed it. Other visitors might have seen the business-card as merely a piece of litter – it could have stayed there, its drawing-pins slowly rusting, for years; but Flaubert gave it function.

And if we are feeling interpretative, we can look further into this brief event. Isn't it, perhaps, a notable historical coincidence that the greatest European novelist of the nineteenth century should be introduced at the Pyramids to one of the twentieth century's most notorious fictional characters? That Flaubert, still damp from skewering boys in Cairo bath-houses, should fall on the name of Nabokov's seducer of underage American girlhood? And further, what is the profession of this single-barrelled version of Humbert Humbert? He is a *frotteur*. Literally, a French polisher; but also, the sort of sexual deviant who loves the rub of the crowd.

And that's not all. Now for the irony about the irony. It turns out, from Flaubert's travel notes, that the business-card wasn't pinned in place by Monsieur Frotteur himself; it was put there by the lithe and thoughtful Maxime du Camp, who had scampered ahead in the purple night and laid out this little mousetrap for his friend's sensibility. The balance of our response shifts with this knowledge: Flaubert becomes plodding and predictable; Du Camp becomes the wit, the dandy, the teaser of modernism before modernism has declared itself.

But then we read on again. If we turn to Flaubert's letters, we discover him, some days after the incident, writing to his mother about the *sublime surprise* of the discovery. 'And to think that I had specially brought that card all the way from Croisset and didn't even get to put it in place! The villain took advantage of my forgetfulness and discovered the wonderfully apposite business-card in the bottom of my folding hat.' So, ever stranger: Flaubert, when he left home, was already preparing the special effects which would later appear entirely characteristic of how he perceived the world. Ironies breed; realities recede. And why, just out of interest, did he take his folding hat to the Pyramids?

2 DESERT ISLAND DISCS

Gustave used to look back on his summer holidays at Trouville – spent between Captain Barbey's parrot and Mme Schlesinger's dog – as among the few tranquil times of his life. Reminiscing from the autumn of his mid-twenties, he told Louise Colet that 'the greatest events of my life have been a few thoughts, reading, certain sunsets by the sea at Trouville, and conversations of five

or six hours on the trot with a friend [Alfred le Poittevin] who
is now married and lost to me.'

In Trouville he met Gertrude and Harriet Collier, daughters
of a British naval attaché. Both, it seems, became enamoured
of him. Harriet gave him her portrait, which hung over the
chimney-piece at Croisset; but it was of Gertrude that he was
fonder. Her feelings for him may be guessed at from a text she
wrote decades later, after Gustave's death. Adopting the style of
romantic fiction, and using disguised names, she boasts that
'I loved him passionately, adoringly. Years have passed over my
head but I have never felt the worship, the love and yet the fear
that took possession of my soul then. Something told me I should
never be his . . . But I knew, in the deepest recesses of my heart,
how truly I could love him, honour him and obey him.'

Gertrude's lush memoir might well be fanciful: what, after all,
is more sentimentally alluring than a dead genius and an adolescent beach holiday? But perhaps it wasn't. Gustave and Gertrude
kept in distant touch along the decades. He sent her a copy
of *Madame Bovary* (she thanked him, pronounced the novel
'hideous', and quoted at him Philip James Bailey, author of
Festus, on the writer's duty to give moral instruction to the
reader); and forty years after that first meeting in Trouville she
came to visit him at Croisset. The handsome, blond cavalier
of her youth was now bald and red-faced, with only a couple of
teeth left in his head. But his gallantry remained in good health.
'My old friend, my youth,' he wrote to her afterwards, 'during
the long years I have lived without knowing your whereabouts,
there was perhaps not a single day when I did not think of you.'

During the course of those long years (in 1847, to be precise,
the year after Flaubert was recalling his Trouville sunsets to
Louise) Gertrude had promised to love, honour and obey someone else: an English economist called Charles Tennant. While
Flaubert slowly attained European fame as a novelist, Gertrude
was herself to publish a book: an edition of her grandfather's
journal, called *France on the Eve of the Great Revolution*. She died in
1918 at the age of ninety-nine; and she had a daughter, Dorothy,
who married the explorer Henry Morton Stanley.

On one of Stanley's trips to Africa, his party got into difficulties. The explorer was obliged gradually to discard all his unnecessary belongings. It was, in a way, a reverse, real-life version
of 'Desert Island Discs': instead of being equipped with things

to make life in the tropics more bearable, Stanley was having to get rid of things to survive there. Books were obviously super-numerary, and he began jettisoning them until he got down to those two which every guest on 'Desert Island Discs' is furnished with as a bare, civilised minimum: the Bible and Shakespeare. Stanley's third book, the one he threw out before reducing him-self to this final minimum, was *Salammbô*.

3 THE SNAP OF COFFINS

The weary, valetudinarian tone of Flaubert's letter to Louise Colet about the sunsets was not a pose. 1846, after all, was the year when first his father and then his sister Caroline had died. 'What a house!' he wrote. 'What a hell!' All night Gustave watched beside his sister's corpse: she lying in her white wedding-dress, he sitting and reading Montaigne.

On the morning of the funeral, he gave her a last farewell kiss as she lay in her coffin. For the second time in three months he heard the battering sound of hobnailed boots climbing the wooden stairs to fetch a body. Mourning was scarcely possible that day: practicalities supervened. There was a lock of Caroline's hair to be cut, and plaster casts of her face and hands to be taken: 'I saw the great paws of those louts touching her and covering her face with plaster.' Great louts are necessary for funerals.

The trail to the cemetery was familiar from the time before. At the graveside Caroline's husband broke down. Gustave watched as the coffin was lowered. Suddenly, it got stuck: the hole had been dug too narrow. The grave-diggers got hold of the coffin and shook it; they pulled it this way and that, twisted it, hacked at it with a spade, levered at it with crowbars; but still it wouldn't move. Finally, one of them placed his foot flat on the box, right over Caroline's face, and forced it down into the grave.

Gustave had a bust made of that face; it presided over his study all his working life, until his own death, in the same house, in 1880. Maupassant helped lay out the body. Flaubert's niece asked for the traditional cast of the writer's hand to be taken. This proved impossible: the fist was too tightly clenched in its terminal seizure.

The procession set off, first to the church at Canteleu, then to the Cimetière Monumental, where the picket of soldiers fired its ludicrous gloss on the last line of *Madame Bovary*. A few words were spoken, then the coffin was lowered. It got stuck. The width had been correctly judged on this occasion; but the grave-diggers had skimped on the length. Sons of louts grappled with the coffin in vain; they could neither cram it in nor twist it out. After a few embarrassed minutes the mourners slowly departed, leaving Flaubert jammed into the ground at an oblique angle.

The Normans are a famously stingy race, and doubtless their grave-diggers are no exception; perhaps they resent every super-fluous sod they cut, and maintained this resentment as a profes-sional tradition from 1846 to 1880. Perhaps Nabokov had read Flaubert's letters before writing *Lolita*. Perhaps H. M. Stanley's admiration for Flaubert's African novel isn't entirely surprising. Perhaps what we read as brute coincidence, silky irony, or brave, far-sighted modernism, looked quite different at the time. Flau-bert took Monsieur Humbert's business-card all the way from Rouen to the Pyramids. Was it meant to be a chuckling adver-tisement for his own sensibility; a tease about the gritty, un-polishable surface of the desert; or might it just have been a joke on us?

6

EMMA BOVARY'S EYES

LET ME TELL YOU why I hate critics. Not for the normal reasons: that they're failed creators (they usually aren't; they may be failed critics, but that's another matter); or that they're by nature carping, jealous and vain (they usually aren't; if anything, they might better be accused of over-generosity, of upgrading the second-rate so that their own fine discriminations thereby appear the rarer). No, the reason I hate critics – well, some of the time – is that they write sentences like this:

> Flaubert does not build up his characters, as did Balzac, by objective, external description; in fact, so careless is he of their outward appearance that on one occasion he gives Emma brown eyes (14); on another deep black eyes (15); and on another blue eyes (16).

This precise and disheartening indictment was drawn up by the late Dr Enid Starkie, Reader Emeritus in French Literature at the University of Oxford, and Flaubert's most exhaustive British biographer. The numbers in her text refer to footnotes in which she spears the novelist with chapter and verse.

I once heard Dr Starkie lecture, and I'm glad to report that she had an atrocious French accent; one of those deliveries full of dame-school confidence and absolutely no ear, swerving between workaday correctness and farcical error, often within the same word. Naturally, this didn't affect her competence to teach at the University of Oxford, because until quite recently the place preferred to treat modern languages as if they were dead: this made them more respectable, more like the distant per-fections of Latin and Greek. Even so, it did strike me as peculiar that someone who lived by French literature should be so calami-tously inadequate at making the basic words of the language sound as they did when her subjects, her heroes (her paymasters, too, you could say) first pronounced them.

You might think this a cheap revenge on a dead lady critic simply for pointing out that Flaubert didn't have a very reliable notion of Emma Bovary's eyes. But then I don't hold with the precept *de mortuis nil nisi bonum* (I speak as a doctor, after all); and it's hard to underestimate the irritation when a critic points out something like that to you. The irritation isn't with Dr Starkie, not at first – she was only, as they say, doing her job – but with Flaubert. So that painstaking genius couldn't even keep the eyes of his most famous character a consistent colour? *Ha*. And then, unable to be cross with him for long, you shift your feelings over to the critic.

I must confess that in all the times *I* read *Madame Bovary*, I never noticed the heroine's rainbow eyes. Should I have? Would you? Was I perhaps too busy noticing things that Dr Starkie was missing (though what they might have been I can't for the moment think)? Put it another way: is there a perfect reader somewhere, a total reader? Does Dr Starkie's reading of *Madame Bovary* contain all the responses which I have when I read the book, and then add a whole lot more, so that my reading is in a way pointless? Well, I hope not. My reading might be pointless in terms of the history of literary criticism; but it's not pointless in terms of pleasure. I can't prove that lay readers enjoy books more than professional critics; but I can tell you one advantage we have over them. We can forget. Dr Starkie and her kind are cursed with memory: the books they teach and write about can never fade from their brains. They become family. Perhaps this is why some critics develop a faintly patronising tone towards their subjects. They act as if Flaubert, or Milton, or Wordsworth were some tedious old aunt in a rocking chair, who smelt of stale powder, was only interested in the past, and hadn't said anything new for years. Of course, it's her house, and everybody's living in it rent free; but even so, surely it is, well, you know . . . *time*?

Whereas the common but passionate reader is allowed to forget; he can go away, be unfaithful with other writers, come back and be entranced again. Domesticity need never intrude on the relationship; it may be sporadic, but when there it is always intense. There's none of the daily rancour which develops when people live bovinely together. I never find myself, fatigue in the voice, reminding Flaubert to hang up the bathmat or use the lavatory brush. Which is what Dr Starkie can't help herself doing. Look, writers aren't *perfect*, I want to cry; any more than husbands and wives are perfect. The only unfailing rule is, if they seem so, they can't be. I never thought my wife was perfect. I loved her, but I never deceived myself. I remember . . . But I'll keep that for another time.

I'll remember instead another lecture I once attended, some years ago at the Cheltenham Literary Festival. It was given by a professor from Cambridge, Christopher Ricks, and it was a very shiny performance. His bald head was shiny; his black shoes were shiny; and his lecture was very shiny indeed. Its theme was Mistakes in Literature and Whether They Matter. Yevtushenko, for example, apparently made a howler in one of his poems about the American nightingale. Pushkin was quite wrong about the sort of military dress worn at balls. John Wain was wrong about the Hiroshima pilot. Nabokov was wrong – rather surprising, this – about the phonetics of the name Lolita. There were other examples: Coleridge, Yeats and Browning were some of those caught out not knowing a hawk from a handsaw, or not even knowing what a handsaw was in the first place.

Two examples particularly struck me. The first was a remarkable discovery about *Lord of the Flies*. In the famous scene where Piggy's spectacles are used for the rediscovery of fire, William Golding got his optics wrong. Completely back to front, in fact. Piggy is short-sighted; and the spectacles he would have been prescribed for this condition could not possibly have been used as burning glasses. Whichever way you held them, they would have been quite unable to make the rays of the sun converge.

The second example concerned 'The Charge of the Light Brigade'. 'Into the valley of Death/Rode the six hundred.' Tennyson wrote the poem very quickly, after reading a report in *The Times* which included the phrase 'someone had blundered'. He also relied on an earlier account which had mentioned '607 sabres'. Subsequently, however, the number of those who took part in what Camille Rousset called *ce terrible et sanglant steeple-chase* was officially corrected to 673. 'Into the valley of Death/ Rode the six hundred and seventy-three'? Not quite enough swing to it, somehow. Perhaps it could have been rounded up to seven hundred – still not quite accurate, but at least more accurate? Tennyson considered the matter and decided to leave the poem as he had written it: 'Six is much better than seven hundred (as I think) metrically so keep it.'

Not putting '673' or '700' or '*c*.700' instead of '600' hardly seems to qualify as a Mistake to me. The shakiness of Golding's optics, on the other hand, must definitely be classed as an error. The next question is, Does it matter? As far as I can remember Professor Ricks's lecture, his argument was that if the factual side of literature becomes unreliable, then ploys such as irony and fantasy become much harder to use. If you don't know what's true, or what's meant to be true, then the value of what isn't true, or isn't meant to be true, becomes diminished. This seems to me a very sound argument; though I do wonder to how many cases of literary mistake it actually applies. With Piggy's glasses, I should think that (a) very few people apart from oculists, opticians and bespectacled professors of English would notice; and (b) when they do notice, they merely detonate the error – like blowing up a small bomb with a controlled explosion. What's more, this detonation (which takes place on a remote beach, with only a dog as witness) doesn't set fire to other parts of the novel.

Mistakes like Golding's are 'external mistakes' – disparities between what the book claims to be the case, and what we know the reality to be; often they merely indicate a lack of specific technical knowledge on the writer's part. The sin is pardonable. What, though, about 'internal mistakes', when the writer claims two incompatible things within his own creation? Emma's eyes are brown, Emma's eyes are blue. Alas, this can be put down only to incompetence, to sloppy literary habits. I read the other day a well-praised first novel in which the narrator – who is both sexually inexperienced and an amateur of French literature – comically rehearses to himself the best way to kiss a girl without being rebuffed: 'With a slow, sensual, irresistible strength, draw her gradually towards you while gazing into her eyes as if you had just been given a copy of the first, suppressed edition of *Madame Bovary*.'

I thought this was quite neatly put, indeed rather amusing. The only trouble is, there's no such thing as a 'first, suppressed edition of *Madame Bovary*'. The novel, as I should have thought was tolerably well known, first appeared serially in the *Revue de Paris*; then came the prosecution for obscenity; and only after the acquittal was the work published in book form. I expect the young novelist (it seems unfair to give his name) was thinking of the 'first, suppressed edition' of *Les Fleurs du mal*. No doubt he'll get it right in time for his second edition; if there is one.

Eyes of brown, eyes of blue. Does it matter? Not, does it matter if the writer contradicts himself; but, does it matter what colour they are anyway? I feel sorry for novelists when they have to mention women's eyes: there's so little choice, and whatever colouring is decided upon inevitably carries banal implications. Her eyes are blue: innocence and honesty. Her eyes are black: passion and depth. Her eyes are green: wildness and jealousy. Her eyes are brown: reliability and common sense. Her eyes are violet: the novel is by Raymond Chandler. How can you escape all this without some haversack of a parenthesis about the lady's character? Her eyes are mud-coloured; her eyes changed hue according to the contact lenses she wore; he never looked her in the eye. Well, take your pick. My wife's eyes were greeny-blue, which makes her story a long one. And so I suspect that in the writer's moments of private candour, he probably admits the pointlessness of describing eyes. He slowly imagines the character, moulds her into shape, and then – probably the last thing of all – pops a pair of glass eyes into those empty sockets. Eyes? Oh yes, she'd better have eyes, he reflects, with a weary courtesy.

Bouvard and Pécuchet, during their investigations into literature, find that they lose respect for an author when he strays into error. I am more surprised by how few mistakes writers make. So the Bishop of Liège dies fifteen years before he should: does this invalidate *Quentin Durward*? It's a trivial offence, something tossed to the reviewers. I see the novelist at the stern rail of a cross-Channel ferry, throwing bits of gristle from his sandwich to the hovering gulls.

I was too far away to observe what colour Enid Starkie's eyes were; all I remember of her is that she dressed like a matelot, walked like a scrum-half, and had an atrocious French accent. But I'll tell you another thing. The Reader Emeritus in French Literature at the University of Oxford and Honorary Fellow of Somerville College, who was 'well known for her studies of the lives and works of writers such as Baudelaire, Rimbaud, Gautier, Eliot and Gide' (I quote her dust-wrapper; first edition, of course), who devoted two large books and many years of her life to the author of *Madame Bovary*, chose as frontispiece to her first volume a portrait of 'Gustave Flaubert by an unknown painter'. It's the first thing we see; it is, if you like, the moment at which Dr Starkie introduces us to Flaubert. The only trouble is, it isn't him. It's a portrait of Louis Bouilhet, as everyone from the *gardienne* of Croisset onwards and upwards will tell you. So what do we make of that once we've stopped chuckling?

Perhaps you still think I'm merely being vengeful towards a dead scholar who can't answer for herself. Well, maybe I am. But then, *quis custodiet ipsos custodes*? And I'll tell you something else. I've just re-read *Madame Bovary*.

> On one occasion he gives Emma brown eyes (14); on another deep black eyes (15); and on another blue eyes (16).

And the moral of it all, I suppose, is: Never take fright at a footnote. Here are the six references Flaubert makes to Emma Bovary's eyes in the course of the book. It is clearly a subject of some importance to the novelist:

1 (Emma's first appearance) 'In so far as she was beautiful, this beauty lay in her eyes: although they were brown, they would appear black because of her lashes...'

2 (Described by her adoring husband early in their marriage) 'Her eyes seemed bigger to him, especially when she was just waking up and fluttered her lids several times in succession; they were black when she was in shadow and dark blue in full daylight; and they seemed to contain layer upon layer of colours, which were thicker in hue deep down, and became lighter towards the enamel-like surface.'

3 (At a candlelit ball) 'Her black eyes appeared even blacker.'

4 (On first meeting Leon) 'Fixing him with her large, wide-open black eyes'.

5 (Indoors, as she appears to Rodolphe when he first examines her) 'Her black eyes'.

6 (Emma looking in a mirror, indoors, in the evening; she has just been seduced by Rodolphe) 'Her eyes had never been so large, so black, nor contained such depth.'

How did the critic put it? 'Flaubert does not build up characters, as did Balzac, by objective, external description; in fact, so careless is he of their outward appearance that ...' It would be interesting to compare the time spent by Flaubert making sure that his heroine had the rare and difficult eyes of a tragic adulteress with the time spent by Dr Starkie in carelessly selling him short.

And one final thing, just to make absolutely sure. Our earliest substantial source of knowledge about Flaubert is Maxime du

Camp's *Souvenirs littéraires* (Hachette, Paris, 1882–3, 2 vols): gossipy, vain, self-justifying and unreliable, yet historically essential. On page 306 of the first volume (Remington & Co., London, 1893, no translator credited) Du Camp describes in great detail the woman on whom Emma Bovary was based. She was, he tells us, the second wife of a medical officer from Bon-Lecours, near Rouen:

> This second wife was not beautiful; she was small, had dull yellow hair, and a face covered with freckles. She was full of pretension, and despised her husband, whom she considered a fool. Round and fair in person, her small bones were well-covered, and in her carriage and her general bearing there were flexible, undulating movements, like those of an eel. Her voice, vulgarised by its Lower Normandy accent, was full of caressing tones, and her eyes, of uncertain colour, green, grey, or blue, according to the light, had a pleading expression, which never left them.

Dr Starkie appears to have been serenely unaware of this enlightening passage. All in all, it seems a magisterial negligence towards a writer who must, one way and another, have paid a lot of her gas bills. Quite simply, it makes me furious. Now do you understand why I hate critics? I could try and describe to you the expression in my eyes at this moment; but they are far too discoloured with rage.

7

CROSS CHANNEL

LISTEN. *RATTARATTARATTARATTA*. And then – shhh – over there. *Fattafattafattafatta*. And again. *Rattarattarattaratta – fatta-fattafattafatta*. A soft November swell has set the tables rattling metallically at one another across the bar. An insistent approach from a table close at hand; a pause while some unheard throb shifts across the boat; and then a softer reply from the other side. Call and response, call and response; like a pair of mechanical birds in a cage. Listen to the pattern: *rattarattarattaratta fattafatta-fattafatta rattarattarattaratta fattafattafattafatta*. Continuity, stability, mutual reliance, it says; yet a change of wind or tide could end it all.

The curving windows at the stern are freckled with spray; through one of them you can make out a set of fat capstans and a listless macaroni of sodden rope. The seagulls have long since given up on this ferry. They cawed us out of Newhaven, had a look at the weather, noted the lack of sandwich packs on the rear promenade, and turned back. Who can blame them? They could have followed us the four hours to Dieppe in the hope of picking up trade on the way back; but that makes for a ten-hour day. By now they will be digging worms on some damp football pitch in Rottingdean.

Beneath the window is a bilingual rubbish bin with a spelling mistake. The top line says PAPIERS (how official the French sounds: 'Driving licence! Identity card!' it seems to command). The English translation underneath reads LITTERS. What a difference a single consonant makes. The first time Flaubert saw his name advertised – as the author of *Madame Bovary*, shortly to be serialised in the *Revue de Paris* – it was spelt Faubert. 'If I make an appearance one day, it will be in full armour,' had been his boast; but even in full armour the armpit and the groin are never completely protected. As he pointed out to Bouilhet, the *Revue*'s version of his name was only a letter away from an unwanted commercial pun: Faubet being the name of a grocer in the rue

Richelieu, just opposite the Comédie-Française. 'Even before I've appeared, they skin me alive.'

I like these out-of-season crossings. When you're young you prefer the vulgar months, the fullness of the seasons. As you grow older you learn to like the in-between times, the months that can't make up their minds. Perhaps it's a way of admitting that things can't ever bear the same certainty again. Or perhaps it's just a way of admitting a preference for empty ferries.

There can't be more than half a dozen people in the bar. One of them is stretched out on a banquette; the lulling rattle of the tables is coaxing its first snore from him. At this time of the year there are no school parties; the video games, disco and cinema are silent; even the barman chats.

This is the third time I've made the trip in a year. November, March, November. Just for a couple of nights in Dieppe: though I sometimes take the car and get down to Rouen. It's not long, but it's enough to make the change. It *is* a change. The light over the Channel, for instance, looks quite different from the French side: clearer, yet more volatile. The sky is a theatre of possibilities. I'm not romanticising. Go into the art galleries along the Normandy coast and you'll see what the local painters liked to paint, over and over again: the view north. A strip of beach, the sea, and the eventful sky. English painters never did the same, clustering at Hastings or Margate or Eastbourne to gaze out at a grumpy, monotonous Channel.

I don't just go for the light. I go for those things you forget about until you see them again. The way they butcher meat. The seriousness of their *pharmacies*. The behaviour of their children in restaurants. The road signs (France is the only country I know where drivers are warned about beetroot on the road: BETTERAVES, I once saw in a red warning triangle, with a picture of a car slipping out of control). *Beaux-arts* town halls. Wine-tasting in smelly chalk-caves by the side of the road. I could go on, but that's enough, or I'll soon be babbling about lime trees and *pétanque* and eating bread dipped in rough red wine – what they call *la soupe à perroquet*, parrot soup. Everyone has a private list, and those of other people quickly appear vain and sentimental. I read a list the other day headed 'What I Like'. It went: 'Salad, cinnamon, cheese, pimento, marzipan, the smell of new-cut hay [would you read on?] ... roses, peonies, lavender, champagne, loosely-held political convictions, Glenn Gould ...' The list, which is by Roland Barthes, continues, as lists do. One item you approve, the next stirs irritation. After 'Médoc wine' and 'having change', Barthes approves of '*Bouvard et Pécuchet*'. Good; fine; we'll read on. What's next? 'Walking in sandals on the lanes of south-west France.' It's enough to make you drive all the way to south-west France and strew some beetroot on the lanes.

My list mentions *pharmacies*. They always seem more single-minded in France. They don't stock beachballs or colour film or snorkelling equipment or burglar alarms. The assistants know what they are doing, and never try to sell you barley sugar on the way out. I find myself deferring to them as if they were consultants.

My wife and I once went into a *pharmacie* in Montauban and requested a packet of bandages. What was it for, they asked. Ellen tapped her heel, where the strap of a new pair of sandals had rubbed up a blister. The *pharmacien* came out from behind his counter, sat her down, removed her sandal with the tenderness of a foot-fetishist, examined her heel, cleaned it with a piece of gauze, stood up, turned to me gravely, as if there were something which really ought to be kept from my wife, and quietly explained, '*That*, Monsieur, is a blister.' The spirit of Homais still reigns, I thought, as he sold us a packet of bandages.

The spirit of Homais: progress, rationalism, science, fraud. 'We must march with the century' are almost his first words; and he marches all the way to the *Légion d'honneur*. When Emma Bovary dies, her body is watched over by two people: the priest, and Homais the *pharmacien*. Representing the old orthodoxy and the new. It's like some piece of nineteenth-century, allegorical sculpture: Religion and Science Watching Together over the Body of Sin. From a painting by G. F. Watts. Except that both the cleric and the man of science manage to fall asleep over the body. United at first only by philosophic error, they quickly establish the deeper unity of joint snorers.

Flaubert didn't believe in progress: especially not in moral progress, which is all that matters. The age he lived in was stupid; the new age, brought in by the Franco-Prussian war, would be even stupider. Of course some things would change: the spirit of Homais was winning. Soon everybody with a club foot would be entitled to a misconceived operation which would lead to an amputated leg; but what did that signify? 'The whole dream of democracy', he wrote, 'is to raise the proletariat to the level of stupidity attained by the bourgeoisie.'

That line often makes people edgy. Isn't it perfectly fair? Over the last hundred years the proletariat has schooled itself in the pretensions of the bourgeoisie; while the bourgeoisie, less confident of its ascendancy, has become more sly and deceitful. Is this progress? Study a packed cross-Channel ferry if you want to see a modern ship of fools. There they all are: working out the profit on their duty-free; having more drinks at the bar than they want; playing the fruit machines; aimlessly circling the deck; making up their minds how honest to be at customs; waiting for the next order from the ship's crew as if the crossing of the Red Sea depended on it. I do not criticise, I merely observe; and I'm not sure what I would think if everyone lined the rail to admire the play of light on the water and started discussing Boudin. I am no different, by the way: I stock up on duty-free and await orders like the rest of them. My point is merely this: Flaubert was right.

The fat lorry-driver on the banquette is snoring like a pasha. I've fetched myself another whisky; I hope you don't mind. Just getting braced to tell you about ... what? about whom? Three stories contend within me. One about Flaubert, one about Ellen, one about myself. My own is the simplest of the three – it hardly amounts to more than a convincing proof of my existence – and yet I find it the hardest to begin. My wife's is more complicated, and more urgent; yet I resist that too. Keeping the best for last, as I was saying earlier? I don't think so; rather the opposite, if anything. But by the time I tell you her story I want you to be prepared: that's to say, I want you to have had enough of books, and parrots, and lost letters, and bears, and the opinions of Dr Enid Starkie, and even the opinions of Dr Geoffrey Braithwaite. Books are not life, however much we might prefer it if they were. Ellen's is a true story; perhaps it is even the reason why I am telling you Flaubert's story instead.

You expect something from me too, don't you? It's like that nowadays. People assume they own part of you, on no matter how small an acquaintance; while if you are reckless enough to write a book, this puts your bank account, your medical records, and the state of your marriage irrevocably into the public domain. Flaubert disapproved. 'The artist must manage to make posterity believe that he never existed.' For the religious, death destroys the body and liberates the spirit; for the artist, death destroys the personality and liberates the work. That's the theory, anyway. Of course, it frequently goes wrong. Look what happened to Flaubert: a century after his death Sartre, like some brawny, desperate lifeguard, spent ten years beating on his chest and blowing into his mouth; ten years trying to yank him back to consciousness, just so that he could sit him up on the sands and tell him exactly what he thought of him.

And what do people think of him now? How do they think of him? As a bald man with a drooping moustache; as the hermit of Croisset, the man who said '*Madame Bovary, c'est moi*'; as the incorrigible aesthete, the bourgeois bourgeoisophobe? Confident scraps of wisdom, hand-me-down summaries for those in a hurry. Flaubert would hardly have been surprised at the lazy rush to understand. It was an impulse out of which he made a whole book (or at least a whole appendix): the *Dictionnaire des idées reçues*.

At the simplest level, his Dictionary is a catalogue of clichés (DOG: *Especially created to save its master's life. A dog is man's best friend*) and cod definitions (CRAYFISH: *Female of the lobster*). Beyond this it's a handbook of fake advice, both social (LIGHT: *Always say* Fiat lux! *when lighting a candle*) and aesthetic (RAILWAY STATIONS: *Always go into ecstasies about them; cite them as models of architecture*). Sometimes the manner is sly and teasing, at others so challengingly straight-faced that you find yourself half-believing it (MACARONI: *When prepared in the Italian style, is served with the fingers*). It reads like a confirmation present specially written by a malicious, rakehell uncle for a serious-minded adolescent with ambitions to get on in society. Study it carefully and you would never say anything wrong, while never getting anything right (HALBERD: *When you see a heavy cloud, never fail to say: 'It's going to rain halberds.' In Switzerland, all the men carry halberds.* ABSINTHE: *Extremely violent poison: a single glass and you're dead. Always drunk by journalists while writing their articles. Has killed more soldiers than the Bedouin*).

Flaubert's Dictionary offers a course in irony: from entry to entry, you can see him applying it in various thicknesses, like a cross-Channel painter darkening the sky with another wash. It tempts me to write a Dictionary of Accepted Ideas about Gustave himself. Just a short one: a booby-trapped pocket guide; something straight-faced yet misleading. The received wisdom in pellet form, with some of the pellets poisoned. This is the attraction, and also the danger, of irony: the way it permits a writer to be seemingly absent from his work, yet in fact hintingly present. You *can* have your cake and eat it; the only trouble is, you get fat.

What might we say of Flaubert in this new Dictionary? We might set him down, perhaps, as a 'bourgeois individualist'; yes, that sounds smug enough, dishonest enough. It's a characterisation which always remains unshaken by the fact that Flaubert loathed the bourgeoisie. And how about 'individualist', or its equivalent? 'In the ideal I have of Art, I think that one must not show one's own, and that the artist must no more appear in his work than God does in nature. Man is nothing, the work of art everything . . . It would be very pleasant for me to say what I think and relieve Monsieur Gustave Flaubert's feelings by means of such utterances; but what is the importance of the said gentleman?'

This demand for authorial absence ran deeper still. Some writers ostensibly agree with the principle, yet sneak in at the back door and cosh the reader with a highly personal style. The murder is perfectly executed, except that the baseball bat left at the scene of the crime is sticky with fingerprints. Flaubert is different. He believed in style; more than anyone. He worked doggedly for beauty, sonority, exactness; perfection – but never the monogrammed perfection of a writer like Wilde. Style is a function of theme. Style is not imposed on subject-matter, but arises from it. Style is truth to thought. The correct word, the true phrase, the perfect sentence are always 'out there' somewhere; the writer's task is to locate them by whatever means he can. For some this means no more than a trip to the supermarket and a loading-up of the metal basket; for others it means being lost on a plain in Greece, in the dark, in snow, in the rain, and finding what you seek only by some rare trick such as barking like a dog.

In our pragmatic and knowing century we probably find such ambition a little provincial (well, Turgenev did call Flaubert naïve). We no longer believe that language and reality 'match up' so congruently – indeed, we probably think that words give birth to things as much as things give birth to words. But if we find Flaubert naïve or – more likely – unsuccessful, we shouldn't patronise his seriousness or his bold loneliness. This was, after all, the century of Balzac and of Hugo, with orchidaceous Romanticism at one end of it and gnomic symbolism at the other.

Flaubert's planned invisibility in a century of babbling personali-
ties and shrieking styles might be characterised in one of two
ways: as classical, or modern. Looking back to the seventeenth
century, or forward to the late twentieth century. Contemporary
critics who pompously reclassify all novels and plays and poems
as texts – the author to the guillotine! – shouldn't skip lightly
over Flaubert. A century before them he was preparing texts and
denying the significance of his own personality.

'The author in his book must be like God in his universe,
everywhere present and nowhere visible.' Of course, this has
been keenly misread in our century. Look at Sartre and Camus.
God is dead, they told us, and therefore so is the God-like
novelist. Omniscience is impossible, man's knowledge is partial,
therefore the novel itself must be partial. That sounds not just
splendid, but logical as well. But is it either? The novel, after
all, didn't arise when belief in God arose; nor, for that matter,
is there much correlation between those novelists who believed
most strongly in the omniscient narrator and those who
believed most strongly in the omniscient creator. I cite George
Eliot alongside Flaubert.

More to the point, the assumed divinity of the nineteenth-
century novelist was only ever a technical device; and the par-
tiality of the modern novelist is just as much a ploy. When a
contemporary narrator hesitates, claims uncertainty, misunder-
stands, plays games and falls into error, does the reader in fact
conclude that reality is being more authentically rendered?
When the writer provides two different endings to his novel
(why two? why not a hundred?), does the reader seriously imagine he is being 'offered a choice' and that the work is reflecting
life's variable outcomes? Such a 'choice' is never real, because the
reader is obliged to consume both endings. In life, we make a
decision – or a decision makes us – and we go one way; had we
made a different decision (as I once told my wife; though I don't
think she was in a condition to appreciate my wisdom), we would
have been elsewhere. The novel with two endings doesn't reproduce this reality: it merely takes us down two diverging paths.
It's a form of cubism, I suppose. And that's all right; but let's not
deceive ourselves about the artifice involved.

After all, if novelists truly wanted to simulate the delta of
life's possibilities, this is what they'd do. At the back of the book
would be a set of sealed envelopes in various colours. Each would

be clearly marked on the outside: Traditional Happy Ending; Traditional Unhappy Ending; Traditional Half-and-Half Ending; Deus ex Machina; Modernist Arbitrary Ending; End of the World Ending; Cliffhanger Ending; Dream Ending; Opaque Ending; Surrealist Ending; and so on. You would be allowed only one, and would have to destroy the envelopes you didn't select. *That's* what I call offering the reader a choice of endings; but you may find me quite unreasonably literal-minded.

As for the hesitating narrator – look, I'm afraid you've run into one right now. It might be because I'm English. You'd guessed that, at least – that I'm English? I . . . I . . . Look at that seagull up there. I hadn't spotted him before. Slipstreaming away, waiting for the bits of gristle from the sandwiches. Listen, I hope you won't think this rude, but I really must take a turn on deck; it's becoming quite stuffy in the bar here. Why don't we meet on the boat back instead? The two o'clock ferry, Thursday? I'm sure I'll feel more like it then. All right? What? No, you can't come on deck with me. For God's sake. Besides, I'm going to the lavatory first. I can't have you following me in there, peering round from the next stall.

I apologise; I didn't mean that. Two o'clock, in the bar, as the ferry sails? Oh, and one last word. The cheese shop in the Grande Rue: don't miss it. I think the name's Leroux. I suggest you get a Brillat-Savarin. You won't get a good one in England unless you bring it back yourself. They're kept too cold, or they have chemicals injected into them to delay the ripening, or something. That is, if you like cheese . . .

How do we seize the past? How do we seize the foreign past? We read, we learn, we ask, we remember, we are humble; and then a casual detail shifts everything. Flaubert was a giant; they all said so. He towered over everybody like a strapping Gallic chieftain. And yet he was only six feet tall: we have this on his own authority. Tall, but not gigantic; shorter than I am, in fact, and when I am in France I never find myself towering over people like a Gallic chieftain.

So Gustave was a six-foot giant, and the world shrinks just a little with that knowledge. The giants were not so tall (were the dwarfs therefore shorter too?). The fat men: were they less fat because they were smaller, and so you needed less stomach to appear fat; or were they more fat, because they developed the same stomachs, but had even less frame to support them? How can we know such trivial, crucial details? We can study files for decades, but every so often we are tempted to throw up our hands and declare that history is merely another literary genre: the past is autobiographical fiction pretending to be a parliamentary report.

I have a small watercolour of Rouen on my wall by Arthur Frederick Payne (born Newarke, Leicester, 1831, working 1849–84). It shows the city from Bonsecours churchyard: the bridges, the spires, the river bending away past Croisset. It was painted on May 4th, 1856. Flaubert finished *Madame Bovary* on April 30th, 1856: there at Croisset, there where I can jab my finger, between two spreading and unknowing sploshes of water-colour. So near and yet so far. Is this history, then – a swift, confident amateur's watercolour?

I'm not sure what I believe about the past. I just want to know if fat people were fatter then. And were mad people madder? There was a lunatic called Mirabeau in the Rouen asylum who was popular with doctors and medical students at the Hôtel-Dieu because of a particular talent: in exchange for a cup of coffee he would copulate on the dissecting table with a female corpse. (Does the cup of coffee make him more, or less, mad?) One day, however, Mirabeau was to prove a coward: Flaubert reports that he funked his task when faced with a woman who had been guillotined. No doubt they offered him two cups of coffee, extra sugar, a slug of cognac? (And does this prove him saner, or madder, this need for a face, however dead?)

Nowadays we aren't allowed to use the word *mad*. What lunacy. The few psychiatrists I respect always talk about people being mad. Use the short, simple, true words. *Dead*, I say, and *dying*, and *mad*, and *adultery*. I don't say *passed on*, or *slipping away*, or *terminal* (oh, he's terminal? Which one? Euston, St Pancras, the Gare St Lazare?), or *personality disorder*, or *fooling around*, *bit on the side*, *well she's away a lot visiting her sister*. I say *mad* and *adultery*, that's what I say. *Mad* has the right sound to it. It's an ordinary word, a word which tells us how lunacy might come and call like a delivery van. Terrible things are also ordinary. Do you know what Nabokov said about adultery in his lecture on *Madame Bovary*? He said it was 'a most conventional way to rise above the conventional'.

Any history of adultery would doubtless quote Emma's seduction in that careering cab: it's probably the most famous act of infidelity in the whole of nineteenth-century fiction. Easy enough for the reader to imagine such a precisely-described scene, and to get it right, you'd think. Yes indeed. But still easy enough to get it just a tiny bit wrong. I cite G. M. Musgrave, sketcher, traveller, memoirist, and vicar of Borden, Kent: author of *The Parson, Pen and Pencil, or, Reminiscences and Illustrations of an Excursion to Paris, Tours, and Rouen, in the Summer of 1847; with a few Memoranda on French Farming* (Richard Bentley, London, 1848) and of *A Ramble Through Normandy, or, Scenes, Characters and Incidents in a Sketching Excursion Through Calvados* (David Bogue, London, 1855). On page 522 of the latter work the Reverend Musgrave is visiting Rouen – 'the Manchester of France', he calls it – at a time when Flaubert is still flailing away at his *Bovary*. His account of the city includes the following aside:

> I was mentioning, just now, the cab-stand. The carriages stationed there are the most dumpy vehicles, I conceive, of their kind, in Europe. I could with ease place my arm on the roof as I stood by one of them in the road. They are well-built, neat, and cleanly little chariots, with two good lamps; and 'cut' about the streets like Tom Thumb's coach.

So our view suddenly lurches: the famous seduction would have been even more cramped, and even less romantic, than we might previously have assumed. This piece of information is, as far as I am aware, hitherto unrecorded in the extensive annotations which have been inflicted on the novel; and I herewith offer it in a spirit of humility for use by professional scholars.

The tall, the fat, the mad. And then there are the colours. When he was researching for *Madame Bovary*, Flaubert spent a whole afternoon examining the countryside through pieces of coloured glass. Would he have seen what we now see? Presumably. But what about this: in 1853, at Trouville, he watched the sun go down over the sea, and declared that it resembled a large disc of redcurrant jam. Vivid enough. But was redcurrant jam the same colour in Normandy in 1853 as it is now? (Would any pots of it have survived, so that we could check? And how would we know the colour had remained the same in the intervening years?) It's the sort of thing you fret about. I decided to write to the Grocers' Company about the matter. Unlike some of my other correspondents, they replied promptly. They were also reassuring: redcurrant jam is one of the purest jams, they said, and though an 1853 Rouennais pot might not have been quite so clear as a modern one because of the use of unrefined sugar, the colour would have been almost exactly the same. So at least that's all right: now we can go ahead and confidently imagine the sunset. But you see what I mean? (As for my other questions: a pot of the jam could indeed have survived until now, but would almost certainly have turned brown, unless kept completely sealed in a dry, airy, pitch-dark room.)

The Reverend George M. Musgrave was a digressive but observant fellow. He was more than a little inclined to pomposity ('I am bound to speak in terms of high eulogium on the subject of Rouen's literary reputation'), but his fussiness over detail makes him a useful informant. He notes the French love of leeks and the French abhorrence of rain. He interrogates everyone: a Rouen merchant who amazes him by not having heard of mint sauce, and a canon of Evreux who informs him that in France the men read too much, while the women read next to nothing (o rarer still Emma Bovary!). While in Rouen he visits the Cimetière Monumental the year after Gustave's father and sister were buried there, and approves its innovative policy of allowing families to buy freehold plots. Elsewhere, he investigates a fertiliser factory, the Bayeux tapestry, and the lunatic asylum at Caen where Beau Brummell died in 1840 (was Brummell mad? The attendants remembered him well: *un bon enfant*, they said, drank only barley water mixed with a very little wine).

Musgrave also went to the fair at Guibray, and there among the freak shows was The Largest Fat Boy in France: Aimable Jouvin, born at Herblay in 1840, now aged fourteen, admission a penny farthing. How fat was the fat boy? Our rambling sketcher didn't, alas, go in himself and record the young phenomenon with his pencil; but he waited while a French cavalryman paid his penny farthing, entered the caravan, and emerged mouthing 'some very choice Norman phraseology'. Though Musgrave did not bring himself to ask the soldier what he had seen, his impression was 'that Aimable had not been fattened up to the mark of the visitor's large expectations'.

At Caen Musgrave went to a regatta, where seven thousand spectators lined the dockside. Most of them were men, and most of these were peasants wearing their best blue blouses. The mass effect was of a light but most brilliant ultramarine. It was a particular, exact colour; Musgrave had seen it only once before, in a special department of the Bank of England where they incinerated notes which had been taken out of circulation. Banknote paper was then prepared with a colouring agent made from cobalt, silex, salt and potash: if you set light to a bundle of money, the cinder would take on the extraordinary tint that Musgrave saw on the Caen dockside. The colour of France.

As he travelled on, this colour and its cruder associates became more apparent. The men's blouses and hose were blue; three-quarters of the women's gowns were blue. The horses' housings and collar-decorations were blue; so were the carts, the name-boards of the villages, the agricultural implements, wheelbarrows and water-butts. In many of the towns the houses displayed the cerulean hue, both inside and out. Musgrave found himself compelled to remark to a Frenchman he met that 'There was more *blue* in his country than in any region of the world with which I was acquainted.'

We look at the sun through smoked glass; we must look at the past through coloured glass.

Thank you. *Santé*. You got your cheese, I hope? You won't mind a word of advice? Eat it. Don't put it in a plastic bag in the fridge and save it for visitors; before you know where you are it'll have swollen to three times its size and smell like a chemical factory. You'll open the bag and be putting your face into a bad marriage.

'Giving the public details about oneself is a bourgeois temptation that I have always resisted' (1879). But here goes. You know my name of course: Geoffrey Braithwaite. Don't miss out the l or you'll start turning me into a Parisian grocer. No; just my joke. Look. You know those personal advertisements in magazines like the *New Statesman*? I thought I might do it like that.

> 60 + widowed doctor, children grown up, active, cheerful if inclined to melancholy, kindly, non-smoker, amateur Flaubert scholar, likes reading, food, travel to familiar places, old films, has friends, but seeks . . .

You see the problem. *But seeks* . . . Do I? What do I seek? A tender fortyish div or wid for companionship stroke marriage? No. Mature lady for country walks, occasional dining? No. Bisexual couple for gleesome threesomes? Certainly not. I always read those pining paragraphs in the back of magazines, though I never feel like replying; and I've just realised why. Because I don't believe any of them. They aren't lying – indeed, they're all trying to be utterly sincere – but they aren't telling the truth. The column distorts the way the advertisers describe themselves. No one would think of himself as an active non-smoker inclined to melancholy if that wasn't encouraged, even demanded, by the form. Two conclusions: first, that you can't define yourself directly, just by looking face-on into the mirror; and secondly, that Flaubert was, as always, right. Style does arise from subject-matter. Try as they might, those advertisers are always beaten down by the form; they are forced – even at the one time they need to be candidly personal – into an unwished impersonality.

You can see, at least, the colour of my eyes. Not as complicated as Emma Bovary's, are they? But do they help you? They might mislead. I'm not being coy; I'm trying to be *useful*. Do you know the colour of Flaubert's eyes? No, you don't: for the simple reason that I suppressed it a few pages ago. I didn't want you to be tempted by cheap conclusions. See how carefully I look after you. You don't like it? I *know* you don't like it. All right. Well, according to Du Camp, Gustave the Gallic chieftain, the six-foot giant with a voice like a trumpet, had 'large eyes as grey as the sea'.

I was reading Mauriac the other day: the *Mémoires intérieurs*, written at the very end of his life. It's the time when the final pellets of vanity accumulate into a cyst, when the self starts up its last pathetic murmur of 'Remember me, remember me . . .'; it's the time when the autobiographies get written, the last boasts are made, and the memories which no one else's brain still holds are written down with a false idea of value.

But that's just what Mauriac declines to do. He writes his '*Mémoires*', but they aren't his memoirs. We are spared the counting-games and spelling-bees of childhood, that first servant-girl in the humid attic, the canny uncle with metal teeth and a headful of stories – or whatever. Instead, Mauriac tells us about the books he's read, the painters he's liked, the plays he's seen. He finds himself by looking in the works of others. He defines his own faith by a passionate anger against Gide the Luciferian. Reading his 'memoirs' is like meeting a man on a train who says, 'Don't look at me, that's misleading. If you want to know what I'm like, wait until we're in a tunnel, and then study my reflection in the window.' You wait, and look, and catch a face against a shifting background of sooty walls, cables and sudden brickwork. The transparent shape flickers and jumps, always a few feet away. You become accustomed to its existence, you move with its movements; and though you know its presence is conditional, you feel it to be permanent. Then there is a wail from ahead, a roar and a burst of light; the face is gone for ever.

Well, you know I've got brown eyes; make of that what you will. Six foot one; grey hair; good health. But what matters about me? Only what I know, what I believe, what I can tell you. Nothing much about my character matters. No, that's not true. I'm honest, I'd better tell you that. I'm aiming to tell the truth; though mistakes are, I suppose, inevitable. And if I make them, at least I'm in good company. *The Times*, in its obituary column, May 10th, 1880, claims that Flaubert wrote a book called *Bouvard et Peluchet*, and that he 'at first adopted his father's profession – that of surgeon'. My *Encyclopaedia Britannica*, eleventh edition (the best, they say), suggests that Charles Bovary is a portrait of the novelist's father. The author of this article, a certain 'E.G.', turns out to have been Edmund Gosse. I snorted a bit when I read that. I have a little less time for 'Mr' Gosse since my encounter with Ed Winterton.

I'm honest, I'm reliable. When I was a doctor I never killed a single patient, which is more of a boast than you might imagine. People trusted me; they kept coming back, at any rate. And I was good with the dying. I never got drunk – that is, I never got too drunk; I never wrote prescriptions for imaginary patients; I never made advances to women in my surgery. I sound like a plaster saint. I'm not.

No, I didn't kill my wife. I might have known you'd think that. First you find out that she's dead; then, a while later, I say that I never killed a single patient. Aha, who *did* you kill, then? The question no doubt appears logical. How easy it is to set off speculation. There was a man called Ledoux who maliciously claimed that Flaubert had committed suicide; he wasted a lot of people's time. I'll tell you about him later. But it all goes to prove my point: what knowledge is useful, what knowledge is true? Either I have to give you so much information about myself that you are forced to admit that I could no more have killed my wife than Flaubert could have committed suicide; or else I merely say, That's all, that's enough. No more. *J'y suis, j'y reste.*

I could play the Mauriac game, perhaps. Tell you how I
brought myself up on Wells, Huxley and Shaw; how I prefer
George Eliot and even Thackeray to Dickens; how I like
Orwell, Hardy and Housman, and dislike the Auden–Spender–
Isherwood crew (preaching socialism as a sideshoot of homo-
sexual law reform); how I'm saving Virginia Woolf for when I'm
dead. The younger fellows? Today's fellows? Well, they each
seem to do one thing well enough, but fail to realise that literature depends on doing several things well at the same time.
I could go on at great length on all these topics; it would be very
pleasant for me to say what I think and relieve Monsieur Geoffrey
Braithwaite's feelings by means of such utterances. But what is
the importance of the said gentleman?

I'd rather play a different version. Some Italian once wrote that
the critic secretly wants to kill the writer. Is that true? Up to a
point. We all hate golden eggs. Bloody golden eggs again, you
can hear the critics mutter as a good novelist produces yet
another good novel; haven't we had enough omelettes this year?

But if not that, then many critics would like to be dictators of
literature, to regulate the past, and to set out with quiet authority
the future direction of the art. This month, everyone must write
about this; next month, nobody is allowed to write about that.
So-and-so will not be reprinted until we say so. All copies of this
seductively bad novel must be destroyed at once. (You think I am
joking? In March 1983, the newspaper *Libération* urged that the
French Minister for Women's Rights should put on her Index
for 'public provocation to sexist hatred' the following works:
Pantagruel, *Jude the Obscure*, Baudelaire's poems, all Kafka, *The
Snows of Kilimanjaro* – and *Madame Bovary*.) Still, let's play. I'll
go first.

1 There shall be no more novels in which a group of people,
isolated by circumstances, revert to the 'natural condition' of
man, become essential, poor, bare, forked creatures. All that may
be written is one short story, the final one of the genre, the cork
in the bottle. I'll write it for you. A group of travellers are shipwrecked, or airwrecked, somewhere, no doubt on an island. One
of them, a large, powerful, dislikeable man, has a gun. He forces
all the others to live in a sandpit of their own digging. Every so
often, he takes one of his prisoners out, shoots him or her, and
eats the carcass. The food tastes good, and he grows fat. When
he has shot and eaten his final prisoner, he begins to worry what

he will do for food; but fortunately a seaplane arrives at this point and rescues him. He tells the world that he was the sole survivor of the original wreck, and that he has sustained himself by eating berries, leaves and roots. The world marvels at his fine physical condition, and a poster bearing his photograph is displayed in the windows of vegetarian food shops. He is never found out.

You see how easy it is to write, how much fun it is? That's why I'd ban the genre.

2 There shall be no more novels about incest. No, not even ones in very bad taste.

3 No novels set in abattoirs. This is, I admit, a rather small genre at the moment; but I have recently noticed increasing use of the abattoir in short stories. It must be nipped in the bud.

4 There is to be a twenty-year ban on novels set in Oxford or Cambridge, and a ten-year ban on other university fiction. No ban on fiction set in polytechnics (though no subsidy to encourage it). No ban on novels set in primary schools; a ten-year ban on secondary-school fiction. A partial ban on growing-up novels (one per author allowed). A partial ban on novels written in the historic present (again, one per author). A total ban on novels in which the main character is a journalist or a television presenter.

5 A quota system is to be introduced on fiction set in South America. The intention is to curb the spread of package-tour baroque and heavy irony. Ah, the propinquity of cheap life and expensive principles, of religion and banditry, of surprising honour and random cruelty. Ah, the daiquiri bird which incubates its eggs on the wing; ah, the fredonna tree whose roots grow at the tips of its branches, and whose fibres assist the hunchback to impregnate by telepathy the haughty wife of the hacienda owner; ah, the opera house now overgrown by jungle. Permit me to rap on the table and murmur 'Pass!' Novels set in the Arctic and the Antarctic will receive a development grant.

6(a) No scenes in which carnal connection takes place between a human being and an animal. The woman and the porpoise, for instance, whose tender coupling symbolises a wider mending of those gossamer threads which formerly bound the world together in peaceable companionship. No, none of that.

(b) No scenes in which carnal connection takes place between man and woman (porpoise-like, you might say) in the shower. My reasons are primarily aesthetic, but also medical.

7 No novels about small, hitherto forgotten wars in distant

parts of the British Empire, in the painstaking course of which we learn first, that the British are averagely wicked; and secondly, that war is very nasty indeed.

8 No novels in which the narrator, or any of the characters, is identified simply by an initial letter. Still they go on doing it!

9 There shall be no more novels which are really about other novels. No 'modern versions', reworkings, sequels or prequels. No imaginative completions of works left unfinished on their author's death. Instead, every writer is to be issued with a sampler in coloured wools to hang over the fireplace. It reads: Knit Your Own Stuff.

10 There shall be a twenty-year ban on God; or rather, on the allegorical, metaphorical, allusive, offstage, imprecise and ambiguous uses of God. The bearded head gardener who is always tending the apple tree; the wise old sea-captain who never rushes to judgment; the character you're not quite introduced to, but who is giving you a creepy feeling by Chapter Four . . . pack them off into storage, all of them. God is permitted only as a verifiable divinity who gets extremely cross at man's transgressions.

So how do we seize the past? As it recedes, does it come into focus? Some think so. We know more, we discover extra documents, we use infra-red light to pierce erasures in the correspondence, and we are free of contemporary prejudice; so we understand better. Is that it? I wonder. Take Gustave's sex-life. For years it was assumed that the bear of Croisset broke out of his bearishness solely with Louise Colet – 'the only sentimental episode of any importance in the life of Flaubert,' Emile Faguet declared. But then Elisa Schlesinger is discovered – the bricked-up royal chamber in Gustave's heart, the slow-burning fire, the adolescent passion never consummated. Next, more letters come into view, and the Egyptian journals. The life begins to reek of actresses; the bedding of Bouilhet is announced; Flaubert himself admits a taste for Cairo bath-house boys. At last we see the whole shape of his carnality; he is ambi-sexual, omni-experienced.

But not so fast. Sartre decrees that Gustave was never homo-sexual; merely passive and feminine in his psychology. The byplay with Bouilhet was just teasing, the outer edge of vivid male friendship: Gustave never committed a single homosexual act in all his life. He says he did, but that was boastful invention: Bouilhet asked for salacities from Cairo, and Flaubert provided them. (Are we convinced by this? Sartre accuses Flaubert of wishful thinking. Might we not accuse Sartre of the same? Wouldn't he prefer Flaubert the trembling bourgeois, joking on the edge of a sin he fears to commit, rather than Flaubert the daredevil, the subversive indulger?) And in the meantime, we are also being encouraged to shift our view of Mme Schlesinger. Current belief among Flaubertistes is that the relationship was consummated after all: either in 1848 or, more probably, in the early months of 1843.

The past is a distant, receding coastline, and we are all in the same boat. Along the stern rail there is a line of telescopes; each brings the shore into focus at a given distance. If the boat is becalmed, one of the telescopes will be in continual use; it will seem to tell the whole, the unchanging truth. But this is an illusion; and as the boat sets off again, we return to our normal activity: scurrying from one telescope to another, seeing the sharpness fade in one, waiting for the blur to clear in another. And when the blur does clear, we imagine that we have made it do so all by ourselves.

Isn't the sea calmer than the other day? And heading north – the light that Boudin saw. What does this journey seem like to those who aren't British – as they head towards the land of embarrassment and breakfast? Do they make nervous jokes about fog and porridge? Flaubert found London scaring; it was an unhealthy city, he declared, where it was impossible to find a *pot-au-feu*. On the other hand, Britain was the home of Shakespeare, clear thinking and political liberty, the land where Voltaire had been welcomed and to which Zola would flee.

Now what is it? First slum of Europe, one of our poets called it not long ago. First hypermarket of Europe might be more like it. Voltaire praised our attitude to commerce, and the lack of snobbery which allowed the younger sons of the gentry to become businessmen. Now the day-trippers arrive from Holland and Belgium, Germany and France, excited about the weakness of the pound and eager to get into Marks & Spencer. Commerce, Voltaire declared, was the base on which the greatness of our nation was built; now it's all that keeps us from going bankrupt.

When I drive off the boat, I always have a desire to go through the Red Channel. I never have more than the permitted amount of duty-free goods; I've never imported plants, or dogs, or drugs, or uncooked meat, or firearms; and yet I constantly find myself wanting to turn the wheel and head for the Red Channel.

It always feels like an admission of failure to come back from the Continent and have nothing to show for it. Would you read this, please, sir? Yes. Have you understood it, sir? Yes. Have you anything to declare? Yes, I'd like to declare a small case of French flu, a dangerous fondness for Flaubert, a childish delight in French road-signs, and a love of the light as you look north. Is there any duty to pay on any of these? There ought to be.

Oh, and I've got this cheese, too. A Brillat-Savarin. That fellow behind me has got one too. I told him you always had to declare your cheese at customs. Say cheese.

I hope you don't think I'm being enigmatic, by the way. If I'm irritating, it's probably because I'm embarrassed; I told you I don't like the full face. But I really am trying to make things easier for you. Mystification is simple; clarity is the hardest thing of all. Not writing a tune is easier than writing one. Not rhyming is easier than rhyming. I don't mean art should be as clear as the instructions on a packet of seeds; I'm saying that you trust the mystifier more if you know he's deliberately choosing not to be lucid. You trust Picasso all the way because he could draw like Ingres.

But what helps? What do we need to know? Not everything. Everything confuses. Directness also confuses. The full-face portrait staring back at you hypnotises. Flaubert is usually looking away in his portraits and photographs. He's looking away so that you can't catch his eye; he's also looking away because what he can see over your shoulder is more interesting than your shoulder.

Directness confuses. I told you my name: Geoffrey Braithwaite. Has that helped? A little; at least it's better than 'B' or 'G' or 'the man' or 'the amateur of cheeses'. And if you hadn't seen me, what would you have deduced from the name? Middle-class professional man; solicitor perhaps; denizen of pine-and-heather country; pepper-and-salt tweeds; a moustache hinting – perhaps fraudulently – at a military past; a sensible wife; perhaps a little boating at weekends; more of a gin than a whisky man; and so on?

I am – was – a doctor, first-generation professional class; as you see, there's no moustache, though I have the military past which men of my age couldn't avoid; I live in Essex, most characterless and therefore most acceptable of the Home Counties; whisky, not gin; no tweed at all; and no boating. Near enough, and yet not near enough, you see. As for my wife, she was not sensible. That was one of the last words anyone would apply to her. They inject soft cheeses, as I said, to stop them ripening too quickly. But they always do ripen; it's in their nature. Soft cheeses collapse; firm cheeses indurate. Both go mouldy.

I was going to put my photograph in the front of the book. Not vanity; just trying to be helpful. But I'm afraid it was rather an old photograph; taken about ten years ago. I haven't got a more recent one. That's something you find: after a certain age, people stop photographing you. Or rather, they photograph you only on formal occasions: birthdays, weddings, Christmas. A flushed and jolly character raises his glass among friends and family – how real, how reliable is *that* evidence? What would the photos of my twenty-fifth wedding anniversary have revealed? Certainly not the truth; so perhaps it's as well they were never taken.

Flaubert's niece Caroline says that towards the end of his life he regretted not having had a wife and family. Her account is, however, rather spare. The two of them were walking by the Seine after a visit to some friends. ' "They got it right," he said to me, alluding to that household with its charming and honest children. "Yes," he repeated to himself gravely, "they got it right." I did not trouble his thoughts, but remained silent at his side. This walk was one of our last.'

I rather wish she *had* troubled his thoughts. Did he really mean it? Should we take the remark as more than the reflex perversity of a man who dreamed of Egypt while in Normandy, and of Normandy while in Egypt? Was he doing more than praise the particular talents of the family they had just visited? After all, had he wanted to praise the institution of marriage itself, he could have turned to his niece and regretted his solitary life by admitting, '*You* got it right.' But he didn't, of course; because she got it wrong. She married a weakling who turned into a bankrupt, and in helping save her husband she bankrupted her uncle. The case of Caroline is instructive – gloomily so to Flaubert.

Her own father had been as much of a weakling as her husband subsequently became; Gustave supplanted him. In her *Souvenirs intimes* Caroline recalls her uncle's return from Egypt when she was a small girl: he arrives home unexpectedly one evening, wakes her, picks her up out of bed, bursts out laughing because her nightdress extends far below her feet, and plants great kisses on her cheeks. He has just come from outdoors: his moustache is cold, and damp with dew. She is frightened, and much relieved

when he puts her down. What is this but a textbook account
of the absent father's alarming return to the household – the
return from the war, from business, from abroad, from philandering, from danger?

He adored her. In London he carried her round the Great
Exhibition; this time she was happy to be in his arms, safe from
the frightening crowds. He taught her history: the story of
Pelopidas and Epaminondas; he taught her geography, taking a
shovel and pail of water into the garden, where he would build
for her instructive peninsulas, islands, gulfs and promontories.
She loved her childhood with him, and the memory of it survived the misfortunes of her adult life. In 1930, when she was
eighty-four, Caroline met Willa Cather in Aix-les-Bains, and
recalled the hours spent eighty years earlier on a rug in the corner
of Gustave's study: he working, she reading, in strict but proudly
observed silence. 'She liked to think, as she lay in her corner, that
she was shut in a cage with some powerful wild animal, a tiger
or a lion or a bear, who had devoured his keeper and would
spring upon anyone else who opened his door, but with whom
she was "quite safe and conceited", as she said with a chuckle.'

But then the necessities of adulthood arrived. He advised her
badly, and she married a weakling. She became a snob; she
thought only of smart society; and finally she tried to turn her
uncle out of the very house in which the most useful things she
knew had been inserted into her brain.

Epaminondas was a Theban general, held to be living proof of
all the virtues; he led a career of principled carnage, and founded
the city of Megalopolis. As he lay dying, one of those present
lamented his lack of issue. He replied, 'I leave two children,
Leuctra and Mantinea' – the sites of his two most famous vic-
tories. Flaubert might have made a similar avowal – 'I leave two
children, Bouvard and Pécuchet' – because his only child, the
niece who became a daughter, had departed into disapproving
adulthood. To her, and to her husband, he had become 'the
consumer'.

Gustave taught Caroline about literature. I quote her: 'He
considered no book dangerous that was well written.' Move
forward seventy years or so to a different household in another
part of France. This time there is a bookish boy, a mother, and a
friend of the mother's called Mme Picard. The boy later wrote
his memoirs; again, I quote: 'Mme Picard's opinion was that a

child should be allowed to read everything. "No book can be dangerous if it is well written".' The boy, aware of Mme Picard's frequently expressed view, deliberately exploits her presence and asks his mother's permission to read a particular and notorious novel. 'But if my little darling reads books like that at his age,' says the mother, 'what will he do when he grows up?' 'I shall live them out!' he replies. It was one of the cleverest retorts of his childhood; it went down in family history, and it won him – or so we are left to assume – readership of the novel. The boy was Jean-Paul Sartre. The book was *Madame Bovary*.

Does the world progress? Or does it merely shuttle back and forth like a ferry? An hour from the English coast and the clear sky disappears. Cloud and rain escort you back to where you belong. As the weather changes, the boat begins to roll a little, and the tables in the bar resume their metallic conversation. *Rattarattarattaratta, fattafattafattafatta.* Call and response, call and response. Now it sounds to me like the final stages of a marriage: two separated parties, screwed to their own particular pieces of floor, uttering routine chatter while the rain begins to fall. My wife . . . Not now, not now.

Pécuchet, during his geological investigations, speculates on what would happen if there were an earthquake beneath the English Channel. The water, he concludes, would rush out into the Atlantic; the coasts of England and France would totter, shift and reunite; the Channel would cease to exist. On hearing his friend's predictions, Bouvard runs away in terror. For myself, I do not think we need to be quite so pessimistic.

You won't forget about the cheese, will you? Don't grow a chemical plant in your fridge. I didn't ask if you were married. My compliments, or not, as the case may be.

I think I shall go through the Red Channel this time. I feel the need for some company. The Reverend Musgrave's opinion was that French *douaniers* behaved like gentlemen, while English customs officers were ruffians. But I find them all quite sympathetic, if you treat them properly.

8

THE TRAIN-SPOTTER'S
GUIDE TO FLAUBERT

I THE HOUSE AT CROISSET — a long, white, eighteenth-century property on the banks of the Seine — was perfect for Flaubert. It was isolated, yet close to Rouen and thence to Paris. It was large enough for him to have a grand study with five windows; yet small enough for him to discourage visitors without obvious discourtesy. It gave him, too, if he wanted it, an unthreatened view of passing life: from the terrace he could train his opera glasses on the pleasure-steamers taking Sunday lunchers to La Bouille. For their part, the lunchers grew accustomed to *cet original de Monsieur Flaubert*, and were disappointed if they didn't spot him, in Nubian shirt and silk skullcap, gazing back at them, taking the novelist's view.

Caroline has described the quiet evenings of her childhood at Croisset. It was a curious ménage: the girl, the uncle, the grand-mother — a solitary representative of each generation, like one of those squeezed houses you sometimes see with a single room on each storey. (The French call such a house *un bâton de perroquet*, a parrot's perch.) The three of them, she recalled, would often sit at the balcony of the little pavilion and watch the confident arrival of the night. On the far bank they might just discern the silhouette of a straining horse on the tow-path; from nearby they might just hear a discreet splosh as the eel-fishermen cast off and slipped out into the stream.

Why did Dr Flaubert sell his property at Déville to buy this house? Traditionally, as a refuge for his invalid son, who had just suffered his first attack of epilepsy. But the property at Déville would have been sold anyway. The Paris to Rouen railway was being extended to Le Havre, and the line cut straight through Dr Flaubert's land; part of it was to be compulsorily purchased. You could say that Gustave was shepherded into creative retreat at Croisset by epilepsy. You could also say he was driven there by the railway.

2 Gustave belonged to the first railway generation in France; and he hated the invention. For a start, it was an odious means of transport. 'I get so fed up on a train that after five minutes I'm howling with boredom. Passengers think it's a neglected dog; not at all, it's M. Flaubert, sighing.' Secondly, it produced a new figure at the dinner table: the railway bore. Conversation on the topic gave Flaubert a *colique des wagons*; in June 1843 he pronounced the railways to be the third most boring subject imaginable after Mme Lafarge (an arsenic poisoner) and the death of the Duc d'Orleans (killed in his carriage the previous year). Louise Colet, striving for modernity in her poem 'La Paysanne', allowed Jean, her soldier returning from the wars in search of his Jeanneton, to notice the running smoke of a train. Flaubert cut the line. 'Jean doesn't give a damn about that sort of thing,' he growled, 'and nor do I.'

But he didn't just hate the railway as such; he hated the way it flattered people with the illusion of progress. What was the point of scientific advance without moral advance? The railway would merely permit more people to move about, meet and be stupid together. In one of his earliest letters, written when he was fifteen, he lists the misdeeds of modern civilisation: 'Railways, poisons, enema pumps, cream tarts, royalty and the guillotine.' Two years later, in his essay on Rabelais, the list of enemies has altered – all except the first item: 'Railways, factories, chemists and mathematicians.' He never changed.

3 'Superior to everything is – Art. A book of poetry is preferable to a railway.'

Intimate Notebook, 1840

4 The function of the railway in Flaubert's affair with Louise Colet has, to my mind, been rather underestimated. Consider the mechanics of their relationship. She lived in Paris, he at Croisset; he wouldn't come to the capital, she wasn't allowed to visit him in the country. So they would meet approximately halfway, at Mantes, where the Hôtel du Grand Cerf would allow them a night or two of lurid rapture and false promises. Afterwards, the following cycle would take place: Louise would assume an early rendezvous; Gustave would put her off; Louise would plead, grow angry, threaten; Gustave would reluctantly give in and agree to another meeting. It would last just long

enough to sate his desires and rekindle her expectations. And
so this grumbling three-legged race was run. Did Gustave ever
reflect on the fate of an earlier visitor to the town? It was at the
capture of Mantes that William the Conqueror fell from his horse
and received the injury from which he later died in Rouen.

The Paris to Rouen railway – built by the English – opened
on May 9th, 1843, barely three years before Gustave and Louise
met. The journey to Mantes, for each of them, was cut from a
day to a couple of hours. Imagine what it would have been like
without the railway. They would have travelled by diligence or
river-steamer; they would have been tired and perhaps irritable
on seeing one another again. Fatigue affects desire. But in view
of the difficulties, more would have been expected of the occasion: more in time – an extra day perhaps – and more in emotional commitment. This is just my theory, of course. But if the
telephone in our century has made adultery both simpler and
harder (assignations are easier, but so is checking up), the railway
in the last century had a similar effect. (Has anyone made a
comparative study of the spread of railways and the spread of
adultery? I can imagine village priests delivering sermons on the
Devil's invention and being mocked for it; but if they did, they
were right.) The railway made it worth while for Gustave: he
could get to Mantes and back without too much trouble; and
Louise's complaints perhaps seemed a reasonable price to pay
for such accessible pleasure. The railway made it worth while for
Louise: Gustave was never really far away, however severe he
sounded in his letters; the next one would surely say that they
could meet again, that only two hours separated them. And the
railway made it worth while for us, who can now read the letters
which resulted from that prolonged erotic oscillation.

5(a) September 1846: the first meeting at Mantes. The only problem was Gustave's mother. She had not as yet been officially
informed of Louise's existence. Indeed, Mme Colet was obliged
to send all her love letters to Gustave via Maxime du Camp, who
then readdressed them in fresh envelopes. How would Mme
Flaubert react to Gustave's sudden nocturnal absence? What
could he tell her? A lie, of course: '*une petite histoire que ma mère a
crue*,' he boasted, like a proud six-year-old, and set off for Mantes.

But Mme Flaubert didn't believe his *petite histoire*. She slept
less that night than Gustave and Louise did. Something had made

her uneasy; perhaps the recent cascade of letters from Maxime du Camp. So the next morning she went to Rouen station, and when her son, still wearing a fresh crust of pride and sex, got off the train, she was waiting for him on the platform. 'She didn't utter any reproach, but her face was the greatest reproach anyone could make.'

They talk about the sadness of departure; what about the guilt of arrival?

(b) Louise, of course, could play the platform scene as well. Her habit of jealously bursting in on Gustave when he was dining with friends was notorious. She always expected to find a rival; but there was no rival, unless you count Emma Bovary. On one occasion, Du Camp records, 'Flaubert was leaving Paris for Rouen when she entered the waiting-room of the station and went through such tragic scenes that the railway officials were obliged to interfere. Flaubert was distressed and begged for mercy, but she gave him no quarter.'

6 It is a little-known fact that Flaubert travelled on the London Underground. I quote items from his skeleton travel diary of 1866:

> *Monday 26 June* (on the train from Newhaven). A few insig-
>   nificant stations with posters, just as at stations on the
>   outskirts of Paris. Arrival at Victoria.
> *Monday 3 July.* Bought a railway timetable.
> *Friday 7 July.* Underground railway – Hornsey. Mrs Farmer
>   ... To Charing Cross station for information.

He does not deign to compare the British and the French railways. This is perhaps a pity. Our friend the Reverend G. M. Musgrave, disembarking at Boulogne a dozen years earlier, was much impressed by the French system: 'The contrivances for receiving, weighing, marking and paying for luggage were simple and excellent. Regularity, precision, and punctuality did the work well in every department. Much civility, much comfort (comfort in *France*!) made every arrangement pleasurable; and all this without more vociferation or commotion than prevails at Paddington; to say nothing of the second-class carriage being nearly equal to our first. Shame to England that it should be thus!'

7 'RAILWAYS: If Napoleon had had them at his disposition, he would have been invincible. Always go into ecstasies about their invention, and say: "I, Monsieur, I who am even now speaking to you, was only this morning at X . . . ; I left by the X-o'clock train; I did the business I had to do there; and by X-o'clock I was back."'

Dictionnaire de idées reçues

8 I took the train from Rouen (Rive Droite). There were blue plastic seats and a warning in four languages not to lean out of the window; English, I noticed, requires more words than French, German or Italian to convey this advice. I sat beneath a metal-framed photograph (black and white) of fishing-boats at the Île d'Oléron. Next to me an elderly couple were reading a story in *Paris-Normandie* about a charcutier, *fou d'amour*, who had killed a family of seven. On the window was a small sticker I hadn't seen before: '*Ne jetez pas l'energie par les fenêtres en les ouvrant en période de chauffage.*' Do not throw energy out of the windows – How unEnglish the phrasing was; logical yet fanciful at the same time.

I was being observant, you see. A single ticket costs 35 francs. The journey takes a minute or so under the hour: half what it took in Flaubert's day. Oissel is the first stop; then Le Vaudreuil – *ville nouvelle*; Gaillon (Aubevoye), with its Grand Marnier warehouse. Musgrave suggested the scenery along this stretch of the Seine reminded him of Norfolk: 'more like English scenery than any district I had seen in Europe.' The ticket-collector raps on the door jamb with his punch: metal on metal, an order you obey. Vernon; then, on your left, the broad Seine conducts you into Mantes.

6, place de la République was a building site. A square block of flats was almost finished; already it exhibited the confident innocence of the usurper. The Grand Cerf? Yes, indeed, they told me at the *tabac*, the old building had stood until a year or so ago. I went back and stared again. All that now remained of the Hôtel was a couple of tall stone gateposts some thirty feet apart. I gazed at them hopelessly. On the train, I had been unable to imagine Flaubert (howling like an impatient dog? grumbling? ardent?) making the same journey; now at this point of pilgrimage, the gateposts were no help in thinking my way back to the hot reunions of Gustave and Louise. Why should they be? We are too impertinent with the past, counting on it in this way for a reliable *frisson*. Why should it play our game?

Grumpily I circled the church (Michelin one star), bought a newspaper, drank a cup of coffee, read about the charcutier, *fou d'amour*, and decided to take the next train back. The road leading to the station is called avenue Franklin Roosevelt, though the reality is a little less grand than the name. Fifty yards from the end, on the left, I came across a café-restaurant. It was called Le Perroquet. Outside, on the pavement, a fretworked wooden parrot with garish green plumage was holding the lunch menu in its beak. The building had one of those brightly timbered exteriors which assert more age than they probably possess. I don't know if it would have been there in Flaubert's day. But I know this. Sometimes the past may be a greased pig; sometimes a bear in its den; and sometimes merely the flash of a parrot, two mocking eyes that spark at you from the forest.

9 Trains play little part in Flaubert's fiction. This shows accuracy, however, not prejudice: most of his work is set before the English navvies and engineers descended on Normandy. *Bouvard et Pécuchet* pokes over into the railway age, but neither of his opinionated copyists, perhaps surprisingly, has a published view on the new mode of transport.

Trains occur only in *L'Education sentimentale*. They are first mentioned as a not very arresting topic of conversation at a soirée given by the Dambreuses. The first real train, and the first real journey, occur in Part Two, chapter three, when Frédéric goes to Creil in the hope of seducing Mme Arnoux. Given the benign impatience of his traveller, Flaubert informs the excursion with an approving lyricism: green plains, stations slipping by like little stage sets, fleecy smoke from the engine dancing briefly on the grass before dispersing. There are several more railway journeys in the novel, and the passengers seem happy enough; at least, none of them howls with boredom like a neglected dog. And though Flaubert aggressively excised from 'La Paysanne' Mme Colet's line about the running smoke on the horizon, this doesn't debar from his own countryside (Part Three, chapter four) 'the smoke of a railway engine stretching out in a horizontal line, like a gigantic ostrich feather whose tip kept blowing away.'

We may detect his private opinion only at one point. Pellerin, the artist among Frédéric's companions, a man who specialises

in complete theories and incomplete sketches, produces one
of his rare finished paintings. Flaubert allows himself a private
smile: 'It represented the Republic, or Progress, or Civilisation,
in the figure of Jesus Christ, driving a locomotive through a
virgin forest.'

10 The penultimate sentence of Gustave's life, uttered as he stood
feeling dizzy but not at all alarmed: 'I think I'm going to have a
kind of fainting fit. It's lucky it should happen today; it would
have been a great nuisance tomorrow, in the train.'

11 At the buffers. Croisset today. The vast paper factory was
churning away on the site of Flaubert's house. I wandered inside;
they were happy to show me round. I gazed at the pistons, the
steam, the vats and the slopping trays: so much wetness to produce something as dry as paper. I asked my guide if they made
the sort of paper that was used for books; she said they made every
sort of paper. The tour, I realised, would not prove sentimental.
Above our heads a huge drum of paper, some twenty feet wide,
was slowly tracking along on a conveyor. It seemed out of proportion to its surroundings, like a piece of pop sculpture on a
deliberately provoking scale. I remarked that it resembled a
gigantic roll of lavatory paper; my guide confirmed that this was
exactly what it was.

Outside the thumping factory things were scarcely quieter.
Lorries bullied past on the road that had once been a tow-path;
pile-drivers banged on both sides of the river; no boat could pass
without hooting. Flaubert used to claim that Pascal had once
visited the house at Croisset; and a tenacious local legend maintained that Abbé Prévost wrote *Manon Lescaut* there. Nowadays
there is no one left to repeat such fictions; and no one to believe
them either.

A sullen Normandy rain was falling. I thought of the horse's
silhouette on the far bank, and the quiet splosh as the eel-
fishermen cast off. Could even eels live in this cheerless commercial conduit? If they did, they would probably taste of diesel and
detergent. My eye moved upriver, and suddenly I noticed it,
squat and shuddering. A train. I'd seen the rails before, a set laid
between the road and the water; the rain was now making them
glisten and smirk. I'd assumed without thinking that they were
for the straddling dock cranes to run on. But no: he hasn't even

been spared this. The swaddled goods train was drawn up about two hundred yards away, ready to make its run past Flaubert's pavilion. It would doubtless hoot derisively as it drew level; perhaps it was carrying poisons, enema pumps and cream tarts, or supplies for chemists and mathematicians. I didn't want to see the event (irony can be heavy-handed as well as ruthless). I climbed into my car and drove off.

9

THE FLAUBERT APOCRYPHA

It is not what they built. It is what they knocked down.
It is not the houses. It is the spaces between the houses.
It is not the streets that exist. It is the streets
that no longer exist.

BUT IT'S ALSO what they didn't build. It's the houses they
dreamed and sketched. It's the brusque boulevards of the imagination; it's that untaken, sauntering path between toupeed
cottages; it's the *trompe-l'oeil* cul-de-sac which bluffs you into the
belief that you're entering some smart avenue.

Do the books that writers don't write matter? It's easy to forget
them, to assume that the apocryphal bibliography must contain
nothing but bad ideas, justly abandoned projects, embarrassing
first thoughts. It needn't be so: first thoughts are often best,
cheeringly rehabilitated by third thoughts after they've been
loured at by seconds. Besides, an idea isn't always abandoned
because it fails some quality control test. The imagination doesn't
crop annually like a reliable fruit tree. The writer has to gather
whatever's there: sometimes too much, sometimes too little,
sometimes nothing at all. And in the years of glut there is always
a slatted wooden tray in some cool, dark attic, which the writer
nervously visits from time to time; and yes, oh dear, while he's
been hard at work downstairs, up in the attic there are puckering
skins, warning spots, a sudden brown collapse and the sprouting
of snowflakes. What can he do about it?

With Flaubert, the apocrypha cast a second shadow. If the
sweetest moment in life is a visit to the brothel which doesn't
come off, perhaps the sweetest moment in writing is the arrival
of that idea for a book which never has to be written, which is
never sullied with a definite shape, which never needs be exposed
to a less loving gaze than that of its author.

Of course, the published works themselves aren't immutable:
they might now look different had Flaubert been awarded time
and money to put his literary estate in order. *Bouvard et Pécuchet*
would have been finished; *Madame Bovary* might have been suppressed (how seriously do we take Gustave's petulance against the
overbearing fame of the book? a little seriously); and *L'Education*

sentimentale might have had a different ending. Du Camp records his friend's dismay at the book's historical misfortune: a year after publication came the Franco-Prussian war, and it seemed to Gustave that the invasion and the débâcle at Sedan would have provided a grand, public and irrebuttable conclusion to a novel which set out to trace the moral failure of a generation.

'Imagine', Du Camp reports him as saying, 'the capital one might have made out of certain incidents. Here, for instance, is one which would have been excellent in calibre. The capitulation has been signed, the army is under arrest, the Emperor, sunk back in a corner of his large carriage, is gloomy and dull-eyed; he smokes a cigarette to keep himself in countenance, and though a tempest is raging within him, tries to appear impassive. Beside him are his aides-de-camp and a Prussian General. All are silent, each glance is lowered; there is pain in every heart.

'Where the two roads cross the procession is stopped by a column of prisoners guarded by some Uhlans, who wear the chapska perched on their ear, and ride with couched lances. The carriage has to be stopped before the human flood, which advances amid a cloud of dust, reddened by the rays of the sun. The men walk dragging their feet and with slouched shoulders. The Emperor's languid eye contemplates this crowd. What a strange way to review his troops. He thinks of previous reviews, of the drums beating, of the waving standards, of his generals covered with gold lace and saluting him with their swords, and of his guard shouting, "Vive l'Empereur!"

'A prisoner recognises him and salutes him, then another and another.

'Suddenly a Zouave leaves the ranks, shakes his fist and cries, "Ah! There you are, you villain; we have been ruined by you!"

'Then ten thousand men yell insults, wave their arms threateningly, spit upon the carriage, and pass like a whirlwind of curses. The Emperor still remains immovable without making a sign or uttering a word, but, he thinks, "Those are the men they used to call my Praetorian Guards!"

'Well, what do you think of that for a situation? It is pretty powerful, is it not? That would have made rather a stirring final scene for my *Education*? I cannot console myself for having missed it.'

Should we mourn such a lost ending? And how do we assess it? Du Camp probably coarsened it in the retelling, and there would have been many Flaubertian redraftings before publication. Its appeal is clear: the *fortissimo* climax, the public conclusion to a nation's private failing. But does the book need such an ending? Having had 1848, do we need 1870 as well? Better to let the novel die away in disenchantment; better the downbeat reminiscing of two friends than a swirling salon-picture.

For the Apocrypha proper, let us be systematic.

1 *Autobiography.* 'One day, if I write my memoirs – the only thing I shall write well, if ever I put myself to the task of doing it – you will find a place in them, and what a place! For you have blown a large breach in the walls of my existence.' Gustave writes this in one of his earliest letters to Louise Colet; and over a seven-year period (1846–53) he makes occasional references to the planned autobiography. Then he announces its official abandonment. But was it ever more than just a project for a project? 'I'll put you in my memoirs' is one of the handier clichés of literary wooing. File it alongside 'I'll put you in motion pictures', 'I could immortalise you in paint', 'I can just see your neck in marble', etc, etc.

2 *Translations.* Lost works, rather than strict apocrypha; but we might note here: (a) Juliet Herbert's translation of *Madame Bovary*, which the novelist oversaw, and which he proclaimed 'a masterpiece'; (b) the translation referred to in a letter of 1844: I have read *Candide* twenty times. I have translated it into English . . .' This does not sound like a school exercise: more like a piece of self-imposed apprenticeship. Judging from Gustave's erratic use of English in his letters, the translation probably added a layer of unintentional comedy to the intentions of the original. He couldn't even copy English place-names accurately: in 1866, making notes on the 'coloured Minton tiles' at the South Kensington Museum, he turns Stoke-upon-Trent into 'Stroke-upon-Trend'.

3 *Fiction.* This section of the Apocrypha contains a large amount of juvenilia, useful mainly to the psychobiographer. But the books a writer fails to write in his adolescence are of a different nature from the books he fails to write once he has announced his profession. These are the not-books for which he must take responsibility.

In 1850, while in Egypt, Flaubert spends two days pondering the story of Mycerinus, a pious king of the fourth dynasty who is credited with reopening temples closed by his predecessors.

In a letter to Bouilhet, however, the novelist characterises his subject more crudely as 'the king who fucks his daughter'. Perhaps Flaubert's interest was encouraged by the discovery (or indeed the memory) that in 1837 the king's sarcophagus had been excavated by the British and shipped back to London. Gustave would have been able to inspect it when he visited the British Museum in 1851.

I tried to inspect it myself the other day. The sarcophagus, they told me, is not one of the Museum's more interesting possessions, and hasn't been on display since 1904. Though believed to be fourth dynasty when it was shipped, it later turned out to be twenty-sixth dynasty: the portions of mummified body inside might, or equally might not, be those of Mycerinus. I felt disappointed, but also relieved: what if Flaubert had continued with his project, and inserted a meticulously-researched description of the king's tomb? Dr Enid Starkie would have been given the chance to swat another Mistake in Literature.

(Perhaps I should award Dr Starkie an entry in my pocket guide to Flaubert; or would that be unnecessarily vindictive? S for Sade, or S for Starkie? It's coming along well, by the way, Braithwaite's Dictionary of Accepted Ideas. All you need to know about Flaubert to know as much as the next person! Only a few more entries and I'll be finished. The letter X is going to be a problem, I can see. There's nothing under X in Flaubert's own Dictionary.)

In 1850, from Constantinople, Flaubert announces three projects: 'Une nuit de Don Juan' (which reaches the planning stage); 'Anubis', the story of 'the woman who wants to be fucked by a god'; and 'My Flemish novel about the young girl who dies a virgin and a mystic ... in a little provincial town, at the bottom of a garden planted with cabbages and bulrushes ...' Gustave complains in this letter to Bouilhet about the dangers of planning a project too thoroughly: 'It seems to me, alas, that if you can so thoroughly dissect your children who are still to be born, you don't get horny enough actually to father them.' In the present cases, Gustave didn't get horny enough; though some see in his third project a vague forerunner of either *Madame Bovary* or *Un cœur simple*.

In 1852–3 Gustave makes serious plans for 'La Spirale', a 'grand, metaphysical, fantastical and bawling novel', whose hero lives a typically Flaubertian double life, being happy in his dreams and unhappy in his real life. Its conclusion, of course: that happiness exists only in the imagination.

In 1853, 'one of my old dreams' is resuscitated: a novel about chivalry. Despite Ariosto such a project is still feasible, Gustave declares: the additional elements he will bring to the subject are 'terror and a broader poetry'.

In 1861: 'I've long been meditating a novel on insanity, or rather on how one becomes insane.' From about this time, or a little later, he was also meditating, according to Du Camp, a novel about the theatre; he would sit in the green room jotting down the confidences of over-candid actresses. 'Only Le Sage in *Gil Blas* has touched upon the truth. I will reveal it in all its nakedness, for it is impossible to imagine how comic it is.'

From this point on, Flaubert must have known that any full-length novel would probably take him five to seven years; and therefore that most of his back-burner projects would inevitably boil themselves dry in the pot. From the last dozen years of his life we find four main ideas, plus an intriguing fifth, a sort of *roman trouvé*.

(a) 'Harel-Bey', an Eastern story. 'If I were younger and had the money, I'd go back to the Orient – to study the modern Orient, the Orient of the Isthmus of Suez. A big book about that is one of my old dreams. I'd like to show a civilised man who turns barbarian, and a barbarian who becomes a civilised man – to develop that contrast between two worlds that end up merging . . . But it's too late.'

(b) A book about the Battle of Thermopylae, which he planned to write after finishing *Bouvard et Pécuchet*.

(c) A novel featuring several generations of a Rouen family.

(d) If you cut a flatworm in half, the head will grow a new tail; more surprisingly, the tail will grow a new head. This is what happened with the regretted ending to *L'Education sentimentale*: it generated an entire novel of its own, called first 'Under Napoleon III', and later 'A Parisian Household'. 'I will write a novel about the Empire [Du Camp reports him saying] and bring in the evening receptions at Compiègne, with all the ambassadors, marshals and senators rattling their decorations as they bend to the ground to kiss the hand of the Prince Imperial. Yes indeed! The period will furnish material for some capital books.'

(e) The *roman trouvé* was found by Charles Lapierre, editor of *Le Nouvelliste de Rouen*. Dining at Croisset one evening, Lapierre told Flaubert the scandalous history of Mademoiselle de P——. She had been born into the Normandy nobility, had connections at Court, and was appointed reader to the Empress Eugénie. Her beauty, they said, was enough to damn a saint. It was certainly enough to damn her: an open liaison with an officer of the Imperial Guard caused her dismissal. Subsequently she became one of the queens of the Parisian demi-monde, ruling in the late 1860s over a loucher version of the Court from which she had been excluded. During the Franco-Prussian war, she disappeared from sight (along with the rest of her profession), and afterwards her star waned. She descended, by all accounts, to the lowest levels of harlotry. And yet, encouragingly (for fiction as well as for herself), she proved able to rise again: she became the established mistress of a cavalry officer, and by the time she died was the legal wife of an admiral.

Flaubert was delighted with the story: 'Do you know, Lapierre, you've just given me the subject of a novel, the counterpart of my *Bovary*, a *Bovary* of high society. What an attractive figure!' He copied down the story at once, and began to make notes on it. But the novel was never written, and the notes have never been found.

All these unwritten books tantalise. Yet they can, to an extent, be filled out, ordered, reimagined. They can be studied in academies. A pier is a disappointed bridge; yet stare at it for long enough and you can dream it to the other side of the Channel. The same is true with these stubs of books.

But what of the unled lives? These, perhaps, are more truly tantalising; these are the real apocrypha. *Thermopylae* instead of *Bouvard et Pécuchet*? Well, it's still a book. But if Gustave himself had changed course? It's easy, after all, not to be a writer. Most people aren't writers, and very little harm comes to them. A phrenologist – that careers master of the nineteenth century – once examined Flaubert and told him he was cut out to be a tamer of wild beasts. Not so inaccurate either. That quote again: 'I attract mad people and animals'.

It is not just the life that we know. It is not just the life that has been successfully hidden. It is not just the lies about the life, some of which cannot now be disbelieved. It is also the life that was not led.

'Am I to be a king, or just a pig?' Gustave writes in his *Intimate Notebook*. At nineteen, it always looks as simple as this. There is the life, and then there is the not-life; the life of ambition served, or the life of porcine failure. Others try and tell you about your future, but you never really believe them. 'Many things', Gustave writes at this time, 'have been predicted to me: (1) that I'll learn to dance; (2) that I'll marry. We'll see – I don't believe it.'

He never married, and he never learned to dance. He was so resistant to dancing that most of the principal male characters in his novels take sympathetic action and refuse to dance as well.

What did he learn instead? Instead he learned that life is not a choice between murdering your way to the throne or slopping back in a sty; that there are swinish kings and regal hogs; that the king may envy the pig; and that the possibilities of the not-life will always change tormentingly to fit the particular embarrassments of the lived life.

At seventeen, he announces that he wants to spend his whole life in a ruined castle by the sea.

At eighteen, he decides that some freakish wind must have mistakenly transplanted him to France: he was born, he declares, to be Emperor of Cochin-China, to smoke 36-fathom pipes, to have 6,000 wives and 1,400 catamites; but instead, displaced by this meteorological hazard, he is left with immense, insatiable desires, fierce boredom, and an attack of the yawns.

At nineteen, he thinks that after he's finished his legal studies he'll go off and become a Turk in Turkey, or a muleteer in Spain, or a cameleer in Egypt.

At twenty, he still wants to become a muleteer, though by now the Spanish location has been narrowed to that of Andalusia. Other career possibilities include the life of a lazzarone in Naples; though he'd settle for being the driver of the coach which plies between Nîmes and Marseilles. Yet is any of this rare enough? The ease with which even the bourgeois travel nowadays comes as an agony to one who has 'the Bosphorus in the soul'.

At twenty-four, with his father and sister newly dead, he plans what to do with his life should his mother die as well: he would sell up everything and live in Rome, Syracuse or Naples.

Still twenty-four, and presenting himself to Louise Colet as a fellow of infinite whim, he claims that he has thought long and *very seriously* about the idea of becoming a bandit in Smyrna. But at the very least 'some day I shall go and live far away from here and never be heard of again'. Perhaps Louise is little amused by Ottoman banditry; for now a more domestic fantasy appears.

If only he were free, he would leave Croisset and come to live with her in Paris. He imagines their life together, their marriage, a sweet existence of mutual love and mutual companionship. He imagines their having a child together; he imagines Louise's death and his own subsequent tenderness in caring for the motherless infant (we do not, alas, have Louise's response to this particular flight). The exotic appeal of the domestic does not, however, last. Within a month the tense of the verb curdles: 'It seems to me that if I had been your husband, we would have been happy together. After we'd been happy, then we would have hated one another. This is normal.' Louise is expected to be grateful that Gustave's far-sightedness has spared her such an unsatisfactory life.

So instead, and still twenty-four, Gustave sits over a map with Du Camp and plans a monster journey to Asia. It would last six years and would cost, at their own rough estimate, three million six hundred thousand and a few odd francs.

At twenty-five he wants to be a Brahmin: the mystic dance, the long hair, the face dripping with holy butter. He officially renounces wanting to be a Camaldolese, a brigand or a Turk. 'Now it's a Brahmin, or nothing at all – which would be simpler.' Go on, be nothing at all, life urges. Being a pig is simple.

At twenty-nine, inspired by Humboldt, he wants to go off and live in South America, among the savannahs, and never be heard of again.

At thirty he muses – as he did throughout his life – on his own previous incarnations, on his apocryphal or metempsychotic lives in the more interesting times of Louis XIV, Nero and Pericles. Of one preincarnation he is certain: he was, at some point during the Roman Empire, the director of a troupe of travelling comedians, the sort of plausible rogue who bought women in Sicily and turned them into actresses, a rowdy mixture of teacher, pimp and artist. (Reading Plautus has reminded Gustave of this previous life: it gives him *le frisson historique*.) Here we should also note Gustave's apocryphal ancestry: he liked to claim that he had Red Indian blood in his veins. This seems to have been not quite the case; though one of his ancestors did emigrate to Canada in the seventeenth century and become a beaver-trapper.

Still thirty, he projects a seemingly more probable life, but one which proves equally to be a not-life. He and Bouilhet play at

imagining themselves old men, patients in some hospice for
incurables: ancients who sweep the streets and babble to one
another of that happy time when they were both thirty and
walked all the way to La Roche-Guyon. The mocked senility
was never attained: Bouilhet died at forty-eight, Flaubert at
fifty-eight.

At thirty-one, he remarks to Louise – a parenthesis to a hypothesis – that if he *had* ever had a son, he would have taken great
pleasure in procuring women for him.

Also at thirty-one, he reports a brief, untypical lapse to Louise:
the desire to chuck in literature. He will come and live with her,
inside her, his head between her breasts; he is fed up, he says,
with masturbating that head of his to make the phrases spurt. But
this fantasy is also a chilling tease: it's recounted in the past tense,
as something which Gustave, in a moment of weakness, fleet-
ingly imagined himself doing. He would always rather have his
head between his own hands than between Louise's breasts.

At thirty-two, he confesses to Louise the manner in which he
has spent many hours of his life: imagining what he would do if
he had an income of a million francs a year. In such dreams
servants would ease him into shoes studded with diamonds; he
would cock an ear to the whinny of his coach-horses, whose
splendour would make England die of jealousy; he would give
oyster banquets, and have his dining-room surrounded by espaliers of flowering jasmine, out of which bright finches would
swoop. But this, at a million a year, was a cheap dream. Du Camp
reports Gustave's plans for 'A Winter in Paris' – an extravaganza
incorporating the luxury of the Roman Empire, the refinement
of the Renaissance, and the faerie of the Thousand and One
Nights. The Winter had been seriously costed, and it came out
at twelve thousand million francs 'at the most'. Du Camp also
adds, more generally, that 'when these dreams took possession of
him, he became almost rigid, and reminded one of an opium-
eater in a state of trance. He seemed to have his head in the
clouds, to be living in a dream of gold. This habit was one reason
why he found steady work difficult.'

At thirty-five, he reveals 'my private dream': to buy a little
palazzo on the Grand Canal. A few months later, a kiosk on the
Bosphorus is added to the real estate in his head. A few months
more, and he is ready to leave for the East, to stay there, to die

there. The painter Camille Rogier, who lives in Beirut, has invited him. He could go; just like that. He could; he doesn't.

At thirty-five, however, the apocryphal life, the not-life, begins to die away. The reason is clear: the real life has really begun. Gustave was thirty-five when *Madame Bovary* came out in book form. The fantasies are no longer needed; or rather, different, particular, practical fantasies are now required. For the world, he will play the Hermit of Croisset; for his friends in Paris, he will play the Idiot of the Salons; for George Sand he will play the Reverend Father Cruchard, a fashionable Jesuit who enjoys hearing the confessions of society women; for his intimate circle he will play Saint Polycarpe, that obscure Bishop of Smyrna, martyred in the nick of time at the age of ninety-five, who pre-echoed Flaubert by stopping up his ears and crying out, 'Oh Lord! Into what an age you have caused me to be born!' But these identities are no longer lurid alibis towards which he might credibly escape; they are playthings, alternative lives issued under licence by the celebrated author. He does not run off to become a bandit in Smyrna; instead, he summons the useful Bishop of Smyrna to live within his skin. He has proved not a tamer of wild beasts, but a tamer of wild lives. Pacification of the apocryphal is complete: writing can begin.

10

THE CASE AGAINST

WHAT MAKES US want to know the worst? Is it that we tire of preferring to know the best? Does curiosity always hurdle self-interest? Or is it, more simply, that wanting to know the worst is love's favourite perversion?

For some, this curiosity operates as baleful fantasy. I had a patient once, a respectable nine-to-fiver otherwise untouched by imagination, who confessed that while making love to his wife he liked to picture her spread blissfully beneath mountainous hidalgos, sleek lascars, rummaging dwarfs. Shock me, the fantasy urges, appal me. For others, the search is real. I have known couples take pride in one another's tawdry behaviour: each pursuing the other's folly, the other's vanity, the other's weakness. What were they really after? Something, evidently, which lay beyond what they appeared to seek. Perhaps some final confirmation that mankind itself was ineradicably corrupt, that life was indeed just a gaudy nightmare in the head of an imbecile?

I loved Ellen, and I wanted to know the worst. I never provoked her; I was cautious and defensive, as is my habit; I didn't even ask questions; but I wanted to know the worst. Ellen never returned this caress. She was fond of me – she would automatically agree, as if the matter weren't worth discussing, that she loved me – but she unquestioningly believed the best about me. That's the difference. She didn't ever search for that sliding panel which opens the secret chamber of the heart, the chamber where memory and corpses are kept. Sometimes you find the panel, but it doesn't open; sometimes it opens, and your gaze meets nothing but a mouse skeleton. But at least you've looked. That's the real distinction between people: not between those who have secrets and those who don't, but between those who want to know everything and those who don't. This search is a sign of love, I maintain.

It's similar with books. Not quite the same, of course (it never is); but similar. If you quite enjoy a writer's work, if you turn the page approvingly yet don't mind being interrupted, then you tend to like that author unthinkingly. Good chap, you assume. Sound fellow. They say he strangled an entire pack of Wolf Cubs and fed their bodies to a school of carp? Oh no, I'm sure he didn't: sound fellow, good chap. But if you love a writer, if you depend upon the drip-feed of his intelligence, if you want to pursue him and find him – despite edicts to the contrary – then it's impossible to know too much. You seek the vice as well. A pack of Wolf Cubs, eh? Was that twenty-seven or twenty-eight? And did he have their little scarves sewn up into a patch-work quilt? And is it true that as he ascended the scaffold he quoted from the Book of Jonah? And that he bequeathed his carp pond to the local Boy Scouts?

But here's the difference. With a lover, a wife, when you find the worst – be it infidelity or lack of love, madness or the suicidal spark – you are almost relieved. Life is as I thought it was; shall we now celebrate this disappointment? With a writer you love, the instinct is to defend. This is what I meant earlier: perhaps love for a writer is the purest, the steadiest form of love. And so your defence comes the more easily. The fact of the matter is, carp are an endangered species, and everyone knows that the only diet they will accept if the winter has been especially harsh and the spring turns wet before St Oursin's Day is that of young minced Wolf Cub. Of course he knew he would hang for the offence, but he also knew that humanity is not an endangered species, and reckoned therefore that twenty-seven (did you say twenty-eight?) Wolf Cubs plus one middle-ranking author (he was always ridiculously modest about his talents) were a trivial price to pay for the survival of an entire breed of fish. Take the long view: did we need so many Wolf Cubs? They would only have grown up and become Boy Scouts. And if you're still mired in sentimentality, look at it this way: the admission fees so far received from visitors to the carp pond have already enabled the Boy Scouts to build and maintain several church halls in the area.

So go on. Read the charge-sheet. I had expected it at some point. But don't forget this: Gustave has been in the dock before. How many offences are there this time?

1 *That he hated humanity.*

Yes, yes, of course. You always say that. I'll give you two sorts of answer. First, let's start with basics. He loved his mother: doesn't that warm your silly, sentimental, twentieth-century heart? He loved his father. He loved his sister. He loved his niece. He loved his friends. He admired certain individuals. But his affections were always specific; they were not given away to all-comers. This seems enough to me. You want him to do more? You want him to 'love humanity', to goose the human race? But that means nothing. Loving humanity means as much and as little as loving raindrops, or loving the Milky Way. You say that you love humanity? Are you sure you aren't treating yourself to easy self-congratulation, seeking approval, making certain you're on the right side?

Secondly, even if he did hate humanity – or was profoundly unimpressed by it, as I would prefer to say – was he wrong? You, clearly, are quite impressed by humanity: it's all clever irrigation schemes, missionary work and micro-electronics to you. Forgive him for seeing it differently. It's clear we're going to have to discuss this at some length. But let me first, briefly, quote to you one of your wise men of the twentieth century: Freud. Not, you will agree, someone with an axe to grind? You want his summing-up on the human race, ten years before his death? 'In the depths of my heart I can't help being convinced that my dear fellow-men, with a few exceptions, are worthless.' This from the man that most people, for most of this century, believed most thoroughly understood the human heart. It is a little embarrassing, is it not?

But come, it's time for you to be rather more specific.

2 *That he hated democracy.*

La democrasserie, as he called it in a letter to Taine. Which do you prefer – democrappery or democrassness? Democrappiness, perhaps? He was, it is true, very unimpressed by it. From which you should not conclude that he favoured tyranny, or absolute monarchy, or bourgeois monarchy, or bureaucratised totalitari-anism, or anarchy, or whatever. His preferred model of govern-ment was a Chinese one – that of the Mandarinate; though he readily admitted that its chances of introduction into France were extremely small. The Mandarinate seems a step back to you? But you forgive Voltaire his enthusiasm for enlightened monarchy: why not forgive Flaubert, a century later, his enthu-siasm for enlightened oligarchy? He did not, at least, entertain the childish fantasy of some literati: that writers are better fitted to run the world than anybody else.

The main point is this: Flaubert thought democracy merely a

stage in the history of government, and he thought it a typical vanity on our part to assume that it represented the finest, proudest way for men to rule one another. He believed in – or rather, he did not fail to notice – the perpetual evolution of humanity, and therefore the evolution of its social forms: 'Democracy isn't mankind's last word, any more than slavery was, or feudalism was, or monarchy was.' The best form of government, he maintained, is one that is dying, because this means it's giving way to something else.

3 *That he didn't believe in progress.*
I cite the twentieth century in his defence.

4 *That he wasn't interested enough in politics.*
Interested 'enough'? You admit, at least, that he was interested. You are suggesting, tactfully, that he didn't like what he saw (correct), and that if he had seen more, he would perhaps have come round to your way of thinking in these matters (incorrect). I should like to make two points, the first of which I shall put into italics, since this seems to be your favourite mode of utterance. *Literature includes politics, and not vice versa.* This isn't a fashionable view, neither with writers nor politicians, but you will forgive me. Novelists who think their writing an instrument of politics seem to me to degrade writing and foolishly exalt politics. No, I'm not saying they should be forbidden from having political opinions or from making political statements. It's just that they should call that part of their work journalism. The writer who imagines that the novel is the most effective way of taking part in politics is usually a bad novelist, a bad journalist, and a bad politician.

Du Camp followed politics carefully, Flaubert sporadically. Which do you prefer? The former. And which of them was the greater writer? The latter. And what were their politics? Du Camp became a lethargic meliorist; Flaubert remained 'an enraged liberal'. Does that surprise you? But even if Flaubert had described himself as a lethargic meliorist, I should make the same point: what a curious vanity it is of the present to expect the past to suck up to it. The present looks back at some great figure of an earlier century and wonders, Was he on our side? Was he a goodie? What a lack of self-confidence this implies: the present wants both to patronise the past by adjudicating on its political acceptability, and also to be flattered by it, to be patted on the back and told to keep up the good work. If this is what you understand by Monsieur Flaubert not being 'interested enough' in politics, then I'm afraid my client must plead guilty.

5 *That he was against the Commune.*

Well, what I've said above is part of the answer. But there is also this consideration, this incredible weakness of character on my client's part: he was on the whole against people killing one another. Call it squeamishness, but he did disapprove. He never killed anyone himself, I have to admit; in fact, he never even tried. He promises to do better in future.

6 *That he was unpatriotic.*

Permit me a short laugh. Ah. That's better. I thought patriotism was a bad thing nowadays. I thought we would all rather betray our country than our friends. Is that not so? Have things turned upside down yet again? What am I expected to say? On September 22nd, 1870, Flaubert bought himself a revolver; at Croisset, he drilled his ragged collection of men in expectation of a Prussian advance; he took them out on night patrols; he told them to shoot him if he tried to run away. By the time the Prussians came, there was not much he could sensibly do except look after his aged mother. He could perhaps have submitted himself to some army medical board, but whether they would have enthused over the application of a 48-year-old epileptic syphilitic with no military experience except that acquired while shooting wild-life in the desert –

7 *That he shot wild-life in the desert.*

Oh, for Christ's sake. We plead *noli contendere*. And besides I haven't finished with the question of patriotism. May I instruct you briefly on the nature of the novelist? What is the easiest, the most comfortable thing for a writer to do? To congratulate the society in which he lives: to admire its biceps, applaud its progress, tease it endearingly about its follies. 'I am as much a Chinaman as a Frenchman,' Flaubert declared. Not, that is, *more* of a Chinaman: had he been born in Peking, no doubt he would have disappointed patriots there too. The greatest patriotism is to tell your country when it is behaving dishonourably, foolishly, viciously. The writer must be universal in sympathy and an outcast by nature: only then can he see clearly. Flaubert always sides with minorities, with 'the Bedouin, the Heretic, the philosopher, the hermit, the Poet'. In 1867 forty-three gypsies pitched camp in the Cours la Reine and aroused much hatred among the Rouennais. Flaubert delighted in their presence and gave them money. No doubt you wish to pat him on the head for this. If he'd known he was gaining the approval of the future, he'd probably have kept the money to himself.

8 *That he didn't involve himself in life.*

'You can depict wine, love, women and glory on the condition that you're not a drunkard, a lover, a husband or a private in the ranks. If you participate in life, you don't see it clearly: you suffer from it too much or enjoy it too much.' This isn't a reply of guilty, it's a complaint that the charge is wrongly phrased. What do you mean by life? Politics? We've dealt with that. The emotional life? Through his family, friends and mistresses, Gustave knew all the stations of the cross. Marriage, you mean perhaps? A curious complaint, though not a new one. Does marriage produce better novels than bachelorhood? Are the philoprogenitive better writers than the childless? I should like to see your statistics.

The best life for a writer is the life which helps him write the best books he can. Are we confident that our judgment in the matter is better than his? Flaubert was more 'involved', to use your term, than many: Henry James by comparison was a nun. Flaubert may have tried to live in an ivory tower –

8(a) *That he tried to live in an ivory tower.*

but he failed. 'I have always tried to live in an ivory tower, but a tide of shit is beating at its walls, threatening to undermine it.'

Three points need to be made. One is that the writer chooses – as far as he can – the extent of what you call his involvement in life: despite his reputation, Flaubert occupied a half-and-half position. 'It isn't the drunkard who writes the drinking song': he knew that. On the other hand, it isn't the teetotaller either. He put it best, perhaps, when he said that the writer must wade into life as into the sea, but only up to the navel.

Secondly, when readers complain about the lives of writers – why didn't he do this; why didn't he protest to the newspapers about that; why wasn't he more involved in life? – aren't they really asking a simpler, and vainer, question: why isn't he more like us? But if a writer were more like a reader, he'd be a reader, not a writer: it's as uncomplicated as that.

Thirdly, what is the thrust of the complaint as far as the books are concerned? Presumably the regret that Flaubert wasn't more involved in life isn't just a philanthropic wish for him: if only old Gustave had had a wife and kiddies, he wouldn't have been so glum about the whole shooting-match? If only he'd got caught up in politics, or good works, or become a governor of his old school, he'd have been taken out of himself more? Presumably you think there are faults in the books which could have been remedied by a change in the writer's life. If so, I think it is up to you to state them. For myself, I cannot think that, for instance, the portrait of provincial manners in *Madame Bovary* is lacking in some particular aspect which would have been remedied had its author clinked tankards of cider every evening with some gouty Norman *bergère*.

9 *That he was a pessimist.*

Ah. I begin to see what you mean. You wish his books were a bit more cheerful, a bit more ... how would you put it, life-enhancing? What a curious idea of literature you do have. Is your PhD from Bucharest? I didn't know one had to defend authors for being pessimists. This is a new one. I decline to do so. Flaubert said: 'You don't make art out of good intentions.' He also said: 'The public wants works which flatter its illusions.'

10 *That he teaches no positive virtues.*

Now you are coming out into the open. So this is how we are to judge our writers – on their 'positive virtues'? Well, I suppose I must play your game briefly: it's what you have to do in the courts. Take all the obscenity trials from *Madame Bovary* to *Lady Chatterley's Lover*: there's always some element of games-playing, of compliance, in the defence. Others might call it tactical hypocrisy. (Is this book sexy? No, M'Lud, we hold that it would have an emetic, not a mimetic, effect on any reader. Does this book encourage adultery? No, M'Lud, look how the miserable sinner who gives herself time and time again to riotous pleasure is punished in the end. Does this book attack marriage? No, M'Lud, it portrays a vile and hopeless marriage so that others may learn that only by following Christian instructions will their own marriages be happy. Is this book blasphemous? No, M'Lud, the novelist's thought is chaste.) As a forensic argument, of course, it has been successful; but I sometimes feel a residual bitterness that one of these defence counsel, when speaking for a true work of literature, did not build his act on simple defiance. (Is this book sexy? M'Lud, we bloody well hope so. Does it encourage adultery and attack marriage? Spot on, M'Lud, that's *exactly* what my client is trying to do. Is this book blasphemous? For Christ's sake, M'Lud, the matter's as clear as the loincloth on

THE CASE AGAINST 117

the Crucifixion. Put it this way, M'Lud: my client thinks that most of the values of the society in which he lives stink, and he hopes with this book to promote fornication, masturbation, adultery, the stoning of priests and, since we've temporarily got your attention, M'Lud, the suspension of corrupt judges by their earlobes. The defence rests its case.)

So, briefly: Flaubert teaches you to gaze upon the truth and not blink from its consequences; he teaches you, with Montaigne, to sleep on the pillow of doubt; he teaches you to dissect out the constituent parts of reality, and to observe that Nature is always a mixture of genres; he teaches you the most exact use of language; he teaches you not to approach a book in search of moral or social pills – literature is not a pharmacopoeia; he teaches the pre-eminence of Truth, Beauty, Feeling and Style. And if you study his private life, he teaches courage, stoicism, friendship; the importance of intelligence, scepticism and wit; the folly of cheap patriotism; the virtue of being able to remain by yourself in your own room; the hatred of hypocrisy; distrust of the doctrinaire; the need for plain speaking. Is that the way you like writers to be described (I do not care for it much myself)? Is it enough? It's all I'm giving you for the moment: I seem to be embarrassing my client.

11 *That he was a Sadist.*

Rubbish. My client was a soft touch. Cite me a single sadistic, or even unkind, thing he did in his whole life. I'll tell you the unkindest thing I know about him: he was caught being beastly to a woman at a party for no obvious reason. When asked why, he replied, 'Because she might want to come into my study.' That's the worst thing I know about my client. Unless you count the occasion in Egypt when he tried to go to bed with a prostitute while suffering from the pox. That was a little deceitful, I admit. But he didn't succeed: the girl, following the normal precautions of her profession, asked to examine him and, when he refused, sent him packing.

He read Sade, of course. What educated French writer doesn't? I gather he is currently popular among Parisian intellectuals. My client told the Goncourt brothers that Sade was 'entertaining nonsense'. He kept a few gruesome mementoes around him, it is true; he enjoyed recounting horrors; there are lurid passages in his early work. But you say he had a 'Sadeian imagination'? I am puzzled. You specify: *Salammbô* contains scenes of shocking violence. I reply: do you think they didn't happen? Do you think the Ancient World was all rose petals, lute music, and plump vats of honey sealed with bear fat?

11(a) *That there are a lot of animals slaughtered in his books.*

He isn't Walt Disney, no. He was interested in cruelty, I agree. He was interested in everything. As well as Sade, there was Nero. But listen to what he says about them: 'These monsters explain history for me.' He is, I must add, all of seventeen at the time. And let me give you another quote: 'I love the vanquished, but I also love the victors.' He strives, as I've said, to be as much a Chinaman as a Frenchman. There is an earthquake in Leghorn: Flaubert doesn't cry out in sympathy. He feels as much sympathy for these victims as he does for slaves who died centuries earlier turning some tyrant's grindstone. You are shocked? It's called having a historical imagination. It's called being a citizen, not just of the world, but of all time. It's what Flaubert described as being 'brother in God to everything that lives, from the giraffe and the crocodile to man.' It's called being a writer.

12 *That he was beastly to women.*

Women loved him. He enjoyed their company; they enjoyed his; he was gallant, flirtatious; he went to bed with them. He just didn't want to marry them. Is that a sin? Perhaps some of his sexual attitudes were pungently those of his time and his class; but who then in the nineteenth century shall escape whipping? He stood, at least, for honesty in sexual dealings: hence his preference for the prostitute over the *grisette*. Such honesty brought him more trouble than hypocrisy would have done – with Louise Colet, for instance. When he told her the truth it sounded like cruelty. But she was a pest, wasn't she? (Let me answer my own question. I think she was a pest; she sounds like a pest; though admittedly we hear only Gustave's side of the story. Perhaps someone should write her account: yes, why not reconstruct Louise Colet's Version? I might do that. Yes, I will.)

If I may say so, a lot of your charges could probably be reclassified under a single heading: *That he wouldn't have liked us if he'd known us.* To which he might be inclined to plead guilty; if only to see the expression on our face.

13 *That he believed in Beauty.*

I think I've got something lodged in my ear. Probably a bit of wax. Just give me a moment to grip my nose and blow out through my eardrums.

14 *That he was obsessed with style.*

You are babbling. Do you still think the novel divides, like Gaul, into three parts – the Idea, the Form and the Style? If so, you are taking your own first tremulous steps into fiction. You want some maxims for writing? Very well. Form isn't an overcoat flung over the flesh of thought (that old comparison, old in Flaubert's day); it's the flesh of thought itself. You can no more imagine an Idea without a Form than a Form without an Idea. Everything in art depends on execution: the story of a louse can be as beautiful as the story of Alexander. You must write according to your feelings, be sure those feelings are true, and let everything else go hang. When a line is good, it ceases to belong to any school. A line of prose must be as immutable as a line of poetry. If you happen to write well, you are accused of lacking ideas.

All these maxims are by Flaubert, except for the one by Bouilhet.

15 *That he didn't believe Art had a social purpose.*

No, he didn't. This is wearying. 'You provide desolation,' wrote George Sand, 'and I provide consolation.' To which Flaubert replied, 'I cannot change my eyes.' The work of art is a pyramid which stands in the desert, uselessly: jackals piss at the base of it, and bourgeois clamber to the top of it; continue this comparison. Do you want art to be a healer? Send for the AMBULANCE GEORGE SAND. Do you want art to tell the truth? Send for the AMBULANCE FLAUBERT: though don't be surprised, when it arrives, if it runs over your leg. Listen to Auden: 'Poetry makes nothing happen.' Do not imagine that Art is something which is designed to give gentle uplift and self-confidence. Art is not a *brassière*. At least, not in the English sense. But do not forget that *brassière* is the French for life-jacket.

11

LOUISE COLET'S VERSION

NOW HEAR MY STORY. I insist. Look, take my arm, like that, and let's just walk. I have tales to tell; you will like them. We'll follow the quai, and cross that bridge – no, the second one – and perhaps we could take a cognac somewhere, and wait until the gas-lamps dim, and then walk back. Come, you're surely not frightened of me? So why that look? You think I am a dangerous woman? Well, that's a form of flattery – I accept the compliment. Or perhaps ... perhaps it's what I might have to *say* that you're frightened of? Aha ... well, it's too late now. You have taken my arm; you cannot drop it. After all, I am older than you. It is your job to protect me.

I have no interest in slander. Slip your fingers down my forearm, if you want to; yes, there, now feel the pulse. I am not vengeful tonight. Some friends say, Louise, you must answer fire with fire, lie with lie. But I do not wish to. Of course I have lied in my time; I have – what is that word your sex favours? – I have schemed. But women scheme when they are weak, they lie out of fear. Men scheme when they are strong, they lie out of arrogance. You don't agree? I only speak from observation; yours may be different, I grant. But you see how calm I am? I am calm because I feel strong. And – what's that? Perhaps, if I am strong, then I am scheming like a man? Come, let's not be complicated.

I did not need Gustave to come into my life. Look at the facts. I was thirty-five, I was beautiful, I was ... renowned. I had conquered first Aix, then Paris. I had won the Académie's poetry prize twice. I had translated Shakespeare. Victor Hugo called me *sister*; Béranger called me *Muse*. As for my private life: my husband was respected in his profession; my ... protector was the most brilliant philosopher of his age. You haven't read Victor Cousin? Then you should. A fascinating mind. The only man who truly understood Plato. A friend of your philosopher Mr Mill. And then, there was – or there was soon to be – Musset, Vigny, Champfleury. I do not boast of my conquests; I do not need to. But you see my point. I was the candle; he was the moth. The mistress of Socrates deigned to cast her smile on this unknown poet. *I* was *his* catch; he wasn't mine.

We met at Pradier's. I could see the banality of that; though of course he couldn't. The sculptor's studio, the free talk, the unclothed model, the mixture of demi-monde and three-quarter-monde. To me it was all familiar (why, only a few years before I'd danced there with a stiff-backed medical student by the name of Achille Flaubert). And, of course, I wasn't present as a spectator; I was there to sit for Pradier. Whereas Gustave? I do not want to be harsh, but when I first set eyes on him I knew the type at once: the big, gangling provincial, so eager and relieved to find himself at last in artistic circles. I know how they talk, out in the provinces, with that mixture of fake self-confidence and real fear: 'Go to Pradier's, my boy, you'll always find some little actress there to be your mistress, and grateful she'll be too.' And the boy in Toulouse or Poitiers or Bordeaux or Rouen, still secretly anxious about the long journey to the capital, feels his head filling up with snobbery and lust. I *understood*, you see, because I had been a provincial myself. I had made the journey from Aix a dozen years earlier. I had come a long way; and I could recognise the signs of travel in others.

Gustave was twenty-four. To my mind, age does not matter; love is what matters. I did not need to have Gustave in my life. If I had been looking for a lover – I admit my husband's fortunes were not at their brightest, and my friendship with the Philosopher was a little turbulent at that time – then I should not have chosen Gustave. But I have no stomach for fat bankers. And besides, you do not look, you do not choose, do you? You are chosen; you are elected into love by a secret ballot against which there is no appeal.

I do not blush at the difference between our ages? Why should I? You men are so conformist in love, so provincial in imagination; that is why we have to flatter you, to prop you up with little lies. So: I was thirty-five, Gustave was twenty-four. I state it and pass on. Perhaps you do not want to pass on; in which case I shall answer your unspoken question. If you wish to examine the mental condition of the couple entering into such a liaison, then you do not need to look at mine. Examine Gustave's. Why? I will give you a pair of dates. I was born in 1810, in September, the 15th day of the month. You remember

Gustave's Madame Schlesinger, the woman who first cicatrised
his adolescent heart, the woman with whom everything was
doomed and hopeless, the woman of whom he used to boast
furtively, the woman for whose sake he had bricked up his heart
(and you accuse *our* sex of vain romance?). Well, this Mme
Schlesinger, I happen to know, was also born in 1810, and also
in September. Eight days after me, to be precise, on the 23rd.
You see?

You look at me in a way that is familiar. I surmise that you
want me to tell you how Gustave was as a lover. Men, I know,
talk of such things with eagerness, with a little contempt; it is as
if they were describing the last meal they had, course by course.
So much detachment. Women are not like that; or at least, the
details, the weaknesses they dwell on in narration are only rarely
the physical ones that men delight in. We look for signs that speak
to us of character – good or bad. Men look only for signs which
flatter them. They are so vain in bed, much more vain than
women. Outside, the sexes are more evenly matched, I admit.

I will reply a little more freely, because you are who you are;
and because it is Gustave of whom I speak. He always used to
lecture people, tell them about the honesty of the artist, the
necessity not to speak like a bourgeois. Well, if I lift the sheets a
little, he has only himself to blame.

He was eager, my Gustave. It was – God knows – never easy
to persuade him to meet me; but once he was there . . . Whatever
the battles that occurred between us, none of them was fought
in the province of the night. There, we embraced by lightning;
there, violent wonder lay entwined with soft playfulness. He
carried a bottle of water from the River Mississippi with which,
he said, he planned to baptise my breast as a sign of love. He was
a strong young man, and I delighted in that strength: he once
signed a letter to me 'Your wild boy of Aveyron'.

He had, of course, the eternal delusion of strong young men,
that women gauge passion by counting the number of times that
the assault is renewed in the course of a single night. Well, to
some extent we do: who would deny that? It is flattering, is it
not? But it is not what counts finally. And after a while, there
seems something almost military about it. Gustave had a way of
talking about the women he had enjoyed. He would recall some
prostitute he had frequented in the rue de la Cigogne: 'I fired
five shots into her,' he would boast to me. It was his habitual turn

of phrase. I found it coarse, but I did not mind: we were artists together, you see. However, I noted the metaphor. The more shots you fire into somebody, the more likely they are to be dead at the end of it. Is that what men want? Do they need a corpse as proof of their virility? I suspect they do, and women, with the logic of flattery, remember to exclaim at the transporting moment, 'Oh, I die! I die!' or some such phrase. After a bout of love, I often find that my brain is at its sharpest; I see things clearly; I feel poetry coming to me. But I know better than to interrupt the hero with my babblings; instead I ape the satisfied cadaver.

In the province of the night there was harmony between us. Gustave was not shy. Nor was he narrow in his tastes. I was – why should I be modest – undoubtedly the most beautiful, the most renowned, the most desirable woman with whom he ever slept (if I had any rival, it was only a strange beast I shall tell you of later). He was, naturally, sometimes nervous in the face of my beauty; and at other times needlessly pleased with himself. I understood. Before me there had been prostitutes, of course, *grisettes*, and friends. Ernest, Alfred, Louis, Max: the band of students, that was how I thought of them. Sodality confirmed by sodomy. No, perhaps that's unfair; I do not know precisely who, precisely when, precisely what; though I do know that Gustave was never tired of *double ententes* about *la pipe*. I also know he was never tired of gazing at me as I lay on my front.

I was different, you see. Prostitutes were uncomplicated; *grisettes* could be paid off too; men were different – friendship, however deep, had its known limits. But love? And losing your-self? And some partnership, some equality? He didn't dare risk it. I was the only woman to whom he was sufficiently drawn; and he chose, out of fear, to humiliate me. I think we should feel sorry for Gustave.

He used to send me flowers. Special flowers; the convention of an unconventional lover. He sent me a rose once. He gathered it one Sunday morning at Croisset, from a hedge in his garden. 'I kiss it,' he wrote. 'Put it quickly to your mouth, and then – you know where ... Adieu! A thousand kisses. I am yours from night to day, from day to night.' Who could resist such senti-ments? I kissed the rose, and that night, in bed, I placed it where he desired me to. In the morning, when I awoke, the rose had by the motions of the night been reduced to its fragrant parts.

The sheets smelt of Croisset – that place which I did not yet know would be forbidden to me; there was a petal between two of my toes, and a thin scratch down the inside of my right thigh. Gustave, eager and clumsy as he was, had forgotten to smooth the stem of the rose.

The next flower was not such a happy one. Gustave went off on his tour of Brittany. Was I wrong to make a fuss? Three months! We had known one another less than a year, all Paris knew of our passion, and he chose three months in the company of Du Camp! We could have been like George Sand and Chopin; greater than them! And Gustave insists on disappearing for three months with that ambitious catamite of his. Was I wrong to make a fuss? Was it not a direct insult, an attempt to humiliate me? And yet *he* said, when I expressed my feelings to him in public (I am not ashamed of love – why should I be? I would declare myself in the waiting-room of a railway station if it were necessary), *he* said that *I* was humiliating *him*. Imagine! He cast me off. *Ultima*, I wrote on the last letter he sent me before his departure.

It wasn't, of course, his last letter. No sooner was he striding across that tedious countryside, pretending to be interested in disused châteaux and drab churches (three months!) than he began to miss me. The letters started to arrive, the apologies, the confessions, the pleas that I should reply to him. He was always like that. When he was at Croisset, he dreamed of the hot sand and the shimmering Nile; when he was on the Nile, he dreamed of damp fogs and shimmering Croisset. He didn't really like travel, of course. He liked the idea of travel, and the memory of travel, but not travel itself. For once I agree with Du Camp, who used to say that Gustave's preferred form of travel was to lie on a divan and have the scenery carried past him. As for that famous Oriental trip of theirs, Du Camp (yes, the odious Du Camp, the unreliable Du Camp) maintained that Gustave spent most of the journey in a state of torpor.

But anyway: while he was tramping through that dull and backward province with his malign companion, Gustave sent me another flower, plucked from beside the tomb of Châteaubriand. He wrote of the calm sea at St Malo, the pink sky, the sweet air. It makes a fine scene, does it not? The romantic grave on that rocky promontory; the great man lying there, his head pointing out to sea, listening for all eternity to the comings and goings of the tide; the young writer, with stirrings of genius inside him, kneels by the tomb, watches the pink drain slowly from the evening sky, reflects – in the way young men are wont to do – on eternity, the fugitive nature of life and the consolations of greatness, then gathers a flower which has rooted itself in Châteaubriand's dust, and sends it to his beautiful mistress in Paris ... Could I be unmoved by such a gesture? Of course not. But I could not help observing that a flower plucked from a grave brings with it certain reverberations when sent to one who has written *Ultima* on a letter received not long before. And I also could not help observing that Gustave's letter was posted from Pontorson, which is forty kilometres from St Malo. Did Gustave pick the flower for himself and then, after forty kilometres, grow weary of it? Or perhaps – such a suggestion arises in me only because I have lain next to the contagious soul of Gustave himself – did he gather it elsewhere? Did he think of the gesture a little too late? Who can resist *l'esprit de l'escalier*, even in love?

My flower – the one that I remember best out of many – was gathered where I said it had been. In Windsor Park. It was after my tragic visit to Croisset and the humiliation of not being received, after the brutality, the pain and the horror of it all. You have heard different versions, no doubt? The truth is simple.

I had to see him. We had to talk. You do not dismiss love in the way you dismiss your hairdresser. He would not come to me in Paris; so I went to him. I took the train (beyond Mantes, this time) to Rouen. I was rowed downstream to Croisset; in my soul, hope struggled with fear, while the ancient oarsman struggled with the current. We came in sight of a charming, low white house in the English style; a laughing house, as it seemed to me. I disembarked; I pushed the iron grille; I was allowed no further. Gustave refused me entrance. Some barnyard crone turned me away. He would not see me there; he condescended to see me at my hotel. My Charon rowed me back. Gustave travelled separately by steamer. He overtook us on the river and arrived ahead of me. It was farce, it was tragedy. We went to my hotel. I talked, but he could not hear. I spoke of possible happiness. The secret of happiness, he told me, is to be happy already. He did not understand my anguish. He embraced me with a self-restraint that was humiliating. He told me to marry Victor Cousin.

I fled to England. I could not bear to be in France a moment longer: my friends confirmed my impulse. I went to London. I was received there with kindness. I was introduced to many

distinguished spirits. I met Mazzini; I met the Countess Guiccioli. My meeting with the Countess was an uplifting occasion
– we became firm friends at once – but also, privately, a sadden-
ing one. George Sand and Chopin, the Countess Guiccioli and
Byron . . . would they ever say Louise Colet and Flaubert? It gave
me, I confess to you frankly, many hours of quiet grief, which
I tried to bear with philosophy. What would become of us? What
would become of me? Is it wrong, I kept asking myself, to be
ambitious in love? Is that *wrong*? Answer me.

I went to Windsor. I remember a fine round tower covered in
ivy. I wandered in the Park and picked a convolvulus for Gustave.
I must tell you that he was always vulgarly ignorant about flowers.
Not their botanical aspect – he probably learned all about that at
some stage, as he learned about most other things (except the
heart of woman) – but their symbolic aspect. It is such an elegant
tongue, the language of flowers: supple, courtly and precise.
When the beauty of the flower resounds with the beauty of the
sentiment which it is hired to communicate . . . well, there is a
happiness which the gift of rubies can rarely surpass. The happiness is made the more poignant by the fact that the flower fades.
But perhaps, by the time the flower fades, *he* will have sent
another one . . .

Gustave understood nothing of this. He was the sort of person
who might, after much hard study, have finally learnt two phrases
from the language of flowers: the gladiolus, which when placed
at the centre of a bouquet indicates by the number of its blooms
the hour for which the rendezvous is set; and the petunia, which
announces that a letter has been intercepted. He would understand such rough and practical uses. Here, take this rose (no
matter what colour, though there are five different meanings for
five different roses in the language of flowers): put it first to your
lips, and then place it between your thighs. Such was the fierce
gallantry of which Gustave was capable. He would not, I am sure,
have understood the significance of the convolvulus; or, if he had
made any effort, he would still have got it wrong. There are three
messages which can be sent by means of the convolvulus. A white
one signifies *Why are you fleeing me?* A pink one signifies *I shall
bind myself to you.* A blue one signifies *I shall wait for better days.*
You must guess the colour of the flower I chose in Windsor Park.

Did he understand women at all? I often doubted it. We
quarrelled, I remember, over that Niotic whore of his, Kuchuk

Hanem. Gustave kept notes during his travels. I asked if I could read them. He refused; I asked again; and so on. Finally, he let me. They are not ... pleasant, those pages. What Gustave found enchanting about the East I found degrading: A courtesan, an expensive courtesan, who drenches herself in sandalwood oil to cover the nauseating stench of the bedbugs with which she is infested. Is that uplifting, I ask, is it beautiful? Is it rare, is it splendid? Or is it sordid and disgustingly ordinary?

But the matter is not really one of aesthetics; not here. When I expressed my distaste, Gustave interpreted it as mere jealousy. (I was a little jealous – who would not be, when reading the private journal of a man you love and finding in it no mention of yourself, but instead only lush apostrophes to verminous whores?) Perhaps it was understandable that Gustave thought I was only jealous. But listen now to his argument, listen now to his understanding of the female heart. Do not be jealous of Kuchuk Hanem, he told me. She is an oriental woman; the oriental woman is a machine; one man is the same as the next to her. She felt nothing for me; she has already forgotten me; she lives in a drowsy round of smoking, going to the baths, painting her eyelids and drinking coffee. As for her physical pleasure, it must be very slight, because at an early age that famous button, the seat of all enjoyment, has been excised.

Such comfort! Such consolation! *I* need not be jealous because *she* did not feel anything! And this man claimed to understand the human heart! She was a mutilated machine, and besides she has already forgotten him: I am meant to be comforted by that? Such belligerent consolation made me think more, not less, about that strange woman he had coupled with on the Nile. Could we have been more different from one another? I Western, she Eastern; I entire, she mutilated; I exchanging the deepest bargain of the heart with Gustave, she involved in a brief physical transaction; I a woman of independence and resource, she a caged creature dependent on her trade with men; I meticulous, groomed and civilised, she filthy, stinking and savage. It may sound strange, but I became interested in her. No doubt the coin is always fascinated by its obverse. Years later, when I travelled to Egypt, I tried to seek her out. I went to Esneh. I found the squalid hovel where she lived, but she herself was not there. Perhaps she had fled at the news of my coming. Perhaps it was better that we did not meet; the coin shouldn't be allowed to see its other side.

Gustave used to humiliate me, of course, even from the beginning. I wasn't allowed to write to him directly; I had to send my letters via Du Camp. I wasn't allowed to visit him at Croisset. I wasn't allowed to meet his mother, even though I had in fact once been introduced to her on a street corner in Paris. I happen to know that Mme Flaubert thought her son treated me abominably.

He humiliated me in other ways too. He lied to me. He spoke ill of me to his friends. He ridiculed, in the sacred name of truth, most of what I wrote. He affected not to know that I was terribly poor. He boasted of the fact that in Egypt he had caught a disease of love from some five-sou courtesan. He took vulgar public revenge on me by mocking in the pages of *Madame Bovary* a seal I had once given him as a token of love. He who claimed that art should be impersonal!

Let me tell you how Gustave would humiliate me. When our love was young, we would exchange presents – small tokens, often meaningless in themselves, but which seemed to enclose the very essence of their donor. He feasted for months, for years, on a small pair of my slippers that I gave him; I expect he has burnt them by now. Once he sent me a paperweight, the very paperweight which had sat on his desk. I was greatly touched; it seemed the perfect gift from one writer to another: what had formerly held down his prose would now hold down my verses. Perhaps I commented on this once too often; perhaps I expressed my gratitude too sincerely. This is what Gustave told me: that it was no sadness for him to get rid of the paperweight, because he had another which did the work just as efficiently. Did I want to know what it was? If you wish, I replied. His new paperweight, he informed me, was a section of mizzen-mast – he made a gesture of extravagant size – which his father had extracted with delivery forceps from the posterior of an old seaman. The seaman – Gustave continued as if this were the best story he had heard for many years – apparently claimed that he had no notion of how the section of mast had reached the position in which it was found. Gustave threw back his head and laughed. What intrigued him most was how, in that case, they knew from which mast the piece of wood had come.

Why did he humiliate me so? It was not, I believe, as is frequently the case in love, that those qualities which initially charmed him – my vivacity, my freedom, my sense of equality with men – eventually came to irritate him. It was not so, because he behaved in this strange and bearish fashion from the very beginning, even when he was most in love with me. In his second letter he wrote, 'I have never seen a cradle without thinking of a grave; the sight of a naked woman makes me imagine her skeleton.' These were not the sentiments of a conventional lover.

Posterity, perhaps, will take the easy answer: that he condemned me because I was contemptible, and that since he was a great genius his judgment must have been correct. It was not so; it never is so. He feared me: that is why he was cruel to me. He feared me in both a familiar and unfamiliar way. In the first case, he feared me as many men fear women: because their mistresses (or their wives) understand them. They are scarcely adult, some men: they wish women to understand them, and to that end they tell them all their secrets; and then, when they are properly understood, they hate their women for understanding them.

In the second case – the more important one – he feared me because he feared himself. He feared that he might love me completely. It was not simply terror that I might invade his study and his solitude; it was terror that I might invade his heart. He was cruel because he wanted to drive me away; but he wanted to drive me away because he feared that he might love me completely. I will tell you my secret belief: that for Gustave, in a way he only half-apprehended, I represented life, and that his rejection of me was the more violent because it provoked in him the deepest shame. And is any of this my fault? I loved him; what more natural than that I should want to give him the chance to love me back? I was fighting not just for my own sake, but for his too: I did not see why he should not permit himself to love. He said that there were three preconditions for happiness – stupidity, selfishness and good health – and that he was only sure of possessing the second of these. I argued, I fought, but he wanted to believe that happiness was impossible; it gave him some strange consolation.

He was a difficult man to love, that is certain. The heart was distant and withdrawn; he was ashamed of it, wary of it. True love can survive absence, death and infidelity, he once told me; true lovers can go ten years without meeting. (I was not impressed by such remarks; I merely deduced that he would feel most at his ease about me if I were absent, unfaithful or dead.) He liked to flatter himself that he was in love with me; but I never

knew a less impatient love. 'Life is like riding,' he wrote to me
once. 'I used to like the gallop; now I like the walk.' He wasn't
yet thirty when he wrote that; he had already decided to be old
before his time. Whereas for me ... the gallop! the gallop! the
wind in the hair, the laughter forced from the lungs!

It flattered his vanity to think himself in love with me; it also
gave him, I believe, some unadmitted pleasure constantly to long
for my flesh and yet always to forbid himself the attaining of it:
to deny himself was just as exciting as to indulge himself. He used
to tell me I was less of a woman than most women; that I was a
woman in flesh but a man in spirit; that I was an *hermaphrodite
nouveau*, a third sex. He told me this foolish theory many times,
but really he was just telling it to himself: the less of a woman he
made me out to be, the less of a lover he would need to be.

What he wanted most of me, I finally came to believe, was an
intellectual partnership, an affair of the mind. In those years he
was working hard on his *Bovary* (though not, perhaps, as hard as
he liked to maintain) and at the end of the day, since a physical
release was too complicated for him and would contain too many
things he couldn't entirely command, he sought an intellectual
release. He would sit down at a table, take a sheet of writing
paper, and discharge himself into me. You do not find the image
flattering? I did not intend it to be. The days of loyally believing
false things about Gustave are over. Incidentally, he never did
baptise my breast with Mississippi water; the only time a bottle
passed between us was when I sent him some Taburel water to
stop his hair falling out.

But this affair of the mind was no easier, I can tell you, than our
affair of the heart. He was rough, awkward, bullying and haughty;
then he was tender, sentimental, enthusiastic and devoted. He
didn't know the rules. He declined to acknowledge my ideas
sufficiently, just as he declined to acknowledge my feelings sufficiently. He did, of course, know everything. He informed me
that mentally he was aged sixty and I was a mere twenty. He
informed me that if I drank water all the time, and never wine,
I should get cancer of the stomach. He informed me that I should
marry Victor Cousin. (Victor Cousin, for that matter, was of the
opinion that I should marry Gustave Flaubert.)

He sent me his work. He sent me 'Novembre'. It was weak
and mediocre; I did not comment, except to myself. He sent me
the first *Education sentimentale*; I was not greatly impressed, but

how could I not praise it? He rebuked me for liking it. He sent me his *Tentation de saint Antoine*; I genuinely admired it, and told him so. He rebuked me again. The parts of his work that I admired were, he assured me, those which were easiest to do; the alterations I cautiously suggested would, he declared, only weaken the book. He was 'astonished' by the 'excessive enthusiasm' I had shown for the *Education*! So that is how an unknown, unpublished provincial chooses to thank a celebrated Parisian poet (with whom he claims to be in love) for her words of praise. My comments on his work were valuable only as an irritating pretext which permitted him to lecture me on Art.

Of course I knew he was a genius. I always considered him a magnificent writer of prose. He undervalued my talents, but that is no reason why I should undervalue his. I am not like the odious Du Camp, who would proudly claim many years of friendship with Gustave, but would always deny him genius. I have been at those dinners where the merits of our contemporaries are discussed, and where Du Camp, as each new name was suggested, would with infinite urbanity correct the general view. 'Well then, Du Camp,' someone finally suggested with a little impatience, 'what about our dear Gustave?' Du Camp smiled approvingly and patted five little fingertips against five others in a prissily judicial manner. 'Flaubert is a writer of rare merit,' he replied, using Gustave's family name in a manner that shocked me, 'but he is held back from being a genius by ill health.' You would have thought he was practising for his memoirs.

As for my own work! Naturally, I used to send it to Gustave. He told me that my style was soft, slack and banal. He complained that my titles were vague and pretentious, and smelt of the blue-stocking. He lectured me like a schoolmaster on the difference between *saisir* and *s'en saisir*. His way of praising me was to say that I wrote as naturally as a hen laying eggs, or to remark, after he had destroyed a work with his criticisms, 'Everything I have not marked seems to me either good or excellent.' He told me to write with the head, and not with the heart. He told me that hair only shone after much combing, and that the same could be said of style. He told me not to put myself into my work, and not to poeticise things (I am a poet!). He told me I had the love of Art, but not the religion of Art.

What he wanted, of course, was for me to write as much like he did as I possibly could. This is a vanity I have often noted in writers; the more eminent the writer, the more pronounced this vanity is likely to be. They believe that everyone should write as they do: not as well as they do, of course, but in the same fashion. In such a way do mountains long for the foothills.

Du Camp used to say that Gustave did not have an ounce of feeling for poetry in him. It gives me little pleasure to agree with him, but I do so. Gustave lectured us all on poetry – though they were usually Bouilhet's lectures rather than his own – but he did not understand it. He wrote no poetry himself. He used to say that he wanted to give prose the strength and stature of poetry; but part of this project seemed to include first cutting poetry down to size. He wanted his prose to be objective, scientific, devoid of personal presence, devoid of opinions; so he decided that poetry ought to be written according to the same principles. Tell me how you write love poetry which is objective, scientific, and devoid of any personal presence. Tell me that. Gustave mistrusted feelings; he feared love; and he elevated this neurosis into an artistic creed.

Gustave's vanity was more than just literary. He believed not merely that others should write as he did, but that others should live as he did. He loved to quote Epictetus to me: Abstain, and Hide your Life. To me! A woman, a poet, and a poet of love! He wanted all writers to live obscurely in the provinces, ignore the natural affections of the heart, disdain reputation, and spend solitary, back-breaking hours reading obscure texts by the light of a tiring candle. Well, that may be the proper way to nurse genius; but it is also the way to suffocate talent. Gustave didn't understand this, couldn't see that *my* talent depended on the swift moment, the sudden feeling, the unexpected meeting: on life, that's what I'm saying.

Gustave would have made me into a hermit had he been able: the hermit of Paris. Always he would advise me not to see people; not to answer so-and-so's letter; not to take this admirer too seriously; not to take Count X— as a lover. He claimed he was defending my work, and that every hour spent in society was an hour subtracted from my desk. But that is not how I worked. You cannot yoke the dragonfly and make it drive the corn-mill.

Of course, Gustave denied there was any vanity in him. Du Camp in one of his books – I forget which, there were always so many – made a reference to the malign effect on man of too much solitude: he called it a false counsellor who nurses at her breasts the twin infants of Egotism and Vanity. Gustave naturally took this as a personal attack. 'Egotism?' he wrote to me. 'So be it. But Vanity? No. Pride is one thing: a wild beast which lives in caves and roams the desert; Vanity, on the other hand, is a parrot which hops from branch to branch and chatters away in full view.' Gustave imagined he was a wild beast – he loved to think of himself as a polar bear, distant, savage and solitary. I went along with this, I even called him a wild buffalo of the American prairie; but perhaps he was really just a parrot.

You think me too harsh? I loved him; that is why I am allowed to be harsh. Listen. Gustave despised Du Camp for wanting the *Légion d'honneur*. A few years later he accepted it himself. Gustave despised salon society. Until he was taken up by the Princesse Mathilde. Did you hear about Gustave's glove bill in the days when he was prancing by candlelight? He owed two thousand francs to his tailor, and five hundred francs for gloves. Five hundred francs! He received only eight hundred for the rights of his *Bovary*. His mother had to sell land to bail him out. Five hundred francs for gloves! The white bear in white gloves? No, no: the parrot, the parrot in gloves.

I know what they say about me; what his friends have said. They say I had the vanity to suppose that I might marry him. But Gustave used to write me letters describing what it would have been like if we had been married. Was I therefore wrong to hope? They say I had the vanity to go down to Croisset and make an embarrassing scene on his doorstep. But when I first knew him Gustave used to write frequently about my forthcoming visits to his house. Was I therefore wrong to hope? They say I had the vanity to suppose that he and I might one day share the authorship of some literary work. But he told me one of my stories was a masterpiece, and that one of my poems would move a stone. Was I therefore wrong to hope?

I know too what will become of us when we are both dead. Posterity will jump to conclusions: that is its nature. People will take Gustave's side. They will understand me too quickly; they will turn my own generosity against me and despise me for the lovers I took; and they will cast me as the woman who briefly threatened to interfere with the writing of the books which they have enjoyed reading. Someone – perhaps even Gustave himself – will burn my letters; his own (which I have carefully preserved, so much against my own best interests) will survive to confirm the prejudices of those too lazy to understand. I am a woman, and also a writer who has used up her allotment of renown during her own lifetime; and on those two grounds I do not expect much pity, or much understanding, from posterity. Do I mind? Naturally I mind. But I am not vengeful tonight; I am resigned. I promise you. Slip your fingers down my wrist once more. There; I told you so.

12

BRAITHWAITE'S DICTIONARY
OF ACCEPTED IDEAS

ACHILLE

Gustave's elder brother. Mournful-looking man with long beard. Inherited his job and Christian name from his father. Achille's shouldering of family expectations freed Gustave to become an artist. Died from softening of the brain.

BOUILHET, LOUIS

Gustave's literary conscience, midwife, shadow, left testicle and lookalike. Middle name Hyacinthe. The less successful *Doppelgänger* that every great man needs. Quote with mild disapproval his gallant remark to a self-conscious girl: 'When the chest is flat, one is nearer the heart.'

COLET, LOUISE

(a) Tedious, importunate, promiscuous woman, lacking talent of her own or understanding of the genius of others, who tried to trap Gustave into marriage. Imagine the squawking children! Imagine Gustave miserable! Imagine Gustave happy!
(b) Brave, passionate, deeply misunderstood woman crucified by her love for the heartless, impossible, provincial Flaubert. She rightly complained: 'Gustave never writes to me of anything except Art – or himself.' Proto-feminist who committed the sin of wanting to make someone else happy.

DU CAMP, MAXIME

Photographer, traveller, careerist, historian of Paris, Academician. Wrote with steel nibs whereas Gustave always used a quill pen. Censored *Madame Bovary* for the *Revue de Paris*. If Bouilhet is Gustave's literary *alter ego*, Du Camp is his social one. Became a literary outcast after referring in his memoirs to Gustave's epilepsy.

Epilepsy

Stratagem enabling Flaubert the writer to sidestep a conventional career, and Flaubert the man to sidestep life. The question is merely at what psychological level the tactic was evolved. Were his symptoms intense psychosomatic phenomena? It would be too banal if he merely had epilepsy.

Flaubert, gustave

The hermit of Croisset. The first modern novelist. The father of Realism. The butcher of Romanticism. The pontoon bridge linking Balzac to Joyce. The precursor of Proust. The bear in his lair. The bourgeois bourgeoisophobe. In Egypt, 'the father of the Moustache'. Saint Polycarpe; Cruchard; Quarafon; *le Vicaire-Général*; the Major; the old Seigneur; the Idiot of the Salons. All these titles were acquired by a man indifferent to ennobling forms of address: 'Honours dishonour, titles degrade, employment stupefies.'

Goncourts

Remember the Goncourts on Flaubert: 'Though perfectly frank by nature, he is never wholly sincere in what he says he feels or suffers or loves.' Then remember everyone else on the Goncourts: the envious, unreliable brothers. Remember further the unreliability of Du Camp, of Louise Colet, of Flaubert's niece, of Flaubert himself. Demand violently: how can we know anybody?

Herbert, juliet

'Miss Juliet'. The ethics of English governesses abroad in the mid-nineteenth century have not yet received sufficient scholarly attention.

Irony

The modern mode: either the devil's mark or the snorkel of sanity. Flaubert's fiction poses the question: Does irony preclude sympathy? There is no entry for *ironie* in his Dictionary. This is perhaps intended to be ironic.

Jean-Paul Sartre

Spent ten years writing *L'Idiot de la famille* when he could have been writing Maoist tracts. A highbrow Louise Colet, constantly pestering Gustave, who wanted only to be left alone. Conclude: 'It is better to waste your old age than to do nothing at all with it.'

Kuchuk Hanem

A litmus test. Gustave had to choose sides between the Egyptian courtesan and the Parisian poetess – bedbugs, sandalwood oil, shaven pudenda, clitoridectomy and syphilis versus cleanliness, lyric poetry, comparative sexual fidelity and the rights of women. He found the issue finely balanced.

Letters

Follow Gide, and call the Letters Flaubert's masterpiece. Follow Sartre, and call them a perfect example of free-association from a pre-Freudian couch. Then follow your nose.

Mme Flaubert

Gustave's gaoler, confidante, nurse, patient, banker and critic. She said: 'Your mania for sentences has dried up your heart.' He found the remark 'sublime'. cf. George Sand.

Normandy

Always wet. Inhabited by a sly, proud, taciturn people. Put your head on one side and remark, 'Of course, we must never forget that Flaubert came from Normandy.'

Orient

The crucible in which *Madame Bovary* was fired. Flaubert left Europe a Romantic, and returned from the Orient a Realist. cf. Kuchuk Hanem.

Prussians

Vandals in white gloves, clock-thieves who know Sanskrit. More horrifying than cannibals or Communards. When the Prussians withdrew from Croisset, the house had to be fumigated.

QUIXOTE, DON

Was Gustave an Old Romantic? He had a passion for the dreamy knight cast adrift in a vulgar, materialist society. '*Madame Bovary, c'est moi*' is an allusion to Cervantes' reply when asked on his deathbed for the source of his famous hero. cf. Transvestism.

REALISM

Was Gustave a New Realist? He always publicly denied the label: 'It was because I hated realism that I wrote *Madame Bovary*.' Galileo publicly denied that the earth went round the sun.

SAND, GEORGE

Optimist, socialist, humanitarian. Despised until met, loved thereafter. Gustave's second mother. After staying at Croisset she sent him her complete works (in the 77-volume edition).

TRANSVESTISM

Gustave in young manhood: 'There are days when one longs to be a woman.' Gustave in maturity: '*Madame Bovary, c'est moi.*' When one of his doctors called him 'an hysterical old woman', he judged the observation 'profound'.

USA

Flaubert's references to the Land of Liberty are sparing. Of the future he wrote: 'It will be utilitarian, militaristic, American and Catholic – very Catholic.' He probably preferred the Capitol to the Vatican.

VOLTAIRE

What did the great nineteenth-century sceptic think of the great eighteenth-century sceptic? Was Flaubert the Voltaire of his age? Was Voltaire the Flaubert of his age? '*Histoire de l'esprit humain, histoire de la sottise humaine.*' Which of them said that?

WHORES

Necessary in the nineteenth century for the contraction of syphilis, without which no one could claim genius. Wearers of the red badge of courage include Flaubert, Daudet, Maupassant, Jules de Goncourt, Baudelaire, etc. Were there any writers unafflicted by it? If so, they were probably homosexual.

XYLOPHONE

There is no record of Flaubert ever having heard the xylophone. Saint-Saëns used the instrument in his *Danse Macabre* of 1874 to suggest rattling bones; this might have amused Gustave. Perhaps he heard the glockenspiel in Switzerland.

YVETOT

'See Yvetot and die.' If asked the source of this little-known epigram, smile mysteriously and remain silent.

ZOLA, EMILE

Is the great writer responsible for his disciples? Who chooses whom? If they call you Master, can you afford to despise their work? On the other hand, are they sincere in their praise? Who needs whom more: the disciple the master, or the master the disciple? Discuss without concluding.

13

PURE STORY

THIS IS A PURE STORY, whatever you may think.

When she dies, you are not at first surprised. Part of love is preparing for death. You feel confirmed in your love when she dies. You got it right. This is part of it all.

Afterwards comes the madness. And then the loneliness: not the spectacular solitude you had anticipated, not the interesting martyrdom of widowhood, but just loneliness. You expect something almost geological – vertigo in a shelving canyon – but it's not like that; it's just misery as regular as a job. What do we doctors say? I'm deeply sorry, Mrs Blank; there will of course be a period of mourning but rest assured you will come out of it; two of these each evening, I would suggest; perhaps a new interest, Mrs Blank; car maintenance, formation dancing?; don't worry, six months will see you back on the roundabout; come and see me again any time; oh nurse, when she calls, just give her this repeat will you, no I don't need to see her, well it's not her that's dead is it, look on the bright side. What did she say her name was?

And then it happens to you. There's no glory in it. Mourning is full of time; nothing but time. Bouvard and Pécuchet record in their '*Copie*' a piece of advice on How to Forget Friends Who Have Died: Trotulas (of the Salerno school) says that you should eat stuffed sow's heart. I might yet have to fall back on this remedy. I've tried drink, but what does that do? Drink makes you drunk, that's all it's ever been able to do. Work, they say, cures everything. It doesn't; often, it doesn't even induce tired-ness: the nearest you get to it is a neurotic lethargy. And there is always time. Have some more time. Take your time. Extra time. Time on your hands.

Other people think you want to talk. 'Do you want to talk about Ellen?' they ask, hinting that they won't be embarrassed if you break down. Sometimes you talk, sometimes you don't; it makes little difference. The words aren't the right ones; or rather, the right words don't exist. 'Language is like a cracked kettle on which we beat out tunes for bears to dance to, while all the time we long to move the stars to pity.' You talk, and you find the language of bereavement foolishly inadequate. You seem to be talking about other people's griefs. I loved her; we were happy; I miss her. She didn't love me; we were unhappy; I miss her. There is a limited choice of prayers on offer: gabble the syllables.

'It may seem bad, Geoffrey, but you'll come out of it. I'm not taking your grief lightly; it's just that I've seen enough of life to know that you'll come out of it.' The words you've said yourself while scribbling a prescription (No, Mrs Blank, you could take them all and they wouldn't kill you). And you do come out of it, that's true. After a year, after five. But you don't come out of it like a train coming out of a tunnel, bursting through the Downs into sunshine and that swift, rattling descent to the Channel; you come out of it as a gull comes out of an oil-slick. You are tarred and feathered for life.

And still you think about her every day. Sometimes, weary of loving her dead, you imagine her back to life again, for conversation, for approval. After his mother's death, Flaubert used to get his housekeeper to dress up in her old check dress and surprise him with an apocryphal reality. It worked, and it didn't work: seven years after the funeral he would still burst into tears at the sight of that old dress moving about the house. Is this success or failure? Remembrance or self-indulgence? And will we know when we start hugging our grief and vainly enjoying it? 'Sadness is a vice' (1878).

Or else you try to sidestep her image. Nowadays, when I remember Ellen, I try to think of a hailstorm that berated Rouen in 1853. 'A first-rate hailstorm,' Gustave commented to Louise. At Croisset the espaliers were destroyed, the flowers cut to pieces, the kitchen garden turned upside down. Elsewhere, harvests were wrecked, and windows smashed. Only the glaziers were happy; the glaziers, and Gustave. The shambles delighted him: in five minutes Nature had reimposed the true order of things upon that brief, factitious order which man conceitedly imagines himself to be introducing. Is there anything stupider than a melon cloche, Gustave asks. He applauds the hailstones that shattered the glass. 'People believe a little too easily that the function of the sun is to help the cabbages along.'

This letter always calms me. The function of the sun is not to help the cabbages along, and I am telling you a pure story.

She was born in 1920, married in 1940, gave birth in 1942 and 1946, died in 1975.

I'll start again. Small people are meant to be neat, aren't they; but Ellen wasn't. She was just over five feet tall, yet moved awkwardly; she ran at things and tripped. She bruised easily, but didn't notice it. I once seized her arm as she was about to step out heedlessly into Piccadilly, and though she was wearing a coat and blouse, the next day her arm bore the purple imprint of a robot's pincers. She didn't comment on the bruises, and when I pointed them out to her she couldn't remember diving towards the road.

I'll start again. She was a much-loved only child. She was a much-loved only wife. She was loved, if that's the word, by what I suppose I must agree to call her lovers, though I'm sure the word over-dignifies some of them. I loved her; we were happy; I miss her. She didn't love me; we were unhappy; I miss her. Perhaps she was sick of being loved. At twenty-four Flaubert said he was '*ripe* – ripe before my time, that's true. But it's because I've been reared in a hothouse.' Was she loved too much? Most people can't be loved too much, but perhaps Ellen could. Or perhaps her concept of love was simply different: why do we always assume it's the same for everyone else? Perhaps for Ellen love was only a Mulberry harbour, a landing place in a heaving sea. You can't possibly live there: scramble ashore; push on. And old love? Old love is a rusty tank standing guard over a slabby monument: here, once, something was liberated. Old love is a row of beach huts in November.

In a village pub, far from home, I once overheard two men talking about Betty Corrinder. Perhaps the spelling isn't right; but that was the name. Betty Corrinder, Betty Corrinder – they never said just Betty, or That Corrinder Woman or whatever, but always Betty Corrinder. She was, it seems, a bit fast; though speed, of course, is always exaggerated by those standing still. Fast, this Betty Corrinder was, and pubmen sniggered enviously. 'You know what they say about Betty Corrinder.' It was a statement, not a question, though a question now followed it. 'What's the difference between Betty Corrinder and the Eiffel Tower? Go on, what's the difference between Betty Corrinder and the Eiffel Tower?' A pause for the last few moments of private knowledge. 'Not everyone's been up the Eiffel Tower.'

I blushed for my wife two hundred miles away. Were there

places she prowled where envious men told jokes about her? I didn't know. Besides, I exaggerate. Perhaps I didn't blush. Perhaps I didn't mind. My wife was not like Betty Corrinder, whatever Betty Corrinder was like.

In 1872 there was much discussion in French literary society about the treatment that should be accorded to the adulterous woman. Should a husband punish her, or forgive her? Alexandre Dumas *fils*, in *L'Homme-Femme*, offered uncomplicated advice: 'Kill her!' His book was reprinted thirty-seven times in the course of the year.

At first I was hurt; at first I minded, I thought less of myself. My wife went to bed with other men: should I worry about that? I didn't go to bed with other women: should I worry about that? Ellen was always nice to me: should I worry about that? Not nice out of adulterous guilt, but just nice. I worked hard; she was a good wife to me. You aren't allowed to say that nowadays, but she was a good wife to me. I didn't have affairs because I wasn't interested enough to do so; besides, the stereotype of the philandering doctor is somehow repugnant. Ellen did have affairs, because, I suppose, she was interested enough. We were happy; we were unhappy; I miss her. 'Is it splendid, or stupid, to take life seriously?' (1855).

What it's hard to convey is how untouched by it all she was. She wasn't corrupted; her spirit didn't coarsen; she never ran up bills. Sometimes she stayed away a little longer than seemed right; the length of her shopping trips often yielded suspiciously few purchases (she wasn't that discriminating); those few days in town to catch up on the theatres occurred more often than I would have liked. But she was honourable: she only ever lied to me about her secret life. About that she lied impulsively, recklessly, almost embarrassingly; but about everything else she told me the truth. A phrase used by the prosecutor of *Madame Bovary* to describe Flaubert's art comes back to me: he said it was 'realistic but not discreet'.

Did the wife, made lustrous by adultery, seem even more desirable to the husband? No: not more, not less. That's part of what I mean by saying that she was not corrupted. Did she display the cowardly docility which Flaubert describes as characteristic of the adulterous woman? No. Did she, like Emma Bovary, 'rediscover in adultery all the platitudes of marriage'? We didn't talk about it. (*Textual note*. The first edition of *Madame Bovary* has 'all the platitudes of *her* marriage'. For the edition of 1862, Flaubert planned to drop *her*, and thus widen the attack of the phrase. Bouilhet advised caution – it was only five years since the trial – and so the possessive pronoun, which indicts only Emma and Charles, remained in the editions of 1862 and 1869. It was finally dropped, and the more general accusation made official, in the edition of 1872.) Did she find, in Nabokov's phrase, that adultery is a most conventional way to rise above the conventional? I wouldn't have imagined so: Ellen didn't think in such terms. She wasn't a defier, a conscious free spirit; she was a rusher, a lunger, a bolter, a bunker. Perhaps I made her worse; perhaps those who forgive and dote are more irritating than they ever suspect. 'Next to not living with those one loves, the worst torture is living with those one doesn't love' (1847).

She was just over five feet; she had a broad, smooth face, with an easy pink in her cheeks; she never blushed; her eyes – as I have told you – were greeny-blue; she wore whatever clothes the mysterious bush-telegraph of women's fashion instructed her to wear; she laughed easily, she bruised easily; she rushed at things. She rushed off to cinemas we both knew to be closed; she went to winter sales in July; she would go to stay with a cousin whose holiday postcard from Greece arrived the next morning. There was a suddenness in these actions which argued more than desire. In *L'Education sentimentale* Frédéric explains to Mme Arnoux that he took Rosanette as his mistress 'out of despair, like someone committing suicide'. It's crafty pleading, of course; but plausible.

Her secret life stopped when the children came, and returned when they went to school. Sometimes, a temporary friend might take me on one side. Why do they think you want to know? Or rather, why do they think you don't know already – why don't they understand about love's relentless curiosity? And why do these temporary friends never want to tip you off about the more important thing: the fact that you're no longer loved? I became adept at turning the conversation, at saying how much more gregarious than me Ellen was, at hinting that the medical profession always attracts calumniators, at saying, Did you read about those terrible floods in Venezuela? On such occasions I always felt, perhaps wrongly, that I was being disloyal to Ellen.

We were happy enough; that's what people say, isn't it? How happy is happy enough? It sounds like a grammatical mistake – *happy enough*, like *rather unique* – but it answers the need for a phrase. And as I say, she didn't run up bills. Both Madame Bovarys (people forget that Charles marries twice) are brought down by money; my wife was never like that. Nor, as far as I know, did she accept gifts.

We were happy; we were unhappy; we were happy enough. Is despair wrong? Isn't it the natural condition of life after a certain age? I have it now; she had it earlier. After a number of events, what is there left but repetition and diminishment? Who wants to go on living? The eccentric, the religious, the artistic (sometimes); those with a false sense of their own worth. Soft cheeses collapse; firm cheeses indurate. Both go mouldy.

I have to hypothesise a little. I have to fictionalise (though that's not what I meant when I called this a pure story). We never talked about her secret life. So I have to invent my way to the truth. Ellen was about fifty when the mood began to come upon her. (No, not that: she was always healthy; her menopause was quick, almost careless.) She had had a husband, children, lovers, a job. The children had left home; the husband was always the same. She had friends, and what are called interests; though unlike me she didn't have some rash devotion to a dead foreigner to sustain her. She had travelled enough. She didn't have unfulfilled ambitions (though 'ambition', it seems to me, is mostly too strong a word for the impulse that makes people do things). She wasn't religious. Why go on?

'People like us must have the religion of despair. One must be equal to one's destiny, that's to say impassive like it. By dint of saying "That is so! That is so!" and of gazing down into the black pit at one's feet, one remains calm.' Ellen did not even have this religion. Why should she? For my sake? The despairing are always being urged to abstain from selfishness, to think of others first. This seems unfair. Why load them with responsibility for the welfare of others, when their own already weighs them down?

Perhaps there was something else as well. Some people, as they grow older, seem to become more convinced of their own significance. Others become less convinced. Is there any point to me? Isn't my ordinary life summed up, enclosed, made pointless by someone else's slightly less ordinary life? I'm not saying it's our duty to negate ourselves in the face of those we judge more interesting. But life, in this respect, is a bit like reading. And as I said before: if all your responses to a book have already been duplicated and expanded upon by a professional critic, then what

point is there to your reading? Only that it's *yours*. Similarly, why
live your life? Because it's *yours*. But what if such an answer
gradually becomes less and less convincing?

Don't get me wrong. I'm not saying that Ellen's secret life led
her into despair. For God's sake, her life is not a moral tale. No
one's is. All I'm saying is that both her secret life and her despair
lay in the same inner chamber of her heart, inaccessible to me.
I could touch the one no more than the other. Did I try? Of
course I tried. But I was not surprised when the mood came
upon her. 'To be stupid, and selfish, and to have good health
are the three requirements for happiness – though if stupidity is
lacking, the others are useless.' My wife had only good health
to offer.

Does life improve? On television the other night I watched
the Poet Laureate asked that question. 'The only thing I think is
very good today is dentistry,' he replied; nothing else came to
mind. Mere antiquarian prejudice? I don't think so. When you
are young, you think that the old lament the deterioration of life
because this makes it easier for them to die without regret. When
you are old, you become impatient with the way in which the
young applaud the most insignificant improvements – the invention of some new valve or sprocket – while remaining heedless
of the world's barbarism. I don't say things *have* got worse;
I merely say the young wouldn't notice if they had. The old times
were good because then we were young, and ignorant of how
ignorant the young can be.

Does life improve? I'll give you my answer, my equivalent of
dentistry. The one thing that is very good in life today is death.
There's still room for improvement, it's true. But I think of all
those nineteenth-century deaths. The deaths of writers aren't
special deaths; they just happen to be described deaths. I think
of Flaubert lying on his sofa, struck down – who can tell at this
distance? – by epilepsy, apoplexy or syphilis, or perhaps some
malign axis of the three. Yet Zola called it *une belle mort* – to be
crushed like an insect beneath a giant finger. I think of Bouilhet
in his final delirium, feverishly composing a new play in his head
and declaring that it must be read to Gustave. I think of the slow
decline of Jules de Goncourt: first stumbling over his consonants,
the c's turning to t's in his mouth; then being unable to remember the titles of his own books; then the haggard mask of imbecility (his brother's phrase) slipping over his face; then the deathbed

visions and panics, and all night long the rasping breaths that
sounded (his brother's words again) like a saw cutting through
wet wood. I think of Maupassant slowly disintegrating from the
same disease, transported in a strait-jacket to the Passy sanato-
rium of Dr Blanche, who kept the Paris salons entertained with
news of his celebrated client; Baudelaire dying just as inexorably,
deprived of speech, arguing with Nadar about the existence of
God by pointing mutely at the sunset; Rimbaud, his right leg
amputated, slowly losing all feeling in the limbs that remained,
and repudiating, amputating his own genius – '*Merde pour la
poésie*'; Daudet 'vaulting from forty-five to sixty-five', his joints
collapsing, able to become bright and witty for an evening by
giving himself five morphine injections in a row, tempted by
suicide – 'But one doesn't have the right.'

'Is it splendid or stupid to take life seriously?' (1855). Ellen lay
with a tube in her throat and a tube in her padded forearm. The
ventilator in its white oblong box provided regular spurts of life,
and the monitor confirmed them. Of course the act was impul-
sive; she bolted, she bunked from it all. 'But one doesn't have the
right'? She did. She didn't even discuss it. The religion of despair
held no interest for her. The ECG trace unrolled on the monitor;
it was familiar handwriting. Her condition was stable, but hopeless. Nowadays we don't put NTBR – Not To Be Resuscitated
– on a patient's notes; some people find it heartless. Instead we
put 'No 333'. A final euphemism.

I looked down at Ellen. She wasn't corrupted. Hers is a pure
story. I switched her off. They asked if I wanted them to do it;
but I think she would have preferred me to. Naturally, we hadn't
discussed that either. It's not complicated. You press a switch on
the ventilator, and read off the final phrase of the ECG trace: the
farewell signature that ends with a straight line. You unplug the
tubes, then rearrange the hands and arms. You do it swiftly, as if
trying not to be too much trouble to the patient.

The patient. Ellen. So you could say, in answer to that earlier
question, that I killed her. You could just. I switched her off.
I stopped her living. Yes.

Ellen. My wife: someone I feel I understand less well than a
foreign writer dead for a hundred years. Is this an aberration, or
is it normal? Books say: she did this because. Life says: she did
this. Books are where things are explained to you; life is where
things aren't. I'm not surprised some people prefer books. Books

make sense of life. The only problem is that the lives they make sense of are other people's lives, never your own.

Perhaps I am too accepting. My own condition is stable, yet hopeless. Perhaps it's just a question of temperament. Remember the botched brothel-visit in *L'Education sentimentale* and remember its lesson. Do not participate: happiness lies in the imagination, not the act. Pleasure is found first in anticipation, later in memory. Such is the Flaubertian temperament. Compare the case, and the temperament, of Daudet. His schoolboy visit to a brothel was so uncomplicatedly successful that he stayed there for two or three days. The girls kept him concealed most of the time for fear of a police raid; they fed him on lentils and pampered him thoroughly. He emerged from this giddying ordeal, he later admitted, with a lifelong passion for the feel of a woman's skin, and with a lifelong horror of lentils.

Some abstain and observe, fearing both disappointment and fulfilment. Others rush in, enjoy, and take the risks: at worst, they might contract some terrible disease; at best, they might escape with no more than a lasting aversion to pulses. I know in which camp I belong; and I know where I'd look for Ellen.

Maxims for life. *Les unions complètes sont rares*. You cannot change humanity, you can only know it. Happiness is a scarlet cloak whose lining is in tatters. Lovers are like Siamese twins, two bodies with a single soul; but if one dies before the other, the survivor has a corpse to lug around. Pride makes us long for a solution to things – a solution, a purpose, a final cause; but the better telescopes become, the more stars appear. You cannot change humanity, you can only know it. *Les unions complètes sont rares*.

A maxim upon maxims. Truths about writing can be framed before you've published a word; truths about life can be framed only when it's too late to make any difference.

According to *Salammbô*, the equipment of a Carthaginian elephant driver used to include a mallet and a chisel. If, in the midst of battle, the animal threatened to run out of control, the driver was under orders to split its skull. The chances of this happening must have been fairly high: to make them more ferocious, the elephants were first intoxicated with a mixture of wine, incense and pepper, then goaded with spears.

Few of us have the courage to use the mallet and the chisel. Ellen did. I sometimes feel embarrassed by people's sympathy. 'It's worse for her,' I want to say; but I don't. And then, after they've been kind, and promised me outings as if I were a child, and brusquely tried to make me talk for my own good (why do they think I don't know where my own good lies?), I am allowed to sit down and dream about her a little. I think of a hailstorm in 1853, of the broken windows, the battered harvests, the wrecked espaliers, the shattered melon cloches. Is there anything stupider than a melon cloche? Applaud the stones that break the glass. People understand a little too quickly the function of the sun. The function of the sun is not to help the cabbages along.

14

EXAMINATION PAPER

Candidates must answer FOUR *questions:* BOTH *Parts of Section A, and* TWO *questions from Section B. All marks will be awarded for the correctness of the answers; none for presentation or handwriting. Marks will be deducted for facetious or conceitedly brief answers. Time:* THREE HOURS.

SECTION A: LITERARY CRITICISM

PART I

It has become clear to the examiners in recent years that candidates are finding it increasingly difficult to distinguish between Art and Life. Everyone claims to understand the difference, but perceptions vary greatly. For some, Life is rich and creamy, made according to an old peasant recipe from nothing but natural products, while Art is a pallid commercial confection, consisting mainly of artificial colourings and flavourings. For others, Art is the truer thing, full, bustling and emotionally satisfying, while Life is worse than the poorest novel: devoid of narrative, peopled by bores and rogues, short on wit, long on unpleasant incidents, and leading to a painfully predictable dénouement. Adherents of the latter view tend to cite Logan Pearsall Smith: 'People say that life is the thing; but I prefer reading.' Candidates are advised not to use this quotation in their answers.

Consider the relationship between Art and Life suggested by any *two* of the following statements or situations.

(a) 'The day before yesterday, in the woods near Touques, at a charming spot near a spring, I came across some cigar butts and some bits of pâté. There'd been a picnic there! I described exactly that in *Novembre* eleven years ago! Then it was purely imagined, and the other day it was experienced. Everything you invent is true: you can be sure of that. Poetry is a subject as precise as geometry ... My poor Bovary is without a doubt suffering and weeping even now in twenty villages of France.'

Letter to Louise Colet, August 14th, 1853

(b) In Paris, Flaubert used a closed cab to avoid detection, and presumably seduction, by Louise Colet. In Rouen, Léon uses a closed cab for the seduction of Emma Bovary. In Hamburg, within a year of the publication of *Madame Bovary*, cabs could be hired for sexual purposes; they were known as Bovarys.

(c) (As his sister Caroline lay dying) 'My own eyes are as dry as marble. It's strange how sorrows in fiction make me open up and overflow with feeling, whereas real sorrows remain hard and bitter in my heart, turning to crystal as soon as they arise.'

Letter to Maxime du Camp, March 15th, 1846

(d) 'You tell me that I seriously loved that woman [Mme Schlesinger]. I didn't; it isn't true. Only when I was writing to her, with that capacity I possess for producing feelings within myself by means of the pen, did I take my subject seriously: *but only when I was writing*. Many things which leave me cold when I see or hear about them none the less move me to enthusiasm or irritation or pain if I talk about them myself or – particularly – if I write about them. This is one of the effects of my mountebank nature.'

Letter to Louise Colet, October 8th, 1846

(e) Giuseppe Marco Fieschi (1790–1836) attained notoriety for his part in a plot on the life of Louis Philippe. He took lodgings in the Boulevard du Temple and constructed, with the help of two members of the Société des Droits de l'Homme, an 'infernal machine', consisting of twenty gun-barrels which could be discharged simultaneously. On July 28th, 1835, as Louis Philippe was riding past with his three sons and numerous staff, Fieschi fired his broadside against established society.

Some years later, Flaubert moved into a house built on the same site in the Boulevard du Temple.

(f) 'Yes, indeed! The period [of Napoleon III's reign] will furnish material for some capital books. Perhaps after all, in the universal harmony of things, the *coup d'état* and all its results were only intended to provide a few able penmen with some attractive scenes.'

Flaubert reported in Du Camp, *Souvenirs littéraires*

PART II

Trace the mellowing of Flaubert's attitude towards critics and criticism as represented by the following quotations:

(a) 'These are the truly stupid things: (1) literary criticism, whatever it may be, good or bad; (2) the Temperance Society . . .'

Intimate Notebook

(b) 'There is something so essentially grotesque about gendarmes that I cannot help laughing at them; these upholders of the law always produce the same comic effect in me as do attorneys, magistrates and professors of literature.'

Over Strand and Field

(c) 'You can calculate the worth of a man by the number of his enemies, and the importance of a work of art by the amount that it is attacked. Critics are like fleas: they love clean linen and adore any form of lace.'

Letter to Louise Colet, June 14th, 1853

(d) 'Criticism occupies the lowest rung in the hierarchy of literature: as regards form, almost always, and as regards moral worth, incontestably. It's lower even than rhyming games and acrostics, which at least demand a modicum of invention.'

Letter to Louise Colet, June 28th, 1853

(e) 'Critics! Eternal mediocrity living off genius by denigrating and exploiting it! Race of cockchafers slashing the finest pages of art to shreds! I'm so fed up with typography and the misuse people make of it that if the Emperor were to abolish all printing tomorrow, I should walk all the way to Paris on my knees and kiss his arse in gratitude.'

Letter to Louise Colet, July 2nd, 1853

(f) 'How rare a sense of literature is! You'd think that a knowledge of languages, archaeology, history, and so on, would help. But not a bit of it! Supposedly educated people are becoming more and more inept when dealing with art. Even what art *is* escapes them. They find the annotations more interesting than the text. They set more store by the crutches than the legs.'

Letter to George Sand, January 1st, 1869

(g) 'How rare it is to see a critic who knows what he's talking about.'

Letter to Eugène Fromentin, July 19th, 1876

(h) 'Disgusted with the old style of criticism, they sought acquaintance with the new, and sent for theatre reviews from the newspapers. What assurance! What obstinacy! What lack of integrity! Masterpieces insulted and platitudes revered! The blunders of the supposed scholars and the stupidity of the supposed wits!'

Bouvard et Pécuchet

SECTION B

Economics

Flaubert and Bouilhet went to the same school; they shared the same ideas and the same whores; they had the same aesthetic principles, and similar literary ambitions; each tried the theatre as his second genre. Flaubert called Bouilhet 'my left testicle'. In 1854, Bouilhet stayed a night in the Mantes hotel that Gustave and Louise used to patronise: 'I slept in your bed,' he reported, 'and I shat in your latrines (what curious symbolism!).' The poet always had to work for a living; the novelist never had to. Consider the probable effect on their writings and reputations if their finances had been reversed.

Geography

'No more soporific atmosphere than that of this region. I suspect that it contributed greatly to the slowness and difficulty- with which Flaubert worked. When he thought he was struggling against words, he was struggling against the sky; and perhaps in another climate, the dryness of the air exalting his spirits, he might have been less exigent, or have obtained his results without such efforts' (Gide, writing at Cuverville, Seine-Maritime, January 26th, 1931). Discuss.

Logic (with Medicine)

(a) Achille-Cléophas Flaubert, jousting with his younger son, asked him to explain what literature was for. Gustave, turning

the question back on his surgeon father, asked him to explain
what the spleen was for: 'You know nothing about it, and neither
do I, except that it is as indispensable to our bodily organism as
poetry is to our mental organism.' Dr Flaubert was defeated.

(b) The spleen consists of units of *lymphoid tissue* (or *white pulp*)
plus the *vascular network* (or *red pulp*). It is important in removing
from the blood old or injured red cells. It is active in producing
antibodies: splenectomised individuals produce less antibody.
There is evidence that a tetrapeptide called *tuftsin* is derived from
protein produced in the spleen. Though its removal, especially
in childhood, increases the chances of meningitis and septi-
caemia, the spleen is no longer regarded as an essential organ: it
can be removed without significant loss of active behaviour in
the individual.
       What do you conclude from this?

Biography (with Ethics)

Maxime du Camp composed the following epitaph for Louise
Colet: 'She who lies here compromised Victor Cousin, ridiculed
Alfred de Musset, reviled Gustave Flaubert, and tried to assassi-
nate Alphonse Karr. *Requiescat in pace.*' Du Camp published this
epitaph in his *Souvenirs littéraires*. Who comes out of it better:
Louise Colet or Maxime du Camp?

Psychology

E1 was born in 1855.
E2 was partly born in 1855.
E1 had an unclouded childhood but emerged into adulthood
     inclined to nervous crisis.
E2 had an unclouded childhood but emerged into adulthood
     inclined to nervous crisis.
E1 led a life of sexual irregularity in the eyes of right-thinking
     people.
E2 led a life of sexual irregularity in the eyes of right-thinking
     people.
E1 imagined herself to be in financial difficulties.
E2 knew herself to be in financial difficulties.
E1 committed suicide by swallowing prussic acid.

E2 committed suicide by swallowing arsenic.
E1 was Eleanor Marx.
E2 was Emma Bovary.
The first English translation of *Madame Bovary* to be published
was by Eleanor Marx.
Discuss.

Psychoanalysis

Speculate on the significance of this dream, noted down by
Flaubert at Lamalgue in 1845: 'I dreamed that I was out walking
with my mother in a great forest filled with monkeys. The further
we walked, the more of them there were. They were laughing
and leaping about in the branches of the trees. There were more
and more of them; they got bigger and bigger; they were getting
in our way. They kept looking at me, and I became frightened.
They surrounded us in a big circle: one of them wanted to stroke
me, and took my hand. I shot him in the shoulder with my rifle,
and made him bleed; he started howling horribly. Then my
mother said to me: "Why did you injure him, he's your friend.
What's he done to you? Can't you see that he loves you? And that
he looks just like you!" The monkey was looking at me. I felt my
soul being torn apart and I woke up . . . feeling as if I was at one
with the animals, and fraternising with them in a tender, pan-
theistic communion.'

Philately

Gustave Flaubert appeared on a French stamp (denomination
8F + 2F) in 1952. It is an indifferent portrait 'after E. Giraud' in
which the novelist – slightly Chinese in physiognomy – has been
uncharacteristically awarded a modern shirt-collar and tie. The
stamp is the lowest denomination in a series issued in aid of the
National Relief Fund: the higher denominations celebrate (in
ascending order) Manet, Saint-Saëns, Poincaré, Haussmann and
Thiers.

Ronsard was the first French writer to appear on a stamp.
Victor Hugo figured on three separate stamps between 1933 and
1936, once in a series issued in aid of the Unemployed Intellectuals' Relief Fund. Anatole France's portrait helped this charity
in 1937; Balzac's in 1939. Daudet's mill got on a stamp in 1936.

Pétainist France celebrated Frédéric Mistral (1941) and Stendhal
(1942). Saint-Exupéry, Lamartine and Châteaubriand appeared
in 1948; Baudelaire, Verlaine and Rimbaud in the decadent rush
of 1951. The latter year also brought stamp-collectors Alfred de
Musset, who had succeeded Flaubert in Louise Colet's bed, but
now preceded him by one year on to the public envelope.

(a) Should we feel slighted on Flaubert's behalf? And if so,
should we feel more, or less, slighted on behalf of Michelet
(1953), Nerval (1955), George Sand (1957), Vigny (1963), Proust
(1966), Zola (1967), Sainte-Beuve (1969), Mérimée and Dumas
père (1970), or Gautier (1972)?

(b) Estimate the chances of *either* Louis Bouilhet *or* Maxime
du Camp *or* Louise Colet appearing on a French stamp.

Phonetics

(a) The co-proprietor of the Hôtel du Nil, Cairo, where Flaubert
stayed in 1850, was called Bouvaret. The protagonist of his first
novel is called Bovary; the co-protagonist of his last novel is
called Bouvard. In his play *Le Candidat* there is a Comte de Bou-
vigny; in his play *Le Château des cœurs* there is a Bouvignard. Is
this all deliberate?

(b) Flaubert's name was first misprinted by the *Revue de Paris* as
Faubert. There was a grocer in the rue Richelieu called Faubet.
When *La Presse* reported the trial of *Madame Bovary*, they called
its author Foubert. Martine, George Sand's *femme de confiance*,
called him Flambart. Camille Rogier, the painter who lived in
Beirut, called him Folbert: 'Do you get the subtlety of the joke?'
Gustave wrote to his mother. (What is the joke? Presumably a
dual-language rendering of the novelist's self-image: Rogier
was calling him Crazy Bear.) Bouilhet also started calling him
Folbert. In Mantes, where he used to meet Louise, there was a
Café Flambert. Is this all coincidence?

(c) According to Du Camp, the name Bovary should be
pronounced with a short o (as in bother). Should we follow his
instruction; and if so, why?

Theatrical History

Assess the technical difficulties involved in implementing the
following stage direction (*Le Château des cœurs*, Act VI, scene viii):

The Stock-Pot, the handles of which have been transformed into wings, rises into the air and turns itself over, and while it increases in size so that it appears to hover over the whole town, the vegetables – carrots, turnips and leeks – that come out of it, remain suspended in the air and turn into luminous constellations.

History (with Astrology)

Consider the following predictions of Gustave Flaubert:

(a) (1850) 'It seems to me almost impossible that before very long England won't take control of Egypt. Aden is already full of her troops. It couldn't be easier: just across Suez, and one fine morning Cairo will be full of redcoats. The news will reach France a couple of weeks later and we'll all be very surprised! Remember my prediction.'

(b) (1852) 'As humanity perfects itself, man becomes degraded. When everything is reduced to the mere counter-balancing of economic interests, what room will there be for virtue? When Nature has been so subjugated that she has lost all her original forms, where will that leave the plastic arts? And so on. In the meantime, things are going to get very murky.'

(c) (1870, on the outbreak of the Franco-Prussian war) 'It will mean the return of racial conflicts. Before a century has passed we'll see millions of men killed in a single go. The East against the West, the old world against the new. Why not?'

(d) (1850) 'From time to time, I open a newspaper. Things seem to be proceeding at a dizzy rate. We are dancing not on the edge of a volcano, but on the wooden seat of a latrine, and it seems to me more than a touch rotten. Soon society will go plummeting down and drown in nineteen centuries of shit. There'll be quite a lot of shouting.'

(e) (1871) 'The Internationals are the Jesuits of the future.'

15

AND THE PARROT . . .

AND THE PARROT? Well, it took me almost two years to solve the Case of the Stuffed Parrot. The letters I had written after first returning from Rouen produced nothing useful; some of them weren't even answered. Anyone would have thought I was a crank, a senile amateur scholar hooked on trivia and pathetically trying to make a name for himself. Whereas in fact the young are much crankier than the old – far more egotistical, self-destructive and even plain bloody odd. It's just that they get a more indulgent press. When someone of eighty, or seventy, or fifty-four commits suicide, it's called softening of the brain, post-menopausal depression, or a final swipe of mean vanity designed to make others feel guilty. When someone of twenty commits suicide, it's called a high-minded refusal to accept the paltry terms on which life is offered, an act not just of courage but of moral and social revolt. Living? The old can do that for us. Pure crankery, of course. I speak as a doctor.

And while we're on the subject, I should say that the notion of Flaubert killing himself is pure crankery as well. The crankery of a single man: a Rouennais called Edmond Ledoux. This fantasist crops up twice in Flaubert's biography; each time all he does is spread gossip. His first unwelcome utterance is the assertion that Flaubert actually became engaged to Juliet Herbert. Ledoux claimed to have seen a copy of *La Tentation de saint Antoine* inscribed by Gustave to Juliet with the words '*A ma fiancée*'. Odd that he saw it in Rouen, rather than in London, where Juliet lived. Odd that nobody else ever saw this copy. Odd that it hasn't survived. Odd that Flaubert never mentioned such an engagement. Odd that the act would run diametrically counter to what he believed in.

Odd, too, that Ledoux's other slanderous assertion – of suicide – also runs counter to the writer's deepest beliefs. Listen to him. 'Let us have the modesty of wounded animals, who withdraw into a corner and remain silent. The world is full of people who bellow against Providence. One must, if only on the score of good manners, avoid behaving like them.' And again, that quotation which roosts in my head: 'People like us must have the religion of despair. By dint of saying "That is so! That is so!" and of gazing down into the black pit at one's feet, one remains calm.'

Those are not the words of a suicide. They are the words of a man whose stoicism runs as deep as his pessimism. Wounded animals don't kill themselves. And if you understand that gazing down into the black pit engenders calm, then you don't jump into it. Perhaps this was Ellen's weakness: an inability to gaze into the black pit. She could only squint at it, repeatedly. One glance would make her despair, and despair would make her seek distraction. Some outgaze the black pit; others ignore it; those who keep glancing at it become obsessed. She chose the exact dosage: the only occasion when being a doctor's wife seemed to help her.

Ledoux's account of the suicide goes like this: Flaubert *hanged himself in his bath*. I suppose it's more plausible than saying that he electrocuted himself with sleeping pills; but really . . . What happened was this. Flaubert got up, took a hot bath, had an apoplectic fit, and stumbled to a sofa in his study; there he was found expiring by the doctor who later issued the death certificate. That's what happened. End of story. Flaubert's earliest biographer talked to the doctor concerned and that's that. Ledoux's version requires the following chain of events: Flaubert got into his hot bath, hanged himself in some as yet unexplained fashion, then climbed out, hid the rope, staggered to his study, collapsed on the sofa and, when the doctor arrived, managed to die while feigning the symptoms of an apoplectic fit. Really, it's too ridiculous.

No smoke without fire, they say. I'm afraid there can be. Edmond Ledoux is a prime example of spontaneous smoke. Who was he, anyway, this Ledoux? Nobody seems to know. He wasn't an authority on anything. He's a complete nonentity. He only exists as the teller of two lies. Perhaps someone in the Flaubert family once did him harm (did Achille fail to cure his bunion?) and this is his effective revenge. Because it means that few books on Flaubert can end without a discussion – always followed by a dismissal – of the suicide claim. As you see, it's happened all over again here. Another long digression whose tone of moral indignation is probably counter-productive. And I intended writing about the parrots. At least Ledoux didn't have a theory about them.

But I have. Not just a theory, either. As I say, it took me a good two years. No, that's boastful: what I really mean is that two years elapsed between the question arising and dissolving. One of the snobbier academics to whom I wrote even suggested that the matter wasn't really of any interest at all. Well, I suppose he has to guard his territory. Someone, however, gave me the name of M. Lucien Andrieu.

I decided not to write to him; after all, my letters so far hadn't proved very successful. Instead, I made a summer trip to Rouen, in August 1982. I stayed at the Grand Hôtel du Nord, abutting the Gros Horloge. In the corner of my room, running from ceiling to floor, was a soil-pipe, inefficiently boxed-in, which roared at me every five minutes or so, and appeared to carry the waste of the entire hotel. After dinner I lay on my bed listening to the sporadic bursts of Gallic evacuation. Then the Gros Horloge struck the hour with a loud and tinny closeness, as if it were inside my wardrobe. I wondered what the chances of sleep might be.

My apprehension was misconceived. After ten o'clock, the soil-pipe went quiet; and so did the Gros Horloge. It may be a tourist attraction in the daytime, but Rouen thoughtfully disconnects its chimes when visitors are trying to sleep. I lay in bed on my back with the lights out and thought about Flaubert's parrot: to Félicité, it was a grotesque but logical version of the Holy Ghost; to me, a fluttering, elusive emblem of the writer's voice. When Félicité lay in bed dying, the parrot came back to her, in magnified form, and welcomed her into Heaven. As I teetered off towards sleep, I wondered what my dreams might be.

They weren't about parrots. I had my railway dream instead. Changing trains at Birmingham, some time during the war. The distant guard's van at the end of the platform, pulling out. My suitcase rubbing at my calf. The blacked-out train; the station dimly lit. A timetable I couldn't read, a blur of figures. No hope anywhere; no more trains; desolation, darkness.

You'd think such a dream would realise when it had made its point? But dreams have no sense of how they're going down with the dreamer, any more than they have a sense of delicacy. The station dream – which I get every three months or so – simply repeats itself, a loop of film endlessly rerunning, until I wake up heavy-chested and depressed. I awoke that morning to the twin sounds of time and shit: the Gros Horloge and my corner soil-pipe. Time and shit: was Gustave laughing?

At the Hôtel-Dieu the same gaunt, white-coated *gardien* showed me round again. In the medical section of the museum, I noticed something I had missed before: a do-it-yourself enema pump. As hated by Gustave Flaubert: 'Railways, poisons, enema pumps, cream tarts...' It consisted of a narrow wooden stool, a hollow spike and a vertical handle. You sat astride the stool, worked your way on to the spike, and then pumped yourself full of water. Well, at least it would give you privacy. The *gardien* and I had a conspiratorial laugh; I told him I was a doctor. He smiled and went to fetch something sure to interest me.

He returned with a large cardboard shoebox containing two preserved human heads. The skin was still intact, though age had turned it brown: as brown as an old jar of redcurrant jam, perhaps. Most of the teeth were in place, but the eyes and hair had not survived. One of the heads had been re-equipped with a coarse black wig and a pair of glass eyes (what colour were they? I can't remember; but less complicated, I'm sure, than the eyes of Emma Bovary). This attempt to make the head more realistic had the opposite effect: it looked like a child's horror mask, a trick-or-treat face from a joke-shop window.

The *gardien* explained that the heads were the work of Jean-Baptiste Laumonier, predecessor of Achille-Cléophas Flaubert at the hospital. Laumonier was looking for new methods of preserving corpses; and the city had allowed him to experiment with the heads of executed criminals. An incident from Gustave's childhood came back to me. Once, out on a walk with his Oncle Parain at the age of six, he had passed a guillotine which had just been used: the cobbles were bright with blood. I mentioned this hopefully; but the *gardien* shook his head. It would have been a nice coincidence, but the dates were incompatible. Laumonier had died in 1818; besides, the two specimens in the shoebox had not in fact been guillotined. I was shown the deep creases just below the jaw where the hangman's noose had once tightened. When Maupassant saw Flaubert's body at Croisset, the neck was dark and swollen. This happens with apoplexy. It's not a sign that someone had hanged himself in the bath.

We continued through the museum until we reached the room containing the parrot. I took out my Polaroid camera, and was allowed to photograph it. As I held the developing print under my armpit, the *gardien* pointed out the Xeroxed letter I had noticed on my first visit. Flaubert to Mme Brainne, July 28th,

1876: 'Do you know what I've had on my table in front of me for the last three weeks? A stuffed parrot. It sits there on sentry duty. The sight of it is beginning to irritate me. But I keep it there so that I can fill my head with the idea of parrothood. Because at the moment I'm writing about the love between an old girl and a parrot.'

'That's the real one,' said the *gardien*, tapping the glass dome in front of us. 'That's the real one.'

'And the other?'

'The other is an impostor.'

'How can you be sure?'

'It's simple. This one comes from the Museum of Rouen.' He pointed to a round stamp on the end of the perch, then drew my attention to a photocopied entry from the Museum register. It recorded a batch of loans to Flaubert. Most of the entries were in some museum shorthand which I couldn't decipher, but the loan of the Amazonian parrot was clearly comprehensible. A series of ticks in the final column of the register showed that Flaubert had returned every item lent to him. Including the parrot.

I felt vaguely disappointed. I had always sentimentally assumed – without proper reason – that the parrot had been found among the writer's effects after his death (this explained, no doubt, why I had secretly been favouring the Croisset bird). Of course the photocopy didn't prove anything, except that Flaubert had borrowed a parrot from the Museum, and that he'd returned it. The Museum stamp was a bit trickier, but not conclusive . . .

'Ours is the real one,' the *gardien* repeated unnecessarily as he showed me out. It seemed as if our roles had been reversed: he needed the reassurance, not me.

'I'm sure you're right.'

But I wasn't. I drove to Croisset and photographed the other parrot. It too sported a Museum stamp. I agreed with the *gardienne* that her parrot was clearly authentic, and that the Hôtel-Dieu bird was definitely an impostor.

After lunch I went to the Cimetière Monumental. 'Hatred of the bourgeois is the beginning of all virtue,' wrote Flaubert; yet he is buried amongst the grandest families of Rouen. During one of his trips to London he visited Highgate Cemetery and found it far too neat: 'These people seem to have died with white gloves on.' At the Cimetière Monumental they wear tails and full decorations, and have been buried with their horses, dogs and English governesses.

Gustave's grave is small and unpretentious; in these surroundings, however, the effect is not to make him look an artist, an anti-bourgeois, but rather to make him look an unsuccessful bourgeois. I leaned against the railings which fence off the family plot – even in death you can own a freehold – and took out my copy of *Un cœur simple*. The description Flaubert gives of Félicité's parrot at the start of chapter four is very brief: 'He was called Loulou. His body was green, the ends of his wings pink, his forehead blue, and his throat golden.' I compared my two photographs. Both parrots had green bodies; both had pink wing-tips (there was more pink in the Hôtel-Dieu version). But the blue forehead and the golden throat: there was no doubting that they belonged to the parrot at the Hôtel-Dieu. The Croisset parrot had it completely back to front: a golden forehead and bluish-green throat.

That seemed to be it, really. All the same, I rang M. Lucien Andrieu and explained my interests in a general way. He invited me to call the next day. As he gave me the address – rue de Lourdines – I imagined the house he was speaking from, the solid, bourgeois house of a Flaubert scholar. The mansard roof pierced with an *oeil-de-boeuf*; the pinkish brick, the Second Empire trimmings; inside, cool seriousness, glass-fronted bookcases, waxed boards and parchment lampshades; I breathed a male, clubby smell.

My briefly-constructed house was an impostor, a dream, a fiction. The real house of the Flaubert scholar was across the river in south Rouen, a run-down area where small industries squat among rows of red-brick terrace houses. Lorries look too big for the streets; there are few shops, and almost as many bars; one was offering *tête de veau* as its *plat du jour*. Just before you get to the rue de Lourdines there is a signpost to the Rouen abattoir.

Monsieur Andrieu was waiting for me on his doorstep. He was a small, elderly man wearing a tweed jacket, tweed carpet slippers and a tweed trilby. There were three ranks of coloured silk in his lapel. He took off his hat to shake hands, then replaced it; his head, he explained, was rather *fragile* in the summer. He was to keep his tweed hat on all the time we were in the house. Some people might have thought this a little cranky, but I didn't. I speak as a doctor.

He was seventy-seven, he informed me, the secretary and oldest surviving member of the Société des Amis de Flaubert. We sat on either side of a table in a front room whose walls were crowded with bric-à-brac: commemorative plates, Flaubert medallions, a painting of the Gros Horloge which M. Andrieu had done himself. It was small and crowded, curious and personal: like a neater version of Félicité's room, or of Flaubert's pavilion. He pointed out a cartoon portrait of himself, drawn by a friend; it showed him as a gunslinger with a large bottle of calvados protruding from his hip pocket. I should have asked the reason for such a ferocious characterisation of my mild and genial host; but I didn't. Instead, I took out my copy of Enid Starkie's *Flaubert: the Making of a Master* and showed him the frontispiece.

'C'est Flaubert, ça?' I asked, just for a final confirmation.

He chuckled.

'C'est Louis Bouilhet. Oui, oui, c'est Bouilhet.' It was clearly not the first time he had been asked. I checked one or two more details with him, and then mentioned the parrots.

'Ah, the parrots. There are two of them.'

'Yes. Do you know which is the true one and which is the impostor?'

He chuckled again.

'They set up the museum at Croisset in 1905,' he replied. 'The year of my birth. Naturally, I was not there. They gathered together what material they could find – well, you've seen it for yourself.' I nodded. 'There wasn't much. Many things had been dispersed. But the curator decided that there was one thing they could have, and that was Flaubert's parrot. Loulou. So they went to the Museum of Natural History and said, Can we please have Flaubert's parrot back. We want it for the pavilion. And the Museum said, Of course, come with us.'

Monsieur Andrieu had told this story before; he knew its pauses.

'So, they took the curator to where they kept the reserve collection. You want a parrot? they said. Then we go to the section of the birds. They opened the door, and they saw in front of them . . . fifty parrots. *Une cinquantaine de perroquets!*'

'What did they do? They did the logical thing, the intelligent thing. They came back with a copy of *Un cœur simple*, and they read to themselves Flaubert's description of Loulou.' Just as I had done the day before. 'And then they chose the parrot which looked most like his description.

'Forty years later, after the last war, they started making the collection at the Hôtel-Dieu. They in their turn went back to the Museum and said, Please can we have Flaubert's parrot. Of course, said the Museum, take your pick, but make sure you get the right one. So they too consulted *Un cœur simple*, and chose the parrot which most resembled Flaubert's description. And that's how there are two parrots.'

'So the pavilion at Croisset, which had the first choice, must have the true parrot?'

M. Andrieu looked non-committal. He pushed his tweed trilby slightly further back on his head. I took out my photographs. 'But if so, what about this?' I quoted the familiar description of the parrot, and pointed to the non-conforming forehead and breast of the Croisset version. Why should the parrot chosen second look more like the one in the book than the parrot chosen first?

'Well. You have to remember two things. One, Flaubert was an artist. He was a writer of the imagination. And he would alter a fact for the sake of a cadence; he was like that. Just because he borrowed a parrot, why should he describe it as it was? Why shouldn't he change the colours round if it sounded better?

'Secondly, Flaubert returned his parrot to the Museum after he'd finished writing the story. That was in 1876. The pavilion was not set up until thirty years later. Stuffed animals get the moth, you know. They fall apart. Félicité's did, after all, didn't it? The stuffing came out of it.'

'Yes.'

'And perhaps they change colour with time. Of course, I am not an expert in the stuffing of animals.'

'So you mean either of them could be the real one? Or, quite possibly, neither?'

He spread his hands slowly on the table, in a conjuror's calming gesture. I had a final question.

'Are there still all those parrots left at the Museum? All fifty of them?'

'I don't know. I don't think so. You have to know that in the Twenties and Thirties, when I was young, there was a great fashion for stuffed animals and birds. People had them in their sitting-rooms. They thought they were pretty. So, a lot of museums sold off parts of their collections which they didn't need. Why should they hold on to fifty Amazonian parrots? They would only decay. I don't know how many they have now. I should think the Museum got rid of most of them.'

We shook hands. On the doorstep M. Andrieu raised his hat to me, briefly uncovering his fragile head to the August sun. I felt pleased and disappointed at the same time. It was an answer and not an answer; it was an ending, and not an ending. As with Félicité's final heartbeats, the story was dying away 'like a fountain running dry, like an echo disappearing'. Well, perhaps that's as it should be.

It was time to pay farewell. Like a conscientious doctor, I made the rounds of Flaubert's three statues. What shape was he in? At Trouville his moustache still needs repair; though the patching on his thigh now looks less conspicuous. At Barentin, his left leg is beginning to split, there is a hole in the corner of his jacket, and a mossy discoloration spots his upper body; I stared at the greenish marks on his chest, half-closed my eyes, and tried to turn him into a Carthaginian interpreter. At Rouen, in the place des Carmes, he is structurally sound, confident in his alloy of 93 per cent copper and 7 per cent tin; but he still continues to streak. Each year he seems to cry a couple more cupreous tears, which brightly vein his neck. This isn't inappropriate: Flaubert was always a great weeper. The tears continue on down his body, giving him a fancy waistcoat and putting thin side-stripes on his legs, as if he were wearing dress-trousers. This too isn't inappropriate: it's a reminder that he enjoyed salon life as well as his Croisset retreat.

A few hundred yards north, at the Museum of Natural History, they took me upstairs. This was a surprise: I'd assumed that reserve collections were always held in cellars. Nowadays they probably have leisure centres down there instead: cafeterias and wall-charts and video-games and everything to make learning easy. Why are they so keen to turn learning into a game? They love to make it childish, even for adults. Especially for adults.

It was a small room, perhaps eight feet by ten, with windows on the right and shelves running away to the left. Despite a few ceiling lights, it remained quite dark, this burial vault on the top floor. Though it wasn't, I suppose, altogether a tomb: some of these creatures would be taken out again into the daylight, and allowed to replace moth-eaten or unfashionable colleagues. So it was an ambivalent room, half-morgue and half-purgatory. It had an uncertain smell, too: somewhere between a surgery and a hardware shop.

Everywhere I looked there were birds. Shelf after shelf of birds, each one covered in a sprinkling of white pesticide. I was directed to the third aisle. I pushed carefully between the shelves and then looked up at a slight angle. There, standing in a line, were the Amazonian parrots. Of the original fifty only three remained. Any gaudiness in their colouring had been dimmed by the dusting of pesticide which lay over them. They gazed at me like three quizzical, sharp-eyed, dandruff-ridden, dishonourable old men. They did look – I had to admit it – a little cranky. I stared at them for a minute or so, and then dodged away.

Perhaps it was one of them.

A HISTORY OF
THE WORLD IN
10½ CHAPTERS

To Pat Kavanagh

CONTENTS

I

THE STOWAWAY

THEY PUT THE Behemoths in the hold along with the rhinos, the hippos and the elephants. It was a sensible decision to use them as ballast; but you can imagine the stench. And there was no one to muck out. The men were overburdened with the feeding rota, and their women, who beneath those leaping fire-tongues of scent no doubt reeked as badly as we did, were far too delicate. So if any mucking-out was to happen, we had to do it ourselves. Every few months they would winch back the thick hatch on the aft deck and let the cleaner-birds in. Well, first they had to let the smell out (and there weren't too many volunteers for winch-work); then six or eight of the less fastidious birds would flutter cautiously around the hatch for a minute or so before diving in. I can't remember what they were all called – indeed, one of those pairs no longer exists – but you know the sort I mean. You've seen hippos with their mouths open and bright little birds pecking away between their teeth like distraught dental hygienists? Picture that on a larger, messier scale. I am hardly squeamish, but even I used to shudder at the scene below decks: a row of squinting monsters being manicured in a sewer.

There was strict discipline on the Ark: that's the first point to make. It wasn't like those nursery versions in painted wood which you might have played with as a child – all happy couples peering merrily over the rail from the comfort of their well-scrubbed stalls. Don't imagine some Mediterranean cruise on which we played languorous roulette and everyone dressed for dinner; on the Ark only the penguins wore tailcoats. Remember: this was a long and dangerous voyage – dangerous even though some of the rules had been fixed in advance. Remember too that we had the whole of the animal kingdom on board: would you have put the cheetahs within springing distance of the antelope? A certain level of security was inevitable, and we accepted double-peg locks, stall inspections, a nightly curfew. But regrettably there were also punishments and isolation cells. Someone at the very top became obsessed with information gathering; and certain of the travellers agreed to act as stool pigeons. I'm sorry to report that ratting to the authorities was at times widespread. It wasn't a nature reserve, that Ark of ours; at times it was more like a prison ship.

Now, I realize that accounts differ. Your species has its much repeated version, which still charms even sceptics; while the animals have a compendium of sentimental myths. But they're not going to rock the boat, are they? Not when they've been treated as heroes, not when it's become a matter of pride that each and every one of them can proudly trace its family tree straight back to the Ark. They were chosen, they endured, they survived: it's normal for them to gloss over the awkward episodes, to have convenient lapses of memory. But I am not constrained in that way. I was never chosen. In fact, like several other species, I was specifically not chosen. I was a stowaway; I too survived; I escaped (getting off was no easier than getting on); and I have flourished. I am a little set apart from the rest of animal society, which still has its nostalgic reunions: there is even a Sealegs Club for species which never once felt queasy. When I recall the Voyage, I feel no sense of obligation; gratitude puts no smear of Vaseline on the lens. My account you can trust.

You presumably grasped that the 'Ark' was more than just a single ship? It was the name we gave to the whole flotilla (you could hardly expect to cram the entire animal kingdom into something a mere three hundred cubits long). It rained for forty days and forty nights? Well, naturally it didn't – that would have been no more than a routine English summer. No, it rained for about a year and a half, by my reckoning. And the waters were upon the earth for a hundred and fifty days? Bump that up to about four years. And so on. Your species has always been hopeless about dates. I put it down to your quaint obsession with multiples of seven.

In the beginning, the Ark consisted of eight vessels: Noah's galleon, which towed the stores ship, then four slightly smaller boats, each captained by one of Noah's sons, and behind them, at a safe distance (the family being superstitious about illness) the hospital ship. The eighth vessel provided a brief mystery: a darting little sloop with filigree decorations in sandalwood all along the stern, it steered a course sycophantically close to that of

Ham's ark. If you got to leeward you would sometimes be teased with strange perfumes; occasionally, at night, when the tempest slackened, you could hear jaunty music and shrill laughter – surprising noises to us, because we had assumed that all the wives of all the sons of Noah were safely ensconced on their own ships. However, this scented, laughing boat was not robust: it went down in a sudden squall, and Ham was pensive for several weeks thereafter.

The stores ship was the next to be lost, on a starless night when the wind had dropped and the lookouts were drowsy. In the morning all that trailed behind Noah's flagship was a length of fat hawser which had been gnawed through by something with sharp incisors and an ability to cling to wet ropes. There were serious recriminations about that, I can tell you; indeed, this may have been the first occasion on which a species disappeared overboard. Not long afterwards the hospital ship was lost. There were murmurings that the two events were connected, that Ham's wife – who was a little short on serenity – had decided to revenge herself upon the animals. Apparently her lifetime output of embroidered blankets had gone down with the stores ship. But nothing was ever proved.

Still, the worst disaster by far was the loss of Varadi. You're familiar with Ham and Shem and the other one, whose name began with a J; but you don't know about Varadi, do you? He was the youngest and strongest of Noah's sons; which didn't, of course, make him the most popular within the family. He also had a sense of humour – or at least he laughed a lot, which is usually proof enough for your species. Yes, Varadi was always cheerful. He could be seen strutting the quarterdeck with a parrot on each shoulder; he would slap the quadrupeds affectionately on the rump, which they'd acknowledge with an appreciative bellow; and it was said that his ark was run on much less tyrannical lines than the others. But there you are: one morning we awoke to find that Varadi's ship had vanished from the horizon, taking with it one fifth of the animal kingdom. You would, I think, have enjoyed the simurgh, with its silver head and peacock's tail; but the bird that nested in the Tree of Knowledge was no more proof against the waves than the brindled vole. Varadi's elder brothers blamed poor navigation; they said Varadi had spent far too much time fraternizing with the beasts; they even hinted that God might have been punishing him for some obscure offence committed when he was a child of eighty-five. But whatever the truth behind Varadi's disappearance, it was a severe loss to your species. His genes would have helped you a great deal.

As far as we were concerned the whole business of the Voyage began when we were invited to report to a certain place by a certain time. That was the first we heard of the scheme. We didn't know anything of the political background. God's wrath with his own creation was news to us; we just got caught up in it willy-nilly. *We* weren't in any way to blame (you don't really believe that story about the serpent, do you? – it was just Adam's black propaganda), and yet the consequences for us were equally severe: every species wiped out except for a single breeding pair, and that couple consigned to the high seas under the charge of an old rogue with a drink problem who was already into his seventh century of life.

So the word went out; but characteristically they didn't tell us the truth. Did you imagine that in the vicinity of Noah's palace (oh, he wasn't poor, that Noah) there dwelt a convenient example of every species on earth? Come, come. No, they were obliged to advertise, and then select the best pair that presented itself. Since they didn't want to cause a universal panic, they announced a competition for twosomes – a sort of beauty contest cum brains trust cum Darby-and-Joan event – and told contestants to present themselves at Noah's gate by a certain month. You can imagine the problems. For a start, not everyone has a competitive nature, so perhaps only the grabbiest turned up. Animals who weren't smart enough to read between the lines felt they simply didn't need to win a luxury cruise for two, all expenses paid, thank you very much. Nor had Noah and his staff allowed for the fact that some species hibernate at a given time of year; let alone the more obvious fact that certain animals travel more slowly than others. There was a particularly relaxed sloth, for instance – an exquisite creature, I can vouch for it personally – which had scarcely got down to the foot of its tree before it was wiped out in the great wash of God's vengeance. What do you call that – natural selection? I'd call it professional incompetence.

The arrangements, frankly, were a shambles. Noah got behind with the building of the arks (it didn't help when the craftsmen realized there weren't enough berths for them to be taken along as well); with the result that insufficient attention was given to choosing the animals. The first normally presentable pair that came along was given the nod – this appeared to be the system; there was certainly no more than the scantiest examination of pedigree. And of course, while they *said* they'd take two of each species, when it came down to it . . . Some creatures were simply Not Wanted On Voyage. That was the case with us; that's why we had to stow away. And any number of beasts, with a perfectly good legal argument for being a separate species, had their claims dismissed. No, we've got two of you already, they were told. Well, what difference do a few extra rings round the tail make, or those bushy tufts down your backbone? We've got *you*. Sorry.

There were splendid animals that arrived without a mate and had to be left behind; there were families which refused to be separated from their offspring and chose to die together; there were medical inspections, often of a brutally intrusive nature; and all night long the air outside Noah's stockade was heavy with the wailings of the rejected. Can you imagine the atmosphere when the news finally got out as to why we'd been asked to submit to this charade of a competition? There was much jealousy and bad behaviour, as you can imagine. Some of the nobler species simply padded away into the forest, declining to survive on the insulting terms offered them by God and Noah, preferring extinction and the waves. Harsh and envious words were spoken about fish; the amphibians began to look distinctly smug; birds practised staying in the air as long as possible. Certain types of monkey were occasionally seen trying to construct crude rafts of their own. One week there was a mysterious outbreak of food poisoning in the Compound of the Chosen, and for some of the less robust species the selection process had to start all over again.

There were times when Noah and his sons got quite hysterical. That doesn't tally with your account of things? You've always been led to believe that Noah was sage, righteous and God-fearing, and I've already described him as a hysterical rogue with a drink problem? The two views aren't entirely incompatible. Put it this way: Noah was pretty bad, but *you should have seen the others*. It came as little surprise to us that God decided to wipe the slate clean; the only puzzle was that he chose to preserve anything at all of this species whose creation did not reflect particularly well on its creator.

At times Noah was nearly on the edge. The Ark was behind

schedule, the craftsmen had to be whipped, hundreds of terrified animals were bivouacking near his palace, and nobody knew when the rains were coming. God wouldn't even give him a date for that. Every morning we looked at the clouds: would it be a westerly wind that brought the rain as usual, or would God send his special downpour from a rare direction? And as the weather slowly thickened, the possibilities of revolt grew. Some of the rejected wanted to commandeer the Ark and save themselves, others wanted to destroy it altogether. Animals of a speculative bent began to propound rival selection principles, based on beast size or utility rather than mere number; but Noah loftily refused to negotiate. He was a man who had his little theories, and he didn't want anyone else's.

As the flotilla neared completion it had to be guarded round the clock. There were many attempts to stow away. A craftsman was discovered one day trying to hollow out a priest's hole among the lower timbers of the stores ship. And there were some pathetic sights: a young elk strung from the rail of Shem's ark; birds dive-bombing the protective netting; and so on. Stowaways, when detected, were immediately put to death; but these public spectacles were never enough to deter the desperate. Our species, I am proud to report, got on board without either bribery or violence; but then we are not as detectable as a young elk. How did we manage it? We had a parent with foresight. While Noah and his sons were roughly frisking the animals as they came up the gangway, running coarse hands through suspiciously shaggy fleeces and carrying out some of the earliest and most unhygienic prostate examinations, we were already well past their gaze and safely in our bunks. One of the ship's carpenters carried us to safety, little knowing what he did.

For two days the wind blew from all directions simultaneously; and then it began to rain. Water sluiced down from a bilious sky to purge the wicked world. Big drops exploded on the deck like pigeons' eggs. The selected representatives of each species were moved from the Compound of the Chosen to their allotted ark: the scene resembled some obligatory mass wedding. Then they screwed down the hatches and we all started getting used to the dark, the confinement and the stench. Not that we cared much about this at first: we were too exhilarated by our survival. The rain fell and fell, occasionally shifting to hail and rattling on the timbers. Sometimes we could hear the crack of thunder from outside, and often the lamentations of abandoned beasts. After a while these cries grew less frequent: we knew that the waters had begun to rise.

Eventually came the day we had been longing for. At first we thought it might be some crazed assault by the last remaining pachyderms, trying to force their way into the Ark, or at least knock it over. But no: it was the boat shifting sideways as the water began to lift it from the cradle. That was the high point of the Voyage, if you ask me; that was when fraternity among the beasts and gratitude towards man flowed like the wine at Noah's table. Afterwards ... but perhaps the animals had been naïve to trust Noah and his God in the first place.

Even before the waters rose there had been grounds for unease. I know your species tends to look down on our world, considering it brutal, cannibalistic and deceitful (though you might acknowledge the argument that this makes us closer to you rather than more distant). But among us there had always been, from the beginning, a sense of equality. Oh, to be sure, we ate one another, and so on; the weaker species knew all too well what to expect if they crossed the path of something that was both bigger and hungry. But we merely recognized this as being the way of things. The fact that one animal was capable of killing another did not make the first animal superior to the second; merely more dangerous. Perhaps this is a concept difficult for you to grasp, but there was a mutual respect amongst us. Eating another animal was not grounds for despising it; and being eaten did not instil in the victim – or the victim's family – any exaggerated admiration for the dining species.

Noah – or Noah's God – changed all that. If you had a Fall, so did we. But we were pushed. It was when the selections were being made for the Compound of the Chosen that we first noticed it. All this stuff about two of everything was true (and you could see it made a certain basic sense); but it wasn't the end of the matter. In the Compound we began to notice that some species had been whittled down not to a couple but to seven (again, this obsession with sevens). At first we thought the extra five might be travelling reserves in case the original pair fell sick. But then it slowly began to emerge. Noah – or Noah's God – had decreed that there were two classes of beast: the clean and the unclean. Clean animals got into the Ark by sevens; the unclean by twos.

There was, as you can imagine, deep resentment at the divisiveness of God's animal policy. Indeed, at first even the clean animals themselves were embarrassed by the whole thing; they knew they'd done little to deserve such special patronage. Though being 'clean', as they rapidly realized, was a mixed blessing. Being 'clean' meant that they could be eaten. Seven animals were welcome on board, but five were destined for the galley. It was a curious form of honour that was being done them. But at least it meant they got the most comfortable quarters available until the day of their ritual slaughter.

I could occasionally find the situation funny, and give vent to the outcast's laugh. However, among the species who took themselves seriously there arose all sorts of complicated jealousies. The pig did not mind, being of a socially unambitious nature; but some of the other animals regarded the notion of uncleanliness as a personal slight. And it must be said that the system – at least, the system as Noah understood it – made very little sense. What was so special about cloven-footed ruminants, one asked oneself? Why should the camel and the rabbit be given second-class status? Why should a division be introduced between fish that had scales and fish that did not? The swan, the pelican, the heron, the hoopoe: are these not some of the finest species? Yet they were not awarded the badge of cleanliness. Why round on the mouse and the lizard – which had enough problems already, you might think – and undermine their self-confidence further? If only we could have seen some glimpse of logic behind it all; if only Noah had explained it better. But all he did was blindly obey. Noah, as you will have been told many times, was a very God-fearing man; and given the nature of God, that was probably the safest line to take. Yet if you could have heard the weeping of the shellfish, the grave and puzzled complaint of the lobster, if you could have seen the mournful shame of the stork, you would have understood that things would never be the same again amongst us.

And then there was another little difficulty. By some unhappy chance, our species had managed to smuggle seven members on board. Not only were we stowaways (which some resented), not only were we unclean (which some had already begun to despise), but we had also mocked those clean and legal species by mimicking their sacred number. We quickly decided to lie about how many of us there were – and we never appeared together in the same place. We discovered which parts of the ship were welcoming to us, and which we should avoid.

So you can see that it was an unhappy convoy from the beginning. Some of us were grieving for those we had been forced to leave behind; others were resentful about their status; others again, though notionally favoured by the title of cleanness, were rightly apprehensive about the oven. And on top of it all, there was Noah and his family.

I don't know how best to break this to you, but Noah was not a nice man. I realize this idea is embarrassing, since you are all descended from him; still, there it is. He was a monster, a puffed-up patriarch who spent half his day grovelling to his God and the other half taking it out on us. He had a gopher-wood stave with which ... well, some of the animals carry the stripes to this day. It's amazing what fear can do. I'm told that among your species a severe shock may cause the hair to turn white in a matter of hours; on the Ark the effects of fear were even more dramatic. There was a pair of lizards, for instance, who at the mere sound of Noah's gopher-wood sandals advancing down the companion-way would actually change colour. I saw it myself: their skin would abandon its natural hue and blend with the background. Noah would pause as he passed their stall, wondering briefly why it was empty, then stroll on; and as his footsteps faded the terrified lizards would slowly revert to their normal colour. Down the post-Ark years this has apparently proved a useful trick; but it all began as a chronic reaction to 'the Admiral'.

With the reindeer it was more complicated. They were always nervous, but it wasn't just fear of Noah, it was something deeper. You know how some of us animals have powers of foresight? Even *you* have managed to notice that, after millennia of exposure to our habits. 'Oh, look,' you say, 'the cows are sitting down in the field, that means it's going to rain.' Well, of course it's all much subtler than you can possibly imagine, and the point of it certainly isn't to act as a cheap weather-vane for human beings. Anyway ... the reindeer were troubled with something deeper than Noah-angst, stranger than storm-nerves; something ... long-term. They sweated up in their stalls, they whinnied neurotically in spells of oppressive heat; they kicked out at the gopher-wood partitions when there was no obvious danger – no subsequently proven danger, either – and when Noah had been, for him, positively restrained in his behaviour. But the reindeer sensed something. And it was something beyond what we then knew. As if they were saying, You think this is the worst? Don't count on it. Still, whatever it was, even the reindeer couldn't be specific about it. Something distant, major . . . long-term.

The rest of us, understandably enough, were far more concerned about the short term. Sick animals, for instance, were always ruthlessly dealt with. This was not a hospital ship, we were constantly informed by the authorities; there was to be no disease, and no malingering. Which hardly seemed just or realistic. But you knew better than to report yourself ill. A little bit of mange and you were over the side before you could stick your tongue out for inspection. And then what do you think happened to your better half? What good is fifty per cent of a breeding pair? Noah was hardly the sentimentalist who would urge the grieving partner to live out its natural span.

Put it another way: what the hell do you think Noah and his family ate in the Ark? They ate *us*, of course. I mean, if you look around the animal kingdom nowadays, you don't think this is all there ever was, do you? A lot of beasts looking more or less the same, and then a gap and another lot of beasts looking more or less the same? I know you've got some theory to make sense of it all – something about relationship to the environment and inherited skills or whatever – but there's a much simpler explanation for the puzzling leaps in the spectrum of creation. One fifth of the earth's species went down with Varadi; and as for the rest that are missing, Noah's crowd ate them. They did. There was a pair of Arctic plovers, for instance – very pretty birds. When they came on board they were a mottled bluey-brown in plumage. A few months later they started to moult. This was quite normal. As their summer feathers departed, their winter coat of pure white began to show through. Of course we weren't in Arctic latitudes, so this was technically unnecessary; still, you can't stop Nature, can you? Nor could you stop Noah. As soon as he saw the plovers turning white, he decided that they were sickening, and in tender consideration for the rest of the ship's health he had them boiled with a little seaweed on the side. He was an ignorant man in many respects, and certainly no ornithologist. We got up a petition and explained certain things to him about moulting and what-have-you. Eventually he seemed to take it in. But that was the Arctic plover gone.

Of course, it didn't stop there. As far as Noah and his family were concerned, we were just a floating cafeteria. Clean and unclean came alike to them on the Ark; lunch first, then piety, that was the rule. And you can't imagine what richness of wildlife Noah deprived you of. Or rather, you can, because that's precisely what you do: you imagine it. All those mythical beasts your poets dreamed up in former centuries: you assume, don't you, that they were either knowingly invented, or else they were alarmist descriptions of animals half-glimpsed in the forest after too good a hunting lunch? I'm afraid the explanation's more simple: Noah and his tribe scoffed them. At the start of the Voyage, as I said, there was a pair of behemoths in our hold. I didn't get much of a look at them myself, but I'm told they were impressive beasts. Yet Ham, Shem or the one whose name began with J apparently proposed at the family council that if you had the elephant and the hippopotamus, you could get by without the behemoth; and besides – the argument combined practicality with principle – two such large carcases would keep the Noah family going for months.

Of course, it didn't work out like that. After a few weeks there were complaints about getting behemoth for dinner every night, and so – merely for a change of diet – some other species was sacrificed. There were guilty nods from time to time in the direction of domestic economy, but I can tell you this: there was a lot of salted behemoth left over at the end of the journey.

The salamander went the same way. The real salamander, I mean, not the unremarkable animal you still call by the same name; our salamander lived in fire. That was a one-off beast and no mistake; yet Ham or Shem or the other one kept pointing out that on a wooden ship the risk was simply too great, and so both the salamanders and the twin fires that housed them had to go. The carbuncle went as well, all because of some ridiculous story Ham's wife had heard about it having a precious jewel inside its skull. She was always a dressy one, that Ham's wife. So they took one of the carbuncles and chopped its head off; split the skull and found nothing at all. Maybe the jewel is only found in the female's head, Ham's wife suggested. So they opened up the other one as well, with the same negative result.

I put this next suggestion to you rather tentatively; I feel I have to voice it, though. At times we suspected a kind of system behind the killing that went on. Certainly there was more extermination than was strictly necessary for nutritional purposes –

far more. And at the same time some of the species that were killed had very little eating on them. What's more, the gulls would occasionally report that they had seen carcases tossed from the stern with perfectly good meat thick on the bone. We began to suspect that Noah and his tribe had it in for certain animals simply for being what they were. The basilisk, for instance, went overboard very early. Now, of course it wasn't very pleasant to look at, but I feel it my duty to record that there was very little eating underneath those scales, and that the bird certainly wasn't sick at the time.

In fact, when we came to look back on it after the event, we began to discern a pattern, and the pattern began with the basilisk. You've never seen one, of course. But if I describe a four-legged cock with a serpent's tail, say that it had a very nasty look in its eye and laid a misshapen egg which it then employed a toad to hatch, you'll understand that this was not the most alluring beast on the Ark. Still, it had its rights like everyone else, didn't it? After the basilisk it was the griffon's turn; after the griffon, the sphinx; after the sphinx, the hippogriff. You thought they were all gaudy fantasies, perhaps? Not a bit of it. And do you see what they had in common? They were all cross-breeds. We think it was Shem – though it could well have been Noah himself – who had this thing about the purity of the species. Cock-eyed, of course; and as we used to say to one another, you only had to look at Noah and his wife, or at their three sons and their three wives, to realize what a genetically messy lot the human race would turn out to be. So why should they start getting fastidious about cross-breeds?

Still, it was the unicorn that was the most distressing. That business depressed us for months. Of course, there were the usual sordid rumours – that Ham's wife had been putting its horn to ignoble use – and the usual posthumous smear campaign by the authorities about the beast's character; but this only sickened us the more. The unavoidable fact is that Noah was jealous. We all looked up to the unicorn, and he couldn't stand it. Noah – what point is there in not telling you the truth? – was bad-tempered, smelly, unreliable, envious and cowardly. He wasn't even a good sailor: when the seas were high he would retire to his cabin, throw himself down on his gopher-wood bed and leave it only to vomit out his stomach into his gopher-wood wash-basin; you could smell the effluvia a deck away. Whereas the unicorn was strong, honest, fearless, impeccably groomed, and a mariner who never knew a moment's queasiness. Once, in a gale, Ham's wife lost her footing near the rail and was about to go overboard. The unicorn – who had deck privileges as a result of popular lobbying – galloped across and stuck his horn through her trailing cloak, pinning it to the deck. Fine thanks he got for his valour; the Noahs had him casseroled one Embarkation Sunday. I can vouch for that. I spoke personally to the carrier-hawk who delivered a warm pot to Shem's ark.

You don't have to believe me, of course; but what do your own archives say? Take the story of Noah's nakedness – you remember? It happened after the Landing. Noah, not surprisingly, was even more pleased with himself than before – he'd saved the human race, he'd ensured the success of his dynasty, he'd been given a formal covenant by God – and he decided to take things easy in the last three hundred and fifty years of his life. He founded a village (which you call Arghuri) on the lower slopes of the mountain, and spent his days dreaming up new decorations and honours for himself: Holy Knight of the Tempest, Grand Commander of the Squalls, and so on. Your sacred text informs you that on his estate he planted a vineyard. Ha! Even the least subtle mind can decode that particular euphemism: he was drunk all the time. One night, after a particularly hard session, he'd just finished undressing when he collapsed on the bedroom floor – not an unusual occurrence. Ham and his brothers happened to be passing his 'tent' (they still used the old sentimental desert word to describe their palaces) and called in to check that their alcoholic father hadn't done himself any harm. Ham went into the bedroom and . . . well, a naked man of six hundred and fifty odd years lying in a drunken stupor is not a pretty sight. Ham did the decent, the filial thing: he got his brothers to cover their father up. As a sign of respect – though even at that time the custom was passing out of use – Shem and the one beginning with J entered their father's chamber backwards, and managed to get him into bed without letting their gaze fall on those organs of generation which mysteriously incite your species to shame. A pious and honourable deed all round, you might think. And how did Noah react when he awoke with one of those knifing new-wine hangovers? He cursed the son who had found him and decreed that all Ham's children should become servants to the family of the two brothers who had entered his room arse-first.

Where is the sense in that? I can guess your explanation: his sense of judgment was affected by drink, and we should offer pity not censure. Well, maybe. But I would just mention this: *we* knew him on the Ark.

He was a large man, Noah – about the size of a gorilla, although there the resemblance ends. The flotilla's captain – he promoted himself to Admiral halfway through the Voyage – was an ugly old thing, both graceless in movement and indifferent to personal hygiene. He didn't even have the skill to grow his own hair except around his face; for the rest of his covering he relied on the skins of other species. Put him side by side with the gorilla and you will easily discern the superior creation: the one with graceful movement, superior strength and an instinct for delousing. On the Ark we puzzled ceaselessly at the riddle of how God came to choose man as His protégé ahead of the more obvious candidates. He would have found most other species a lot more loyal. If He'd plumped for the gorilla, I doubt there'd have been half so much disobedience – probably no need to have had the Flood in the first place.

And the smell of the fellow . . . Wet fur growing on a species which takes pride in grooming is one thing; but a dank, salt-encrusted pelt hanging ungroomed from the neck of a negligent species to whom it doesn't belong is quite another matter. Even when the calmer times came, old Noah didn't seem to dry out (I am reporting what the birds said, and the birds could be trusted). He carried the damp and the storm around with him like some guilty memory or the promise of more bad weather.

There were other dangers on the Voyage apart from that of being turned into lunch. Take our species, for instance. Once we'd boarded and were tucked away, we felt pretty smug. This was, you understand, long before the days of the fine syringe filled with a solution of carbolic acid in alcohol, before creosote and metallic naphthenates and pentachlorphenol and benzene and para-dichlor-benzene and ortho-di-chloro-benzene. We happily did not run into the family Cleridae or the mite Pediculoides or parasitic wasps of the family Braconidae. But even so we had an enemy, and a patient one: time. What if time exacted from us our inevitable changes?

It came as a serious warning the day we realized that time and nature were happening to our cousin *xestobium rufo-villosum*. That set off quite a panic. It was late in the Voyage, during calmer times, when we were just sitting out the days and waiting for God's pleasure. In the middle of the night, with the Ark becalmed and silence everywhere – a silence so rare and thick that all the beasts stopped to listen, thereby deepening it still further – we heard to our astonishment the ticking of *xestobium rufo-villosum*. Four or five sharp clicks, then a pause, then a distant reply. We the humble, the discreet, the disregarded yet sensible *anobium domesticum* could not believe our ears. That egg becomes larva, larva chrysalis, and chrysalis imago is the inflexible law of our world: pupation brings with it no rebuke. But that our cousins, transformed into adulthood, should choose this moment, this moment of all, to advertise their amatory intentions, was almost beyond belief. Here we were, perilously at sea, final extinction a daily possibility, and all *xestobium rufo-villosum* could think about was sex. It must have been a neurotic response to fear of extinction or something. But even so . . .

One of Noah's sons came to check up on the noise as our stupid cousins, hopelessly in thrall to erotic publicity, struck their jaws against the wall of their burrows. Fortunately, the offspring of 'the Admiral' had only a crude understanding of the animal kingdom with which they had been entrusted, and he took the patterned clicks to be a creaking of the ship's timbers. Soon the wind rose again and *xestobium rufo-villosum* could make its trysts in safety. But the affair left the rest of us much more cautious. *Anobium domesticum*, by seven votes to none, resolved not to pupate until after Disembarkation.

It has to be said that Noah, rain or shine, wasn't much of a sailor. He was picked for his piety rather than his navigational skills. He wasn't any good in a storm, and he wasn't much better when the seas were calm. How would I be any judge? Again, I am reporting what the birds said – the birds that can stay in the air for weeks at a time, the birds that can find their way from one end of the planet to the other by navigational systems as elaborate as any invented by your species. And the *birds* said Noah didn't know what he was doing – he was all bluster and prayer. It wasn't difficult, what he had to do, was it? During the tempest he had to survive by running from the fiercest part of the storm; and during calm weather he had to ensure we didn't drift so far from our original map-reference that we came to rest in some un-inhabitable Sahara. The best that can be said for Noah is that he survived the storm (though he hardly needed to worry about reefs and coastlines, which made things easier), and that when the waters finally subsided we didn't find ourselves by mistake in the middle of some great ocean. If we'd done that, there's no knowing how long we'd have been at sea.

Of course, the birds offered to put their expertise at Noah's disposal; but he was too proud. He gave them a few simple reconnaissance tasks – looking out for whirlpools and tornadoes – while disdaining their proper skills. He also sent a number of species to their deaths by asking them to go aloft in terrible weather when they weren't properly equipped to do so. When Noah despatched the warbling goose into a Force Nine gale (the bird did, it's true, have an irritating cry, especially if you were trying to sleep), the stormy petrel actually volunteered to take its place. But the offer was spurned – and that was the end of the warbling goose.

All right, all right, Noah had his virtues. He was a survivor – and not just in terms of the Voyage. He also cracked the secret of long life, which has subsequently been lost to your species. But he was not a nice man. Did you know about the time he had the ass keel-hauled? Is that in your archives? It was in Year Two, when the rules had been just a little relaxed, and selected travellers were allowed to mingle. Well, Noah caught the ass trying to climb up the mare. He really hit the roof, ranted away about no good coming of such a union – which rather confirmed our theory about his horror of cross-breeding – and said he would make an example of the beast. So they tied his hooves together, slung him over the side, dragged him underneath the hull and up the other side in a stampeding sea. Most of us put it down to sexual jealousy, simple as that. What was amazing, though, was how the ass took it. They know all about endurance, those guys. When they pulled him over the rail, he was in a terrible state. His poor old ears looked like fronds of slimy seaweed and his tail like a yard of sodden rope and a few of the other beasts who by this time weren't too crazy about Noah gathered round him, and the goat I think it was butted him gently in the side to see if he was still alive, and the ass opened one eye, rolled it around the circle of concerned muzzles, and said, 'Now I know what it's like to be a seal.' Not bad in the circumstances? But I have to tell you, that was nearly one more species you lost.

I suppose it wasn't altogether Noah's fault. I mean, that God of his was a really oppressive role-model. Noah couldn't do anything without first wondering what *He* would think. Now that's no way to go on. Always looking over your shoulder for approval – it's not adult, is it? And Noah didn't have the excuse of being a young man, either. He was six hundred-odd, by the way your species reckons these things. Six hundred years should have produced some flexibility of mind, some ability to see both sides of the question. Not a bit of it. Take the construction of the Ark. What does he do? He builds it in gopher-wood. *Gopher*-wood? Even Shem objected, but no; that was what he wanted and that was what he had to have. The fact that not much gopher-wood grew nearby was brushed aside. No doubt he was merely following instructions from his role-model; but even so. Anyone who knows anything about wood – and *I* speak with some authority in the matter – could have told him that a couple of dozen other tree-types would have done as well, if not better; and what's more, the idea of building all parts of a boat from a single wood is ridiculous. You should choose your material according to the purpose for which it is intended; everyone knows that. Still, this was old Noah for you – no flexibility of mind at all. Only saw one side of the question. Gopher-wood bathroom fittings – have you ever heard of anything more ridiculous?

He got it, as I say, from his role-model. What would God think? That was the question always on his lips. There was something a bit sinister about Noah's devotion to God; creepy, if you know what I mean. Still, he certainly knew which side his bread was buttered; and I suppose being selected like that as the favoured survivor, knowing that your dynasty is going to be the only one on earth – it must turn your head, mustn't it? As for his sons – Ham, Shem, and the one beginning with J – it certainly didn't do much good for their egos. Swanking about on deck like the Royal Family.

You see, there's one thing I want to make quite clear. This Ark business. You're probably still thinking that Noah, for all his faults, was basically some kind of early conservationist, that he collected the animals together because he didn't want them to die out, that he couldn't endure not seeing a giraffe ever again, that he was doing it for *us*. This wasn't the case at all. He got us together because his role-model told him to, but also out of self-interest, even cynicism. *He wanted to have something to eat after the Flood had subsided.* Five and a half years under water and most of the kitchen gardens were washed away, I can tell you; only rice prospered. And so most of us knew that in Noah's eyes we were just future dinners on two, four or however many legs. If not now, then later; if not us, then our offspring. That's not a nice feeling, as you can imagine. An atmosphere of paranoia and terror held sway on that Ark of Noah's. Which of us would he come for next? Fail to charm Ham's wife today and you might be a fricassee by tomorrow night. That sort of uncertainty can provoke the oddest behaviour. I remember when a couple of lemmings were caught making for the side of the ship – they said they wanted to end it once and for all, they couldn't bear the suspense. But Shem caught them just in time and locked them up in a packing-case. Every so often, when he was feeling bored, he would slide open the top of their box and wave a big knife around inside. It was his idea of a joke. But if it didn't traumatize the entire species I'd be very surprised.

And of course once the Voyage was over, God made Noah's dining rights official. The pay-off for all that obedience was the permission to eat whichever of us Noah chose for the rest of his life. It was all part of some pact or covenant botched together between the pair of them. A pretty hollow contract, if you ask me. After all, having eliminated everyone else from the earth, God had to make do with the one family of worshippers he'd got left, didn't he? Couldn't very well say, No you aren't up to scratch either. Noah probably realized he had God over a barrel (what an admission of failure to pull the Flood and then be obliged to ditch your First Family), and we reckoned he'd have eaten us anyway, treaty or no treaty. This so-called covenant had absolutely nothing in it for us – except our death-warrant. Oh yes, we were thrown one tiny sop – Noah and his crowd weren't permitted to eat any females that were in calf. A loophole which led to some frenzied activity around the beached Ark, and also to some strange psychological side-effects. Have you ever thought about the origins of the hysterical pregnancy?

Which reminds me of that business with Ham's wife. It was all rumour, they said, and you can see how such rumours might have started. Ham's wife was not the most popular person in the Ark; and the loss of the hospital ship, as I've said, was widely attributed to her. She was still very attractive – only about a hundred and fifty at the time of the Deluge – but she was also wilful and short-tempered. She certainly dominated poor Ham. Now the facts are as follows. Ham and his wife had two children – two male children, that is, which was the way they counted – called Cush and Mizraim. They had a third son, Phut, who was born on the Ark, and a fourth, Canaan, who arrived after the Landing. Noah and his wife had dark hair and brown eyes; so did Ham and his wife; so, for that matter, did Shem and Varadi and the one beginning with J. And all the children of Shem and Varadi and the one whose name began with J had dark hair and brown eyes. And so did Cush, and Mizraim, and Canaan. But Phut, the one born on the Ark, had red hair. Red hair and green eyes. Those are the facts.

At this point we leave the harbour of facts for the high seas of rumour (that's how Noah used to talk, by the way). I was not myself on Ham's ark, so I am merely reporting, in a dispassionate way, the news the birds brought. There were two main stories, and I leave you to choose between them. You remember the case of the craftsman who chipped out a priest's hole for himself on the stores ship? Well, it was said – though not officially confirmed – that when they searched the quarters of Ham's wife they discovered a compartment nobody had realized was there. It certainly wasn't marked on the plans. Ham's wife denied all knowledge of it, yet it seems one of her yakskin undervests was found hanging on a peg there, and a jealous examination of the floor revealed several red hairs caught between the planking.

The second story – which again I pass on without comment – touches on more delicate matters, but since it directly concerns a significant percentage of your species I am constrained to go on. There was on board Ham's ark a pair of simians of the most extraordinary beauty and sleekness. They were, by all accounts, highly intelligent, perfectly groomed, and had mobile faces which you could swear were about to utter speech. They also had flowing red fur and green eyes. No, such a species no longer exists: it did not survive the Voyage, and the circumstances surrounding its death on board have never been fully cleared up. Something to do with a falling spar . . . But what a coincidence, we always thought, for a falling spar to kill both members of a particularly nimble species at one and the same time.

The public explanation was quite different, of course. There were no secret compartments. There was no miscegenation. The spar which killed the simians was enormous, and also carried away a purple muskrat, two pygmy ostriches and a pair of flat-tailed aardvarks. The strange colouring of Phut was a sign from God – though what it denoted lay beyond human decipherability at the time. Later its significance became clear: it was a sign that the Voyage had passed its half-way mark. Therefore Phut was a blessed child, and no subject for alarm and punishment. Noah himself announced as much. God had come to him in a dream and told him to stay his hand against the infant, and Noah, being a righteous man as he pointed out, did so.

I don't need to tell you that the animals were pretty divided about what to believe. The mammals, for instance, refused to countenance the idea that the male of the red-haired, green-eyed simians could have been carnally familiar with Ham's wife. To be sure, we never know what is in the secret heart of even our closest friends, but the mammals were prepared to swear on their mammalhood that it would never have happened. They knew the male simian too well, they said, and could vouch for his high standards of personal cleanliness. He was even, they hinted, a bit of a snob. And supposing – just supposing – he had wanted a bit of rough trade, there were far more alluring specimens on offer than Ham's wife. Why not one of those cute little yellow-tailed monkeys who were anybody's for a pawful of mashed nutmeg?

That is nearly the end of my revelations. They are intended – you must understand me – in a spirit of friendship. If you think I am being contentious, it is probably because your species – I hope you don't mind my saying this – is so hopelessly dogmatic. You believe what you want to believe, and you go on believing it. But then, of course, you all have Noah's genes. No doubt this also accounts for the fact that you are often strangely incurious. You never ask, for instance, this question about your early history: what happened to the raven?

When the Ark landed on the mountaintop (it was more complicated than that, of course, but we'll let details pass), Noah sent out a raven and a dove to see if the waters had retreated from the face of the earth. Now, in the version that has come down to you, the raven has a very small part; it merely flutters hither and thither, to little avail, you are led to conclude. The dove's three journeys, on the other hand, are made a matter of heroism. We weep when she finds no rest for the sole of her foot; we rejoice when she returns to the Ark with an olive leaf. You have elevated this bird, I understand, into something of symbolic value. So let me just point this out: the raven always maintained

that *he* found the olive tree; that *he* brought a leaf from it back to
the Ark; but that Noah decided it was 'more appropriate' to say
that the dove had discovered it. Personally, I always believed the
raven, who apart from anything else was much stronger in the air
than the dove; and it would have been just like Noah (modelling
himself on that God of his again) to stir up a dispute among the
animals. Noah had it put about that the raven, instead of returning as soon as possible with evidence of dry land, had been
malingering, and had been spotted (by whose eye? not even the
upwardly mobile dove would have demeaned herself with such
a slander) gourmandising on carrion. The raven, I need hardly
add, felt hurt and betrayed at this instant rewriting of history, and
it is said – by those with a better ear than mine – that you can
hear the sad croak of dissatisfaction in his voice to this day. The
dove, by contrast, began sounding unbearably smug from the
moment we disembarked. She could already envisage herself on
postage stamps and letterheads.

Before the ramps were lowered, 'the Admiral' addressed the
beasts on his Ark, and his words were relayed to those of us on
other ships. He thanked us for our co-operation, he apologized
for the occasional sparseness of rations, and he promised that
since we had all kept our side of the bargain, he was going to get
the best *quid pro quo* out of God in the forthcoming negotiations.
Some of us laughed a little doubtingly at that: we remembered
the keel-hauling of the ass, the loss of the hospital ship, the
exterminatory policy with cross-breeds, the death of the unicorn
. . . It was evident to us that if Noah was coming on all Mister
Nice Guy, it was because he sensed what any clear-thinking
animal would do the moment it placed its foot on dry land: make
for the forests and the hills. He was obviously trying to soft-soap
us into staying close to New Noah's Palace, whose construction
he chose to announce at the same time. Amenities here would
include free water for the animals and extra feed during harsh
winters. He was obviously scared that the meat diet he'd got
used to on the Ark would be taken away from him as fast as its
two, four or however many legs could carry it, and that the Noah
family would be back on berries and nuts once again. Amaz-
ingly, some of the beasts thought Noah's offer a fair one: after
all, they argued, he can't eat all of us, he'll probably just cull the
old and the sick. So some of them – not the cleverest ones, it has
to be said – stayed around waiting for the Palace to be built and

the water to flow like wine. The pigs, the cattle, the sheep, some of the stupider goats, the chickens ... We warned them, or at least we tried. We used to mutter derisively, 'Braised or boiled?' but to no avail. As I say, they weren't very bright, and were probably scared of going back into the wild; they'd grown dependent on their gaol, and their gaoler. What happened over the next few generations was quite predictable: they became shadows of their former selves. The pigs and sheep you see walking around today are zombies compared to their effervescent ancestors on the Ark. They've had the stuffing knocked out of them. And some of them, like the turkey, have to endure the further indignity of having the stuffing put back into them – before they are braised or boiled.

And of course, what did Noah actually deliver in his famous Disembarkation Treaty with God? What did he get in return for the sacrifices and loyalty of his tribe (let alone the more considerable sacrifices of the animal kingdom)? God said – and this is Noah putting the best possible interpretation on the matter – that He promised not to send another Flood, and that as a sign of His intention He was creating for us the rainbow. The rainbow! Ha! It's a very pretty thing, to be sure, and the first one he produced for us, an iridescent semi-circle with a paler sibling beside it, the pair of them glittering in an indigo sky, certainly made a lot of us look up from our grazing. You could see the idea behind it: as the rain gave reluctant way to the sun, this flamboyant symbol would remind us each time that the rain wasn't going to carry on and turn into a Flood. But even so. It wasn't much of a deal. And was it legally enforceable? Try getting a rainbow to stand up in court.

The cannier animals saw Noah's offer of half-board for what it was; they took to the hills and the woods, relying on their own skills for water and winter feed. The reindeer, we couldn't help noticing, were among the first to take off, speeding away from 'the Admiral' and all his future descendants, bearing with them their mysterious forebodings. You are right, by the way, to see the animals that fled – ungrateful traitors, according to Noah – as the nobler species. Can a pig be noble? A sheep? A chicken? If only you had seen the unicorn ... That was another contentious aspect of Noah's post-Disembarkation address to those still loitering at the edge of his stockade. He said that God, by giving us the rainbow, was in effect promising to keep the world's supply of miracles topped up. A clear reference, if ever I heard one, to the scores of original miracles which in the course of the Voyage had been slung over the side of Noah's ships or had disappeared into the guts of his family. The rainbow in place of the unicorn? Why didn't God just restore the unicorn? We animals would have been happier with that, instead of a big hint in the sky about God's magnanimity every time it stopped raining.

Getting off the Ark, I think I told you, wasn't much easier than getting on. There had, alas, been a certain amount of ratting by some of the chosen species, so there was no question of Noah simply flinging down the ramps and crying 'Happy land'. Every animal had to put up with a strict body-search before being released; some were even doused in tubs of water which smelt of tar. Several female beasts complained of having to undergo internal examination by Shem. Quite a few stowaways were discovered: some of the more conspicuous beetles, a few rats who had unwisely gorged themselves during the Voyage and got too fat, even a snake or two. We got off – I don't suppose it need be a secret any longer – in the hollowed tip of a ram's horn. It was a big, surly, subversive animal, whose friendship we had deliberately cultivated for the last three years at sea. It had no respect for Noah, and was only too happy to help outsmart him after the Landing.

When the seven of us climbed out of that ram's horn, we were euphoric. We had survived. We had stowed away, survived and escaped – all without entering into any fishy covenants with either God or Noah. We had done it by ourselves. We felt ennobled as a species. That might strike you as comic, but we did: we felt ennobled. That Voyage taught us a lot of things, you see, and the main thing was this: that man is a very unevolved species compared to the animals. We don't deny, of course, your cleverness, your considerable potential. But you are, as yet, at an early stage of your development. We, for instance, are always ourselves: that is what it means to be evolved. We are what we are, and we know what that is. You don't expect a cat suddenly to start barking, do you, or a pig to start lowing? But this is what, in a manner of speaking, those of us who made the Voyage on the Ark learned to expect from your species. One moment you bark, one moment you mew; one moment you wish to be wild, one moment you wish to be tame. You knew where you were with Noah only in this one respect: that you never knew where you were with him.

You aren't too good with the truth, either, your species. You keep forgetting things, or you pretend to. The loss of Varadi and his ark – does anyone speak of that? I can see there might be a positive side to this wilful averting of the eye: ignoring the bad things makes it easier for you to carry on. But ignoring the bad things makes you end up believing that bad things never happen. You are always surprised by them. It surprises you that guns kill, that money corrupts, that snow falls in winter. Such naïvety can be charming; alas, it can also be perilous.

For instance, you won't even admit the true nature of Noah, your first father – the pious patriarch, the committed conservationist. I gather that one of your early Hebrew legends asserts that Noah discovered the principle of intoxication by watching a goat get drunk on fermented grapes. What a brazen attempt to shift responsibility on to the animals; and all, sadly, part of a pattern. The Fall was the serpent's fault, the honest raven was a slacker and a glutton, the goat turned Noah into an alkie. Listen: you can take it from me that Noah didn't need any cloven-footed knowledge to help crack the secret of the vine.

Blame someone else, that's always your first instinct. And if you can't blame someone else, then start claiming the problem isn't a problem anyway. Rewrite the rules, shift the goalposts. Some of those scholars who devote their lives to your sacred texts have even tried to prove that the Noah of the Ark wasn't the same man as the Noah arraigned for drunkenness and indecent exposure. How could a drunkard possibly be chosen by God? Ah, well, he wasn't, you see. Not *that* Noah. Simple case of mistaken identity. Problem disappears.

How could a drunkard possibly be chosen by God? I've told you – because all the other candidates were a damn sight worse. Noah was the pick of a very bad bunch. As for his drinking: to tell you the truth, it was the Voyage that tipped him over the edge. Old Noah had always enjoyed a few horns of fermented liquor in the days before Embarkation: who didn't? But it was the Voyage that turned him into a soak. He just couldn't handle the responsibility. He made some bad navigational decisions, he lost four of his eight ships and about a third of the species entrusted to him – he'd have been court-martialled if there'd been anyone around to sit on the bench. And for all his bluster, he felt guilty about losing half the Ark. Guilt, immaturity, the constant struggle to hold down a job beyond your capabilities –

it makes a powerful combination, one which would have had the same ruinous effect on most members of your species. You could even argue, I suppose, that God drove Noah to drink. Perhaps this is why your scholars are so jumpy, so keen to separate the first Noah from the second: the consequences are awkward. But the story of the 'second' Noah – the drunkenness, the indecency, the capricious punishment of a dutiful son – well, it didn't come as a surprise to those of us who knew the 'first' Noah on the Ark. A depressing yet predictable case of alcoholic degeneration, I'm afraid.

As I was saying, we were euphoric when we got off the Ark. Apart from anything else, we'd eaten enough gopher-wood to last a lifetime. That's another reason for wishing Noah had been less bigoted in his design of the fleet: it would have given some of us a change of diet. Hardly a consideration for Noah, of course, because we weren't meant to be there. And with the hindsight of a few millennia, this exclusion seems even harsher than it did at the time. There were seven of us stowaways, but had we been admitted as a seaworthy species only two boarding-passes would have been issued; and we would have accepted that decision. Now, it's true Noah couldn't have predicted how long his Voyage was going to last, but considering how little we seven ate in five and a half years, it surely would have been worth the risk letting just a pair of us on board. And after all, it's not our fault for being woodworm.

2
THE VISITORS

FRANKLIN HUGHES HAD come on board an hour earlier to extend some necessary bonhomie towards those who would make his job easier over the next twenty days. Now, he leaned on the rail and watched the passengers climb the gangway: middle-aged and elderly couples for the most part, some bearing an obvious stamp of nationality, others, more decorous, preserving for the moment a sly anonymity of origin. Franklin, his arm lightly but unarguably around the shoulder of his travelling companion, played his annual game of guessing where his audience came from. Americans were the easiest, the men in New World leisure-wear of pastel hues, the women unconcerned by throbbing paunches. The British were the next easiest, the men in Old World tweed jackets hiding short-sleeved shirts of ochre or beige, the women sturdy-kneed and keen to tramp any mountain at the sniff of a Greek temple. There were two Canadian couples whose towelling hats bore a prominent maple-leaf emblem; a rangy Swedish family with four heads of blond hair; some confusable French and Italians whom Franklin identified with a simple mutter of *baguette* or *macaroni*; and six Japanese who declined their stereotype by not displaying a single camera between them. With the exception of a few family groups and the occasional lone aesthetic-looking Englishman, they came up the gangway in obedient couples.

'The animals came in two by two,' Franklin commented. He was a tall, fleshy man somewhere in his forties, with pale gold hair and a reddish complexion which the envious put down to drink and the charitable to an excess of sun; his face seemed familiar in a way which made you forget to ask whether or not you judged it good-looking. His companion, or assistant, but not, she would insist, secretary, was a slim, dark girl displaying clothes newly bought for the cruise. Franklin, ostentatiously an old hand, wore a khaki bush-shirt and a pair of rumpled jeans. While it was not quite the uniform some of the passengers expected of a distinguished guest lecturer, it accurately suggested the origin of such distinction as Franklin could command. If he'd been an American academic he might have dug out a seersucker suit; if a British academic, perhaps a creased linen jacket the colour of ice-cream. But Franklin's fame (which was not quite as extensive as he thought it) came from television. He had started as a mouthpiece for other people's views, a young man in a corduroy suit with an affable and unthreatening way of explaining culture. After a while he realized that if he could speak this stuff there was no reason why he shouldn't write it as well. At first it was no more than 'additional material by Franklin Hughes', then a co-script credit, and finally the achievement of a full 'written and presented by Franklin Hughes'. What his special area of knowledge was nobody could quite discern, but he roved freely in the worlds of archaeology, history and comparative culture. He specialized in the contemporary allusion which would rescue and enliven for the average viewer such dead subjects as Hannibal's crossing of the Alps, or Viking treasure hoards in East Anglia, or Herod's palaces. 'Hannibal's elephants were the panzer divisions of their age,' he would declare as he passionately straddled a foreign landscape; or, 'That's as many foot-soldiers as could be fitted into Wembley Stadium on Cup Final Day'; or, 'Herod wasn't just a tyrant and a unifier of his country, he was also a patron of the arts – perhaps we should think of him as a sort of Mussolini with good taste.'

Franklin's television fame soon brought him a second wife, and a couple of years later a second divorce. Nowadays, his contracts with Aphrodite Cultural Tours always included the provision of a cabin for his assistant; the crew of the *Santa Euphemia* noted with admiration that the assistants tended not to last from one voyage to the next. Franklin was generous towards the stewards, and popular with those who had paid a couple of thousand pounds for their twenty days. He had the engaging habit of sometimes pursuing a favourite digression so fervently that he would have to stop and look around with a puzzled smile before reminding himself where he was meant to be. Many of the passengers commented to one another on Franklin's obvious enthusiasm for his subject, how refreshing it was in these cynical times, and how he really made history come alive for them. If his bush-shirt was often carelessly buttoned and his denim trousers occasionally stained with lobster, this was no more than corroboration of his beguiling zeal for the job. His clothes hinted, too, at the admirable democracy of learning in the modern age: you evidently did not have to be a stuffy professor in a wing-collar to understand the principles of Greek architecture.

'The Welcome Buffet's at eight,' said Franklin. 'Think I'd better put in a couple of hours on my spiel for tomorrow morning.'

'Surely you've done that lots of times before?' Tricia was half-hoping he would stay on deck with her as they sailed out into the Gulf of Venice.

'Got to make it different each year. Otherwise you go stale.' He touched her lightly on the forearm and went below. In fact, his opening address at ten the next morning would be exactly the same as for the previous five years. The only difference – the only thing designed to prevent Franklin from going stale – was the presence of Tricia instead of . . . of, what was that last girl's name? But he liked to maintain the fiction of working on his lectures beforehand, and he could easily pass up the chance of seeing Venice recede yet again. It would still be there the following year, a centimetre or two nearer the waterline, its pinky complexion, like his own, flaking a little more.

On deck, Tricia gazed at the city until the campanile of San Marco became a pencil-stub. She had first met Franklin three months ago, when he'd appeared on the chat-show for which she was a junior researcher. They'd been to bed a few times, but not much so far. She had told the girls at the flat she was going away with a schoolfriend; if things went well, she'd let on when she got back, but for the moment she was a little superstitious. Franklin Hughes! And he'd been really considerate so far, even allotting her some nominal duties so that she wouldn't look too much like just a girlfriend. So many people in television struck her as a bit fake – charming, yet not altogether honest. Franklin was just the same offscreen as on: outgoing, jokey, eager to tell you things. You believed what he said. Television critics made fun of his clothes and the tuft of chest-hair where his shirt parted, and sometimes they sneered at what he said, but that was just envy, and she'd like to see some of those critics get up and try to perform like Franklin. Making it look easy, he had explained to her at their first lunch, was the hardest thing of all. The other secret about television, he said, was how to know when to shut up and let the pictures do the work for you – 'You've got to get that fine balance between word and image.' Privately, Franklin was hoping for the ultimate credit: 'Written, narrated and produced by Franklin Hughes'. In his dreams he sometimes choreographed for himself a gigantic walking shot in the Forum which would take him from the Arch of Septimus Severus to the Temple of Vesta. Where to put the camera was the only problem.

The first leg of the trip, as they steamed down the Adriatic, went much as usual. There was the Welcome Buffet, with the crew sizing up the passengers and the passengers warily circling one another; Franklin's opening lecture, in which he flattered his audience, deprecated his television fame and announced that it was a refreshing change to be addressing real people instead of a glass eye and a cameraman shouting 'Hair in the gate, can we do it again, love?' (the technical reference would be lost on most of his listeners, which was intended by Franklin: they were allowed to be snobbish about TV, but not to assume it was idiots' business); and then there was Franklin's other opening lecture, one just as necessary to bring off, in which he explained to his assistant how the main thing they must remember was to have a good time. Sure he'd have to work – indeed, there'd be times when much as he didn't want to he'd be forced to shut himself away in his cabin with his notes – but mostly he felt they should treat it as two weeks holiday from the filthy English weather and all that backstabbing at Television Centre. Tricia nodded agreement, though as a junior researcher she had not yet witnessed, let alone endured, any backstabbing. A more worldly-wise girl would have readily understood Franklin to mean 'Don't expect anything more out of me than this'. Tricia, being placid and optimistic, glossed his little speech more mildly as 'Let's be careful of building up false expectations' – which to do him credit was roughly what Franklin Hughes intended. He fell lightly in love several times each year, a tendency in himself which he would occasionally deplore but regularly indulge. However, he was far from heartless, and the moment he felt a girl – especially a nice girl – needing him more than he needed her a terrible flush of apprehension would break out in him. This rustling panic would usually make him suggest one of two things – either that the girl move into his flat, or that she move out of his life – neither of which he exactly wanted. So his address of welcome to Jenny or Cathy or in this case Tricia came more from prudence than cynicism, though when things subsequently went awry it was unsurprising if Jenny or Cathy or in this case Tricia remembered him as more calculating than in fact he had been.

The same prudence, murmuring insistently at him across numerous gory news reports, had made Franklin Hughes acquire an Irish passport. The world was no longer a welcoming place where the old dark-blue British job, topped up with the words 'journalist' and 'BBC', got you what you wanted. 'Her Britannic Majesty's Secretary of State,' Franklin could quote from memory, 'Requests and requires in the Name of Her Majesty all those whom it may concern to allow the bearer such assistance and protection as may be necessary.' Wishful thinking. Nowadays Franklin travelled on a green Irish passport with a gold harp on the cover, which made him feel like a Guinness rep every time he produced it. Inside, the word 'journalist' was also missing from Hughes's largely honest self-description. There were countries in the world which didn't welcome journalists, and who thought that white-skinned ones pretending interest in archaeological sites were obviously British spies. The less compromising 'Writer' was also intended as a piece of self-encouragement. If Franklin described himself as a writer, then this might nudge him into becoming one. Next time round, there was a definite chance for a book-of-the-series; and beyond that he was toying with something serious but sexy – like a personal history of the world – which might roost for months in the bestseller lists.

The *Santa Euphemia* was an elderly but comfortable ship with a courtly Italian captain and an efficient Greek crew. These Aphrodite Tours brought a predictable clientèle, disparate in nationality but homogeneous in taste. The sort of people who preferred reading to deck quoits, and sun-bathing to the disco. They followed the guest lecturer everywhere, took most of the supplementary trips, and disdained straw donkeys in the souvenir shops. They had not come for romance, though a string trio occasionally incited some old-fashioned dancing. They took their turn at the captain's table, were inventive when it came to fancy-dress night, and dutifully read the ship's newspaper, which printed their daily route alongside birthday messages and non-controversial events happening on the European continent.

The atmosphere seemed a little torpid to Tricia, but it was a well-organized torpor. As in the address to his assistant, Franklin had emphasized in his opening lecture that the purpose of the next three weeks was pleasure and relaxation. He hinted tactfully that people had different levels of interest in classical antiquity, and that he for one wouldn't be keeping an attendance book and marking down absentees with a black X. Franklin engagingly admitted that there were occasions when even he could tire of yet another row of Corinthian columns standing against a cloudless sky; though he did this in a way which allowed the passengers to disbelieve him.

The tail end of the Northern winter had been left behind; and at a stately pace the *Santa Euphemia* took its contented passengers into a calm Mediterranean spring. Tweed jackets gave way to linen ones, trouser-suits to slightly outdated sun-dresses. They passed through the Corinth Canal at night, with some of the passengers jammed against a porthole in their nightclothes, and the hardier ones on deck, occasionally letting off ineffectual bursts of flash from their cameras. From the Ionian to the Aegean: it was a little fresher and choppier in the Cyclades, but nobody minded. They went ashore at chichi Mykonos, where an elderly headmaster twisted his ankle while climbing among the ruins; at marbled Paros and volcanic Thira. The cruise was ten days old when they stopped at Rhodes. While the passengers were ashore the *Santa Euphemia* took on fuel, vegetables, meat and more wine. It also took on some visitors, although this did not become apparent until the following morning.

They were steaming towards Crete, and at eleven o'clock Franklin began his usual lecture on Knossos and Minoan Civilization. He had to be a little careful, because his audience tended to know about Knossos, and some of them would have their personal theories. Franklin liked people asking questions; he didn't mind pieces of obscure and even correct information being added to what he had already imparted – he would offer thanks with a courtly bow and a murmur of 'Herr Professor', implying that as long as some of us have an overall grasp of things, it was fine for others to fill their heads with recondite detail; but what Franklin Hughes couldn't stand were bores with pet ideas they couldn't wait to try out on the guest lecturer. Excuse me, Mr Hughes, it looks very Egyptian to me – how do we know the Egyptians didn't build it? Aren't you assuming that Homer wrote when people think he (a little laugh) – or she – did? I don't have any actual expert knowledge, yet surely it would make more sense if . . . There was always at least one of them, playing the puzzled yet reasonable amateur; unfooled by received opinion, he – or she – knew that historians were full of bluff, and that complicated matters were best understood using zestful intuition untainted by any actual knowledge or research. 'I appreciate what you're saying, Mr Hughes, but surely it would be more logical ...' What Franklin occasionally wanted to say, though never did, was that these brisk guesses about earlier civilizations seemed to him to have their foundation as often as not in Hollywood epics starring Kirk Douglas or Burt Lancaster. He imagined himself hearing out one of these jokers and replying, with a skirl of irony on the adverb, 'Of course, you realize that the film of Ben Hur isn't *entirely* reliable?' But not this trip. In fact, not until he knew it was going to be his last trip. Then he could let go a little. He could be franker with his audience, less careful with the booze, more receptive to the flirting glance.

The visitors were late for Franklin Hughes's lecture on Knossos, and he had already done the bit in which he pretended to be Sir Arthur Evans when they opened the double doors and fired a single shot into the ceiling. Franklin, still headily involved in his own performance, murmured, 'Can I have a translation of that?' but it was an old joke, and not enough to recapture the passengers' attention. They had already forgotten Knossos and were watching the tall man with a moustache and glasses who was coming to take Franklin's place at the lectern. Under normal circumstances, Franklin might have yielded him the microphone after a courteous inquiry about his credentials. But given that the man was carrying a large machine-gun and wore one of those red check head-dresses which used to be shorthand for lovable desert warriors loyal to Lawrence of Arabia but in recent years had become shorthand for baying terrorists eager to massacre the innocent, Franklin simply made a vague 'Over to you' gesture with his hands and sat down on his chair.

Franklin's audience – as he still thought of them in a brief pro-prietorial flurry – fell silent. Everyone was avoiding an incautious movement; each breath was discreetly taken. There were three visitors, and the other two were guarding the double doors into the lecture room. The tall one with the glasses had an almost scholarly air as he tapped the microphone in the manner of lecturers everywhere: partly to see if it was working, partly to attract attention. The second half of this gesture was not strictly necessary.

'I apologize for the inconvenience,' he began, setting off a nervous laugh or two. 'But I am afraid it is necessary to interrupt your holiday for a while. I hope it will not be a long interruption. You will all stay here, sitting exactly where you are, until we tell you what to do.'

A voice, male, angry and American, asked from the middle of the auditorium, 'Who are you and what the hell do you want?' The Arab swayed back to the microphone he had just left, and with the contemptuous suavity of a diplomat, replied, 'I am sorry, I am not taking questions at this juncture.' Then, just to make sure he was not mistaken for a diplomat, he went on. 'We are not people who believe in unnecessary violence. However, when I fired the shot into the ceiling to attract your attention, I had set this little catch here so that the gun only fires one shot at a time. If I change the catch' – he did so while holding the weapon half-aloft like an arms instructor with an exceptionally ignorant class – 'the gun will continue to fire until the magazine is empty. I hope that is clear.'

The Arab left the hall. People held hands; there were occasional sniffs and sobs, but mostly silence. Franklin glanced across to the far left of the auditorium at Tricia. His assistants were allowed to come to his lectures, though not to sit in direct line of sight – 'Mustn't start me thinking about the wrong thing.' She didn't appear frightened, more apprehensive about what the form was. Franklin wanted to say, 'Look, this hasn't happened to me before, it isn't normal, I don't know what to do,' but settled instead for an indeterminate nod. After ten minutes of stiff-necked silence, an American woman in her mid-fifties stood up. Immediately one of the two visitors guarding the door shouted at her. She took no notice, just as she ignored the whispers and grabbing hand of her husband. She walked down the central aisle to the gunmen, stopped a couple of yards short, and said in a clear, slow voice suppurating with panic, 'I have to go to the goddam bathroom.'

The Arabs neither replied nor looked her in the eye. Instead, with a small gesture of their guns, they indicated as surely as such things can be that she was currently a large target and that any further advance would confirm the fact in an obvious and final way. She turned, walked back to her seat and began to cry. Another woman on the right of the hall immediately started sobbing. Franklin looked across at Tricia again, nodded, got to his feet, deliberately didn't look at the two guards, and went across to the lectern. 'As I was saying . . .' He gave an authoritative cough and all eyes reverted to him. 'I was saying that the Palace of Knossos was not by any means the first human settlement on the site. What we think of as the Minoan strata reach down to about seventeen feet, but below this there are signs of human habitation down to twenty-six feet or so. There was life where the palace was built for at least ten thousand years before the first stone was laid . . .'

It seemed normal to be lecturing again. It also felt as if some feathered cloak of leadership had been thrown over him. He decided to acknowledge this, glancingly at first. Did the guards understand English? Perhaps. Had they ever been to Knossos? Unlikely. So Franklin, while describing the council chamber at the palace, invented a large clay tablet which, he claimed, had probably hung over the gypsum throne. It read – he looked towards the Arabs at this point – 'We are living in difficult times'. As he continued describing the site, he unearthed more tablets, many of which, as he now fearlessly began to point out, had a universal message. 'We must above all not do anything rash', one said. Another: 'Empty threats are as useless as empty scabbards'. Another: 'The tiger always waits before it springs' (Hughes wondered briefly if Minoan Civilization knew about tigers). He was not sure how many of his audience had latched on to what he was doing, but there came an occasional assenting growl. In a curious way, he was also enjoying himself. He ended his tour of the palace with one of the least typically Minoan of his many inscriptions: 'There is a great power where the sun sets which will not permit certain things'. Then he shuffled his notes together and sat down to warmer applause than usual. He looked across at Tricia and winked. She had tears in her eyes. He glanced towards the two Arabs and thought, that's shown you, now you can see what we're made of, there's some stiff upper lip for you. He rather wished he'd made up some Minoan aphorism about people who wore red tea-towels on their heads, but recognized he wouldn't have had the nerve. He'd keep that one for later, after they were all safe.

They waited for half an hour in a silence that smelt of urine before the leader of the visitors returned. He had a brief word with the guards and walked up the aisle to the lectern. 'I understand that you have been lectured on the palace of Knossos,' he began, and Franklin felt sweat burst into the palms of his hands.

'That is good. It is important for you to understand other civilizations. How they are great, and how' – he paused meaningly –
'they fall. I hope very much that you will enjoy your trip to
Knossos.'

He was leaving the microphone when the same American
voice, this time more conciliatory in tone, as if heedful of the
Minoan tablets, said, 'Excuse me, would you be able to tell us
roughly who you are and roughly what you want?'

The Arab smiled. 'I am not sure that would be a good idea at
this stage.' He gave a nod to indicate he had finished, then
paused, as if a civil question at least deserved a civil answer. 'Let
me put it this way. If things go according to plan, you will soon
be able to continue your explorations of the Minoan Civilization. We shall disappear just as we came, and we shall seem to
you simply to have been a dream. Then you can forget us. You
will remember only that we were a small delay. So there is no
need for you to know who we are or where we come from or
what we want.'

He was about to leave the low podium when Franklin, rather
to his own surprise, said, 'Excuse me.' The Arab turned. 'No
more questions.' Hughes went on, 'This is not a question. I just
think … I'm sure you've got other things on your mind …
if we're going to have to stay here you ought to let us go to the
lavatory.' The leader of the visitors frowned. 'The bathroom,'
Franklin explained; then again, 'the toilet.'

'Of course. You will be able to go to the toilet when we
move you.'

'When will that be?' Franklin felt himself a little carried away
by his self-appointed role. For his part the Arab noted some
unacceptable lack of compliance. He replied brusquely, 'When
we decide.'

He left. Ten minutes later an Arab they had not seen before
came in and whispered to Hughes. He stood up. 'They are going
to move us from here to the dining-room. We are to be moved
in twos. Occupants of the same cabin are to identify themselves
as such. We will be taken to our cabins, where we will be allowed
to go to the lavatory. We are also to collect our passports, but
nothing else.' The Arab whispered again. 'And we are not allowed
to lock the lavatory door.' Without being asked, Franklin went
on, 'I think these visitors to the ship are quite serious. I don't think
we should do anything which might upset them.'

Only one guard was available to move the passengers, and the process took several hours. As Franklin and Tricia were being taken to C deck, he remarked to her, in the casual tone of one commenting on the weather, 'Take the ring off your right hand and put it on your wedding finger. Turn the stone round so that you can't see it. Don't do it now, do it when you're having a pee.'

When they reached the dining-room their passports were examined by a fifth Arab. Tricia was sent to the far end, where the British had been put in one corner and the Americans in another. In the middle of the room were the French, the Italians, two Spaniards and the Canadians. Nearest the door were the Japanese, the Swedes, and Franklin, the solitary Irishman. One of the last couples to be brought in were the Zimmermanns, a pair of stout, well-dressed Americans. Hughes had at first placed the husband in the garment business, some master cutter who had set up on his own; but a conversation on Paros had revealed him to be a recently retired professor of philosophy from the mid-West. As the couple passed Franklin's table on their way to the American quarter, Zimmermann muttered lightly, 'Separating the clean from the unclean.'

When they were all present, Franklin was taken off to the purser's office, where the leader was installed. He found himself wondering if the slightly bulbous nose and the moustache were by any chance attached to the glasses; perhaps they all came off together.

'Ah, Mr Hughes. You seem to be their spokesman. At any event, now your position is official. You will explain to them the following. We are doing our best to make them comfortable, but they must realize that there are certain difficulties. They will be allowed to talk to one another for five minutes at each hour. At the same time those who wish to go to the toilet will be allowed to do so. One person at a time. I can see that they are all sensible people and would not like them to decide not to be sensible. There is one man who says he cannot find his passport. He says he is called Talbot.'

'Mr Talbot, yes.' A vague, elderly Englishman who tended to ask questions about religion in the Ancient World. A mild fellow with no theories of his own, thank God.

'He is to sit with the Americans.'

'But he's British. He comes from Kidderminster.'

'If he remembers where his passport is and he is British he can sit with the British.'

'You can tell he's British. I can vouch for him being British.' The Arab looked unimpressed. 'He doesn't talk like an American, does he?'

'I have not talked to him. Still, talking is not proof, is it? You, I think, talk like a British but your passport says you are not a British.' Franklin nodded slowly. 'So we will wait for the passport.'

'Why are you separating us like this?'

'We think you will like to sit with one another.' The Arab made a sign for him to go.

'There's one other thing. My wife. Can she sit with me?'

'Your wife?' The man looked at a list of passengers in front of him. 'You have no wife.'

'Yes I do. She's travelling as Tricia Maitland. It's her maiden name. We were married three weeks ago.' Franklin paused, then added in a confessional tone, 'My third wife, actually.'

But the Arab seemed unimpressed by Franklin's harem. 'You were married three weeks ago? And yet it seems you do not share the same cabin. Are things going so badly?'

'No, I have a separate cabin for my work, you see. The lecturing. It's a luxury, having another cabin, a privilege.'

'She is your wife?' The tone gave nothing away.

'Yes she is,' he replied, mildly indignant.

'But she has a British passport.'

'She's Irish. You become Irish if you marry an Irishman. It's Irish law.'

'Mr Hughes, she has a British passport.' He shrugged as if the dilemma were insoluble, then found a solution. 'But if you wish to sit with your wife, then you may go and sit with her at the British table.'

Franklin smiled awkwardly. 'If I'm the passengers' spokesman, how do I get to see you to pass on the passengers' demands?'

'The passengers' demands? No, you have not understood. The passengers do not have demands. You do not see me unless I want to see you.'

After Franklin had relayed the new orders, he sat at his table by himself and thought about the position. The good part was that so far they had been treated with reasonable civility; no one had yet been beaten up or shot, and their captors didn't seem to be the hysterical butchers they might have expected. On the other hand, the bad part lay quite close to the good part: being unhysterical, the visitors might also prove reliable, efficient, hard to divert from their purpose. And what was their purpose? Why had they hijacked the *Santa Euphemia*? Who were they negotiating with? And who was steering the sodding ship, which as far as Franklin could tell was going round in large, slow circles?

From time to time, he would nod encouragingly to the Japanese at the next table. Passengers at the far end of the dining-room, he couldn't help noting, would occasionally look up in his direction, as if checking that he was still there. He'd become the liaison man, perhaps even the leader. That Knossos lecture, in the circumstances, had been little short of brilliant; a lot more ballsy than he'd imagined possible. It was the sitting alone like this that got him down; it made him brood. His initial burst of emotion – something close to exhilaration – was seeping away; in its place came lethargy and apprehension. Perhaps he should go and sit with Tricia and the Brits. But then they might take his citizenship away from him. This dividing-up of the passengers: did it mean what he feared it might mean?

Late that afternoon they heard a plane fly over, quite low. There was a muted cheer from the American section of the dining-room; then the plane went away. At six o'clock one of the Greek stewards appeared with a large tray of sandwiches; Franklin noted the effect of fear on hunger. At seven, as he went for a pee, an American voice whispered, 'Keep up the good work.' Back at his table, he tried to look soberly confident. The trouble was, the more he reflected, the less cheerful he felt. In recent years Western governments had been noisy about terror-ism, about standing tall and facing down the threat; but the threat never seemed to understand that it was being faced down, and continued much as before. Those in the middle got killed; governments and terrorists survived.

At nine Franklin was summoned again to the purser's office. The passengers were to be moved for the night: the Americans back to the lecture hall, the British to the disco, and so on. These separate encampments would then be locked. It was necessary: the visitors had to get their sleep as well. Passports were to be held ready for inspection at all times.

'What about Mr Talbot?'

'He has become an honourary American. Until he finds his passport.'

'What about my wife?'

'Miss Maitland. What about her?'

'Can she join me?'

'Ah. Your British wife.'

'She's Irish. You marry an Irishman you become Irish. It's the law.'

'The law, Mr Hughes. People are always telling *us* what is the law. I am often puzzled by what they consider is lawful and what is unlawful.' He looked away to a map of the Mediterranean on the wall behind Franklin. 'Is it lawful to drop bombs on refugee camps, for instance? I have often tried to discover the law which says this is permissible. But it is a long argument, and sometimes I think argument is pointless, just as the law is pointless.' He gave a dismissive shrug. 'As for the matter of Miss Maitland, let us hope that her nationality does not become, how shall I put it, relevant.'

Franklin tried to damp down a shudder. There were times when euphemism could be much more frightening than direct threat. 'Are you able to tell me when it might become…relevant?'

'They are stupid, you see. They are stupid because they think we are stupid. They lie in the most obvious way. They say they do not have the authority to act. They say arrangements cannot be made quickly. Of course they can. There is such a thing as the telephone. If they think they have learned something from previous incidents of this kind, they are stupid not to realize that we have too. We know about their tactics, the lying and the delays, all this establishing of some kind of relationship with the freedom fighters. We know all that. And we know about the limits of the body for taking action. So we are obliged by your governments to do what we say we will do. If they started negotiating at once, there would be no problem. But they only start when it is too late. It is on their heads.'

'No,' said Franklin. 'It's on our heads.'

'You, Mr Hughes, I think, do not have to worry so soon.'

'How soon is soon?'

'Indeed, I think you may not have to worry at all.'

'How soon is soon?'

The leader paused, then made a regretful gesture. 'Tomorrow

some time. The timetable, you see, is fixed. We have told them from the beginning.'

Part of Franklin Hughes could not believe he was having this conversation. Another part wanted to say he had always supported the cause of his captors – whatever that cause might be – and by the way the Gaelic on his passport meant that he was a member of the IRA, and for Christ's sake could he please go to his cabin and lie down and forget all about it. Instead, he repeated, 'Timetable?' The Arab nodded. Without thinking, Franklin said, 'One an hour?' Immediately, he wished he hadn't asked. For all he knew he was giving the fellow ideas.

The Arab shook his head. 'Two. A pair every hour. Unless you raise the stakes they do not take you seriously.'

'Christ. Just coming on board and killing people just like that. Just like that?'

'You think it would be better if we explained to them why we were killing them?' The tone was sarcastic.

'Well, yes, actually.'

'Do you think they would be sympathetic?' Now there was more mockery than sarcasm. Franklin was silent. He wondered when the killing was due to start. 'Goodnight, Mr Hughes,' said the leader of the visitors.

Franklin was put for the night in a stateroom with the Swedish family and the three Japanese couples. They were, he deduced, the safest group among the passengers. The Swedes because their nation was famously neutral; Franklin and the Japanese presumably because in recent times Ireland and Japan had produced terrorists. How ludicrous. The six Japanese who had come on a cultural cruise in Europe hadn't been asked whether they supported the various political killers in their own country; nor had Franklin been quizzed about the IRA. A Guinness passport awarded through some genealogical fluke suggested the possibility of sympathy with the visitors, and this was his protection. In fact, Franklin hated the IRA, just as he hated any political group which interfered, or might interfere, with the full-time job of being Franklin Hughes. For all he knew – and in accordance with his annual policy he had not asked – Tricia was far more sympathetic to the various worldwide groups of homicidal maniacs indirectly committed to interrupting the career of Franklin Hughes. Yet she was herded in with the diabolic British.

There was little talk in the stateroom that night. The Japanese kept to themselves; the Swedish family spent the time trying to distract their children by talking of home and Christmas and British football teams; while Franklin felt burdened by what he knew. He was scared and sickened; but isolation seemed to breed complicity with his captors. He tried thinking of his two wives and the daughter who must be – what? – fifteen now: he always had to remember the year of her birth and work it out from there. He should get down to see her more often. Perhaps he could take her with him when they filmed the next series. She could watch his famous walking shot in the Forum; she'd like that. Now where could he place the camera? Or perhaps a tracking shot. And some extras in toga and sandals – yes, he liked it . . .

Next morning Franklin was taken to the purser's office. The leader of the visitors waved him to sit down. 'I have decided to take your advice.'

'My advice?'

'The negotiations, I fear, are going badly. That is to say, there are no negotiations. We have explained our position but they are extremely unwilling to explain their position.'

'They?'

'They. So, unless things change very quickly, we shall be forced to put some pressure on them.'

'Pressure?' Even Franklin, who could not have made a career in television without skill in trading euphemisms, was enraged. 'You mean killing people.'

'That is the only pressure, sadly, which they understand.'

'What about trying other sorts?'

'But we have. We have tried sitting on our hands and waiting for world opinion to come to our help. We have tried being good and hoping that we would be rewarded by getting our land back. I can assure you that these systems do not work.'

'Why not try something in between?'

'An embargo on American goods, Mr Hughes? I do not think they would take us seriously. A lack of Chevrolets being imported to Beirut? No, regrettably there are people who only understand certain kinds of pressure. The world is only advanced . . .'

'. . . by killing people? A cheerful philosophy.'

'The world is not a cheerful place. I would have thought your investigations into the ancient civilizations would have taught you that. But anyway . . . I have decided to take your advice. We shall explain to the passengers what is happening. How they are mixed up in history. What that history is.'

'I'm sure they'll appreciate that.' Franklin felt queasy. 'Tell them what's going on.'

'Exactly. You see at four o'clock it will become necessary to ... to start killing them. Naturally we hope it will not be necessary. But if it is ... You are right, things must be explained to them if it is possible. Even a soldier knows why he is fighting. It is fair that the passengers be told as well.'

'But they're not fighting.' The Arab's tone, as much as what he said, riled Franklin. 'They're civilians. They're on holiday. They're not fighting.'

'There are no civilians any more,' replied the Arab. 'Your governments pretend, but that is not the case. Those nuclear weapons of yours, they are only to be let off against an army? The Zionists, at least, understand this. All their people are fighting. To kill a Zionist civilian is to kill a soldier.'

'Look, there aren't any Zionist civilians on the ship, for Christ's sake. They're people like poor old Mr Talbot who's lost his passport and has been turned into an American.'

'All the more reason why things must be explained.'

'I see,' said Franklin, and he let the sneer come through. 'So you're going to assemble the passengers and explain to them how they're all really Zionist soldiers and that's why you've got to kill them.'

'No, Mr Hughes, you misunderstand. I am not going to explain anything. They would not listen. No, Mr Hughes, *you* are going to explain things to them.'

'Me?' Franklin didn't feel nervous. Indeed, he felt decisive. 'Certainly not. You can do your own dirty work.'

'But Mr Hughes, you are a public speaker. I have heard you, if only for a short time. You do it so well. You could introduce a historical view of the matter. My second-in-command will give you all the information you require.'

'I don't require any information. Do your own dirty work.'

'Mr Hughes, I really cannot negotiate in two directions at the same time. It is nine-thirty. You have half an hour to decide. At ten you will say that you do the lecture. You will then have two hours, three hours if that is required, with my second-in-command for the briefing.' Franklin was shaking his head, but the Arab continued regardless. 'Then you have until three o'clock to prepare the lecture. I suggest that you make it last forty-five minutes. I shall listen to you, of course, with the greatest interest and attention. And at three forty-five, if I am satisfied with how you explain matters, we shall in return accept the Irish nationality of your recently married wife. That is all I have to say, you will send me your reply at ten o'clock.'

Back in the stateroom with the Swedes and the Japanese, Franklin remembered a TV series about psychology he'd once been asked to present. It had folded directly after the pilot, a loss nobody much regretted. One item in that show reported an experiment for measuring the point at which self-interest takes over from altruism. Put like this, it sounded almost respectable; but Franklin had been revolted by the actual test. The researchers had taken a female monkey who had recently given birth and put her in a special cage. The mother was still feeding and grooming her infant in a way presumably not too dissimilar from the maternal behaviour of the experimenters' wives. Then they turned a switch and began heating up the metal floor of the monkey's cage. At first she jumped around in discomfort, then squealed a lot, then took to standing on alternate legs, all the while holding her infant in her arms. The floor was made hotter, the monkey's pain more evident. At a certain point the heat from the floor became unbearable, and she was faced with a choice, as the experimenters put it, between altruism and self-interest. She either had to suffer extreme pain and perhaps death in order to protect her offspring, or else place her infant on the floor and stand on it to keep herself from harm. In every case, sooner or later self-interest had triumphed over altruism.

Franklin had been sickened by the experiment, and glad the TV series hadn't got beyond the pilot, if that was what he would have had to present. Now he felt a bit like that monkey. He was being asked to choose between two equally repellent ideas: that of abandoning his girlfriend while retaining his integrity, or rescuing his girlfriend by justifying to a group of innocent people why it was right that they should be killed. And would that rescue Trish? Franklin hadn't even been promised his own safety; perhaps the pair of them, reclassified as Irish, would merely be moved to the bottom of the killing list, but still remain on it. Who would they start with? The Americans, the British? If they started with the Americans, how long would that delay the killing of the British? Fourteen, sixteen Americans – he translated that brutally into seven or eight hours. If they started at four, and the governments stood firm, by midnight they would start killing the British. What order would they do it in? Men first? Random? Alphabetical? Trish's surname was Maitland. Right in the middle of the alphabet. Would she see the dawn?

He imagined himself standing on Tricia's body to protect his own burning feet and shuddered. He would have to do the lecture. That was the difference between a monkey and a human being. In the last analysis, humans were capable of altruism. This was why he was not a monkey. Of course, it was more than probable that when he gave the lecture his audience would conclude the exact opposite – that Franklin was operating out of self-interest, saving his own skin by a foul piece of subservience. But this was the thing about altruism, it was always liable to be misunderstood. And he could explain everything to them all afterwards. If there was an afterwards. If there was a them all.

When the second-in-command arrived, Franklin asked to see the leader again. He intended demanding safe-conduct for Tricia and himself in exchange for the lecture. However, the second-in-command had only come for a reply, not for renewed conversation. Dully, Franklin nodded his head. He'd never been much good at negotiating anyway.

At two forty-five Franklin was taken to his cabin and allowed to wash. At three o'clock he entered the lecture hall to find the most attentive audience he had ever faced. He filled a glass from the carafe of stale water that nobody had bothered to change. He sensed below him the swell of exhaustion, a rip-tide of panic. After only a day the men seemed almost bearded, the women crumpled. They had already begun not to look like themselves, or the selves that Franklin had spent ten days with. Perhaps this made them easier to kill.

Before he got his own writing credit Franklin had become expert at presenting the ideas of others as plausibly as possible. But never had he felt such apprehension at a script; never had a director imposed such conditions; never had his fee been so bizarre. When first agreeing to the task he had persuaded himself that he could surely find a way of tipping off his audience that he was acting under duress. He would think up some ploy like that of the false Minoan inscriptions; or he would make his lecture so exaggerated, pretend such enthusiasm for the cause thrust upon him, that nobody could possibly miss the irony.

No, that wouldn't work. 'Irony', an ancient TV producer had once confided to him, 'may be defined as what people miss.' And the passengers certainly wouldn't be on the lookout for it in their present circumstances. The briefing had made things yet harder: the second-in-command had given precise instructions, and added that any deviation from them would result not just in Miss Maitland remaining British, but in Franklin's Irish passport no longer being recognized. They certainly knew how to negotiate, these bastards.

'I had been hoping,' he began, 'that the next time I addressed you I would be taking up again the story of Knossos. Unfortunately, as you are aware, the circumstances have changed. We have visitors amongst us.' He paused and looked down the aisle at the leader who stood before the double doors with a guard on each side. 'Things are different. We are in the hands of others. Our . . . destiny is no longer our own.' Franklin coughed. This wasn't very good. Already he was straying into euphemism. The one duty, the one intellectual duty he had, was to speak as directly as he could. Franklin would freely admit he was a showman and would stand on his head in a bucket of herrings if that would raise viewing figures a few thousand; but there was a residual feeling in him – a mixture of admiration and shame – which made him hold in special regard those communicators who were deeply unlike him: the ones who spoke quietly, in their own simple words, and whose stillness gave them authority. Franklin, who knew he could never be like them, tried to acknowledge their example as he spoke.

'I have been asked to explain things to you. To explain how you – we – find ourselves in the position we are now in. I am not an expert on the politics of the Middle East, but I shall try to make things as clear as I can. We should perhaps begin by going back to the nineteenth century, long before the establishment of the state of Israel . . .' Franklin found himself back in an easy rhythm, a bowler pitching on a length. He felt his audience begin to relax. The circumstances were unusual, but they were being told a story, and they were offering themselves to the story-teller in the manner of audiences down the ages, wanting to see how things turned out, wanting to have the world explained to them. Hughes sketched in an idyllic nineteenth century, all nomads and goat-farming and traditional hospitality which allowed you to stay in someone else's tent for three days before being asked what the purpose of your visit might be. He talked of early Zionist settlers and Western concepts of land-ownership. The Balfour Declaration. Jewish immigration from Europe. The Second World War. European guilt over the Holocaust being paid for by the Arabs. The Jews having learned from their persecution by the Nazis that the only way to survive was to be like Nazis. Their militarism, expansionism, racism. Their pre-emptive attack on the Egyptian air force at the start of the Six Day War being the exact moral equivalent of Pearl Harbor (Franklin deliberately did not look at the Japanese – or the Americans – at this moment, nor for some time thereafter). The refugee camps. The theft of land. The artificial support of the Israeli economy by the dollar. The atrocities committed against the dispossessed. The Jewish lobby in America. The Arabs only asking from the Western Powers for the same justice in the Middle East as had already been accorded to the Jews. The regrettable necessity of violence, a lesson taught the Arabs by the Jews, just as it had been taught the Jews by the Nazis.

Franklin had used up two-thirds of his time. If he could feel a brooding hostility in some parts of the audience, there was also, strangely, a wider drowsiness, as if they'd heard this story before and had not believed it then either. 'And so we come to the here and now.' That brought them back to full attention; despite the circumstances, Franklin felt a bubble of pleasure. He was the hypnotist who snaps his fingers. 'In the Middle East, we must understand, there are no civilians any more. The Zionists understand this, the Western governments do not. We, alas, are not civilians. The Zionists have made this happen. You – we – are being held hostage by the Black Thunder group to secure the release of three of their members. You may remember' (though Franklin doubted it, since incidents of this kind were frequent, almost interchangeable) 'that two years ago a civilian aircraft carrying three members of the Black Thunder group was forced down by the American air force in Sicily, that the Italian authorities in contravention of international law compounded this act of piracy by arresting the three freedom fighters, that Britain defended America's action at the United Nations, and that the three men are now in prison in France and Germany. The Black Thunder group does not turn the other cheek, and this legitimate . . . hijack' – Franklin used the word carefully, with a glance at the leader as if to demonstrate how he disdained euphemism –

'is in response to that act of piracy. Unfortunately the Western governments do not show the same concern for their citizens as the Black Thunder group shows for its freedom fighters. Unfortunately they are so far declining to release the prisoners. Regrettably the Black Thunder group has no alternative but to carry out its intended threat which was made very clear from the beginning to the Western governments...'

At this moment a large, unathletic American in a blue shirt got to his feet and started running down the aisle towards the Arabs. Their guns had not been set to fire only one shot at a time. The noise was very loud and immediately there was a lot of blood. An Italian sitting in the line of fire received a bullet in the head and fell across his wife's lap. A few people got up and quickly sat down again. The leader of the Black Thunder group looked at his watch and waved at Hughes to continue. Franklin took a long swig of stale water. He wished it were something stronger. 'Because of the stubbornness of the Western governments,' he went on, trying to sound now more like an official spokesman than Franklin Hughes, 'and their reckless disregard for human life, it is necessary for sacrifices to be made. You will have understood the historical inevitability of this from what I have said before. The Black Thunder group has every confidence that the Western governments will swiftly come to the negotiating table. In a final effort to make them do so it will be necessary to execute two of you ... of us ... every hour until that point. The Black Thunder group finds this course of action regrettable, but the Western governments leave them no alternative. The order of executions has been decided according to the guilt of the Western nations for the situation in the Middle East.' Franklin could no longer look at his audience. He dropped his voice, yet could not avoid being heard as he went on. 'Zionist Americans first. Then other Americans. Then British. Then French, Italians and Canadians.'

'What the fuck has Canada ever done in the Middle East? What the fuck?' shouted a man still wearing a towelling maple-leaf hat. He was restrained from getting up by his wife. Franklin, who felt the heat from the metal floor of his cage to be unendurable, shuffled his notes together automatically, stepped off the podium without looking at anyone, walked up the aisle getting blood on his crêpe soles as he stepped past the dead American, ignored the three Arabs who could shoot him if they wanted to, and went without escort or opposition to his cabin. He locked the door and lay down on his bunk.

Ten minutes later there came the noise of shooting. From five o'clock to eleven o'clock, punctually on the hour like some terrible parody of a municipal clock, gunfire pealed. Splashes followed, as the bodies were flung over the rail in pairs. Shortly after eleven, twenty-two members of the American Special Forces, who had been trailing the *Santa Euphemia* for fifteen hours, managed to get on board. In the battle six more passengers, including Mr Talbot, the honorary American citizen from Kidderminster, were shot dead. Out of the eight visitors who had helped load supplies at Rhodes, five were killed, two after they had surrendered.

Neither the leader nor the second-in-command survived, so there remained no witness to corroborate Franklin Hughes's story of the bargain he had struck with the Arabs. Tricia Maitland, who had become Irish for a few hours without realizing it, and who in the course of Franklin Hughes's lecture had returned her ring to the finger where it originally belonged, never spoke to him again.

3

THE WARS OF RELIGION

SOURCE: *the Archives Municipales de Besançon (section CG, boîte 377a). The following case, hitherto unpublished, is of particular interest to legal historians in that the* procureur pour les insectes *was the distinguished jurist Bartholomé Chassenée (also Chassanée and Chasseneux), later first president of the Parlement de Provence. Born in 1480, Chassenée made his name before the ecclesiastical court of Autun defending rats which had been charged with feloniously destroying a crop of barley. The following documents, from the opening* pétition des habitans *to the final judgment of the court, do not represent the entire proceedings — for instance, the testimony of witnesses, who might be anything from local peasants to distinguished experts on the behavioural patterns of the defendants, has not been recorded — but the legal submissions embody and often specifically refer to the evidence, and thus there is nothing absent from the essential structure and argument of the case. As was normal at the time, the pleas and the* conclusions du procureur épiscopal *were made in French, while the sentence of the court was solemnly delivered in Latin.*

(Translator's note: The manuscript is continuous and all in the same hand. Thus we are not dealing with the original submissions as penned by each lawyer's clerk, but with the work of a third party, perhaps an official of the court, who may have omitted sections of the pleas. Comparison with the contents of boîtes 371–379 suggests that the case as it exists in this form was perhaps part of a set of exemplary or typical proceedings used in the training of jurists. This conjecture is supported by the fact that only Chassenée among the participants is identified by name, as if students were being directed to examine the instructive dexterity of a distinguished defence counsel, regardless of the result of the case. The handwriting belongs to the first half of the sixteenth century, so that if, as may be, the document is a copy of someone else's version of the trial, it is still contemporary. I have done my best to render the sometimes extravagant style of pleading — especially of the unnamed procureur des habitans *— into a comparable English.)*

Pétition de habitans

We, the inhabitants of Mamirolle in the diocese of Besançon, being fearful of Almighty God and humbly dutiful to his spouse the Church, and being furthermore most regular and obedient in the payment of our tithes, do hereby on this the 12th day of August 1520 most pressingly and urgently petition the court to relieve and disburden us of the felonious intervention of those malefactors which have infested us already for many seasons, which have brought upon us God's wrath and a shameful libel upon our habitation, and which threaten all of us, God-fearing and obedient in our duties to the Church as we are, with immediate and catastrophic death being flung down at us from above like clamorous thunder, which will surely come to pass unless the court in its solemn wisdom do not speedily and justly expel these malefactors from our village, conjuring them to depart, hateful and intolerable as they are, under pain of condemnation, anathema, and excommunication from the Holy Church and the Dominion of God.

Plaidoyer des habitans

Gentlemen, these poor and humble petitioners, wretched and distressed, come before you as once did the inhabitants of the isles of Minorca and Majorca before the mighty Augustus Caesar, begging him in his justice and power to rid their islands of those rabbits which were destroying their crops and ruining their livelihood. If Augustus Caesar was able to help those dutiful subjects, how much more easily may this court lift the oppressive burden which lies upon the shoulders of your petitioners as heavily as when the great Aeneas did carry his father Anchises from the burning city of Troy. The old Anchises was blinded by a bolt of lightning, and these your petitioners are even now as if blinded, cast into darkness out of the light of the Lord's blessing, by the felonious behaviour of those who stand accused in this case, and yet who have not even appeared before the court to answer the charges, being contemptuous of this tribunal and blaspheming towards God, preferring instead to bury themselves in sinful darkness rather than face the truth of light.

Know, gentlemen, what has already been put before you by witnesses of humble faith and unimpeachable honesty, simple petitioners too trepid of this court to let anything but the clear fountain of truth flow from their mouths. They have testified to the events of the twenty-second day of the month of April in this year of Our Lord, which being the day of the annual pilgrimage of Hugo, Bishop of Besançon, to the humble church of Saint-Michel in their village. They have described to you, in detail which burns in your memory like the fiery furnace from which Shadrach, Meshach and Abednego came unscathed, how as in every year they had adorned and beautified their church to make it worthy for the eye of the Bishop to behold, how they had caused flowers to be placed upon the altar and the door to be made freshly safe against the irruption of animals, but how, though they might bar the door to the pig and the cow, they were unable to bar the door to those diabolic *bestioles* which crawl through the smallest hole even as David found the chink in Goliath's armour. They have told you how they lowered by rope from the rafters the Bishop's throne which is tethered there from one year's end to the next and is descended only for the day of the Bishop's pilgrimage, lest any child or stranger might by chance sit on it and thereby profane it, this being a humble and devout tradition, fully worthy of the praise of God and of this court. How the throne, being lowered, was placed before the altar as it has been every year since the oldest Methuselah in the habitation can remember, and how the prudent villagers set a guard upon it through the night before the arrival of the Bishop, so heedful were they that the throne be not defiled. And how the next day Hugo, Bishop of Besançon, did come in his annual pilgrimage, like Gracchus coming among his beloved people, to the humble church of Saint-Michel, and was pleased by their devotion and true faith. And how, having first as was his custom given his general blessing to the villagers of Mamirolle from the step of the church, he went in procession up the nave of the church, followed at subservient distance by his flock, and prostrated himself, even in the finery of his apparel, before the altar, just as Jesus Christ prostrated himself before his Almighty Father. Then he rose, ascended the simple step to the altar, turned to face the congregation, and lowered himself upon his throne. Oh malevolent day! Oh malevolent invaders! And how the Bishop fell, striking his head upon the altar step and being hurled against his will into a state of imbecility. And how, when the Bishop and his retinue had departed, bearing off the Bishop in a state of imbecility, the terrified petitioners did examine the Bishop's throne and discover in the leg that had tumbled down like the walls of Jericho a vile and unnatural infestation of woodworm, and how these woodworm, having secretly and darkly gone about their devilish work, had so devoured the leg that the Bishop did fall like mighty Daedalus from the heavens of light into the darkness of imbecility. And how, being much fearful of the wrath of God, the petitioners did climb up to the roof of the church of Saint-Michel and examine the cradle in which the throne had rested for three hundred and sixty-four days of the year, and how they found that woodworm had also infested the cradle so that it broke apart when they touched it and fell sacrilegiously down upon the altar steps, and how the timbers of the roof were all found to be vilely tainted by those diabolic *bestioles*, which made the petitioners apprehensive for their own lives, since they are both poor and devout, and their poverty would not permit them to build a new church, while their devotion commands them to worship their Holy Father as fervently as they have always done and in a sacred place not among the fields and woods.

Hear, Gentlemen, therefore, the petition of these humble villagers, wretched as the grass beneath the foot. They are accustomed to many plagues, to the locusts that darken the sky like the hand of God passing over the sun, to the ravages of rats that lay waste as did the boar to the environs of Calydon as narrated by Homer in the first book of the Iliad, to the weevil which devours the grain in their winter storehouse. How much more vile and malevolent, therefore, is this plague which attacks the grain which the villagers have stored up in Heaven by their humble piety and their payment of tithes. For these malefactors, disrespectful even to this day of your court, have offended God by attacking his House, they have offended his spouse the Church by casting Hugo, Bishop of Besançon, into the darkness of imbecility, they have offended these petitioners by threatening to bring the framework and fabric of their church tumbling down upon the innocent heads of children and infants even as the village is at prayer, and it is therefore right and reasonable and necessary for the court to injunct and enjoin these animals to quit their habitation, to withdraw from the House of God, and for the court to pronounce upon them the necessary anathemata and excommunications prescribed by our Holy Mother, the Church, for which your petitioners do ever pray.

Plaidoyer des insectes

Since, Gentlemen, it has pleased you to appoint me procurator for the *bestioles* in this case, I shall endeavour to explain to the court how the charges against them are null and void, and how the case must be non-suited. To begin with, I confess I am astonished that my clients, who have committed no crime, have been treated as if they were the worst criminals known to this court, and that my clients, though notoriously dumb, have been summoned to explain their behaviour as if they were accustomed to employ the human tongue while going about their daily business. I shall, in all humility, attempt to make my speaking tongue do service for their silent tongue.

Since you have permitted me to speak on behalf of these unfortunate animals, I will state, in the first place, that this court lacks the jurisdiction to try the defendants, and that the summons issued against them has no validity, for it implies that the recipients are endowed with reason and volition, being thereby capable both of committing a crime and of answering a summons for the trial of the said crime. Which is not the case, since my clients are brute beasts acting only from instinct, and which is confirmed by the first book of the *Pandects*, at the paragraph *Si quadrupes*, where it is written *Nec enim potest animal injuriam fecisse, quod sensu caret.*

In the second place, additionally and alternatively, I will submit that even if the court were to have jurisdiction over the *bestioles*, it would be unreasonable and unlawful for the present tribunal to consider their case, for it is a well-known and long-established principle that the accused may not be tried *in absentia*. It has been stated that the woodworm have been formally summoned by writ to appear before this court on this particular day, and have insolently refused to appear, thereby forfeiting their normal rights and permitting them to be tried *in absentia*. Against this argument I propose two counter-arguments. First, that while the summons for attendance was properly issued, have we any proof that it was accepted by the *bestioles*? For it is established that a writ must not just be issued but delivered, and the procurator *pour les habitans* has failed to indicate in what manner the woodworm did acknowledge the writ. Secondly, and further, it is a principle even more firmly established in the annals of the law that a defendant may be excused default or non-appearance if it can be shown that the length or difficulty or danger of the journey render it impossible for attendance at the court safely to be made. If you summoned a rat before you, would you expect it to proceed to your court while passing through a town full of cats? And on this point, not only is the distance from the abode of the *bestioles* to the court a monstrous league for them to travel, it is also one which they would accomplish under mortal threat from those predators which attend on their humble lives. They may, therefore, in safety and in legality and with all respect to this tribunal courteously refuse to obey the writ.

In the third place, the summons is incorrectly drawn, since it refers to the woodworm who currently have their habitation in the church of Saint-Michel in the village of Mamirolle. Does this mean every single *bestiole* that is in the church? But there are many who live peaceable lives offering no threat whatsoever to the *habitans*. Must a whole village be summoned to court because there is a gang of robbers living within it? This is no sound law. Further, it is an established principle that defendants should be identified to the court. We have under examination two particular felonious acts, the injury to the leg of the Bishop's throne, and the injury to the roof of the church, and it is plain from any scant knowledge of the nature of the animals being charged that those woodworm which currently make their habitation in the leg could not possibly have had anything to do with the roof, and that those woodworm which make their habitation in the roof cannot possibly have had anything to do with the leg. Thus it is that two parties are charged with two crimes without separation in the writ of party and crime, which renders the summons invalid for failure of specificity.

In the fourth place, and without prejudice to the aforesaid, I will argue that not only, as we have proposed, is it contrary to Man's law and the Church's law to try the *bestioles* in this fashion, it is also contrary to God's law. For whence came these tiny creatures against whom the solemn might of this court is being flung? Who created them? None other than Almighty God who created us all, the highest and the lowest. And do we not read in the first chapter of the sacred book of Genesis that God made the beast of the earth after his kind, the cattle after their kind, and every living thing that creepeth upon the earth after his kind, and God saw that it was good? And further did not God give unto the beasts of the earth and unto every creeping thing every seed upon the face of the earth, and every tree upon the face of the earth, and every fruit of every tree as meat? And yet further, did he not give order unto them all to be fruitful and multiply and replenish the earth? The Creator would not have instructed the beasts of the earth and every creeping thing to multiply had He not, in His infinite wisdom, provided them with food, which He did so, expressly giving the seeds and the fruit and the trees as meat. What have these humble *bestioles* done since the day of Creation but exercise the inalienable rights conferred on them at that time, rights which Man has no power to curtail or abrogate? That the woodworm make their habitation where they do may prove inconvenient to Man, but that is not sufficient reason to seek to rebel against the rules of Nature laid down at the Creation, such rebellion being a direct and insolent disobedience to the Creator. The Lord breathed life into the woodworm, and gave him the trees of the earth for meat: how presumptuous and how perilous it would be for us to seek to countermand the will of God. No, rather, I submit to the court that we should direct our attention not to the supposed felonies of God's humblest creation, but to the felonies of man himself. God does nothing without a purpose, and the purpose in permitting the *bestioles* to take up their habitation in the church of Saint-Michel can have been none other than as a warning and a punishment against the wickedness of mankind. That the woodworm were allowed to infest the church rather than any other building is, I further submit, an even more severe warning and punishment. Are those who come before the court as petitioners so certain of their obedience to God, so sure of their humility and Christian virtue that they would accuse the humblest animal before accusing themselves? Beware the sin of pride, I tell those petitioners. Cast out the beam from your own eye before you seek to extract the mote from the eye of another.

In the fifth and final place, the procurator *pour les habitans* asks the court to hurl against the *bestioles* that bolt of lightning known as excommunication. It is my duty to submit to you, and without prejudice to any of the aforesaid, that such a punishment is both inappropriate and unlawful. Excommunication being the separation of the sinner from communion with God, a refusal to permit him to eat of the bread and drink of the wine that are the body and blood of Christ, a casting-out from the Holy Church and its light and its warmth, how therefore can it be lawful to excommunicate a beast of the field or a creeping thing from upon the earth which has never been a communicant of the Holy Church? It cannot be a fit and proper punishment to deprive a defendant of that which he has never possessed in the first place. This makes bad law. And secondly, excommunication is a process of great terror, a casting of the sinner into fearsome darkness, an eternal separation of the sinner from the light and from the goodness of God. How can this be an appropriate punishment for a *bestiole* which does not possess an immortal soul? How is it possible to condemn a defendant to eternal torment when he does not have eternal life? These animals cannot be expelled from the Church since they are not members of it, and as the Apostle Paul says, 'Ye judge them that are within and not them also that are without.'

I ask, therefore, that the case be rejected and non-suited, and without prejudice to the foregoing, that the defendants be acquitted and exempted from all further prosecution.

Bartholomé Chassenée, Jurist

Réplique des habitans

Gentlemen, it does me honour to appear again before your solemn court, to plead for justice as did that poor offended mother who appeared before Solomon to claim her child. Like Ulysses against Ajax I shall fight the procurator for the *bestioles*, who has produced before you many arguments as bedizened as Jezebel.

In the first place, he contends that this court has no power and jurisdiction to try the bestial felonies that have taken place at Mamirolle, and towards this end argues that we are no better in God's eye than the woodworm, no higher and no lower, therefore we do not have the right to sit in judgment on them like Jupiter whose temple was on the Tarpeian rock from whence were traitors flung. But I shall refute this as Our Lord turned the moneylenders out of the Temple at Jerusalem, and in this way. Is man not higher than the animals? Is it not clear from the holy book of Genesis that the animals which were created before man, were so created in order to be subservient to his use? Did not the Lord give unto Adam dominion over the fish of the sea, and over the fowl of the air, and over every living thing that moveth upon the earth? Did not Adam give the names to all the cattle, and to

the fowl of the air, and to every beast of the field? Was not the
dominion of man over the animals asserted by the Psalmist and
reiterated by the apostle Paul? And how may man have dominion
over the animals and such dominion not include the right to
punish them for their misdeeds? Furthermore, this right to sit in
judgment over the animals, which the procurator for the *bestioles*
so actively denies, is specifically given to man by God himself, as
appears in the sacred book of Exodus. Did not the Lord lay down
unto Moses the sacred law of an eye for an eye and a tooth for a
tooth? And did he not continue thus, if an ox gore a man or a
woman, that they die, then the ox shall be surely stoned, and his
flesh shall not be eaten. Does the holy book of Exodus not thus
make clear the law? And does it not go on further, that if one
man's ox hurt another's, that he die, then they shall sell the live
ox, and divide the money of it, and the dead ox also they shall
divide? Has not the Lord laid it down thus, and given man the
judgment over the animals?

In the second place, that the woodworm are to be excused
trial because of their failure to attend court. But they have been
correctly summoned in accordance with all due process. They
have been summoned as the Jews were summoned to be taxed by
Augustus Caesar. And did not the Israelites obey? Which among
those present here would prevent the *bestioles* from coming to
court? My humble petitioners might have wished to do so, and
to this end they might have sought to burn in the flames the leg
of the throne that cast Hugo, Bishop of Besançon into a state of
imbecility by striking his head on the altar step, but like Christians stayed their hand, preferring instead to submit the matter
to your solemn judgment. What enemy, therefore, might the
accused *bestioles* encounter? The distinguished procurator has
made reference to cats eating rats. I was not aware, Gentlemen,
that cats had taken to devouring woodworm on their way to
court, yet no doubt I shall be corrected if I am in error. No, there
is only one explanation of the refusal of the accused to appear
before you, and that is a blind and most wilful disobedience, a
hateful silence, a guilt that blazes as the burning bush which did
appear unto Moses, a bush which blazed but was not consumed,
even as their guilt continues to blaze with every hour that they
obstinately refuse to appear.

In the third place, it is argued that God created the woodworm
even as he created Man, and that he gave him the seeds and the

fruit and the trees as meat, and that whatever they might choose to eat therefore has the blessing of God. Which is indeed the main and essential pleading of the procurator for the *bestioles*, and I hereby refute it thus. The sacred book of Genesis tells us that God in his infinite mercy and generosity gave unto the beasts of the field and unto the creeping things all the seeds and the fruit and the trees as meat. He gave the trees unto those creatures which have the instinct to devour trees, even though this might be a hindrance and a discomfort to Man. But He did not give them the cut wood. Where in the Holy Book of Genesis is it allowed that the creeping things of the earth may inhabit the cut wood? Did the Lord intend when He permitted a creature to burrow within the oak tree that the same creature had the right to burrow within the House of the Lord? Where in the Holy Scripture does the Lord give unto the animals the right to devour His temples? And does the Lord instruct His servants to pass by on the other side while His temples are devoured and His Bishops reduced to a state of imbecility? The pig that eats the holy sacramental wafer is hanged for its blasphemy, and the *bestiole* that makes his own habitation in the habitation of the Lord is no less blasphemous.

Furthermore, and without prejudice to the foregoing, it has been argued that the Lord created the woodworm even as He created Man, and that therefore everything the Lord might do has the Lord's blessing, however pestilential and maleficent it might be. But did the Almighty Lord, in His matchless wisdom and beneficence, create the weevil in order that it destroy our crops, and the woodworm in order that it destroy the Lord's house? The wisest doctors of our Church for many centuries have examined every verse of the Holy Scripture just as Herod's soldiers searched for innocent children, and they have found no chapter, no line, no phrase wherein there is mention of the woodworm. Therefore the question which I lay before the court as the essential question in this case is the following: was the woodworm ever upon Noah's Ark? Holy writ makes no mention of the woodworm embarking upon or disembarking from the mighty vessel of Noah. And indeed how could it have been so, for was not the Ark constructed of wood? How can the Lord in his eternal wisdom have allowed on board a creature whose daily habits might cause the shipwreck and disastrous death of Man and all the beasts of the Creation? How could such a thing

be so? Therefore, it follows that the woodworm was not upon
the Ark, but is an unnatural and imperfect creature which did
not exist at the time of the great bane and ruin of the Deluge.
Whence its generation came, whether from some foul spon-
taneity or some malevolent hand, we know not, yet its hateful
malice is evident. This vile creature has given over its body to
the Devil and thereby put itself beyond the protection and shelter
of the Lord. What greater proof could there be but the manner
of its desecrations, the cunning odiousness with which it hurled
Hugo, Bishop of Besançon, into imbecility? Was this not the
work of the Devil, to proceed thus in darkness and secrecy for
many years, and then make triumph of his foul purpose? Yet the
procurator for the *bestioles* argues that the woodworm have the
blessing of the Lord in all that they do and all that they eat. He
contends, therefore, that what they did in devouring the leg of
the Bishop's throne had the blessing of the Lord. He contends
further that the Lord by his own hand smote down one of
the Bishops of his own Holy Church just as He smote down Bel-
shazzar, as He smote down Amalek, as He smote down the Midi-
anites, as He smote down the Canaanites, as He smote down
Sihon the Amorite. Is this not a vile blasphemy which the court
must extirpate even as Hercules did cleanse the stables of Augeas?

And in the fourth place, it is contended that the court does
not have the power and the right to pronounce the decree of
excommunication. But this is to deny the very authority conferred by God upon his dear spouse, the Church, whom He has
made sovereign of the whole world, having put all things under
Her feet, as the Psalmist affirms, all sheep and oxen, the beasts of
the field, the fowl of the air, the fish of the sea, and whatsoever
passeth through the paths of the seas. Guided by the Holy Spirit,
the Church can do nothing wrong. Indeed, do we not read in
our sacred texts of serpents and poisonous reptiles whose venom
has been conjured from them? Do we not read in the sacred book
of Ecclesiastes that 'Surely the serpent will bite without enchantment'? Therefore it is in holy concord with God's teaching that
the Church has for centuries used its mighty but righteous power
to hurl anathemata and excommunication against those noxious
animals whose foul presence is an offence to the eye of the Lord.
Did not David's maledictions on the mountains of Gilboa cause
the rain and the dew to cease there? Did not Jesus Christ the son
of God ordain that every tree that bringeth not forth good fruit

should be hewn down and cast into the fire? And if an irrational thing shall be destroyed because it does not produce fruit, how much more is it permitted to curse it, since the greater penalty includes the less: *cum si liceat quid est plus, debet licere quid est minus.* Was not the serpent cursed in the Garden of Eden, making it to crawl upon its belly for the rest of its life? And when the town of Aix was infested by serpents which inhabited the warm baths and killed many of the inhabitants by biting them, did not the holy Bishop of Grenoble excommunicate the serpents, where-upon they departed? And thus did the Bishop of Lausanne free Lake Leman from the infestation of eels. And thus did the same Bishop expel from the waters of the same lake those blood-suckers which fed on the salmon which the devout were wont to consume on fast-days. And did not Egbert, Bishop of Trier, anathematize the swallows whose chirping interrupted the prayers of the devout? And did not St Bernard likewise and for like reason excommunicate swarms of flies, which on the mor-row, like Sennacherib's host, were all dead corpses? And did not the crozier of St Magnus, the apostle of Algau, expel and exterminate all manner of rats, mice and cockchafers? Therefore is it not right and established that this court may cast the bolt of excommunication upon these defilers and assassins of God's holy temple? The procurator for the *bestioles* argues that since a wood-worm has no immortal soul it cannot be excommunicated. But have we not shown, firstly that the woodworm is no natural beast, having not been on the Ark of Noah, and second that the actions for which it has been summoned to appear before the court are clear evidence that it has been taken over by a malign spirit, namely that of Lucifer. How much more necessary, there-fore, is the order of excommunication which I hereby beg and demand from this court.

Réplique des insectes

Gentlemen, we have been treated to many points of argument thus far, some blown away by the wind like the winnowed chaff, some resting on the ground before you like the valuable grain. I hereby prevail upon your patience a little further to make re-joinder to the contentions of the procurator *des habitans*, whose arguments will fall like the walls of Jericho before the trumpet of truth.

In the first place, the procurator makes mention of the length of time the *bestioles* had been making their habitation in the leg of the Bishop's throne, storing up their dark purpose, and offers this as proof that the work was diabolically inspired. It was for this reason that I called before you the good Brother Frolibert who is wise in the ways of the creeping things of the earth, and indeed you know he makes the honey at the Abbey of St Georges. And did he not assert that wise men believe the *bestioles* do not live for more than a few brief summers? Yet we all know that an infestation of woodworm may proceed for many human generations before it cause the wood to break apart as it did under Hugo, Bishop of Besançon, reducing him to a condition of imbecility. From which we must conclude that the woodworm summoned before this court are merely the descendants of many generations of woodworm who have made their habitation in the church of Saint-Michel. If malign intent is to be ascribed to the *bestioles*, it is surely only to be ascribed to the first generation of *bestioles* and not to their innocent posterity who without fault find themselves living where they do? On this ground, therefore, I apply again for the case to be non-suited. And further, there has been no evidence from the prosecution as to the occasion and date upon which the woodworm are alleged to have entered the wood. The procurator has attempted to maintain that the *bestioles* are not granted by Holy Scripture the right to inhabit cut wood. To which we reply, firstly that the Scripture does not in any patent form forbid them from so doing, secondly that if God had not intended them to eat the cut wood He would not have given them the instinct to do so, and thirdly that in the absence of evidence to the contrary, an accused being innocent until proved guilty, an assumption of priority of possession in the matter of the wood must be granted to the *bestioles*, namely that they were in the wood when it was cut by the woodsman who sold it to the joiner who fashioned it into the throne. Far from the woodworm infesting what Man has constructed, it is Man who has wilfully destroyed the woodworm's habitation and taken it for his own purpose. On which ground also we ask that the case be non-suited.

In the second place it is argued that the woodworm did not have passage on the Ark of Noah and therefore must be diabolically possessed. To which we reply, firstly that the Holy Scripture does not list every species of God's creation, and that the legal presumption should be that any creature was upon the Ark unless it be specifically stated that he was not. And secondly, that if as the procurator alleges the woodworm was not upon the Ark, then it is even more evident that Man has not been given dominion over this creature. God sent the baneful Flood to purge the world, and when the waters receded and the world was new-born, He gave Man dominion over the animals. But where is it written that He also gave him dominion over any animals which had not travelled upon the Ark?

In the third place, it is a monstrous libel upon our pleading to claim that Hugo, Bishop of Besançon, according to our allegation, was thrust into the darkness of imbecility by God's own hand. We make no such allegation, for it would be the contention of a blasphemer. But indeed is it not the case that the ways of God are often most mysteriously hid from our gaze? When the Bishop of Grenoble fell from his horse and was killed we did not blame either the Lord or the horse or the woodworm. When the Bishop of Constance was lost overboard in the lake we did not conclude that God had hurled him into the water or that woodworm had destroyed the keel of the boat. When the pillar in the cloister of Saint Théodoric collapsed on the foot of the Bishop of Lyons causing him to walk ever thereafter with a staff, we did not blame the Lord or the pillar or the woodworm. The Lord's ways are indeed frequently hidden from us, but is it not also the case that the Lord has called down many plagues upon the unworthy? Did He not send a plague of frogs against Pharaoh? Did He not send lice and grievous swarms of flies upon the land of Egypt? Did He not, against that Pharaoh, send also a plague of boils, and thunder and hail, and a grievous plague of locusts? Did He not send hailstones against the Five Kings? Did He not strike even his own servant Job with boils? And it was for this reason that I called before you Father Godric and enquired of him for the records of the payment of tithes by the inhabitants of Mamirolle. And were there not many excuses proffered about the inclemency of the weather, and the crops that had failed, and the sickness there had been in the village, and the band of soldiers who had passed by and murdered several of the strong young men of the village? But for all this it was evident and plain that the tithes have not been paid as the Church lays down, that there has been wilful neglect amounting to disobedience of the Lord God and his spouse on earth the

Church. And is it not therefore the case that, just as He sent a plague of locusts to scourge Pharaoh and grievous swarms of flies upon the land of Egypt, so he sent woodworm into the church to scourge the inhabitants for their disobedience? How can this have been done without the Lord's permission? Do we think Almighty God is so weak and timorous a creature that He is unable to protect His temple against these tiny *bestioles*? Surely it is a blasphemy to doubt God's power to do this. And therefore we must conclude that the infestation was either divinely ordered or divinely permitted, that God sent the woodworm to punish the disobedient sinners and that the sinners should cower before His rage and scourge themselves for their sins and pay their tithes as they have been commanded. Truly, this is a matter for prayer and fasting and scourging and the hope of God's mercy rather than one for anathemata and excommunication against the agents, the very conduits of the Lord's purpose and intent.

In the fourth place, therefore, acknowledging as we do that the woodworm are God's creatures and as such are entitled to sustenance even as man is entitled to sustenance, and acknowledging also that justice shall be tempered by mercy, we submit, without prejudice to the foregoing, that the court demand of the *habitans* of Mamirolle, who have been so tardy in their payment of tithes, to nominate and set aside for the said *bestioles* alternative pasture, where they may graze peacefully without future harm to the church of Saint-Michel, and that the *bestioles* be commanded by the court, which has all such powers, to move to the said pasture. For what do my humble clients hope for and demand except to be allowed to live peaceably and in the dark without interference and wrongful accusation. Gentlemen, I make my final plea that the case be non-suited, and without prejudice that the *bestioles* be declared innocent, and without prejudice again that they be required to move to fresh pasture. I submit on their behalf to the judgment of the court.

Bartholemé Chassenée, Jurist

Conclusions du procureur épiscopal

The arguments offered by the counsel for the defence have been truly and weightily delivered, and must be accorded great and serious thought, for it is not lightly or at random that the court should hurl the bolt of excommunication, for being lightly or at random hurled, it may, by reason of its particular energy and force, if it fails to strike the object at which it is aimed, return against him who hurled it. The arguments offered by the counsel for the prosecution have also been delivered with much learning and education, and it is truly a deep sea in which it is impossible to touch bottom.

In the matter raised by the procurator for the *bestioles* regarding the many generations of woodworm and whether this genera-tion of woodworm summoned before us was the generation who committed the crime, we have this to say. Firstly, that it is stated in Holy Scripture in the book of Exodus that the Lord shall visit the iniquities of the fathers upon the children unto the third and fourth generation, and therefore in this matter the court has the power most piously to bring to judgment several generations of woodworm all of whom have offended against the Lord, which would indeed be a mighty act of justice to perform. And secondly, that if we accept the argument of the procurator *pour les habitans* that the *bestioles* are diabolically possessed, what could be more natural – in this case more foully unnatural – than that such possession should allow the woodworm to outlive their normal span of years, and thus it might be that only a single generation of creeping things have wrought all the damage unto the throne and the roof. In either case we have been much swayed by the argument of the procurator *pour les habitans* that the woodworm could not have been upon the Ark of Noah – for what prudent sea captain in his wisdom would permit such agents of shipwreck to board his vessel? – and therefore are not to be numbered among God's prime creations. What their status in the mighty hierarchy shall be – whether they be partly natural, whether they be living corruption, or whether they be creations of the devil – is a matter for those great doctors of the Church who weigh such matters.

Neither can we know all of the myriad reasons why God should have permitted a plague of woodworm to infest this humble church. Perhaps beggars have been turned away from the door. Perhaps the tithes have not been paid regularly. Perhaps there has been frivolity inside the church, and the mansion of the Lord has been turned into a place of assignation, whereupon God sent the insects. We must never forget the duty of charity and the requirement to give alms, and did not Eusebius liken hell to a

cold place where the wailing and gnashing of teeth are caused by
the dreadful frost not the everlasting fire, and is not charity one
of the means by which we throw ourselves upon the mercy of
the Lord? Therefore, in recommending the sentence of excommunication on these *bestioles* who have so vilely and viciously
ravaged the temple of the Lord, we do also recommend that all
the penances and prayers customary in such cases be required of
the *habitans*.

Sentence du juge d'Église

In the name and by virtue of God, the omnipotent, Father, Son
and Holy Spirit, and of Mary, the most blessed Mother of our
Lord Jesus Christ, and by the authority of the Holy Apostles
Peter and Paul, as well as by that which has made us a functionary
in this case, having fortified ourselves with the Holy Cross, and
having before our eyes the fear of God, we admonish the aforesaid woodworm as detestable vermin and command them, under
pain of malediction, anathema and excommunication, to quit
within seven days the church of Saint-Michel in the village of
Mamirolle in the diocese of Besançon and to proceed without
delay or hindrance to the pasture offered to them by the *habitans*,
there to have their habitation and never again to infest the
church of Saint-Michel. In order to make lawful this sentence,
and to render effective any malediction, anathema and excommunication that may at any time be pronounced, the *habitans*
of Mamirolle are hereby instructed to pay heedful attention to
the duty of charity, to yield up their tithes as commanded by the
Holy Church, to refrain from any frivolity in the House of
the Lord, and once a year, on the anniversary of that hateful
day when Hugo, Bishop of Besançon, was cast down into the
darkness of imbecility . . .

*Here the manuscript in the Archives Municipales de Besançon breaks off,
without giving details of the annual penance or remembrance imposed by
the court. It appears from the condition of the parchment that in the course
of the last four and a half centuries it has been attacked, perhaps on more
than one occasion, by some species of termite, which has devoured the
closing words of the juge d'Église.*

4
THE SURVIVOR

> In fourteen hundred and ninety-two
> Columbus sailed the ocean blue.

AND THEN WHAT? She couldn't remember. All those years ago, obedient ten-year-olds with arms crossed, they had chanted it back to the mistress. All except Eric Dooley who sat behind her and chewed her pigtail. Once she'd been asked to get up and recite the next two lines but she was only a few inches out of her seat when her head snapped back and the class laughed. Eric was hanging on to her plait with his teeth. Perhaps that was why she could never remember the next two lines.

She remembered the reindeer well enough, though. It all began with the reindeer, which flew through the air at Christmas. She was a girl who believed what she was told, and the reindeer flew.

She must have seen them first on a Christmas card. Six, eight, ten of them, harnessed side by side. She always imagined that each pair was man and wife, a happy couple, like the animals that went into the Ark. That would be right wouldn't it, that would be natural? But her Dad said you could tell from the antlers that the reindeer pulling the sleigh were stags. At first she only felt disappointed, but later resentment grew. Father Christmas ran an all-male team. Typical. Absolutely bloody typical, she thought.

They flew, that was the point. She didn't believe that Father Christmas squeezed down the chimney and left presents at the end of your bed, but she did believe that the reindeer flew. People tried to argue her out of it, they said if you believe that you'll believe anything. However, she was fourteen now, short-haired and stubborn, and she always had her reply ready. No, she would say, if only you could believe that the reindeer can fly, then you'd realize anything is possible. Anything.

Around that time she went to the zoo. It was their horns that fascinated her. They were all silky, as if they'd been covered with some posh material from a smart shop. They looked like branches in some forest where nobody had trodden for centuries; soft, sheeny, mossy branches. She imagined a sloping bit of wood with a gentle light and some fallen nuts cracking beneath her foot. Yeah, and a cottage made out of gingerbread at the end of the path, said her best friend Sandra when she told her. No, she thought, the antlers turn into branches, the branches into antlers. Everything's connected, and the reindeer *can* fly.

She saw them fighting once, on television. They butted and raged at one another, charged headlong, tangled horns. They fought so hard they rubbed the skin off their antlers. She thought that underneath there'd be just dry bone, and their horns would look like winter branches stripped of their bark by hungry animals. But it wasn't like that. Not at all. They bled. The skin was torn off and underneath was blood as well as bone. The antlers turned scarlet and white, standing out in the soft greens and browns of the landscape like a tray of bones at the butcher's. It was horrible, she thought, yet we ought to face it. Everything *is* connected, even the parts we don't like, especially the parts we don't like.

She watched the television a lot after the first big accident. It wasn't a very serious accident, they said, not really, not like a bomb going off. And anyway it was a long way away, in Russia, and they didn't have proper modern power stations over there like we do, and even if they did their safety standards were obviously much lower so it couldn't happen here and there wasn't anything to worry about, was there? It might even teach the Russians a lesson, people said. Make them think twice about dropping the big one.

In a strange way people were excited by it. Something bigger than the latest unemployment figures or the price of a stamp. Besides, most of the nasty things were happening to other people. There was a cloud of poison, and everyone tracked its course like they'd follow the drift of quite an interesting area of low pressure on the weather map. For a while people stopped buying milk, and asked the butcher where the meat came from. But soon they stopped worrying, and forgot about it all.

At first the plan had been to bury the reindeer six feet down. It wasn't much of a news story, just an inch or two on the foreign page. The cloud had gone over where the reindeer grazed, poison had come down in the rain, the lichen became radioactive, the reindeer had eaten the lichen and got radioactive themselves. What did I tell you, she thought, everything is connected.

People couldn't understand why she got so upset. They said she shouldn't be sentimental, and after all it wasn't as if she had to live off reindeer meat, and if she had some spare sympathy going shouldn't she save it for human beings? She tried to explain, but she wasn't very good at explaining and they didn't understand. The ones who thought they understood said, Yes, we see, it's all about your childhood and the silly romantic ideas you had when you were a kid, but you can't go on having silly romantic ideas all your life, you've got to grow up in the end, you've got to be realistic, please don't cry, no maybe that's a good idea, here, have a good cry, it'll probably be good for you in the long run. No, it's not like that, she said, it's not like that at all. Then cartoonists started making jokes, about how the reindeer were so gleaming with radioactivity that Father Christmas didn't need headlights on his sleigh, and Rudolf the Red-Nosed Reindeer had a very shiny nose because he came from Chernobyl; but she didn't think it was funny.

Listen, she'd tell people. The way they measure the level of radioactivity is in something called becquerels. When the accident happened the Norwegian government had to decide what amount of radiation in meat was safe, and they came up with a figure of 600 becquerels. But people didn't like the idea of their meat being poisoned, and the Norwegian butchers didn't do such good business, and the one sort of meat no one would buy was reindeer, which was hardly surprising. So this is what the government did. They said that as people obviously weren't going to eat reindeer very often because they were so scared, then it would be just as safe for them to eat meat that was more con- taminated every once in a while as to eat less contaminated meat more often. So they raised the permitted limit for reindeer meat to 6,000 becquerels. Hey presto! One day it's harmful to eat meat with 600 becquerels in it, the next day it's safe with ten times that amount. This only applied to reindeer, of course. At the same time it's still officially dangerous to eat a pork chop or scrag end of lamb with 601 becquerels in it.

One of the TV programmes showed a couple of Lapp farmers bringing a reindeer corpse in for inspection. This was just after the limit had been raised ten times. The official from the Depart- ment of whatever it was, Agriculture or something, chopped up the little bits of reindeer innards and did the usual tests on them. The reading came out at 42,000 becquerels. 42 *thousand*.

At first the plan was to bury them, six feet down. Still, there's nothing like a good disaster to get people thinking clever thoughts. *Bury* the reindeer? No, that makes it look as if there's been a problem, like something's actually gone wrong. There must be a more useful way of disposing of them. You couldn't feed the meat to humans, so why not feed it to animals? That's a good idea – but which animals? Obviously not the sort which end up getting eaten by humans, we've got to protect number one. So they decided to feed it to the mink. 'What a clever idea. Mink aren't supposed to be very nice, and anyway the sort of people who can afford mink coats probably don't mind a little dose of radioactivity on top of it. Like a dash of scent behind the ears or something. Rather chic, really.

Most people had stopped paying attention to what she was telling them by now, but she always carried on. Listen, she said, so instead of burying the reindeer they're now painting a big blue stripe down the carcases and feeding them to mink. I think they should have buried them. Burying things gives you a proper sense of shame. Look what we've done to the reindeer, they'd say as they dug the pit. Or they might, at least. They might think about it. Why are we always punishing animals? We pretend we like them, we keep them as pets and get soppy if we think they're reacting like us, but we've been punishing animals from the beginning, haven't we? Killing them and torturing them and throwing our guilt on to them?

She gave up eating meat after the accident. Every time she found a slice of beef on her plate or a spoonful of stew she thought of reindeer. The poor beasts with their horns stripped bare and all bloody from fighting. Then the row of carcases each with a stripe of blue paint down its back, clanking past on a row of shiny hooks.

That, she explained, was when she first came here. Down south, that is. People said she was silly, she was running away, wasn't being realistic, if she felt that strongly about things she ought to stay and argue against them. But it depressed her too much. People didn't listen enough to her arguments. Besides, you should always go where you believe the reindeer can fly: *that* was being realistic. They couldn't fly up in the north any more.

*   *   *

I wonder what's happened to Greg. I wonder if he's safe. I wonder what he thinks about me, now he knows I was right. I hope he doesn't hate me for it. Men often hate you for being right. Or perhaps he'll pretend nothing has even happened; that way he can be sure he was right. Yes, it wasn't what you thought, it was just a comet burning out in the sky, or a summer storm, or a hoax on TV. Silly cow.

Greg was an ordinary bloke. Not that I wanted anything different when I met him. He went to work, came home, sat around, drank beer, went out with his mates and drank some more beer, sometimes slapped me around a bit on pay-night. We got on fair enough. Argued about Paul, of course. Greg said I ought to get him fixed so he'd be less aggressive and stop scratching the furniture. I said it wasn't anything to do with that, all cats scratched the furniture, maybe we should get him a scratching pole. Greg said how did I know that wouldn't encourage him, like giving him permission to scratch everything a whole lot more? I said don't be daft. He said it was scientifically proved that if you castrate cats they're less aggressive. I said wasn't the opposite more likely – that if you mutilated them it'd make them angry and violent? Greg picked up this big pair of scissors and said well why don't we bloody find out then? I screamed.

I wouldn't let him have Paul fixed, even if he did mess up the furniture quite a bit. Later I remembered something. They castrate reindeer, you know. The Lapps do. They pick out a big stag and castrate it and that makes it tame. Then they hang a bell round its neck and this bell-bull as they call it leads the rest of the reindeer around, wherever the herdsmen decide they want them to go. So the idea probably does work, but I still think it's wrong. It's not a cat's fault that it's a cat. I didn't tell any of this to Greg of course, about the bell-bulls. Sometimes, when he slapped me around, I'd think, maybe we ought to get you fixed first, that might make you less aggressive. But I never did say it. It wouldn't have helped.

We used to row about animals. Greg thought I was soft. Once I told him they were turning all the whales into soap. He laughed and said that was a bloody good way of using them up. I burst into tears. I suppose as much because he could think of something like that as because he said it.

We didn't row about the Big Thing. He just said politics was men's business and I didn't know what I was talking about. That

was as far as our conversations about the extinction of the planet
went. If I said I was worried what America might do if Russia
didn't back down or vice versa, or the Middle East or whatever,
he said did I think it might be pre-menstrual tension. You can't
talk to anyone like that, can you? He wouldn't even discuss it,
wouldn't row about it. Once I said maybe it *was* pre-menstrual
tension, and he said yes I thought so. I said no, listen, maybe
women are more in touch with the world. He said what did
I mean, and I said, well, everything's connected, isn't it, and
women are more closely connected to all the cycles of nature and
birth and rebirth on the planet than men, who are only impregnators after all when it comes down to it, and if women are in
tune with the planet then maybe if terrible things are going on
up in the north, things which threaten the whole existence of
the planet, then maybe women get to feel these things, like the
way some people know earthquakes are coming, and perhaps
that's what sets off PMT. He said silly cow, that's just why politics is men's business, and got another beer out of the fridge.
A few days later he said to me, what happened about the end of
the world? I just looked at him and he said, as far as I can see all
that pre-menstrual tension you had was about the fact that you
were getting your period. I said you make me so angry I almost
want the end of the world to come just so you'll be proved
wrong. He said he was sorry, but what did he know, after all he
was just an impregnator as I'd pointed out, and he reckoned those
other impregnators up in the north would sort something out.

Sort something out? That's what the plumber says, or the man
who comes to nail the roof back on. 'Reckon we'll be able to
sort something out,' they say with one of those confident winks.
Well, they didn't sort something out on this occasion, did they?
They bloody didn't. And in the last days of the crisis, Greg didn't
always come home at nights. Even he'd finally noticed and
decided to have some fun before it was all over. In a way I
couldn't blame him, except for the fact that he wouldn't admit
it. He said he was staying out because he couldn't stand coming
home and getting nagged at by me. I told him I understood and
it was all right, yet when I explained he got very uptight. He said
if he wanted a bit on the side then it wouldn't be because of the
world situation but because I was on his back all the time. They
just don't see the connections, do they? When men in dark-grey
suits and striped ties up there in the north start taking certain

strategic precautions as they term it, men like Greg in thongs and T-shirts down here in the south begin staying out late in bars trying to pick up girls. They should understand that, shouldn't they? They should admit it.

So when I knew what had happened, I didn't wait for Greg to come home. He was out there knocking back another beer, saying how those fellows up there would sort something out, and in the meantime why don't you come and sit on my knee, darling? I just took Paul and put him in his basket and got on the bus with as much tinned food as I could carry and some bottles of water. I didn't leave a note because there wasn't anything to say. I got off at the terminal on Harry Chan Avenue and started walking towards the Esplanade. Then guess what I saw, sunning herself on the roof of a car? A sleepy, friendly, tortoiseshell cat. I stroked her, she purred, I sort of scooped her up in my arm, one or two people stopped to look but I was round the corner into Herbert Street before they could say anything.

Greg would have been angry about the boat. Still, he only had a quarter share in her, and if the four of them were going to spend their last days drinking in bars and picking up girls because of the men in dark-grey suits who in my opinion should have been fixed themselves years ago, then they weren't going to miss the boat, were they? I filled her up, and as I cast off I saw that the tortoiseshell I'd put down just anywhere was sitting on top of Paul's basket, looking at me. 'You'll be Linda,' I said.

She left the world behind from a place called Doctor's Gully. At the end of the Esplanade at Darwin, behind the modern YMCA building, a zig-zag road runs down to a disused boat ramp. The big hot car-park is mostly empty, except when tourists come to watch the fish feed. Nothing else goes on nowadays at Doctor's Gully. Every day at high tide hundreds, thousands of fish come right up to the water's edge to be fed.

She thought how trusting the fish were. They must think these huge two-legged creatures are giving them food out of the kindness of their hearts. Maybe that's how it started, but now it's $2.50 admission for adults, $1.50 for children. She wondered why none of the tourists who stayed in the big hotels along the Esplanade thought it odd. But nobody stops to think about the world any more. We live in a world where they make children pay to see the fish eat. Nowadays even fish are exploited, she thought. Exploited, and then poisoned. The ocean out there is filling up with poison. The fish will die too.

Doctor's Gully was deserted. Hardly anyone sailed from there any more; they'd all moved off to the marina years ago. But there were still a couple of boats pulled up on the rocks, looking abandoned. One of them, pink and grey, with not much of a mast, had NOT FOR SALE painted along its side. This always made her laugh. Greg and his friends kept their little boat behind this one, away from the fish-feeding place. The rocks over here were strewn with discarded bits of metal – engines, boilers, valves, pipes, all turning orangey-brown with rust. As she walked, she stirred up flocks of orangey-brown butterflies which had started to live among the scrap metal, using it as camouflage. What have we done to the butterflies, she thought; look where we've made them live. She gazed out to sea, across the scrubby bits of mangrove pushing up by the shore, towards a line of small tankers, and beyond them low, humpy islands on the horizon. This was the place from which she left the world behind.

Past Melville Island, through Dundas Strait, and out into the Arafura Sea; after that she let the wind govern her direction. Mostly they seemed to be heading east, but she didn't attend too carefully. You only followed where you were going if you wanted to get back to where you had started from, and she knew that was impossible.

She hadn't expected neat mushroom clouds on the horizon. She knew it wouldn't be like it was in the films. Sometimes there was a shifting of the light, sometimes a distant rumbling noise. Such things could have meant nothing at all; but somewhere it had happened, and the winds that circled the planet were doing the rest. At night she slackened sail and went below to the little cabin, leaving the deck to Paul and Linda. At first Paul had wanted to fight the newcomer – all the old territorial stuff. But after a day or two the cats became accustomed to one another.

She thought she might have caught the sun a little. She'd been out in the heat all day with only one of Greg's old baseball caps for protection. He had this collection of stupid caps with silly slogans on them. This one was red with white lettering on it, an advertisement for a restaurant somewhere. It read UNTIL YOU'VE ATE AT BJ'S YOU AINT SHIT. Some drinking mate of Greg's had given it him for a birthday, and Greg could never tire of the joke. He'd sit there on the boat with a can of beer in his hand and his cap on his head and just start chuckling to himself. Then he'd laugh a lot more until everyone was watching, and finally announce 'Until you've ate at BJ's you aint shit.' That would crack him up, time and again. She hated the cap but it made sense to wear it. She'd forgotten the zinc cream and all the other tubes of stuff.

She knew what she was doing. She knew probably nothing would come of what Greg would have referred to as her little venture. Whenever she had a plan of any sort – especially something that didn't involve him – he would always refer to it as her little venture. She didn't think she was going to land on some undamaged island where you only had to throw a bean over your shoulder for a row of them to spring up and wave their pods at you. She didn't expect a coral reef, a strip of sand from the holiday brochures, and a nodding palm. She didn't imagine some good-looking fellow turning up after a couple of weeks in a dinghy with two dogs on board; then a girl with two chickens, a bloke with two pigs, and so on. Her expectations were not high. She just thought you had to try it, whatever the result. It was your duty. You weren't allowed to get out of it.

I couldn't tell last night. I was coming out of a dream, or maybe I was still in it, but I heard the cats, I swear I did. Or rather, the sound of a cat on heat, calling. Not that Linda would have had far to call. By the time I was fully awake there was only the sound of the waves against the hull. I went up the steps and pushed open the doors. In the moonlight I could see the pair of them, sitting smugly on their paws, side by side, looking back at me. Just like a couple of kids who'd almost got caught necking by the girl's mum. A cat on heat sounds like a baby crying, doesn't it? That ought to tell us something.

I don't keep count of the days. There isn't any point, is there? We aren't going to measure things in days any more. Days and weekends and holidays – that's how the men in grey suits measure things. We'll have to go back to some older cycle, sunrise to sunset for a start, and the moon will come into it, and the seasons, and the weather – the new, terrible weather we shall have to live under. How do tribes in the jungle measure the days? It's not too late to learn from them. People like that have the key to living with nature. They wouldn't castrate their cats.

They might worship them, they might even eat them, but they wouldn't have them fixed.

I just eat enough to keep me going. I'm not going to calculate how long I might be at sea and then divide the rations into forty-eight portions or anything like that. That's the old sort of thinking, the thinking that led us into all this. I eat enough to keep going, that's all. I fish, of course. I'm sure it's safe. But when I catch something I can't help giving it to Paul and Linda. Still tins for me, while the cats grow plump.

I must be more careful. Must have passed out in the sun. Came to lying on my back with the cats licking my face. Felt very parched and feverish. Too much tinned food, perhaps. Next time I catch a fish I'd better eat it myself, even if it makes me unpopular.

I wonder what Greg's up to. Is he up to anything? I sort of see him there, with a beer in his hand, laughing and pointing. 'Until you've ate at BJ's you aint shit,' he says. He's reading it off my cap, staring at me. He's got a girl on his knee. My life with Greg seems as far away from me now as my life in the north.

I saw a flying fish the other day. I'm sure I did. I couldn't have made it up, could I? It made me happy. Fish can fly, and so can reindeer.

Definitely got some fever. Managed to catch a fish and even cook it. Big trouble from Paul and Linda. Dreams, bad dreams. Still heading more or less east, I think.

I'm sure I'm not alone. I mean, I'm sure everywhere in the world there are people like me. It can't be just me, just me alone in a boat with two cats and everyone else on dry land shouting silly cow. I bet there are hundreds, thousands of boats with people in and animals doing what I'm doing. Abandon ship, that was the old cry. Now it's abandon land. There's danger everywhere, but more on land. We all crawled out of the sea once, didn't we? Maybe that was a mistake. Now we're going back to it.

I imagine all the other people doing what I'm doing and that gives me hope. It must be an instinct in the human race, mustn't it? When threatened, scatter. Not just running away from the danger, but raising our chances of survival as a species. If we spread out over the whole globe, the poison won't be able to harm everyone. Even if they fired off all their poison, there must be a chance.

In the night I hear the cats. A hopeful sound.

*   *   *

Bad dreams. Nightmares, I suppose. When does a dream become a nightmare? These dreams of mine go on after I've woken up. It's like having a hangover. The bad dreams won't let the rest of life go on.

She thought she saw another boat on the horizon, and steered towards it. She didn't have any flares, and it was too far away for shouting, so she just steered towards it. It was sailing parallel to the horizon, and she had it in view for half an hour or so. Then it went away. Perhaps it wasn't a boat anyway, she said to herself; but whatever it was, its disappearance left her feeling depressed.

She remembered a terrible thing she'd once read in a newspaper story about life on board a supertanker. Nowadays the ships had got bigger and bigger, while the crew had got smaller and smaller, and everything was done by technology. They programmed a computer in the Gulf or wherever, and the ship practically sailed itself all the way to London or Sydney. It was much nicer for the owners, who saved lots of money, and much nicer for the crew, who only had to worry about the boredom. Most of the time they sat around below deck drinking beer like Greg, as far as she could make out. Drinking beer and watching videos.

There was one thing she couldn't ever forget from the article. It said that in the old days there was always someone up in the crow's nest or on the bridge, watching for trouble. But nowadays the big ships didn't have a lookout any more, or at least the lookout was just a man staring from time to time at a screen with a lot of blips on it. In the old days if you were lost at sea in a raft or a dinghy or something, and a boat came along, there was a pretty good chance of being rescued. You waved and shouted and fired off any rockets you had; you ran your shirt up to the top of the mast; and there were always people keeping an eye out for you. Nowadays you can drift in the ocean for weeks, and a supertanker finally comes along, and it goes right past. The radar won't pick you up because you're too small, and it's pure luck if anybody happens to be hanging over the rail being sick. There had been lots of cases where castaways who would have been rescued in the old days simply weren't picked up; and even incidents of people being run down by the ships they thought were coming to rescue them. She tried to imagine how awful it would be, the terrible wait, and then the feeling as the ship goes past and there's nothing you can do, all your shouts drowned by the engines. That's what's wrong with the world, she thought. We've given up having lookouts. We don't think about saving other people, we just sail on by relying on our machines. Everyone's below deck, having a beer with Greg.

So maybe that ship on the horizon wouldn't have spotted her anyway. Not that she wanted to be rescued or anything. There just might have been some news about the world, that was all.

She began to have more nightmares. The bad dreams hung over longer into the day. She felt she was on her back. There was a pain in her arm. She was wearing white gloves. She was in a sort of cage, as far as she could tell: on either side of her metal bars rose vertically. Men came and saw her, always men. She thought she must write down the nightmares, write them down as well as the true things that were happening. She told the men in the nightmares that she was going to write about them. They smiled and said they would give her a pencil and paper. She refused. She said she would use her own.

She knew the cats were getting a good diet of fish. She knew they didn't get much exercise and were putting on weight. But it just seemed to her that Linda was putting on more weight than Paul. She didn't like to believe it was happening. She didn't dare.

One day she saw land. She started the engine and steered towards it. She got close enough to see mangroves and palms, then the fuel ran out and the winds carried her away. It was a surprise to find no sadness or disappointment within her as the island receded. In any case, she thought, it would have been cheating to find the new land with the help of a diesel engine. The old ways of doing things had to be rediscovered: the future lay in the past. She would allow the winds to guide and guard her. She threw the empty fuel cans overboard.

I'm crazy. I should have got pregnant before I left. Of course. How didn't I see that was the answer? All these jokes from Greg about him being just an impregnator and I couldn't see what was obvious. That was what he was there for. That's why I met him. All that side of things seems odd now. Bits of rubber and tubes to squeeze and pills to swallow. There won't be any of that any more. We're going to give ourselves back to nature now.

I wonder where Greg is; *whether* Greg is. He could be dead. I've always wondered about that phrase the survival of the fittest. Anyone would think, looking at us, that Greg was the fitter to survive: he's bigger, stronger, more practical in our terms anyway, more conservative, more easy-going. I'm a worrier, I've never done carpentry, I'm not so good at being on my own. But I'm the one that's going to survive, or have the chance to anyway. The Survival of the Worriers – is that what it means? People like Greg will die out like the dinosaurs. Only those who can see what's happening will survive, that must be the rule. I bet there were animals who sensed the Ice Age was coming and set off on some long and dangerous journey to find a safer, warmer climate. And I bet the dinosaurs thought they were neurotic, put it down to pre-menstrual tension, said, Silly cow. I wonder if the reindeer saw what was going to happen to them. Do you think they ever sensed it somehow?

They say I don't understand things. They say I'm not making the right connections. Listen to them, listen to them and their connections. This happened, they say, and as a consequence that happened. There was a battle here, a war there, a king was deposed, famous men – always famous men, I'm sick of famous men – made events happen. Maybe I've been out in the sun too long, but I can't see their connections. I look at the history of the world, which they don't seem to realize is coming to an end, and I don't see what they see. All I see is the old connections, the ones we don't take any notice of any more because that makes it easier to poison the reindeer and paint stripes down their backs and feed them to mink. Who made that happen? Which famous man will claim the credit for that?

It's laughable. Listen to this dream. I was in bed, and I couldn't move. Things were a bit blurry. I didn't know where I was. There was a man. I don't remember what he looked like – just a man. He said, 'How are you feeling?'

I said, 'I'm fine.'

'Are you really?'

'Of course I am. Why shouldn't I be?'

He didn't reply, just nodded, and seemed to be looking up and down my body, which was under the bedclothes of course. Then he said, 'None of these urges?'

262 A HISTORY OF THE WORLD IN 10½ CHAPTERS

'What urges?'

'You know what I'm talking about.'

'Excuse me,' I replied – it's funny how you come over all formal in dreams, where you wouldn't in real life – 'Excuse me, but I really haven't the faintest notion of what it is you are referring to.'

'You've been attacking men.'

'Oh, yes? What was I after, their wallets?'

'No. It seems you were after sex.'

I began to laugh. The man frowned; I can remember the frown even if the rest of his face has gone. 'This really is too transparent,' I said, a frosty actress in an old film. I laughed some more. You know that moment, like a break in the cloud, when you realize inside a dream that you're only dreaming? He frowned again. I said, 'Don't be so obvious.' He didn't like that, and went away.

I woke up grinning to myself. Thinking about Greg and the cats and whether I should have got pregnant, and I have a sex-dream. The mind can be pretty straightforward, can't it? What made it think it could get away with something like that?

I'm stuck with this rhyme as we head in whatever direction we're heading:

> In fourteen hundred and ninety-two
> Columbus sailed the ocean blue

And then what? They always make it sound so simple. Names, dates, achievements. I hate dates. Dates are bullies, dates are know-alls.

She was always confident of reaching the island. She was asleep when the wind brought her there. All she had to do was steer between two knuckles of rock and run the boat aground on some pebbles. There was no perfect sweep of sand ready for the tourist's footprint, no coral breakwater, not even a nodding palm. She was relieved and grateful about this. It was better that the sand was rock, the lush jungle a scrub, the fertile soil a dustheap. Too much beauty, too much verdure might make her forget the rest of the planet.

Paul jumped ashore, but Linda waited to be carried. Yes, she thought, it was time we found land. She decided to sleep in the

boat at first. You were supposed to start building a log cabin as
soon as you arrived, but that was silly. The island might not prove
suitable.

She thought that landing on the island would make the nightmares stop.

It was very hot. Anyone would think the place had central
heating, she said to herself. There were no breezes, no change in
the weather. She watched over Paul and Linda. They were her
consolation.

   She wondered if the nightmares were caused by sleeping in the
boat, by being cooped up all night after having the freedom to
walk around all day. She thought her mind could be protesting,
asking to be let out. So she made a little shelter above the tideline
and began sleeping there.

   This didn't make any difference.

   Something terrible was happening to her skin.

The nightmares got worse. She decided this was normal, as far
as you could use the word *normal* any more. At least, it was to
be expected, given her condition. She had been poisoned. How
bad the poison was she didn't know. In her dreams the men
were always very polite, even gentle. This was how she knew
not to trust them: they were tempters. The mind was producing
its own arguments against reality, against itself, what it knew.
There was obviously something chemical behind it all, like
antibodies or whatever. The mind, being in a state of shock
because of what had happened, was creating its own reasons
for denying what had happened. She should have expected
something like that.

I'll give you an example. I'm quite cunning in my nightmares.
When the men come I pretend not to be surprised. I act as if it's
normal that they should be there. I call their bluff. Last night we
had the following exchange. Make of it what you will.

   'Why am I wearing white gloves?' I asked.

   'Is that what you think they are?'

   'What do you think they are?'

   'We had to put a drip in your arm.'

'Is that why I have to wear white gloves? This isn't the opera.'
'They aren't gloves. They're bandages.'
'I thought you said I had a drip in my arm.'
'That's right. The bandages are to hold the drip in place.'
'But I can't move my fingers.'
'That's normal.'
'*Normal?*' I said. 'What's normal nowadays?' He couldn't find an answer to that, so I carried on. 'Which arm is the drip in?'
'The left. You can see that for yourself.'
'Then why have you bandaged my right arm as well?'
He had to think about that for a long time. Finally he said, 'Because you were trying to pull the drip out with your free arm.'
'Why should I want to do that?'
'I should think only you can tell us.'
I shook my head. He went away defeated. But I gave as good as I got, didn't I? And the next night I took them on again. My mind obviously thought I'd seen off that tempter too easily, so it produced a different one, who kept calling me by name.
'How are you tonight, Kath?'
'I thought you always said *we*. That is, if you're who you pretend you are.'
'Why should I say *we*, Kath? I know how I am. I was asking about you.'
'*We*,' I said sarcastically, 'we in the zoo are fine, thank you very much.'
'What do you mean, the zoo?'
'The bars, stupid.' I didn't really think it was a zoo; I wanted to find out what they thought it was. Fighting your own mind isn't always an easy business.
'The bars? Oh, they're just part of your bed.'
'My bed? Excuse me, so it isn't a cot and I'm not a baby?'
'It's a special bed. Look.' He flicked a catch and folded one set of bars down and out of my sight. Then he pulled them up again and latched them shut.
'Oh, I see, you're locking me up, is that the idea?'
'No, no, no, Kath. We just don't want you to fall asleep and roll out of bed. If you had a nightmare, for instance.'
That was a crafty tactic. *If you had a nightmare* . . . But it would take a lot more than this to trick me. I think I know what my mind is doing. It *is* a sort of zoo I'm imagining, because a zoo is the only place I've seen reindeer. Live, I mean. So I associate

them with bars. My mind knows that for me it all started with the reindeer; that's why it invented this deception. It's very plausible, the mind.

'I don't *have* nightmares,' I said firmly, as if they were spots or something. I thought that was good, telling him he didn't exist.

'Well, in case you started sleep-walking or something.'

'Have I been sleep-walking?'

'We can't watch everybody, Kath. There are many others in the same boat as you.'

'I know!' I shouted. 'I know!' I was shouting because I felt triumphant. He was clever, that one, but he'd given himself away. *In the same boat.* Naturally he meant *in other boats*, but he – or rather my mind – had tripped up.

I slept well that night.

She had a terrible thought. What if the kittens weren't all right? What if Linda gave birth to freaks, to monsters? Could it happen this soon? What winds had blown them all here, what poison was in those winds?

She seemed to sleep a lot. The flat heat continued. She felt parched much of the time, and drinking from the stream didn't help. Perhaps there was something wrong with the water. Her skin was falling off. She held up her hands and her fingers looked like the antlers of a fighting stag. Her depressions continued. She tried to cheer herself up with the thought that at least she didn't have a boyfriend on the island. What would Greg say if he saw her like this?

It was the mind, she decided; that was the cause of it all. The mind simply got too clever for its own good, it got carried away. It was the mind that invented these weapons, wasn't it? You couldn't imagine an animal inventing its own destruction, could you?

She told herself the following story. There was a bear in the forest, an intelligent, lively bear, a . . . *normal* bear. One day it started digging a great pit. When it had finished it broke a branch from a tree, pulled off the leaves and twigs, gnawed one end to a sharp point and planted this stake in the bottom of the pit, sticking upwards. Then the bear covered the hole it had dug with branches and undergrowth so that it looked like any other part of the forest floor, and went away. Now where do you think the bear had dug its pit? Right in the middle of one of its own favourite trails, a spot it regularly crossed on its way to drink honey from the trees, or whatever it is bears do. So the next day the bear lolloped along the path, fell into the pit and got impaled on the stake. As it died it thought, My, my, this is a surprise, what a curious way things have turned out. Perhaps it was a mistake to dig a trap where I did. Perhaps it was a mistake to dig a trap in the first place.

You can't imagine a bear doing that, can you? But that's what it's like with us, she reflected. The mind just got carried away. Never knew when to stop. But then the mind never does. It's the same with these nightmares – the sleeping mind just gets carried away. She wondered if primitive people had nightmares. She bet they didn't. Or at least, not the sort we have.

She didn't believe in God, but now she was tempted. Not because she was afraid of dying. It wasn't that. No, she was tempted to believe in someone watching what was going on, watching the bear dig its own pit and then fall into it. It wouldn't be such a good story if there was no one around to tell it. Look what they went and did – they blew themselves up. Silly cows.

The one I had the argument with about the gloves was here again. I caught him out.

'I've still got my gloves on,' I said.

'Yes,' he replied, humouring me but getting it wrong.

'I haven't got a drip in my arm.'

He obviously wasn't prepared for that. 'Ah, no.'

'So why am I wearing my white gloves?'

'Ah.' He paused while deciding which lie to tell. It wasn't a bad one he came up with. 'You were pulling your hair out.'

'Nonsense. It's falling out. It falls out every day.'

'No, I'm afraid you were pulling it out.'

'Nonsense. I only have to put my hand to it and it falls out in great hanks.'

'I'm afraid not,' he said patronizingly.

'Go away,' I shouted. 'Go away, go away.'

'Of course.'

And he went. It was a very devious thing he came up with about my hair, a lie as close to the truth as possible. Because I have been touching my hair. Well, that's not surprising, is it?

Still, it was a good sign that I told him to go and he went.

I feel I'm getting on top of things, I'm beginning to control my nightmares. This is just a period I've been going through. I'll be glad when it ends. The next period may be worse, of course, but at least it'll be different. I wish I knew how much I was poisoned. Enough to put a blue stripe down my back and feed me to the mink?

The mind got carried away, she found herself repeating. Everything was connected, the weapons and the nightmares. That's why they'd had to break the cycle. Start making things simple again. Begin at the beginning. People said you couldn't turn the clock back, but you could. The future was in the past.

She wished she could put a stop to the men and their temptations. She thought they would stop when she reached the island. She thought they would stop when she gave up sleeping in the boat. But they only became more persistent and more cunning. At night she was afraid to fall asleep because of the nightmares; yet she needed rest so much, and each morning she woke later and later. The flat heat continued, a stale, institutional heat; it was like being surrounded by radiators. Would it ever end? Perhaps the seasons had been killed off by what had happened, or at least reduced from four to two – that special winter they'd all been warned about, and this unbearable summer. Maybe the world had to earn the spring and autumn back by good behaviour over many centuries.

I don't know which of the men it was. I've started closing my eyes. That's harder than you think. If you've already got your eyes closed in sleep, try closing them again to shut out a nightmare. It's not easy. But if I can learn this, then perhaps I'll be able to learn putting my hands over my ears as well. That would help.

'How are you feeling this morning?'

'Why do you say *morning*? It's always night when you call.' You see how I don't let them get away with anything?

'If you say so.'

'What do you mean, if I say so?'

'You're the boss.' That's right, I am the boss. You've got to keep control of your own mind, otherwise it'll run away with you. And that's what's caused the peril we're in at the moment. Keep the mind under control.

So I answer, 'Go away.'

'You keep saying that.'

'Well if I'm the boss I'm allowed to, aren't I?'

'You'll have to talk about it one day.'

'*Day*. There you go again.' I kept my eyes closed. 'What's *it*, anyway?' I thought I was still pursuing him, but this may have been a tactical mistake.

'*It*? Oh, everything . . . How you got yourself into this situation, how we're going to help you get out of it.'

'You really are a very ignorant man, you know that?'

He ignored this. I hate the way they pretend not to have heard the things they can't deal with. 'Greg,' he said, clearly changing the subject. 'Your feelings of guilt, rejection, things like that . . .'

'Is Greg alive?' The nightmare was so real I somehow thought the man might know the answer.

'Greg? Yes, Greg's fine. But we thought it wouldn't help . . .'

'Why should I have guilt feelings? I'm not guilty about taking the boat. He just wanted to drink beer and get off with girls. He didn't need a boat for that.'

'I don't think the boat's central to the matter.'

'What do you mean, not central? I wouldn't be here without the boat.'

'I mean you're offloading a lot on to the boat. So that you can avoid thinking about what happened before the boat. Do you think that's what you might be doing?'

'How would I know? *You're* meant to be the expert.' This was very sarcastic of me, I know, but I couldn't resist it. I was angry with him. As if *I* was ignoring what had happened before I took the boat. *I* was one of the few people that noticed, after all. The rest of the world behaved like Greg. 'Well, I think we seem to be making some progress.'

'Go away.'

I knew he'd be back. In a way I was sort of waiting for him to return. Just to get it over with, I suppose. And he had me intrigued, I'll admit that. I mean, I know exactly what's happened, and more or less why and more or less how. But I wanted to see how clever his – well, my own, really – explanation would be.

'So you think you might be ready to talk about Greg.'

'*Greg?* What's it got to do with Greg?'

'Well, it seems to us, and we'd like your confirmation on this one, that your ... your break-up with Greg has a lot to do with your present ... problems.'

'You really are a very ignorant man.' I liked saying that.

'Then help cure me of my ignorance, Kath. Explain things to me. When did you first notice things were going wrong with Greg?'

'Greg, Greg. There's been a bloody nuclear war and all you want to talk about is *Greg*.'

'Yes, the war, of course. But I thought we'd better take one thing at a time.'

'And Greg is more important than the war? You certainly have an odd system of priorities. Perhaps Greg caused the war. You know he's got a baseball cap that says MAKE WAR NOT LOVE on it? Perhaps he sat there drinking beer and pressed the button just for something to do.'

'That's an interesting approach. I think we could get some-where with that.' I didn't respond. He went on, 'Would we be right in thinking that with Greg you sort of were putting all your eggs in one basket? You thought he was your last chance? Perhaps you were laying too many expectations on him?'

I'd had enough of this. 'My name is Kathleen Ferris,' I said, as much to myself as to anybody else. 'I'm thirty-eight years old. I left the north and came to the south because I could see what was happening. But the war pursued me. It came anyway. I got in the boat, I let the winds carry me. I took two cats, Paul and Linda. I found this island. I am living here. I don't know what will happen to me, but I know it's the duty of those of us who care about the planet to go on living.' When I stopped I found I'd burst into tears without realizing. The tears ran down the sides of my face and into my ears. I couldn't see, I couldn't hear. I felt I was swimming, drowning.

Eventually, very quietly – or was it just that my ears were full of water? – the man said, 'Yes, we thought you might be seeing things like that.'

'I have been through the bad winds. My skin is falling off. I am thirsty all the time. I don't know how serious it is, but I know I have to go on. If only for the cats. They might need me.'

'Yes.'

'What do you *mean*, Yes?'

'Well, psychosomatic symptoms can be very convincing.'

'Can't you get it into your head? There's been a bloody nuclear war.'

'Hmmm,' said the man. He was being deliberately provocative.

'All right,' I replied. 'I may as well listen to your version. I can feel you wanting to tell me.'

'Well, we think it goes back to your break-up with Greg. And to your relationship of course. The possessiveness, the violence. But the break-up . . .'

Though I'd been meaning to play along with him, I couldn't help interrupting. 'It wasn't really a break-up. I just took the boat when the war started.'

'Yes, of course. But things between you . . . you wouldn't say they were going well?'

'No worse than with other blokes. He's just a bloke, Greg. He's normal for a bloke.'

'Precisely.'

'What do you mean, *precisely*?'

'Well, we called in your files from the north, you see. There does seem to be a pattern. You like putting all your eggs in one basket. With the same type of man. And that's always a bit dangerous, isn't it?' When I didn't reply, he went on, 'We call it the persistent victim syndrome. PVS.'

I decided to ignore that too. For a start, I didn't know what he was talking about. Spinning some tale or other.

'There's a lot of denial in your life, isn't there? You . . . deny a lot of things.'

'Oh no I don't,' I said. This was ridiculous. I made up my mind to force him out into the open. 'Are you telling me, are you telling me there hasn't been a war?'

'That's right. I mean, it was very worrying. It looked as if there might well be one. But they sorted something out.'

'*They sorted something out!*' I said it in a sarcastic shout, because this proved everything. My mind had been remembering that phrase of Greg's which I'd found so complacent. I enjoyed shouting, I wanted to shout something else, so I did. 'Until you've ate at BJ's you aint shit!' I yelled. I was feeling triumphant, but the man didn't seem to understand, and he laid a hand on my arm as if I needed comforting.

'Yes, they really sorted something out. It never happened.'

'I see,' I replied, still victorious. 'So of course I'm not on the island?'

'Oh no.'

'I imagined it.'

'Yes.'

'And so of course the boat doesn't exist either?'

'Oh yes, you went on the boat.'

'But there weren't any cats on it.'

'Yes, you had two cats with you when they found you. They were terribly thin. They only just survived.'

It was cunning of him not to contradict me entirely. Cunning, but predictable. I decided on a switch of tactics. I'd be puzzled, and a bit pathetic. 'I don't understand,' I said, reaching out and taking his hand. 'If there wasn't any war, why was I in the boat?'

'Greg,' he said, with a sort of nasty confidence, as if I'd finally admitted something. 'You were running away. We find that those with persistent victim syndrome often experience acute guilt when they finally take flight. Then there was the bad news from the north. That was your excuse. You were exteriorizing things, transferring your confusion and anxiety on to the world. It's normal,' he added patronizingly, though it was obvious he didn't think so. 'Quite normal.'

'I'm not the only persistent victim around here,' I replied. 'The whole bloody world's a persistent victim.'

'Of course.' He agreed without really listening.

'They said there was going to be a war. They said the war had started.'

'They're always saying that. But they sorted something out.'

'So you keep saying. Well. So, in your *version*' – I stressed the word – 'where did they find me?'

'About a hundred miles east of Darwin. Going round in circles.'

'Going round in circles,' I repeated. 'That's what the world does.' First he tells me I'm projecting myself on to the world, then he tells me I'm doing what we all know the world does all the time. This really wasn't very impressive.

'And how do you explain my hair falling out?'

'You've been pulling it out, I'm afraid.'

'And my skin falling off?'

'It's been a bad time for you. You've been under severe stress. It's not unusual. But it'll get better.'

'And how do you explain that I remember very clearly everything that's happened from the news of the war breaking out in the north to my time here on the island?'

'Well, the technical term is fabulation. You make up a story to cover the facts you don't know or can't accept. You keep a few true facts and spin a new story round them. Particularly in cases of double stress.'

'Meaning?'

'Severe stress in the private life coupled with a political crisis in the world outside. We always get an increase in admissions when things are going badly in the north.'

'You'll be telling me next there were dozens of crazy people going round in circles in the sea.'

'A few. Four or five maybe. Most of the admissions didn't make it as far as a boat, though.' He sounded as if he was impressed by my tenacity.

'And how many . . . admissions have you had this time?'

'A couple of dozen.'

'Well, I admire your fabulation,' I said, using the technical term back to him. That put him in his place. 'I really think it's quite clever.' He'd given himself away, of course. *You keep a few true facts and spin a new story round them* – exactly what he'd done.

'I'm glad we're making some progress, Kath.'

'Go away and sort something out,' I said. 'By the way, is there any news of the reindeer?'

'What sort of news did you want?'

'Good news!' I shouted. 'Good news!'

'I'll see what I can do.'

She felt tired when the nightmare left; tired but victorious. She had drawn out the worst the tempter had to offer. She would be safe now. Of course, he'd made a whole series of blunders. *I'm glad we're making some progress*: he should never have said that. Nobody likes to be patronized by their own mind. The one that really gave him away was about the cats getting thin. That had been the most noticeable thing about the whole voyage, the way the cats got fatter, the way they loved the fish she caught.

She made a decision not to speak to the men again. She couldn't stop them coming – and she was sure they would visit her for many more nights – but she wouldn't speak to them. She had learnt how to shut her eyes in her nightmares; now she would learn to stop her ears and her mouth. She wouldn't be tempted. She wouldn't.

If she had to die then she would. They must have come through some very bad winds; how bad she would only find out when she either recovered or died. She worried about the cats, but believed they'd be able to fend for themselves. They would return to nature. They already had. When the food from the boat ran out they took to hunting. Or rather Paul did: Linda was too fat to hunt. Paul brought back small creatures for her, things like voles and mice. Tears bubbled into Kath's eyes when he did so.

It was all about her mind being afraid of its own death, that's what she finally decided. When her skin got bad and her hair started falling out, her mind tried to think up an alternative explanation. She even knew the technical term for it now: fabulation. Where had she picked that up from? She must have read it in a magazine somewhere. Fabulation. You keep a few true facts and spin a new story round them.

She remembered an exchange she'd had the previous night. The man in the dream said you deny a lot of things in your life don't you, and she'd answered oh no I don't. That was funny, looking back; but it was also serious. You mustn't fool yourself. That's what Greg did, that's what most people did. We've got to look at things how they are; we can't rely on fabulation any more. It's the only way we'll survive.

The next day, on a small, scrubby island in the Torres Strait, Kath Ferris woke up to find that Linda had given birth. Five tortoise-shell kittens, all huddling together, helpless and blind, yet quite without defect. She felt such love. The cat wouldn't let her touch the kittens, of course, but that was all right, that was normal. She felt such happiness! Such hope!

5
SHIPWRECK

I

IT BEGAN WITH a portent.

They had doubled Cape Finisterre and were sailing south before a fresh wind when a school of porpoises surrounded the frigate. Those on board crowded the poop and the breastwork, marvelling at the animals' ability to circle a vessel already gaily proceeding at nine or ten knots. As they were admiring the sports of the porpoises, a cry was raised. A cabin boy had fallen through one of the fore portholes on the larboard side. A signal gun was fired, a life-raft thrown out, and the vessel hove to. But these manoeuvres were cumbrously done, and by the time the six-oared barge was let down, it was in vain. They could not find the raft, let alone the boy. He was only fifteen years old, and those who knew him maintained that he was a strong swimmer; they conjectured that he would most probably have reached the raft. If so, he doubtless perished upon it, after having experienced the most cruel sufferings.

The expedition for Senegal consisted of four vessels: a frigate, a corvette, a flute and a brig. It had set sail from the Island of Aix on 17th June 1816 with 365 people on board. Now it continued south with its complement reduced by one. They provisioned at Tenerife, taking on precious wines, oranges, lemons, banian figs and vegetables of all kinds. Here they noted the depravity of the local inhabitants: the women of Saint Croix stood at their doors and urged the Frenchmen to enter, confident that their husbands' jealousies would be cured by the monks of the Inquisition who would speak disapprovingly of conjugal mania as the blinding gift of Satan. Reflective passengers ascribed such behaviour to the southern sun, whose power, it is known, weakens both natural and moral bonds.

From Tenerife they sailed south-south-west. Fresh winds and navigational ineptitude scattered the flotilla. Alone, the frigate

passed the tropic and rounded Cape Barbas. It was running close
to the shore, at times no more than half a cannon shot away. The
sea was strewn with rocks; brigantines could not frequent these
seas at low water. They had doubled Cape Blanco, or so they
believed, when they found themselves in shallows; the lead was
cast every half-hour. At daybreak Mr Maudet, ensign of the
watch, made out the reckoning upon a chicken coop, and judged
that they were on the edge of the Arguin reef. His advice was discounted. But even those unschooled in the sea could observe that
the water had changed colour; weed was apparent at the ship's
side, and a great many fish were being taken. In calm seas and
clear weather, they were running aground. The lead announced
eighteen fathoms, then shortly afterwards six fathoms. The
frigate luffing, almost immediately gave a heel; a second and third,
then stopped. The sounding line showed a depth of five metres
and sixty centimetres.

By misfortune, they had struck the reef at high tide; and the
seas growing violent, attempts to free the ship failed. The frigate
was assuredly lost. Since the boats it carried were not capacious
enough to contain the whole personnel, it was decided to build
a raft and embark upon it those who could not be put into the
boats. The raft would then be towed to the shore and all would
be saved. This plan was perfectly well-laid; but as two of the company were later to affirm, it was traced upon loose sand, which
was dispersed by the breath of egotism.

The raft was made, and well made, places in the boats allotted,
provisions made ready. At daybreak, with two metres and seventy
centimetres of water in the hold and the pumps failing, the order
was given to abandon ship. Yet disorder quickly embraced the
well-laid plan. The allotment of places was ignored, and the provisions were carelessly handled, forgotten or lost in the waters.
One hundred and fifty was to be the complement of the raft: one
hundred and twenty soldiers including officers, twenty-nine men
sailors and passengers, one woman. But scarcely had fifty men got
on board this machine – whose extent was twenty metres in
length and seven in breadth – than it sank to at least seventy centimetres under water. They cast off the barrels of flour which had
been embarked, whereupon the level of the raft rose; the remaining people descended upon it, and it sank again. When the
machine was fully laden, it was a metre beneath the surface, and
those on board so crowded that they could not take a single step;

at the back and front, they were in water up to the waist. Loose flour barrels were cast against them by the waves; a twenty-five-pound bag of biscuit was thrown down to them, which the water converted at once into a paste.

It had been intended that one of the naval officers should take command of the raft; but this officer declined to come on board. At seven o'clock in the morning the signal for departure was given, and the little flotilla pulled away from the abandoned frigate. Seventeen persons had refused to leave the vessel, or had concealed themselves away, and thus remained on board to discover their fate.

The raft was towed by four boats in line astern, preceded by a pinnace, which made soundings. As the boats took up their positions, cries of *Vive le roi!* arose from the men on the raft, and a small white flag was raised upon the end of a musket. But it was at this instant of greatest hope and expectation for those upon the raft that the breath of egotism was added to the normal winds of the seas. One by one, whether for reason of self-interest, incompetence, misfortune or seeming necessity, the tow-ropes were cast aside.

The raft was barely two leagues from the frigate when it was abandoned. Those on board had wine, a little brandy, some water and a small portion of sodden biscuit. They had been given no compass or chart. With neither oars nor rudder, there was no means of controlling the raft, and little means either of controlling those upon it, who were constantly flung against one another as the waters rolled over them. In the first night, a storm got up and threw the machine with great violence; the cries of those on board mingled with the roaring of the billows. Some attached ropes to the timbers of the craft, and held fast to these; all were buffeted without mercy. By daybreak the air was filled with lamentable cries, vows which could never be fulfilled were offered up to Heaven, and all prepared themselves for imminent death. It was impossible to form an idea of that first night which was not below the truth.

The next day the seas were calm, and for many hope was rekindled. Nevertheless, two young lads and a baker, convinced that there was no escape from death, bade farewell to their companions and willingly embraced the sea. It was during this day that those on the raft began to experience their first delusions. Some fancied that they saw land, others espied vessels come to

save them, and the dashing of these deceptive hopes upon the
rocks provoked greater despondency.

The second night was more terrible than the first. The seas
were mountainous and the raft constantly near to being overthrown; the officers, clustered by the short mast, ordered the
soldiery from one side of the machine to the other to counterbalance the energy of the waves. A group of men, certain that
they were lost, broke open a cask of wine and resolved to soothe
their last moments by abandoning the power of reason; in which
they succeeded, until the sea water coming in through the
hole they had made in the cask spoiled the wine. Thus doubly
maddened, these disordered men determined to send all to a
common destruction, and to this end attacked the ropes that
bound the raft together. The mutineers being resisted, a pitched
battle took place amid the waves and the darkness of the night.
Order was restored, and there was an hour of tranquillity upon
that fatal machine. But at midnight the soldiery rose again and
attacked their superiors with knives and sabres; those without
weapons were so deranged that they attempted to tear at the
officers with their teeth, and many bites were endured. Men were
thrown into the sea, bludgeoned, stabbed; two barrels of wine
were thrown overboard and the last of the water. By the time the
villains were subdued, the raft was laden with corpses.

During the first uprising, a workman by the name of Dominique, who had joined the mutineers, was cast into the sea. On
hearing the piteous cries of this treacherous underling, the engineer in charge of the workmen threw himself into the water, and
taking the villain by the hair, succeeded in dragging him back on
board. Dominique's head had been split open by a sabre. In the
darkness the wound was bound up and the wretch restored to
life. But no sooner was he so revived than, ungrateful as he was,
he rejoined the mutineers and rose with them again. This time
he found less fortune and less mercy; he perished that night.

Delirium now menaced the unhappy survivors. Some threw
themselves into the sea; some fell into torpor; some unfortunate
wretches rushed at their comrades with sabres drawn demanding
to be given *the wing of a chicken*. The engineer whose bravery
had saved the workman Dominique pictured himself travelling
the fine plains of Italy, and one of the officers saying to him,
'I remember that we have been deserted by the boats; but fear
nothing; I have just written to the governor, and in a few hours

we shall be saved.' The engineer, calm in his delirium, responded thus: 'Have you a pigeon to carry your orders with as much celerity?'

Only one cask of wine remained for the sixty still on board the raft. They collected tags from the soldiers and fashioned them into fish-hooks; they took a bayonet and bent it into such shape as to catch a shark. Whereupon a shark arrived, and seized the bayonet, and with a savage twist of its jaw straightened it fully out again, and swam away.

An extreme resource proved necessary to prolong their miserable existence. Some of those who had survived the night of the mutiny fell upon the corpses and hacked pieces from them, devouring the flesh on the instant. Most of the officers refused this meat; though one proposed that it should first be dried to make it more palatable. Some tried chewing swordbelts and cartouche boxes, and the leather trimmings to their hats, with little benefit. One sailor attempted to eat his own excrements, but he could not succeed.

The third day was calm and fine. They took repose, but cruel dreams added to the horrors already inflicted by hunger and thirst. The raft, which now carried less than one half its original complement, had risen up in the water, an unforeseen benefit of the night's mutinies. Yet those on board remained in water to the knees, and could only repose standing up, pressed against one another in a solid mass. On the fourth morning they perceived that a dozen of their fellows had died in the night; the bodies were given to the sea, except for one that was reserved against their hunger. At four o'clock that afternoon a shoal of flying fish passed over the raft, and many became ensnared in the extremities of the machine. That night they dressed the fish, but their hunger was so great and each portion so exiguous, that many of them added human flesh to the fish, and the flesh being dressed was found less repugnant. Even the officers began to eat it when presented in this form.

It was from this day onwards that all learned to consume human flesh. The next night was to bring a fresh supply. Some Spaniards, Italians and Negroes, who had remained neutral during the first mutinies, conspired together with the plan of throwing their superiors overboard and escaping to the shore, which they believed to be at hand, with those valuables and possessions which had been placed into a bag and hung upon the mast. Once more, a terrible combat ensued, and blood washed over the fatal raft. When this third mutiny was finally suppressed, there remained no more than thirty on board, and the raft had risen yet again in the water. Barely a man lay without wounds, into which salt water constantly flowed, and piercing cries were heard.

On the seventh day two soldiers concealed themselves behind the last barrel of wine. They struck a hole in it and began to drink the wine through a straw. On being discovered, the two tres-passers were instantly cast into the water, in accordance with the necessary law that had been promulgated.

It was now that the most terrible decision came to be taken. On counting their numbers, it was found that they were twenty-seven. Fifteen of these were likely to live for some days; the rest, suffering from large wounds and many of them delirious, had but the smallest chance of survival. In the time that might elapse before their deaths, however, they would surely diminish further the limited supply of provisions. It was calculated that they could well drink between them as many as thirty or forty bottles of wine. To put the sick on half allowance was but to kill them by degrees. And thus, after a debate in which the most dreadful despair presided, it was agreed among the fifteen healthy persons that their sick comrades must, for the common good of those who might yet survive, be cast into the sea. Three sailors and a soldier, their hearts now hardened by the constant sight of death, performed these repugnant but necessary executions. The healthy were separated from the unhealthy like the clean from the unclean.

After this cruel sacrifice, the last fifteen survivors threw all their arms into the water, reserving only a sabre lest some rope or wood might need cutting. There was sustenance left for six days while they awaited death.

There came a small event which each interpreted according to his nature. A white butterfly, of a species common in France, appeared over their heads fluttering, and settled upon the sail. To some, crazed with hunger, it seemed that even this could make a morsel. To others, the ease with which their visitor moved appeared a very mockery when they lay exhausted and almost motionless beneath it. To yet others, this simple butterfly was a sign, a messenger from Heaven as white as Noah's dove. Even those sceptical ones who declined to recognize a divine instrument knew with cautious hope that butterflies travel little distance from the dry land.

Yet no dry land appeared. Under the burning sun a raging thirst consumed them, until they began to moisten their lips with their own urine. They drank it from little tin cups which first they placed in water to cool their inner liquid the quicker. It happened that a man's cup might be stolen and restored to him later, but without the urine it had previously held. There was one who could not bring himself to swallow it, however thirsty he might be. A surgeon amongst them remarked that the urine of some men was more agreeable to swallow than that of others. He further remarked that the one immediate effect of drinking urine was an inclination to produce urine anew.

An officer of the army discovered a lemon, which he intended to reserve entirely for himself; violent entreaties persuaded him of the perils of selfishness. Thirty cloves of garlic were also found, from which arose further disputation; had all weapons but a sabre not been discarded, blood might have been shed once more. There were two phials filled with spirituous liquor for cleaning the teeth; one or two drops of this liquor, dispensed with reluctance by its possessor, produced on the tongue a delightful sensation which for a few seconds cast out thirst. Some pieces of pewter on being placed in the mouth effected a kind of coolness. An empty phial which had once contained essence of roses was passed among the survivors; they inhaled, and the remnants of perfume made a soothing impression.

On the tenth day several of the men, upon receiving their allotment of wine, conceived the plan of becoming intoxicated and then destroying themselves; they were with difficulty persuaded from this notion. Sharks surrounded the raft, and some soldiers, in their derangement, openly bathed within sight of the great fish. Eight of the men, reckoning that land could not be far distant, constructed a second raft upon which to escape. They built a narrow machine with a low mast and a hammock cloth for a sail; but as they made a trial of it, the frailty of the craft proved to them the temerity of their enterprise, and they abandoned it.

On the thirteenth day of their ordeal, the sun rose entirely free from clouds. The fifteen wretches had put up their prayers to the Almighty, and divided amongst them their portion of wine, when a captain of infantry, looking towards the horizon, descried a ship and announced it with an exclamation. All offered thanks to the Lord and gave way to transports of joy. They straightened barrel hoops and attached handkerchiefs to the end; one of their number mounted to the top of the mast and waved these little flags. All watched the vessel on the horizon and guessed at its progress. Some estimated that it was coming closer by the minute; others asserted that its course lay in a contrary direction. For half an hour they lay suspended between hope and fear. Then the ship disappeared from the sea.

From joy they fell into despondency and grief; they envied the fate of those who had died before them. Then, to find some consolation from their despair in sleep, they rigged a piece of cloth as shelter from the sun, and lay down beneath it. They proposed to write an account of their adventures, which they would all sign, and nail it to the top of the mast, hoping that it might by some means reach their families and the Government.

They had passed two hours among the most cruel reflections when the master gunner, wishing to go to the front of the raft, went out of the tent and saw the *Argus* half a league distant, carrying a full press of sail, and bearing down upon them. He could scarcely breathe. His hands stretched towards the sea. 'Saved!' he said. 'See the brig close upon us!' All rejoiced; even the wounded made to crawl towards the back part of the machine, the better to see their saviours approaching. They embraced one another, and their delight redoubled when they saw that they owed their deliverance to Frenchmen. They waved handkerchiefs and thanked Providence.

The *Argus* clewed up her sails and lay on to their starboard, half a pistol shot away. The fifteen survivors, the strongest of whom could not have lived beyond the next forty-eight hours, were taken up on board; the commander and officers of the brig, by their reiterated care, rekindled in the survivors the flame of life. Two who later wrote their account of the ordeal concluded that the manner in which they were saved was truly miraculous, and that the finger of Heaven was conspicuous in the event.

The voyage of the frigate had begun with a portent, and it ended with an echo. When the fatal raft, towed by its attendant vessels, had put to sea, there were seventeen persons left behind. Thus abandoned by their own choice, they straightaway examined the ship for everything that the departing had not taken and the sea had not penetrated. They found biscuit, wine, brandy

and bacon, enough to subsist for a while. At first tranquillity prevailed, for their comrades had promised to return to their rescue. But when forty-two days had passed without relief, twelve of the seventeen determined to reach land. To this end they constructed a second raft from some of the frigate's remaining timbers, which they bound together with strong ropes, and they embarked upon it. Like their predecessors, they lacked oars and navigational equipment, and possessed no more than a rudimentary sail. They took with them a small supply of provisions and what hope there was remaining. But many days later some Moors who live beside the Saharan coast and are subjects of King Zaide discovered the vestiges of their craft, and came to Andar with this information. It was believed that the men on this second raft were doubtless the prey of those sea-monsters which are found in great numbers off the shores of Africa.

And then finally, as if in mockery, there came the echo of an echo. Five men remained upon the frigate. Several days after the second raft had departed, a sailor who had refused to go upon it also attempted to reach the shore. Unable to construct a third raft for himself, he put to sea in a chicken coop. Perhaps it was the very cage upon which Mr Maudet had verified the frigate's fatal course on that morning when they had struck the reef. But the chicken coop sank and the sailor perished when no more than half a cable's length from the *Medusa*.

II

How do you turn catastrophe into art?

Nowadays the process is automatic. A nuclear plant explodes? We'll have a play on the London stage within a year. A President is assassinated? You can have the book or the film or the filmed book or the booked film. War? Send in the novelists. A series of gruesome murders? Listen for the tramp of the poets. We have to understand it, of course, this catastrophe; to understand it, we have to imagine it, so we need the imaginative arts. But we also need to justify it and forgive it, this catastrophe, however minimally. Why did it happen, this mad act of Nature, this crazed human moment? Well, at least it produced art. Perhaps, in the end, that's what catastrophe is *for*.

He shaved his head before he started the picture, we all know that. Shaved his head so he wouldn't be able to see anyone, locked himself in his studio and came out when he'd finished his masterpiece. Is that what happened?

The expedition set off on 17th June 1816.

The *Medusa* struck the reef in the afternoon of 2nd July 1816.

The survivors were rescued from the raft on 17th July 1816.

Savigny and Corréard published their account of the voyage in November 1817.

The canvas was bought on 24th February 1818.

The canvas was transferred to a larger studio and restretched on 28th June 1818.

The painting was finished in July 1819.

On 28th August 1819, three days before the opening of the Salon, Louis XVIII examined the painting and addressed to the artist what the *Moniteur Universel* called 'one of those felicitous remarks which at the same time judge the work and encourage the artist'. The King said, 'Monsieur Géricault, your shipwreck is certainly no disaster.'

It begins with truth to life. The artist read Savigny and Corréard's account; he met them, interrogated them. He compiled a dossier of the case. He sought out the carpenter from the *Medusa*, who had survived, and got him to build a scale model of his original machine. On it he positioned wax models to represent the survivors. Around him in his studio he placed his own paintings of severed heads and dissected limbs, to infiltrate the air with mortality. Recognizable portraits of Savigny, Corréard and the carpenter are included in the final picture. (How did they feel about posing for this reprise of their sufferings?)

He was perfectly calm when painting, reported Antoine Alphonse Montfort, the pupil of Horace Vernet; there was little perceptible motion of the body or the arms, and only a slight flushing of the face to indicate his concentration. He worked directly on to the white canvas with only a rough outline to guide him. He painted for as long as there was light with a remorselessness which was also rooted in technical necessity: the heavy, fast-drying oils he used meant that each section, once begun, had to be completed that day. He had, as we know, had his head shaved of its reddish-blond curls, as a Do Not Disturb sign. But he was not solitary: models, pupils and friends continued coming to the house, which he shared with his young assistant Louis-Alexis Jamar. Among the models he used was the young Delacroix, who posed for the dead figure lying face down with his left arm extended.

Let us start with what he did not paint. He did not paint:

(1) The *Medusa* striking the reef;
(2) The moment when the tow-ropes were cast off and the raft abandoned;
(3) The mutinies in the night;
(4) The necessary cannibalism;
(5) The self-protective mass murder;
(6) The arrival of the butterfly;
(7) The survivors up to their waists, or calves, or ankles in water;
(8) The actual moment of rescue.

In other words his first concern was not to be (1) political; (2) symbolic; (3) theatrical; (4) shocking; (5) thrilling; (6) senti-mental; (7) documentational; or (8) unambiguous.

Notes

(1) The *Medusa* was a shipwreck, a news story and a painting; it was also a cause. Bonapartists attacked Monarchists. The behav-iour of the frigate's captain illuminated (a) the incompetence and corruption of the Royalist Navy; (b) the general callousness of the ruling class towards those beneath them. Parallels with the ship of state running aground would have been both obvious and heavy-handed.

 (2) Savigny and Corréard, survivors and co-authors of the first account of the shipwreck, petitioned the government, seeking compensation for the victims and punishment for the guilty officers. Rebuffed by institutional justice, they applied to the wider courts of public opinion with their book. Corréard sub-sequently set up as a publisher and pamphleteer with a shop called At The Wreck of The *Medusa*; it became a meeting-place for political malcontents. We can imagine a painting of the moment when the tow-ropes are loosed: an axe, glittering in the sun, is being swung; an officer, turning his back on the raft, is casually slipping a knot . . . It would make an excellent painted pamphlet.

(3) The Mutiny was the scene that Géricault most nearly painted. Several preliminary drawings survive. Night, tempest, heavy seas, riven sail, raised sabres, drowning, hand-to-hand combat, naked bodies. What's wrong with all this? Mainly that it looks like one of those saloon-bar fights in B-Westerns where every single person is involved – throwing a punch, smashing a chair, breaking a bottle over an enemy's head, swinging heavy-booted from the chandelier. Too much is going on. You can tell more by showing less.

The sketches of the Mutiny that survive are held to resemble traditional versions of the Last Judgment, with its separation of the innocent from the guilty, and with the fall of the mutinous into damnation. Such an allusion would have been misleading. On the raft, it was not virtue that triumphed, but strength; and there was little mercy to be had. The sub-text of this version would say that God was on the side of the officer-class. Perhaps he used to be in those days. Was Noah officer-class?

(4) There is very little cannibalism in Western art. Prud-ishness? This seems unlikely: Western art is not prudish about gouged eyes, severed heads in bags, sacrificial mastectomy, cir-cumcision, crucifixion. What's more, cannibalism was a heathen practice which could be usefully condemned in paint while surreptitiously enflaming the spectator. But some subjects just seem to get painted more than others. Take officer-class Noah, for instance. There seem to be surprisingly few pictures of his Ark around. There is the odd jocular American primitive, and a murky Giacomo Bassano in the Prado, yet not much else springs to mind. Adam and Eve, the Expulsion, the Annuncia-tion, the Last Judgment – you can have all these by major artists. But Noah and his Ark? A key moment in human history, a storm at sea, picturesque animals, divine intervention in human affairs: surely the necessary elements are there. What could account for this iconographical deficiency? Perhaps the lack of a single Ark painting great enough to give the subject impetus and popularity. Or is it something in the story itself: maybe artists agreed that the Flood doesn't show God in the best possible light?

Géricault made one sketch of cannibalism on the raft. The spotlit moment of anthropophagy shows a well-muscled survivor gnawing the elbow of a well-muscled cadaver. It is almost comic. Tone was always going to be the problem here.

(5) A painting is a moment. What would we think was happening in a scene where three sailors and a soldier were throwing people off a raft into the sea? That the victims were already dead? Or if not, that they were being murdered for their jewellery? Cartoonists having trouble explaining the background to their jokes often give us newsvendors standing by billboards on which some convenient headline is inscribed. With painting, the equivalent information would have to be given in the title: A GRIEVOUS SCENE ABOARD THE RAFT OF THE MEDUSA IN WHICH DESPERATE SURVIVORS, WRACKED BY CONSCIENCE, REALIZE THAT PROVISIONS ARE INSUFFICIENT AND TAKE THE TRAGIC BUT NECESSARY DECISION TO SACRIFICE THE WOUNDED IN ORDER THAT THEY THEMSELVES MIGHT HAVE A GREATER CHANCE OF SURVIVAL. That should just about do it.

The title of 'The Raft of the Medusa', incidentally, is not 'The Raft of the Medusa'. The painting was listed in the Salon catalogue as *Scène de naufrage* – 'Scene of Shipwreck'. A cautious political move? Perhaps. But it's equally a useful instruction to the spectator: this is a painting, not an opinion.

(6) It's not hard to imagine the arrival of the butterfly as depicted by other painters. But it sounds fairly coarse in its emotional appeal, doesn't it? And even if the question of tone could be overcome, there are two major difficulties. First, it wouldn't look like a true event, even though it was; what is true is not necessarily convincing. Second, a white butterfly six or eight centimetres across, alighting on a raft twenty metres long by seven metres broad, does give serious problems of scale.

(7) If the raft is under water, you can't paint the raft. The figures would all be sprouting from the sea like a line-up of Venus Anadyomenes. Further, the lack of a raft presents formal problems: with everyone standing up because if they lay down they would drown, your painting is stiff with verticals; you have to be extra-ingenious. Better to wait until more on board have died, the raft has risen out of the water, and the horizontal plane becomes fully available.

(8) The boat from the *Argus* pulling alongside, the survivors holding out their arms and clambering in, the pathetic contrast between the condition of the rescued and that of the rescuers, a scene of exhaustion and joy – all very affecting, no doubt about

it. Géricault made several sketches of this moment of rescue. It could make a strong image; but it's a bit . . . straightforward.

That's what he didn't paint.

What did he paint, then? Well, what does it look as if he painted? Let us reimagine our eye into ignorance. We scrutinize 'Scene of Shipwreck' with no knowledge of French naval history. We see survivors on a raft hailing a tiny ship on the horizon (the distant vessel, we can't help noticing, is no bigger than that butterfly would have been). Our initial presumption is that this is the moment of sighting which leads to a rescue. This feeling comes partly from a tireless preference for happy endings, but also from posing ourselves, at some level of consciousness, the following question: how would we know about these people on the raft if they had *not* been rescued?

What backs up this presumption? The ship is on the horizon; the sun is also on the horizon (though unseen), lightening it with yellow. Sunrise, we deduce, and the ship arriving with the sun, bringing a new day, hope and rescue; the black clouds overhead (very black) will soon disappear. However, what if it were sunset? Dawn and dusk are easily confused. 'What if it were sunset, with the ship about to vanish like the sun, and the castaways facing hopeless night as black as that cloud overhead? Puzzled, we might look at the raft's sail to see if the machine was being blown towards or away from its rescuer, and to judge if that baleful cloud is about to be dispelled; but we get little help – the wind is blowing not up and down the picture but from right to left, and the frame cuts us off from further knowledge of the weather to our right. Then, still undecided, a third possibility occurs: it could be sunrise, yet even so the rescuing vessel is not coming towards the shipwrecked. This would be the plainest rebuff of all from fate: the sun is rising, *but not for you*.

The ignorant eye yields, with a certain testy reluctance, to the informed eye. Let's check 'Scene of Shipwreck' against Savigny and Corréard's narrative. It's clear at once that Géricault hasn't painted the hailing that led to the final rescue: that happened differently, with the brig suddenly close upon the raft and everyone rejoicing. No, this is the first sighting, when the *Argus* appeared on the horizon for a tantalizing half hour. Comparing paint with print, we notice at once that Géricault has not represented the survivor up the mast holding straightened-out barrel-hoops with handkerchiefs attached to them. He has opted instead for a man being held up on top of a barrel and waving a large cloth. We pause over this change, then acknowledge its advantage: reality offered him a monkey-up-a-stick image; art suggested a solider focus and an extra vertical.

But let us not inform ourselves too quickly. Return the question to the tetchy ignorant eye. Forget the weather; what can be deduced from the personnel on the raft itself? Why not start with a head-count. There are twenty figures on board. Two are actively waving, one actively pointing, two vigorously supplicating, plus one offering muscular support to the hailing figure on the barrel: six in favour of hope and rescue. Then there are five figures (two prone, three supine) who look either dead or dying, plus an old greybeard with his back to the sighted *Argus* in a posture of mourning: six against. In between (we measure space as well as mood) there are eight more figures: one half-supplicating, half-supporting; three watching the hailer with non-committal expressions; one watching the hailer agonizingly; two in profile examining, respectively, waves past and waves to come; plus one obscure figure in the darkest, most damaged part of the canvas, with head in hands (and clawing at his scalp?). Six, six and eight: no overall majority.

(Twenty? queries the informed eye. But Savigny and Corréard said there were only fifteen survivors. So all those five figures who might only be unconscious are definitely dead? Yes. But then what about the culling which took place, when the last fifteen healthy survivors pitched their thirteen wounded comrades into the sea? Géricault has dragged some of them back from the deep to help out with his composition. And should the dead lose their vote in the referendum over hope versus despair? Technically, yes; but not in assessing the mood of the picture.)

So the structure is balanced, six for, six against, eight don't knows. Our two eyes, ignorant and informed, squintily roam. Increasingly, they are drawn back from the obvious focus of attention, the hailer on the barrel, towards the mourning figure front left, the only person looking out at us. He is supporting on his lap a younger fellow who is – we have done our sums – certainly dead. The old man's back is turned against every living person on the raft: his pose is one of resignation, sorrow, despair; he is further marked out by his grey hair and the red cloth worn as a neck-protector. He might have strayed in from a different genre – some Poussin elder who had got lost, perhaps. (Non-sense, snaps the informed eye. Poussin? Guérin and Gros, if you must know. And the dead 'Son'? A medley of Guérin, Girodet and Prud'hon.) What is this 'Father' doing? (a) lamenting the dead man (his son? his chum?) on his lap; (b) realizing they will never be rescued; (c) reflecting that even if they are rescued it doesn't matter a damn because of the death he holds in his arms? (By the way, says the informed eye, there really are handicaps to being ignorant. You'd never, for instance, guess that the Father and Son are an attentuated cannibalistic motif, would you? As a group they first appear in Géricault's only surviving sketch of the Cannibalism scene; and any educated contemporary spectator would be assuredly reminded of Dante's description of Count Ugolino sorrowing in his Pisan tower among his dying children – whom he ate. Is that clear now?)

Whatever we decide that the old man is thinking, his presence becomes as powerful a force in the painting as that of the hailer. This counterbalance suggests the following deduction: that the picture represents the mid-point of that first sighting of the *Argus*. The vessel has been in view for a quarter of an hour and has another fifteen minutes to offer. Some believe it is still coming towards them; some are uncertain and waiting to see what happens; some – including the wisest head on board – know that it is heading away from them, and that they will not be saved. This figure incites us to read 'Scene of Shipwreck' as an image of hope being mocked.

Those who saw Géricault's painting on the walls of the 1819 Salon knew, almost without exception, that they were looking at the survivors of the *Medusa*'s raft, knew that the ship on the horizon did pick them up (if not at the first attempt), and knew that what had happened on the expedition to Senegal was a major political scandal. But the painting which survives is the one that outlives its own story. Religion decays, the icon remains; a narrative is forgotten, yet its representation still magnetizes (the ignorant eye triumphs – how galling for the informed eye). Nowadays, as we examine 'Scene of Shipwreck', it is hard to feel much indignation against Hugues Duroy de Chaumareys, captain of the expedition, or against the minister who appointed him captain, or the naval officer who refused to skipper the raft, or the sailors who loosed the tow-ropes, or the soldiery who mutinied. (Indeed, history democratizes our sympathies. Had not the

soldiers been brutalized by their wartime experiences? Was not
the captain a victim of his own pampered upbringing? Would
we bet on ourselves to behave heroically in similar circumstances?) Time dissolves the story into form, colour, emotion.
Modern and ignorant, we reimagine the story: do we vote for the
optimistic yellowing sky, or for the grieving greybeard? Or do we
end up believing both versions? The eye can flick from one
mood, and one interpretation, to the other: is this what was
intended?

(8a) He very nearly painted the following. Two oil studies of
1818, which in composition are closest of any preparatory
sketches to the final image, show this significant difference: the
vessel which is being hailed is much closer. We can see its outline,
sails and masts. It is in profile, on the extreme right of the canvas,
and has just begun a painful voyage across the painted horizon.
It has clearly not yet seen the raft. The impact of these preliminary sketches is more active, kinetic: we feel as if the frantic
waving by those on the raft might have some effect over the next
few minutes, and that the picture, instead of being an instant of
time, propels itself into its own future, asking the question, Will
the ship sail off the edge of the canvas without seeing the raft?
In contrast, the final version of 'Shipwreck' is less active, offers
a less articulated question. The signalling seems more futile, and
the hazard on which the survivors' fate depends more terrifying.
What is their chance of rescue? A drop in the ocean.

He was eight months in his studio. Around this time he drew a
self-portrait, from which he stares out at us with the sullen, rather
suspicious gaze that painters often assume when faced by a
mirror; guiltily, we assume that the disapproval is aimed at us,
whereas in fact it is mostly directed back at the sitter. His beard
is short, and a tasselled Greek cap covers his shorn hair (we only
hear of it being cropped when he began the picture, but hair
grows a long way in eight months: how many extra trims did he
need?). He strikes us as a piratical figure, determined and ferocious enough to take on, to board his enormous Shipwreck. The
width of his brushes, by the way, was surprising. From the
breadth of his manner, Montfort supposed that Géricault used
very thick brushes; yet they were small compared to those of
other artists. Small brushes, and heavy, fast-drying oils.

We must remember him at work. It is a normal temptation to schematize, reducing eight months to a finished picture and a series of preliminary sketches; but we must resist this. He is tallish, strong and slender, with admirable legs which were compared to those of the ephebe restraining the horse in the centre of his 'Barberi Race'. Standing before the Shipwreck, he works with an intensity of concentration and a need for absolute silence: the scratch of a chair was enough to break the invisible thread between eye and brush-tip. He is painting his large figures directly on to the canvas with only an outline drawing for assistance. When the work is half done it looks like a row of sculptures hanging on a white wall.

We must remember him in the confinement of his studio, at work, in motion, making mistakes. When we know the final result of his eight months, his progress towards it seems irresistible. We start with the masterpiece and work backwards through the discarded ideas and near-misses; but for him the discarded ideas began as excitements, and he saw only at the very end what we take for granted at the beginning. For us the conclusion was inevitable; not for him. We must try to allow for hazard, for lucky discovery, even for bluff. We can only explain it in words, yet we must also try to forget words. A painting may be represented as a series of decisions labelled (1) to (8a), but we should understand that these are just the annotations of feeling. We must remember nerves and emotions. The painter isn't carried fluently downstream towards the sunlit pool of that finished image, but is trying to hold a course in an open sea of contrary tides.

Truth to life, at the start, to be sure; yet once the process gets under way, truth to art is the greater allegiance. The incident never took place as depicted; the numbers are inaccurate; the cannibalism is reduced to a literary reference; the Father and Son group has the thinnest documentary justification, the barrel group none at all. The raft has been cleaned up as if for the state visit of some queasy-stomached monarch: the strips of human flesh have been housewifed away, and everyone's hair is as sleek as a painter's new-bought brush.

As Géricault approaches his final image, questions of form predominate. He pulls the focus, crops, adjusts. The horizon is raised and lowered (if the hailing figure is below the horizon, the whole raft is gloomily engulfed by the sea; if he breaks the horizon, it is like the raising of hope). Géricault cuts down the surrounding areas of sea and sky, hurling us on to the raft whether we like it or not. He stretches the distance from the shipwrecked to the rescuing vessel. He readjusts the positions of his figures. How often in a picture do so many of the chief participants have their backs to the spectator?

And what splendidly muscular backs they are. We feel embarrassed at this point, yet we shouldn't be. The naïve question often proves to be the central one. So go on, let's ask. *Why do the survivors look so healthy?* We admire the way Géricault sought out the *Medusa*'s carpenter and had him build a scale model of the raft ... but ... but if he bothered to get the raft right, why couldn't he do the same with its inhabitants? We can understand why he fiddled the hailing figure into a separate vertical, why he added some supernumerary corpses to assist the formal structure. But why does everyone – even the corpses – look so muscled, so ... healthy? Where are the wounds, the scars, the haggardness, the disease? These are men who have drunk their own urine, gnawed the leather from their hats, consumed their own comrades. Five of the fifteen did not survive their rescue very long. So why do they look as if they have just come from a body-building class?

When television companies make drama-docs about concentration camps, the eye – ignorant or informed – is always drawn to those pyjamaed extras. Their heads may be shaven, their shoulders hunched, all nail varnish removed, yet still they throb with vigour. As we watch them queue on screen for a bowl of gruel into which the camp guard contemptuously spits, we imagine them offscreen gorging themselves at the catering van. Does 'Scene of Shipwreck' prefigure this anomaly? With some painters we might pause and wonder. But not with Géricault, the portrayer of madness, corpses and severed heads. He once stopped a friend in the street who was yellow with jaundice and told him how handsome he was looking. Such an artist would hardly shrink from flesh at the limit of its endurance.

So let's imagine something else he didn't paint – 'Scene of Shipwreck' with the casting redistributed among the emaciated. Shrivelled flesh, suppurating wounds, Belsen cheeks: such details would move us, without trouble, to pity. Salt water would gush from our eyes to match the salt water on the canvas. But this would be precipitate: the painting would be acting on us too directly. Withered castaways in tattered rags are in the same emotional register as that butterfly, the first impelling us to an easy desolation as the second impels us to an easy consolation. The trick is not hard to work.

Whereas the response Géricault seeks is one beyond mere pity and indignation, though these emotions might be picked up *en route* like hitchhikers. For all its subject-matter, 'Scene of Shipwreck' is full of muscle and dynamism. The figures on the raft are like the waves: beneath them, yet also through them surges the energy of the ocean. Were they painted in lifelike exhaustion they would be mere dribbles of spume rather than formal conduits. For the eye is washed – not teased, not persuaded, but tidetugged – up to the peak of the hailing figure, down to the trough of the despairing elder, across to the recumbent corpse front right who links and leaks into the real tides. It is because the figures are sturdy enough to transmit such power that the canvas unlooses in us deeper, submarinous emotions, can shift us through currents of hope and despair, elation, panic and resignation.

What has happened? The painting has slipped history's anchor. This is no longer 'Scene of Shipwreck', let alone 'The Raft of the Medusa'. We don't just imagine the ferocious miseries on that fatal machine; we don't just become the sufferers. They become us. And the picture's secret lies in the pattern of its energy. Look at it one more time: at the violent waterspout building up through those muscular backs as they reach for the speck of the rescuing vessel. All that straining – to what end? There is no formal response to the painting's main surge, just as there is no response to most human feelings. Not merely hope, but any burdensome yearning: ambition, hatred, love (especially love) – how rarely do our emotions meet the object they seem to deserve? How hopelessly we signal; how dark the sky; how big the waves. We are all lost at sea, washed between hope and despair, hailing something that may never come to rescue us. Catastrophe has become art; but this is no reducing process. It is freeing, enlarging, explaining. Catastrophe has become art: that is, after all, what it is for.

And what of that earlier catastrophe, the Flood? Well, the iconography of officer-class Noah begins as we might imagine. For the first dozen or more Christian centuries the Ark (usually represented as a mere box or sarcophagus to indicate that Noah's salvation was a premonstration of Christ's escape from his sepulchre) appears widely in illuminated manuscripts, stained-glass windows, cathedral sculpture. Noah was a very popular fellow:

we can find him on the bronze doors of San Zeno in Verona, on Nîmes cathedral's west façade and Lincoln's east; he sails into fresco at the Campo Santo in Pisa and Santa Maria Novella in Florence; he anchors in mosaic at Monreale, the Baptistery in Florence, St Mark's in Venice.

But where are the great paintings, the famous images that these are leading up to? What happens – does the Flood dry up? Not exactly; but the waters are diverted by Michelangelo. In the Sistine Chapel the Ark (now looking more like a floating bandstand than a ship) for the first time loses its compositional pre-eminence; here it is pushed right to the back of the scene. What fills the foreground are the anguished figures of those doomed antediluvians left to perish when the chosen Noah and his family were saved. The emphasis is on the lost, the abandoned, the discarded sinners, God's detritus. (Should we allow ourselves to postulate Michelangelo the rationalist, moved by pity to subtle condemnation of God's heartlessness? Or Michelangelo the pious, fulfilling his papal contract and showing us what might happen if we failed to mend our ways? Perhaps the decision was purely aesthetic – the artist preferring the contorted bodies of the damned to yet another dutiful representation of yet another wooden Ark.) Whatever the reason, Michelangelo reoriented – and revitalized – the subject. Baldassare Peruzzi followed him, Raphael followed him; painters and illustrators increasingly concentrated on the forsaken rather than the saved. And as this innovation became a tradition, the Ark itself sailed further and further away, retreating towards the horizon just as the *Argus* did when Géricault was approaching his final image. The wind continues to blow, and the tides to run: the Ark eventually reaches the horizon, and disappears over it. In Poussin's 'The Deluge' the ship is nowhere to be seen; all we are left with is the tormented group of non-swimmers first brought to prominence by Michelangelo and Raphael. Old Noah has sailed out of art history.

Three reactions to 'Scene of Shipwreck':
(a) Salon critics complained that while they might be familiar with the events the painting referred to, there was no internal evidence from which to ascertain the nationality of the victims, the skies under which the tragedy was taking place, or the date at which it was all happening. This was, of course, the point.

(b) Delacroix in 1855 recalled his reactions nearly forty years earlier to his first sight of the emerging Medusa: 'The impression it gave me was so strong that as I left the studio I broke into a run, and kept running like a madman all the way back to the rue de la Planche where I then lived, at the far end of the faubourg Saint-Germain.'

(c) Géricault, on his death-bed, in reply to someone who mentioned the painting: 'Bah, une vignette!'

And there we have it – the moment of supreme agony on the raft, taken up, transformed, justified by art, turned into a sprung and weighted image, then varnished, framed, glazed, hung in a famous art gallery to illuminate our human condition, fixed, final, always there. Is that what we have? Well, no. People die; rafts rot; and works of art are not exempt. The emotional structure of Géricault's work, the oscillation between hope and despair, is reinforced by the pigment: the raft contains areas of bright illumination violently contrasted with patches of the deepest darkness. To make the shadow as black as possible, Géricault used quantities of bitumen to give him the shimmeringly gloomy black he sought. Bitumen, however, is chemically unstable, and from the moment Louis XVIII examined the work a slow, irreparable decay of the paint surface was inevitable. 'No sooner do we come into this world', said Flaubert, 'than bits of us start to fall off.' The masterpiece, once completed, does not stop: it continues in motion, downhill. Our leading expert on Géricault confirms that the painting is 'now in part a ruin'. And no doubt if they examine the frame they will discover woodworm living there.

6

THE MOUNTAIN

Tick, tick, tick, tick. Tock. Tick, tick, tick, tick. Tock. It sounded like a clock gently misfiring, time entering a delirium. This might have been appropriate, the Colonel reflected, but it wasn't the case. It was important to stick to what you knew, right to the end, especially at the end. He knew it wasn't the case. It wasn't time, it wasn't even a distant clock.

Colonel Fergusson lay in the cold square bedroom of his cold square house three miles outside Dublin and listened to the clicking overhead. It was one o'clock in the morning on a windless November night of 1837. His daughter Amanda sat at his bedside in stiff, pout-lipped profile, reading some piece of religious mumbo-jumbo. At her elbow the candle burned with a steady flame, which was more than that perspiring fool of a doctor with letters after his name had been able to say about the Colonel's heart.

It was a provocation, that's what it was, thought the Colonel. Here he was on his deathbed, preparing for oblivion, and she sits over there reading Parson Noah's latest pamphlet. Actively disagreeing right to the end. Colonel Fergusson had long since given up trying to understand the business. How could the child he loved most have failed to inherit either his instincts or the opinions he had with such difficulty acquired? It was vexing. If he hadn't adored her he would have treated her as a credulous imbecile. And still, despite it all, despite this living, fleshly rebuttal, he believed in the world's ability to progress, in man's ascent, in the defeat of superstition. It was all finally very puzzling.

Tick, tick, tick, tick. Tock. The clicking continued overhead. Four, five loud ticks, a silence, then a fainter echo. The Colonel could tell that the noise was distracting Amanda from her pamphlet, though she gave no outward sign. It was simply that he could judge such things after living so closely with her for however many years. He could tell she hadn't really got her nose in the Reverend Abraham. And it was her fault that he could tell, that he knew her so thoroughly. He'd told her to go off and get married when that lieutenant whose name he could never recall had asked her. She'd argued about that, too. She'd said she loved her father more than her uniformed claimant. He'd replied that this wasn't a sound reason, and anyway he'd only die on her. She'd wept and said he wasn't to talk like that. But he'd been right, hadn't he? He was bound to be, wasn't he?

Amanda Fergusson now rested her book on her lap and looked at the ceiling in alarm. The beetle was a harbinger. Everyone knew that its sound portended the death of someone in the house within the year. It was the wisdom of ages. She looked across to see if her father was still awake. Colonel Fergusson had his eyes closed and was breathing out through his nose in long smooth puffs like a bellows. But Amanda knew him well enough to suspect that he might be bluffing. It would be just like him. He had always played tricks on her.

Like that time he'd taken her to Dublin, one blustery day in February of 1821. Amanda was seventeen, and everywhere carried with her a sketching book as she now carried her religious pamphlets. She had lately been excited by reports of the exhibition at Bullock's Egyptian Hall in Piccadilly, London, of Monsieur Jerricault's Great Picture, 24 feet long by 18 feet high, representing the Surviving Crew of the Medusa French Frigate on the Raft. Admission 1s, Description 6d, and 50,000 spectators had paid to see this new masterpiece of foreign art, shown alongside such permanent displays as Mr Bullock's magnificent collection of 25,000 fossils and his Pantherion of stuffed wild beasts. Now the canvas had come to Dublin, where it was put on view at the Rotunda: Admission 1s 8d, Description 5d.

Amanda had been chosen above her five siblings by reason of her precocity with watercolour – at least, this was Colonel Fergusson's official excuse for indulging his natural preference once again. Except that they did not go, as promised, to the Rotunda, but went instead to a rival attraction advertised in *Saunder's News-Letter & Daily Advertiser*: one, indeed, which ensured that Monsieur Jerricault's Great Picture did not triumph in Dublin as it had done in London. Colonel Fergusson took his daughter to the Pavilion, where they witnessed Messrs Marshall's Marine Peristrephic Panorama of the Wreck of the Medusa French Frigate and the Fatal Raft: Admission front seats 1s 8d,

back seats 10d, children in the front seats at half price. 'The Pavilion is always rendered perfectly comfortable by patent stoves'.

Whereas the Rotunda displayed a mere twenty-four feet by
eighteen of stationary pigment, here they were offered some
10,000 square feet of mobile canvas. Before their eyes an
immense picture, or series of pictures, gradually unwound: not
just one scene, but the entire history of the shipwreck passed
before them. Episode succeeded episode, while coloured lights
played upon the unreeling fabric, and an orchestra emphasized
the drama of events. The audience was constantly moved to
applause by the spectacle, and Colonel Fergusson would nudge
his daughter heavily at some particularly felicitous aspect of the
display. In the sixth scene those poor French wretches on the raft
were represented in very much the same posture as that in which
they had been first delineated by Monsieur Jerricault. But how
much grander, Colonel Fergusson observed, to picture their tragic plight with movement and coloured lights, accompanied by
music which he identified quite unnecessarily to his daughter as
'Vive Henrico!'

'That is the way forward,' remarked the Colonel with enthusiasm as they left the Pavilion. 'Those painters will have to look
to their brushes.'

Amanda did not reply, but the following week she returned to
Dublin with one of her five siblings and this time visited
the Rotunda. There she greatly admired Monsieur Jerricault's
canvas, which though static contained for her much motion and
lighting and, in its own way, music – indeed, in some fashion it
contained more of these things than did the vulgar Panorama.
Upon her return she told her father as much.

Colonel Fergusson nodded indulgently at such pertness and
obstinacy, but held his peace. On the 5th of March, however,
he jauntily indicated to his favourite daughter a fresh advertisement in *Saunder's News-Letter* announcing that Mr Bullock had
reduced – had clearly been *obliged* to reduce, the Colonel interpreted – the price of admission into his immobile spectacle to
a mere ten pence. At the end of that month Colonel Fergusson
imparted the news that the Frenchy picture at the Rotunda
had closed for lack of spectators, whereas Messrs Marshall's
Peristrephic Panorama was still being shown three times a day
to audiences rendered perfectly comfortable by patent stoves.

'It is the way forward,' the Colonel repeated in June of that year, after attending by himself the farewell performance at the Pavilion.

'Mere novelty is no proof of value,' his daughter had replied, sounding a little too smug for one so young.

Tick, tick, tick, tick. Tock. Colonel Fergusson's faked sleep became more choleric. God damn it, he was thinking, this dying business is difficult. They just won't let you get on with it, not on your own terms, anyway. You have to die on other people's terms, and that's a bore, love them as you might. He opened his eyes and prepared to correct his daughter for the several hundredth occasion in their lives together.

'It's love,' he said suddenly. 'That's all it is.' Amanda's gaze was surprised from the ceiling, and she looked across with brimming eyes. 'It's the love-call of *xestobium rufo-villosum*, for God's sake, girl. Simple as that. Put one of the little fellows in a box and tap on the table with a pencil and he behaves in exactly the same way. Thinks you're a female and butts his head against the box trying to get to you. Speaking of which, why didn't you marry that lieutenant when I told you to? Sheer damn insubordination.' He reached across and took her hand.

But his daughter didn't reply, her eyes continued to overflow, the ticking carried on overhead, and Colonel Fergusson was duly buried before the year's end. On this prediction the doctor and the death-watch beetle had managed to agree.

Amanda's grief for her father was compounded by anxiety over his ontological status. Did his obstinate refusal to acknowledge the divine plan – and his careless use of the Almighty's name even on his deathbed – mean that he was now consigned to outer darkness, to some chilly region unheated by patent stoves? Miss Fergusson knew the Lord to be just, yet merciful. Those who accepted his commandments were to be judged in punctilious accordance with the law, whereas the ignorant savage in the darkened jungle who could not possibly have known the light would be treated with gentleness and given a second chance. But did the category of ignorant savage extend to occupants of cold square houses outside Dublin? Was the pain which unbelievers bore all their lives at the prospect of oblivion to be extended into further pain inflicted for having denied the Lord? Miss Fergusson feared that it might be.

How could her father have failed to recognize God, His eternal design, and its essential goodness? The proof of this plan and of this benevolence lay manifest in Nature, which was provided by God for Man's enjoyment. This did not mean, as some had assumed, that Man might recklessly pillage Nature for what he sought; indeed, Nature was deserving of the more respect because it was a divine creation. But God had created both Man and Nature, placing Man into that Nature as a hand is placed into a glove. Amanda frequently reflected upon the fruits of the field, how various they were, and yet how perfectly each was adapted for Man's enjoyment. For instance, trees bearing edible fruits were made easy to climb, being much lower than forest trees. Fruits which were soft when ripe, such as the apricot, the fig or the mulberry, which might be bruised by falling, presented themselves at a small distance from the ground; whereas hard fruit, which ran no risk of sustaining an injury by a fall, like the cocoa, the walnut or the chestnut, presented themselves at a considerable height. Some fruit – like the cherry and the plum – were moulded for the mouth; others – the apple and the pear – for the hand; others still, like the melon, were made larger, so as to be divided among the family circle. Yet others, like the pumpkin, were made of a size to be shared amongst the whole neighbourhood, and many of these larger fruits were marked on their outer rind with vertical divisions, so as to make apportionment the easier.

Where Amanda discovered in the world divine intent, benevolent order and rigorous justice, her father had seen only chaos, hazard and malice. Yet they were both examining the same world. In the course of their many arguments, Amanda once asked him to consider the domestic condition of the Fergusson family, who lived together with strong bonds of affection, and declare whether they too were the consequence of chaos, hazard and malice. Colonel Fergusson, who could not quite bear to inform his daughter that the human family sprang from the same impulse which animated a beetle striking its head against the walls of its box, replied that in his view the Fergussons were a happy accident. His daughter replied that there were too many happy accidents in the world for them to be accidental.

In part, Amanda reflected, it was a matter of how you perceived things. Her father saw in a vulgar simulacrum of coloured lights and trilling music a true portrayal of a great maritime tragedy; whereas for her the reality was best conveyed by a simple, static canvas adorned with pigment. Mainly, however, it was a question of faith. A few weeks after their visit to the Peristrephic Panorama, her father was rowing her slowly across the serpentine lake on the neighbouring estate of Lord F—. Some connection having been made in his mind, he began to rebuke her for a belief in the reality of Noah's Ark, which he referred to sarcastically as the Myth of the Deluge. Amanda was not discountenanced by the accusation. She replied by asking her father if he believed in the reality of Mr Bullock's Pantherion of stuffed wild beasts at his Egyptian Hall in Piccadilly, London. The Colonel, taken aback, responded that naturally he did; whereupon his daughter exhibited a humorous astonishment. She believed in the reality of something ordained by God and described in a book of Holy Scripture read and remembered for thousands of years; whereas he believed in the reality of something described in the pages of *Saunder's News-Letter & Daily Advertiser*, which people were unlikely to remember the very next morning. Which of them, she insisted upon knowing, with a continuing and unnecessary mockery in her eye, was the more credulous?

It was in the autumn of 1839, after long meditation, that Amanda Fergusson proposed to Miss Logan the expedition to Arghuri. Miss Logan was a vigorous and seemingly practical woman some ten years older than Miss Fergusson, and had been fond of the Colonel without any zephyr of indiscretion arising. More to the point, she had travelled to Italy a few years previously while in the employment of Sir Charles B—.

'I regret that I am unacquainted with the place,' replied Miss Logan when first interviewed. 'Is it far beyond Naples?'

'It is on the lower slopes of Mount Ararat,' Miss Fergusson responded. 'The name Arghuri is derived from two Armenian words signifying *he planted the vine*. It is where Noah returned to his agricultural labours after the Flood. An ancient vine stock planted by the Patriarch's own hands still flourishes.'

Miss Logan concealed her astonishment at this curious lecture, but felt bound to enquire further. 'And why might we be going there?'

'To intercede for the soul of my father. There is a monastery upon the mountain.'

'It is a long way to go.'

'I believe it to be appropriate.'

'I see.' Miss Logan was pensive at first, but then brightened.

'And shall we drink the wine there?' She was remembering her travels in Italy.

'It is forbidden,' replied Miss Fergusson. 'Tradition forbids it.'

'Tradition?'

'Heaven, then. Heaven has forbidden it, in memory of the fault into which the grapes betrayed the Patriarch.' Miss Logan, who would complaisantly allow the Bible to be read to her but was not diligent in turning the pages herself, exhibited a momentary confusion. 'Drunkenness,' explained Miss Fergusson. 'Noah's drunkenness.'

'Of course.'

'The monks of Arghuri are permitted to eat the grapes, but not to ferment them.'

'I see.'

'There is also an ancient willow tree, sprung from one of the planks of Noah's Ark, which grows there.'

'I see.'

And thus it was agreed. They would depart in the spring, to avoid the malarial menace of the later seasons. Each would require a portable bedstead, an air mattress and a pillow; they would take some Oxley's essence of ginger, some good opium, quinine and Sedlitz powders; a portable inkstand, a match-box and supply of German tinder; umbrellas against the sun and flannel belts to ward off cramps of the stomach during the night. After some discussion they decided not to travel with either a portable bath or a patent coffee-machine. But they counted as necessary a pair of iron-pointed walking sticks, a clasp-knife, stout hunting-whips to beat off the legions of dogs they were prepared to encounter, and a policeman's small lantern, since they had been warned that Turkish paper lanterns were useless in a hurricane. They took mackintoshes and heavy greatcoats, anticipating that Lady Mary Wortley Montagu's dream of perennial sunshine was unlikely to be fulfilled for lesser voyagers. Miss Logan understood gunpowder to be the most acceptable offering for the Turkish peasant, and writing-paper for the superior classes. A common box-compass, she had further been advised, would afford pleasure by directing the Mussulman to the point of his prayers; but Miss Fergusson was disinclined to assist the heathen in his false adorations. Finally, the ladies packed two small glass bottles, which they intended to fill with grape juice crushed from the fruit of Noah's vineyard.

They travelled by Government steam-packet from Falmouth to Marseilles, thereafter entrusting themselves to the French conveyances. In early May they were received by the British Ambassador in Constantinople. As Miss Fergusson explained the extent and purpose of their journey, the diplomat studied her: a dark-haired woman in early middle age, with protuberant black eyes and rather full, reddish cheeks which pushed her lips forward into a pout. Yet she was in no wise a flirt: her natural expression appeared to mix prudishness with certainty, a combination which left the Ambassador indifferent. He grasped most of what she was saying without ever quite bestowing upon her his full attention.

'Ah,' he said at the finish, 'there was a rumour a few years ago that some Russo had managed to get to the top of the mountain.'

'Parrot,' replied Miss Fergusson without a smile. 'Not a Russo, I think. Dr Friedrich Parrot. Professor in the University of Dorpat.'

The Ambassador gave a diagonal nod of the head, as if it were slightly impertinent to know more than he did about local matters.

'It seems to me appropriate and just,' went on Miss Fergusson, 'that the first traveller to ascend the mountain upon which the Ark rested should bear the name of an animal. No doubt part of the Lord's great design for us all.'

'No doubt,' replied the Ambassador, looking away to Miss Logan for some clue as to the personality of her employer. 'No doubt.'

They remained a week in the Ottoman capital, by no means long enough for Miss Logan to become accustomed to the coarse stares she received at the *tables d'hôte*. Then the two ladies gave themselves up to the Favaid-i-Osmaniyeh, a Turkish company running steamers to Trebizond. The accommodation was crowded and to Miss Logan's mind far filthier than anything she had previously encountered. She ventured upon deck the first morning, and was approached by not one but three potential beaux, each with his hair curled and exuding a powerful odour of bergamot. Thereafter Miss Logan, despite having been engaged for her experience, confined herself to the cabin. Miss Fergusson professed not to notice such inconveniences and to be positively intrigued by the scrum of third-class passengers on board; she would occasionally return with an observation or a question designed to stir Miss Logan from her dismal state of mind. Why, her employer wished to know, were the Turkish women all accommodated on the left-hand side of the quarter-deck? Was there some purpose, be it of society or of religion, behind such positioning? Miss Logan was unable to furnish a reply. Now that they had left Naples way behind them she felt increasingly less secure. At the faintest whiff of bergamot she shuddered.

When Miss Logan had permitted herself to become engaged for the voyage to Asiatic Turkey, she had under-estimated Miss Fergusson's pertinacity. The absconding muleteer, the swindling innkeeper and the devious customs-house officer were all treated to the same display of unthwartable will. Miss Logan lost count of the times their luggage was detained, or they were told that a *buyurulda* or special permit would be necessary in addition to the *tezkare* they had already procured; but Miss Fergusson, with assistance from a dragoman whose own brief display of inde-pendent thought had been snuffed out early on, harried, demanded and succeeded. She was tirelessly willing to discuss things in the manner of the country; to sit down with a landlord, for example, and answer such questions as whether England was smaller than London, and which of the two belonged to France, and how much larger the Turkish navy was than those of Eng-land, France and Russia put together.

Miss Logan had further imagined that their journey, while devotional in its final purpose, might afford pleasant opportuni-ties for sketching, the activity which had first established a bond between employer and companion. But antiquities held no charm for Amanda Fergusson; she had no desire to examine heathen temples to Augustus, or half-surviving columns suppos-edly erected in honour of the apostate Emperor Julian. At least she evinced an interest in the natural landscape. As they rode inland from Trebizond, hunting-whips at the ready against the expected dog-packs, they viewed mohair goats on hillsides of dwarf oak, dull yellow vines, lush apple orchards; they heard grasshoppers whose ringing note seemed sharper and more insistent than that of their British cousins; and they witnessed sunsets of the rarest purple and rose. There were fields of corn, opium and cotton; bursts of rhododendron and yellow azalea; red-legged partridge, hoopoes and blue crows. In the Zirgana mountains large red deer softly returned their gaze from an apprehensive distance.

At Erzerum Miss Logan prevailed upon her employer to visit the Christian church. The impulse proved at first a happy one, for in the graveyard Miss Fergusson discovered tombstones and crosses whose Celtic air recalled those of her native Ireland; a smile of approval crossed her dutiful features. But this unexpected lenity was short-lived. Leaving the church, the two ladies noticed a young peasant woman placing a votive offering in a crevice by the main door. It proved to be a human tooth, no doubt her own. The crevice, upon further examination, was found to be stuffed full of yellowing incisors and weathered molars. Miss Fergusson expressed herself forcibly on the subject of popular superstition and the responsibility of the clergy. Those who preached the word of God, she maintained, should be judged according to the word of God, and punished the more severely if found wanting.

They crossed into Russia, engaging at the frontier post a new guide, a large and bearded Kurd who claimed familiarity with the requirements of foreigners. Miss Fergusson addressed him in what seemed to Miss Logan a mixture of Russo and Turk. The days when Miss Logan's fluent Italian had been of use to them were long past; having begun the journey as guide and interpreter, she felt she had dwindled into a mere hanger-on, with little greater status than the discarded dragoman or the newly-appointed Kurd.

As the three of them proceeded into Caucasia, they disturbed flocks of pelican, whose earthbound ungainliness was miraculously transfigured by flight. Miss Fergusson's irritation over the incident in Erzerum began to calm. Passing the eastern spur of Mount Alageuz, they gazed intently as the broad bulk of Great Ararat slowly revealed itself. The summit was hidden, enfolded in a circle of white cloud which glittered brilliantly in the sun.

'It has a halo,' exclaimed Miss Logan. 'Like an angel.'

'You are correct,' Miss Fergusson replied, with a little nod. 'People like my father would not agree, of course. They would tell us that such comparisons are all hot air. Literally.' She gave a pursed smile and Miss Logan, with an enquiring glance, invited her to continue. 'They would explain that the halo of cloud is a perfectly natural phenomenon. During the night and for several hours after dawn the summit remains clearly visible,

but as the plain warms up in the morning sun, the hot air rises
and becomes vapour at a given height. At the day's end, when
everything cools down again, the halo disappears. It comes as no
surprise to ... science,' she said with a disapproving emphasis
upon the final word.

'It is a magic mountain,' commented Miss Logan.

Her employer corrected her. 'It is a *holy* mountain.' She gave
an impatient sigh. 'There always appear to be two explanations
of everything. That is why we have been given free will, in order
that we may choose the correct one. My father failed to compre-
hend that his explanations were based as much upon faith as
mine. Faith in nothing. It would be all vapour and clouds and
rising air to him. But who created the vapour, who created the
clouds? Who ensured that Noah's mountain of all mountains
would be blessed each day with a halo of cloud?'

'Exactly,' said Miss Logan, not entirely in agreement.

That day they encountered an Armenian priest who informed
them that the mountain towards which they were heading had
never been ascended and, moreover, never would be. When Miss
Fergusson politely suggested the name of Dr Parrot, the priest
assured her that she was mistaken. Perhaps she was confusing
Massis – as he referred to Great Ararat – with the volcano far to
the south which the Turks called Sippan Dagh. The Ark of
Noah, before it found its final resting-place, had struck the
summit of Sippan Dagh and removed its cap, thereby exposing
the inner fires of the earth. That mountain, he understood, was
accessible to man, but not Massis. On this subject, if on nothing
else, Christian and Mussulman agreed. And furthermore, went
on the priest, was it not so proven by Holy Scripture? The mountain before them was the birthplace of mankind; and he referred
the ladies, while excusing himself with an ingratiating laugh for
mentioning an indelicate subject, to the authority of Our
Saviour's words to Nicodemus, where it is stated that a man
cannot enter a second time into his mother's womb and be born
once more.

As they were parting, the priest drew from his pocket a small
black amulet, worn smooth over many centuries. It was, he
claimed, a piece of bitumen which assuredly had once formed
part of the hull of Noah's Ark, and had great value in the averting
of mischief. Since the ladies had expressed such interest in the
mountain of Massis, then perhaps ...

Miss Fergusson courteously responded to the suggested transaction by pointing out that if indeed it was impossible to ascend the mountain, then the likelihood of their believing that the amulet could be a piece of bitumen from the Patriarch's vessel was not very great. The Armenian, however, saw no incompatibility between his two propositions. Perhaps a bird had carried it down, as the dove had borne the olive branch. Or it might have been brought by an angel. Did not tradition relate how Saint James had three times attempted to ascend Massis, and on the third occasion been told by an angel that it was forbidden, but that the angel had given him a plank of wood from the Ark, and there where he had received it was founded the monastery of Saint James?

They parted without a bargain being struck. Miss Logan, embarrassed by Our Lord's words to Nicodemus, was instead thinking about bitumen: was that not the material used by artists to blacken the shadows in their paintings? Miss Fergusson, on the other hand, had merely been put into a temper: first by the attempt to thrust some foolish meaning on to the scriptural verse; and secondly by the priest's brazen commercial behaviour. She had yet to be impressed by the Eastern clergy, who not only countenanced belief in the miraculous powers of human teeth, but actually traded in bogus religious relics. It was monstrous. They should be punished for it. No doubt they would be. Miss Logan examined her employer apprehensively.

The next day they crossed a relentless plain of reeds and coarse grass, relieved only by colonies of bustard and the black tents of Kurdish tribesmen. They stopped for the night in a small village a day's ride from the foot of the mountain. After a meal of cream cheese and salted salmon trout from the Gokchai, the two women stood in the dark air scented with apricot and looked towards the mountain of Noah. The range before them contained two separate crescendi: Great Ararat, a bulky, broad-shouldered mass like a buttressed dome, and Little Ararat, some four thousand feet lower, an elegant cone with smooth and regular sides. Miss Fergusson did not think it fanciful to perceive in the comparative design and height of the two Ararats a bodying-forth of that primal divide in the human race between the two sexes. She did not communicate this reflection to Miss Logan, who had so far proved dismally unreceptive to the transcendental.

As if to confirm her pedestrian turn of mind, Miss Logan at

this point revealed that it had been a matter of curiosity to her since childhood how the Ark had succeeded in resting upon the top of a mountain. Had the peak risen up from the waters and punctured the keel, thereby skewering the vessel in place? For if not, how otherwise had the Ark avoided a precipitous descent as the waters had retreated?

'Others before you have had similar reflections,' replied Miss Fergusson with distinct lack of indulgence. 'Marco Polo insisted that the mountain was made in the shape of a cube, which would certainly have explained the matter. My father would probably have agreed with him, had he given the subject his attention. But we can see that this is not the case. Those who have ascended to the peak of Great Ararat inform us that close below the summit there is a gently sloping valley. It is,' she specified, as if Miss Logan could not otherwise understand the matter, 'approximately half the size of Green Park in London. As a place of disembarkation it would be both natural and safe.'

'So the Ark did not land on the very summit?'

'Scripture makes no such claim.'

As they approached Arghuri, which lay at a height of more than six thousand feet above sea level, the temperature of the air became more genial. Three miles below the village they came upon the first of the hallowed plantations of Father Noah. The vines had just finished flowering, and tiny dark green grapes hung intermittently among the foliage. A peasant put down his rough hoe and conducted the unexpected party to the village elder, who received their offering of gunpowder with formal thanks yet little surprise. Miss Logan was sometimes irked by such civility. The elder was behaving as if parties of white women were constantly presenting him with gunpowder.

Miss Fergusson, however, remained her dutiful and efficient self. It was arranged that later in the afternoon they would be conducted to the Monastery of Saint James; they would be lodged that night in the village, and would return again to the church the following day for their devotions.

The monastery lay beside the Arghuri rivulet in the lower part of a great chasm which extended almost to the very summit of the mountain. It consisted of a cruciform church whose stone was hewn from hardened lava. Various small dwellings pressed against its sides like the farrow of a sow. As the party entered the courtyard a middle-aged priest stood waiting for them, the cupola of Saint James rising behind him. He was dressed in a plain gown of blue serge, with a pointed Capuchin cowl; his beard was long, its blackness intertwined with grey; on his feet he wore woollen Persian socks and common slippers. One hand bore the rosary; the other was folded across his chest in a gesture of welcome. Something urged Miss Logan to kneel before the pastor of Noah's church; but the presence and certain disapproval of Miss Fergusson, who dismissed as 'Romish' a large category of religious behaviour, prevented her.

The courtyard spoke less of a monastery than a farm. Sacks of corn were piled loosely against a wall; three sheep had wandered in from the nearby pasture and had not been expelled; there was a rank smell from underfoot. Smiling, the Archimandrite invited them to his cell, which proved to be one of the tiny dwellings built hard against the outer wall of the church. As he was conducting them across the dozen or so yards, the Archimandrite appeared to touch Miss Fergusson's elbow by way of courteous but strictly unnecessary guidance.

The monk's cell had stout clay walls and a plaster roof supported by a sturdy central prop. There was a rough icon of some unidentifiable saint hanging above a straw pallet; the courtyard odours continued here. To Miss Logan it seemed admirably simple, to Miss Fergusson squalid. The behaviour of the Archimandrite also provoked differing interpretations: Miss Logan discerned an amiable candour where Miss Fergusson saw only sly obsequiousness. It seemed to Miss Logan that her employer had perhaps exhausted her stock of civility on the long journey to Mount Ararat, and had now retreated into a stony carelessness. When the Archimandrite suggested that the two ladies might like to lodge at the monastery that night, she was briefly dismissive; when he pressed his offer of hospitality further, she was brusque.

The Archimandrite continued to smile, and his mood still appeared to Miss Logan a gracious one. At this point a servant appeared bearing a rough tray on which were set three horn beakers. Water from the Arghuri brook, thought Miss Logan; or perhaps that sourish milk which they had already received many times on their travels from obliging shepherds. But the servant returned with a wineskin, and at a signal poured a liquor from it into the horn vessels. The Archimandrite raised his beaker towards the women, and drank fully; whereupon his servant poured for him again.

Miss Fergusson sipped. Then she put questions to the Archimandrite which provoked a severe apprehension in Miss Logan. This feeling was exacerbated by waiting for the guide to translate.

'This is wine?'

'Indeed.' The priest smiled, as if encouraging the women to indulge in this local taste which was still clearly unknown in their distant land.

'It is made from grapes?'

'You are correct, lady.'

'Tell me, the grapes from which this wine has been made, where are they grown?'

The Archimandrite spread both hands and circled to indicate the neighbouring countryside.

'And the vines from which the grapes were plucked, who first planted them?'

'Our great ancestor and forefather, parent of us all, Noah.'

Miss Fergusson summed up the exchange so far, needless as this seemed to her companion. 'You are serving us the fermented grapes from Noah's vines?'

'It is my honour, Madam.' He smiled again. He seemed to expect if not especial thanks, at least some expression of wonder. Instead, Miss Fergusson stood up, took the untasted wine from Miss Logan, and returned both beakers to the servant. Without a word she left the Archimandrite's cell, swept from the court-yard in a manner which made three sheep instinctively follow her, and started down the mountainside. Miss Logan made indeterminate gestures to the priest, then set off in pursuit of her employer. They traversed lush apricot orchards without comment; they ignored a shepherd holding out a bowl of milk; wordlessly they returned to the village where Miss Fergusson, her calculated civility now restored to her, asked the elder if lodgings could be supplied to them without delay. The old man proposed his own house, the largest in Arghuri. Miss Fergusson thanked him, and offered in return a small parcel of sugar, which was gravely accepted.

That evening in their room a low table no bigger than a music stool was set with food. They were given *losh*, the thin local bread, cold mutton cut in pieces, hard-boiled eggs taken from their shells and halved, and the fruit of the arbutus. They were served no wine, either because such was the custom of the house, or because intelligence of their visit to the monastery had reached the elder. Instead, they drank sheep's milk once more.

'It is a blasphemy,' said Miss Fergusson eventually. 'A blasphemy. On Noah's mountain. He lives like a farmer. He invites women to stay with him. He ferments the grape of the Patriarch. It is a blasphemy.'

Miss Logan knew better than to reply, let alone plead the cause of the amiable Archimandrite. She recalled to herself that the circumstances of their visit had deprived them of an opportunity to examine the ancient willow tree sprung from a plank of Noah's Ark.

'We shall ascend the mountain,' said Miss Fergusson.

'But we do not know how to do such a thing.'

'We shall ascend the mountain. Sin must be purged with water. The sin of the world was purged by the waters of the flood. It is a double blasphemy that the monk commits. We shall fill our bottles with snow from the holy mountain. The pure juice of Noah's vine we came in search of has been rendered impure. We shall bring back purging water instead. That is the only way to salvage the journey.'

Miss Logan nodded, in startled acquiescence rather than agreement.

They set off from the village of Arghuri on the morning of June 20th, in the year of Our Lord 1840, accompanied only by their Kurdish guide. The elder regretfully explained the villagers' belief that the mountain was sacred, and that no one should venture upon it higher than the Monastery of Saint James. He himself shared these beliefs. He did not try to dissuade the party from their ascent, but he did insist on loaning Miss Fergusson a pistol. This she displayed at her belt, though she had neither the intention nor the resource to use it. Miss Logan carried a small bag of lemons, which had also been advised.

The ladies rode with white umbrellas raised against the morning sun. Looking upwards, Miss Fergusson observed the halo of cloud beginning to form itself around the summit of the mountain. A daily miracle, she noted to herself. For several hours they appeared to make little progress; they were traversing a barren region of fine sand and yellowish clay, broken only by a few stunted, prickly bushes. Miss Logan observed several butterflies and numerous lizards, but was secretly disappointed that so few

of the creatures which had descended from the Ark were mani-
festing themselves. She had, she admitted to herself, foolishly
pictured the slopes of the mountain as a kind of zoological
garden. But the animals had been told to go forth and multiply.
They must have obeyed.

They dipped into rocky ravines, none of which contained the
smallest stream. It seemed an arid mountain, as dry as a chalk
down in Sussex. Then, a little higher, it surprised them, suddenly
unveiling green pasture and rose bushes with delicate pink blos-
som. They rounded a spur and came upon a small encampment
– three or four rude tents, with matting walls and black roofs
made from goats' hair. Miss Logan was slightly alarmed by the
sudden presence of this group of nomads, whose flock could be
seen lower down the slope, but Miss Fergusson directed her horse
straight towards them. A ferocious-looking man whose tangled
hair resembled the roof of his own tent held up to them a rough
bowl. It contained sourish milk mixed with water, and Miss
Logan drank somewhat nervously. They nodded, smiled, and
continued on their way.

'Did you judge that a natural gesture of hospitality?' asked
Amanda Fergusson suddenly.

Miss Logan considered this strange question. 'Yes,' she
responded, for they had previously come across many similar
instances of such behaviour.

'My father would have said it was merely an animal bribe to
turn away the wrath of strangers. It would be an article of faith
with him to believe that. He would have said those nomads were
just like beetles.'

'Like beetles?'

'My father was interested in beetles. He told me that if you put
one in a box and tapped on the lid, it would knock back, thinking
you were another beetle offering itself in marriage.'

'I do not consider that they were behaving like beetles,' said
Miss Logan, while carefully indicating by her tone that this was
only her private opinion and in no way derogatory of Colonel
Fergusson.

'Nor do I.'

Miss Logan did not fully understand her employer's condition
of mind. Having come this great distance to intercede for her
father, she now seemed instead to be constantly arguing with
his shade.

At the first steep slope of Great Ararat they tethered their horses to a thorn tree and hobbled them. They were to proceed from here on foot. Miss Fergusson, umbrella aloft and pistol at her belt, led the way with the certain tread of the righteous; Miss Logan, dangling her bag of lemons, struggled to keep up as the terrain grew more precipitous; their Kurdish guide, weighed down with baggage, brought up the rear. They would be obliged to spend two nights on the mountain if they were to reach the snowline.

They had climbed hard all afternoon, and shortly before seven o'clock, with the sky softening towards apricot, were resting on a rocky outcrop. At first they did not identify the noise, or what it signified. They were aware of a low rumble, a granite growl, though whence it came, whether from above or below them, was not evident. Then the ground beneath their feet began to vibrate, and there came a noise like thunder – but internal, suppressed, terrifying thunder, the sound of a primeval, subterranean god raging against his confinement. Miss Logan glanced fearfully at her employer. Amanda Fergusson was directing her field-glasses at the Monastery of Saint James, and her face bore an expression of prim pleasure which shocked her companion. Miss Logan was near-sighted, and consequently it was from Miss Fergusson's features rather than from personal observation that she grasped what was happening. When the field-glasses were finally passed to her she was able to confirm that every roof and every wall of the monastery church and of the little community they had left only that morning had been thrown down by the violent commotion.

Miss Fergusson got to her feet and briskly began to continue the ascent.

'Are we not to help the survivors?' asked Miss Logan in perplexity.

'There will not be any,' replied her employer. Adding in a sharper tone, 'It was a punishment they should have foreseen.'

'A punishment?'

'For disobedience. For fermenting the fruit of Noah's vine. For building a church and then blaspheming within it.' Miss Logan looked at Amanda Fergusson cautiously, unsure how to express the view that to her humble and ignorant mind the punishment seemed excessive. 'This is a holy mountain,' said Miss Fergusson coldly. 'The mountain upon which Noah's Ark rested. A small sin is a great sin in this place.'

Miss Logan did not break her alarmed silence; she merely followed her employer who was pushing on ahead up a gully of rock. At the top Miss Fergusson waited and then turned to her. 'You expect God to be like the Lord Chief Justice in London. You expect a whole speech of explanation. The God of this mountain is the God who saved only Noah and his family out of the whole world. Remember that.'

Miss Logan grew seriously perturbed at these observations. Was Miss Fergusson comparing the earthquake which had thrown down the village of Arghuri to the great Flood itself? Was she likening the salvation of two white women and a Kurd to that of Noah's family? When preparing for their expedition they had been told that the magnetic compass was useless on such mountains as these, for the rocks were loaded with iron. It seemed evident that you could lose your bearing here in other ways as well.

What was she doing on Noah's mountain alongside a pilgrim turned fanatic and a bearded peasant with whom she could not communicate, while the rock below them exploded like the gunpowder they had brought to ingratiate themselves with the local chieftains? Everything urged them to go down, yet they were continuing upwards. The Kurd, whom she had expected to flee at the first shaking of the ground, was staying with them. Perhaps he intended to slit their throats while they slept.

They rested that night and continued climbing as soon as the sun rose. Their white umbrellas stood out vividly against the harsh terrain of the mountain. Here was only bare rock and gravel; nothing grew but lichen; all was utterly dry. They might have been upon the surface of the moon.

They climbed until they reached the first pocket of snow, which lay in a long, dark slash on the mountain's side. They were three thousand feet from the peak, just below a cornice of ice which encircled Great Ararat. It was here that the rising air from the plain turned to vapour and formed the miraculous halo. The sky above them was beginning to turn a brightish green, scarcely blue at all any more. Miss Logan felt very cold.

The two bottles were filled with snow and entrusted to the guide. Later, Miss Logan would try picturing to herself her employer's curious serenity of face and confidence of carriage as they started down the mountain; she exhibited contentment bordering on smugness. They had travelled no more than a few

hundred yards – the Kurd leading, Miss Logan bringing up the
rear – and were crossing a patch of rough scree, a descent more
tiring than dangerous, when Miss Fergusson fell. She pitched
forwards and sideways, sliding a dozen yards down the slope
before the Kurd was able to arrest her progress. Miss Logan
halted, initially in surprise, for it appeared that Miss Fergusson
had lost her footing on a little stretch of solid rock which should
have afforded no peril.

She was smiling when they reached her, apparently unconcerned by the blood. Miss Logan would not allow the Kurd to
bandage Miss Fergusson; she accepted pieces of his shirt for the
purpose, but then insisted that he turn his back. After half an hour
or so, the two of them restored their employer to her feet, and
they set off again, Miss Fergusson leaning on the guide's arm with
a strange nonchalance, as if she were being conducted round a
cathedral or a zoological garden.

They made only a short distance in the remainder of that day,
for Miss Fergusson demanded frequent rests. Miss Logan calculated how far away their horses were tethered, and was not
encouraged. Towards nightfall they came upon a pair of small
caves, which Miss Fergusson compared to the pressing of God's
thumb into the mountainside. The Kurd entered the first of them
cautiously, sniffing for wild beasts, then beckoned them in. Miss
Logan prepared the bedding and administered some opium; the
guide, after making gestures incomprehensible to her, vanished.
He returned an hour later with a few stunted bushes he had managed to prise from the rock. He made a fire; Miss Fergusson lay
down, took some water, and slept.

When she awoke she pronounced herself feeble, and said her
bones were stiff in her skin. She had neither strength nor hunger.
They waited through that day in the cave, trusting that Miss
Fergusson's condition would improve by the next morning.
Miss Logan began to reflect upon the changes in her employer
since they had arrived on the mountain. Their purpose in coming here had been to intercede for the soul of Colonel Fergusson.
Yet so far they had not prayed; Amanda Fergusson appeared still
to be arguing with her father; while the God she had taken to
proclaiming did not sound the kind of God who would lightly
forgive the Colonel's obstinate sinning against the light. Had
Miss Fergusson realized, or at least decided, that her father's soul
was lost, cast out, condemned? Is that what had happened?

As evening fell, Miss Fergusson told her companion to leave the cave while she spoke to the guide. This seemed unnecessary, for Miss Logan had not a word of Turk or Russo or Kurdish or whatever mixture it was the other two communicated in; but she did as she was told. She stood outside looking up at a creamy moon, fearful lest some bat might fly into her hair.

'You are to move me so that I may see the moon.' They lifted her gently, as if she were an old lady, and placed her nearer the mouth of the cave. 'You are to set off at first light tomorrow. Whether you return or not is immaterial.' Miss Logan nodded. She did not argue because she knew she would not win; she did not weep because she knew she would be rebuked. 'I shall remember the Holy Scripture and wait for God's will. On this mountain God's will is quite manifest. I cannot imagine a happier place from which to be taken unto Him.'

Miss Logan and the Kurd took turns watching over her that night. The moon, now almost full, illuminated the floor of the cave where Amanda Fergusson lay. 'My father would have wanted music with it,' she said at one point. Miss Logan smiled an agreement which irritated her employer. 'You cannot possibly know to what I am referring.' Miss Logan immediately agreed a second time.

There was a silence. The dry cold air was scented with wood-smoke. 'He thought pictures should move. With lights and music and patent stoves. He thought that was the future.' Miss Logan, little better informed than before, considered it safest not to respond. 'But it was not the future. Look at the moon. The moon does not require music and coloured lights.'

Miss Logan did win one small, final argument – by forceful gesture rather than words – and Miss Fergusson was left with both bottles of molten snow. She also accepted a couple of lemons. At daybreak Miss Logan, now wearing the pistol at her belt, set off down the mountain with the guide. She felt resolved in spirit but uncertain how best to proceed. She imagined, for instance, that if the inhabitants of Arghuri had been unwilling to venture on to the mountain before the earthquake, any survivors would scarcely be ready to do so now. She might be compelled to seek help in a more distant village.

The horses were gone. The Kurd made a long noise in his throat which she presumed to indicate disappointment. The tree to which they had been tethered was still there, but the horses had disappeared. Miss Logan imagined them panicking as the ground raged beneath them, tearing themselves free and violently bearing away their hobbles as they fled from the mountain. Later, as she trudged behind the Kurd towards the village of Arghuri, Miss Logan envisaged an alternative explanation: the horses being stolen by those hospitable nomads encountered that first morning.

The Monastery of Saint James had been quite destroyed, and they passed it without halting. As they neared the ruins of Arghuri, the Kurd indicated that Miss Logan was to wait for him while he investigated the village. Twenty minutes later he returned, shaking his head in a universal gesture. As they skirted the wrecked houses, Miss Logan could not help observing to herself that the earthquake had killed all the inhabitants while leaving intact those vines which – if Miss Fergusson should be believed – were the very source of their temptation and their punishment.

It took them two days before they reached human habitation. In a hill village to the south-west, the guide delivered her to the house of an Armenian priest who spoke passable French. She explained the need to raise an immediate rescue party and return to Great Ararat. The priest replied that no doubt the Kurd was organizing the relief at that very moment. Something in his demeanour indicated that perhaps he did not quite believe her story of having climbed most of the way up Massis, which peasants and holy men alike knew to be inaccessible.

She waited all day for the Kurd to return, but he failed to do so; and when she made enquiries the next morning she was told that he had left the town within minutes of conducting her to the priest's house. Miss Logan was angry and distressed at such Judas-like behaviour, and expressed herself forcibly on the subject to the Armenian priest, who nodded and offered to say prayers for Miss Fergusson. Miss Logan accepted, while wondering about the efficacy of mere unadorned prayer in a region where people yielded up their teeth as votive offerings.

Only several weeks later, as she lay stifling in her cabin on a filthy steamer from Trebizond, did she reflect that the Kurd, in the whole time he had been with them, had executed Miss Fergusson's commands with punctiliousness, and honour; further, that she had no means of knowing what had passed between the two of them that last night in the cave. Perhaps Miss Fergusson had instructed the guide to lead her companion to a place of safety, and then desert.

Miss Logan also reflected upon Miss Fergusson's fall. They had been crossing a scree; there had been many loose stones, and footing was difficult, but surely at that point they had been traversing a gentler slope, and her employer had actually been standing on a flattish stretch of granite when she had fallen. It was a magnetic mountain where a compass did not work, and it was easy to lose your bearing. No, that was not it. The question she was avoiding was whether Miss Fergusson might not have been the instrument of her own precipitation, in order to achieve or confirm whatever it was she wanted to achieve or confirm. Miss Fergusson had maintained, when they first stood before the haloed mountain, that there were two explanations of everything, that each required the exercise of faith, and that we had been given free will in order that we might choose between them. This dilemma was to preoccupy Miss Logan for years to come.

7
THREE SIMPLE STORIES

I

I WAS A NORMAL eighteen-year-old: shuttered, self-conscious, untravelled and sneering; violently educated, socially crass, emotionally blurting. At least, all the other eighteen-year-olds I knew were like this, so I presumed it was normal. I was waiting to go up to university and had just got a job as a prep-school master. The fiction I had read predicted gaudy roles for me – as private tutor at the old stone mansion where peacocks roost in the yew hedges and chalky bones are discovered in the sealed-up priest's hole; as gullible ingénu at an eccentric private establishment on the Welsh borders stuffed with robust drunkards and covert lechers. There would be careless girls and unimpressable butlers. You know the social moral of the story: the meritocrat becomes infected with snobbery.

Reality proved more local. I taught for a term at a crammer half a mile from my home, and instead of passing lazy days with charming children whose actively hatted mothers would smile, condescend and yet flirt during some endless pollen-spattered sports day, I spent my time with the son of the local bookmaker (he lent me his bike: I crashed it) and the daughter of the suburb's solicitor. Yet half a mile is a fine distance to the untravelled; and at eighteen the smallest gradations of middle-class society thrill and daunt. The school came with a family attached; the family lived in a house. Everything here was different and therefore better: the stiff-backed brass taps, the cut of the banister, the genuine oil paintings (we had a genuine oil painting too, but not as genuine as that), the library which somehow was more than just a roomful of books, the furniture old enough to have wood-worm in it, and the casual acceptance of inherited things. In the hall hung the amputated blade of an oar: inscribed in gold lettering on its black scoop were the names of a college eight, each of whom had been awarded such a trophy in sun-ridden pre-war days; the item seemed impossibly exotic. There was an air-raid shelter in the front garden which at home would have provoked embarrassment and been subjected to vigorous camouflage with hardy perennials; here it evoked no more than amused pride. The family matched the house. The father was a spy; the mother had been an actress; the son wore tab collars and double-breasted waistcoats. Need I say more? Had I read enough French novels at the time, I would have known what to expect; and of course it was here that I fell in love for the first time. But that is another story, or at least another chapter.

It was the grandfather who had founded the school, and he still lived on the premises. Although in his mid-eighties, he had only recently been written out of the curriculum by some crafty predecessor of mine. He was occasionally to be seen wandering through the house in his cream linen jacket, college tie – Gonville and Caius, you were meant to know – and flat cap (in our house a flat cap would have been common; here it was posh and probably indicated that you used to go beagling). He was searching for 'his class', which he never found, and talked about 'the laboratory', which was no more than a back kitchen with a bunsen burner and running water. On warm afternoons he would sit outside the front door with a Roberts portable radio (the all-wood construction, I learned, gave better sound quality than the plastic or metal bodies of the transistors I admired), listening to the cricket commentary. His name was Lawrence Beesley.

Apart from my great-grandfather, he was the oldest man I had ever met. His age and status induced in me the normal mixture of deference, fear and cheek. His decrepitude – the historically stained clothes, that dangle of egg-white slobber from the chin – set off in me a general adolescent anger against life and its inevitable valedictory condition; a feeling which smoothly translated itself into hatred of the person undergoing that condition. His daughter fed him on tins of baby food, which again confirmed for me the sour joke of existence and the particular contemptibility of this old man. I used to tell him invented cricket scores. '84 for 2, Mr Beesley,' I would shout as I passed him snoozing in the sun beneath the gangling wistaria. 'West Indies 790 for 3 declared,' I would insist as I delivered him his child's dinner on a tray. I would tell him scores from matches that were not being played, scores from matches that could never have been played, fanciful scores, impossible scores. He would nod in reply, and I would creep away, sniggering at my tiny cruelty, pleased that I was not such a nice young man as he might have imagined.

Fifty-two years before I met him, Lawrence Beesley had been a second-class passenger on the maiden voyage of the *Titanic*. He was thirty-five, had recently given up his job as science master at Dulwich College, and was crossing the Atlantic – according to subsequent family legend, at least – in half-hearted pursuit of an American heiress. When the *Titanic* struck its iceberg, Beesley escaped in the underpopulated Lifeboat 13, and was picked up by the *Carpathia*. Among the souvenirs this octogenarian survivor kept in his room was a blanket embroidered with the name of the rescuing ship. The more sceptical members of his family maintained that the blanket had acquired its lettering at a date considerably later than 1912. They also amused themselves with the speculation that their ancestor had escaped from the *Titanic* in women's clothing. Was it not the case that Beesley's name had been omitted from the initial list of those saved, and actually included among the drowned in the final casualty bulletin? Surely this was solid confirmation of the hypothesis that the false corpse turned mystery survivor had taken to petticoats and a high voice until safely landed in New York, where he surreptitiously discarded his drag in a subway toilet?

I supported this theory with pleasure, because it confirmed my view of the world. In the autumn of that year I was to wedge into the mirror of my college bedsitting-room a piece of paper bearing the following lines: 'Life's a cheat and all things shew it/I thought so once and now I know it'. Beesley's case offered corroboration: the hero of the *Titanic* was a blanket-forger and transvestite imposter; how just and appropriate, therefore, that I fed him false cricket scores. And on a wider scale, theorists maintained that life amounted to the survival of the fittest: did not the Beesley hypothesis prove that the 'fittest' were merely the most cunning? The heroes, the solid men of yeoman virtue, the good breeding stock, even the captain (especially the captain!) – they all went down nobly with the ship; whereas the cowards, the panickers, the deceivers found reasons for skulking in a life-boat. Was this not deft proof of how the human gene-pool was constantly deteriorating, how bad blood drove out good?

Lawrence Beesley made no mention of female dress in his book *The Loss of the Titanic*. Installed at a Boston residential club by the American publishers Houghton Mifflin, he wrote the account in six weeks; it came out less than three months after the sinking it describes, and has been reprinted at intervals ever since. It made Beesley one of the best-known survivors of the disaster, and for fifty years – right up to the time I met him – he was regularly consulted by maritime historians, film researchers, journalists, souvenir hunters, bores, conspiracy theorists and vexatious litigants. When other ships were sunk by icebergs he would be telephoned by newsmen eager for him to imagine the fate of the victims.

Forty or so years after his escape he was engaged as a consultant on the film *A Night to Remember*, made at Pinewood. Much of the movie was shot after dark, with a half-size replica of the vessel poised to sink into a sea of ruckled black velvet. Beesley watched the action with his daughter on several successive evenings, and what follows is based upon the account she gave to me. Beesley was – not surprisingly – intrigued by the reborn and once-again-teetering *Titanic*. In particular, he was keen to be among the extras who despairingly crowded the rail as the ship went down – keen, you could say, to undergo in fiction an alternative version of history. The film's director was equally determined that this consultant who lacked the necessary card from the actors' union should not appear on celluloid. Beesley, adept in any emergency, counterfeited the pass required to let him board the facsimile *Titanic*, dressed himself in period costume (can echoes prove the truth of the thing being echoed?) and installed himself among the extras. The film lights were turned on and the crowd briefed about their imminent deaths in the ruckled black velvet. Right at the last minute, as the cameras were due to roll, the director spotted that Beesley had managed to insinuate himself to the ship's rail; picking up his megaphone, he instructed the amateur imposter kindly to disembark. And so, for the second time in his life, Lawrence Beesley found himself leaving the *Titanic* just before it was due to go down.

Being a violently-educated eighteen-year-old, I was familiar with Marx's elaboration of Hegel: history repeats itself, the first time as tragedy, the second time as farce. But I had yet to come across an illustration of this process. Years later I have still to discover a better one.

II

What was Jonah doing inside the whale in the first place? It's a fishy story, as you might expect.

It all began when God instructed Jonah to go and preach against Nineveh, a place which, despite God's substantial record of annihilating wicked cities, was still – obstinately, unaccountably – a wicked city. Jonah, disliking the task for unexplained reasons which might have had something to do with a fear of being stoned to death by the partying Ninevites, ran away. At Joppa he embarked on a boat to the farthest end of the known world: Tarshish, in Spain. He failed to understand, of course, that the Lord knew exactly where he was, and what's more had operative control over the winds and waters of the Eastern Mediterranean. When a storm of rare violence blew up the mariners, being superstitious folk, cast lots to determine which of those on board was the cause of the evil, and the short straw, broken domino or queen of spades was drawn by Jonah. He was promptly pitched overboard and just as promptly swallowed by a great fish or whale which the Lord had directed through the waters for this especial purpose.

Inside the whale, for three days and three nights, Jonah prayed to the Lord and swore his future obedience so convincingly that God ordered the fish to vomit up the penitent. Not surprisingly, the next time the Almighty posted him to Nineveh, Jonah did as he was told. He went and denounced the wicked city, saying that like all other wicked cities of the Eastern Mediterranean it was about to be annihilated. Whereupon the partying Ninevites, just like Jonah inside the whale, repented; whereupon God decided after all to spare the city; whereupon Jonah became incredibly irritated, which was only normal in one who'd been put to a lot of trouble to bring the message of destruction, only for the Lord, despite a well-known, indeed historic taste for wrecking cities, to turn round and change his mind. As if this wasn't enough, God, tireless to prove himself top dog, now pulled a fancy parable on his minion. First he made a gourd spring up to protect Jonah from the sun (by 'gourd' we are to understand something like the castor-oil plant or *Palma Christi*, with its rapid growth and all-sheltering leaves); then, with no more than a wave of the silk handkerchief, he sent a maggot to destroy the said gourd, leaving Jonah painfully exposed to the heat. God's explanation of this little piece of street theatre ran as follows: you didn't punish the gourd when it failed you, did you; and in the same way I'm not going to punish Nineveh.

It's not much of a story, is it? As in most of the Old Testament, there's a crippling lack of free will around – or even the illusion of free will. God holds all the cards and wins all the tricks. The only uncertainty is how the Lord is going to play it this time: start with the two of trumps and lead up to the ace, start with the ace and run down to the two, or mix them around. And since you never can tell with paranoid schizophrenics, this element does give the narrative some drive. But what do we make of that gourd business? It's not very convincing as a logical argument: anyone can see there's a world of difference between a castor-oil plant and a city of 120,000 people. Unless, of course, this is the whole point, and the God of the Eastern Mediterranean values his creation no higher than vegetable matter.

If we examine God not as protagonist and moral bully but as author of this story, we have to mark him down for plot, motivation, suspense and characterization. Yet in his routine and fairly repellent morality there is one sensational stroke of melodrama – the business with the whale. Technically, the cetacean side of things isn't at all well handled: the beast is evidently as much of a pawn as Jonah; its providential appearance just as the sailors are tossing Jonah overboard smacks far too heavily of a *deus ex machina*; and the great fish is casually dismissed from the story the moment its narrative function has been fulfilled. Even the gourd comes off better than the poor whale, who is no more than a floating prison where Jonah spends three days purging his contempt of court. God finger-flips the blubbery jail hither and thither like a war-game admiral nudging his fleet across maps of the sea.

And yet, despite all this, the whale steals it. We forget the allegorical point of the story (Babylon engulfing disobedient Israel), we don't much care whether or not Nineveh was saved, or what happened to the regurgitated penitent; but we remember the whale. Giotto shows him chomping on Jonah's thighs, with only the knees and the flailing feet to go. Brueghel, Michelangelo, Correggio, Rubens and Dali emblazoned the tale. In Gouda there is a stained-glass window of Jonah leaving the fish's mouth like a foot-passenger stepping from the jaws of a car-ferry. Jonah (portrayed as everything from muscular faun to bearded elder) has an iconography whose pedigree and variety would make Noah envious.

What is it about Jonah's escapade that transfixes us? Is it the moment of swallowing, the oscillation between danger and salvation, when we imagine ourselves miraculously rescued from the peril of drowning only to be cast into the peril of being eaten alive? Is it the three days and three nights in the whale's belly, that image of enclosure, smothering, live burial? (Once, taking the night train from London to Paris, I found myself in the locked sleeping compartment of a locked coach in a locked hold beneath the waterline on a cross-channel ferry; I didn't think of Jonah at the time, but perhaps my panic was related to his. And is a more textbook fear involved: does the image of pulsing blubber set off some terror of being transported back to the womb?) Or are we most struck by the third element in the story, the deliverance, the proof that there is salvation and justice after our purgatorial incarceration? Like Jonah, we are all storm-tossed by the seas of life, undergo apparent death and certain burial, but then attain a blinding resurrection as the car-ferry doors swing open and we are delivered back into the light and into a recognition of God's love. Is this why the myth swims through our memory?

Perhaps: or perhaps not at all. When the film *Jaws* came out, there were many attempts to explain its hold over the audience. Did it draw on some primal metaphor, some archetypal dream known the world over? Did it exploit the clashing elements of land and water, feeding on our anxiety at the concept of amphibianism? Did it relate in some way to the fact that millions of years ago our gill-bearing ancestors crawled out of the pond, and ever since we have been paralysed by the thought of a return to it? The English novelist Kingsley Amis, considering the film and its possible interpretations, came to the following conclusion: 'It's about being bloody frightened of being eaten by a bloody great shark.'

At bottom, this is the grip which the story of Jonah and the whale still has on us: fear of being devoured by a large creature, fear of being chomped, slurped, gargled, washed down with a draught of salt water and a school of anchovies as a chaser; fear of being blinded, darkened, suffocated, drowned, hooded with blubber; fear of sensory deprivation which we know drives people mad; fear of being dead. Our response is as vivid as that of every other death-dreading generation since the tale was first invented by some sadistic mariner keen to terrify the new cabin-boy.

Of course, we recognize that the story can't have any basis in truth. We are sophisticated people, and we can tell the difference between reality and myth. A whale might swallow a man, yes, we can allow that as plausible; but once inside he could not possibly live. For a start he would drown, or if he didn't drown he would suffocate; and most probably he would have died of a heart attack when he felt the great mouth gape for him. No, it is impossible for a man to survive in a whale's belly. We know how to distinguish myth from reality. We are sophisticated people.

On 25th August 1891, James Bartley, a thirty-five-year-old sailor on the *Star of the East*, was swallowed by a sperm whale off the Falkland Islands:

> I remember very well from the moment that I fell from the boat and felt my feet strike some soft substance. I looked up and saw a big-ribbed canopy of light pink and white descending over me, and the next moment I felt myself drawn downward, feet first, and I realized that I was being swallowed by a whale. I was drawn lower and lower; a wall of flesh surrounded me and hemmed me in on every side, yet the pressure was not painful and the flesh easily gave way like soft india-rubber before my slightest movement.
>
> Suddenly I found myself in a sack much larger than my body, but completely dark. I felt about me; and my hands came in contact with several fishes, some of which seemed to be still alive, for they squirmed in my fingers, and slipped back to my feet. Soon I felt a great pain in my head and my breathing became more and more difficult. At the same time I felt a terrible heat; it seemed to consume me, growing hotter and hotter. My eyes became coals of fire in my head, and I believed every moment that I was condemned to perish in the belly of a whale. It tormented me beyond all endurance, while at the same time the awful silence of the terrible prison weighed me down. I tried to rise, to move my arms and legs, to cry out. All action was now impossible, but my brain seemed abnormally clear; and with a full comprehension of my awful fate, I finally lost all consciousness.

The whale was later killed and taken alongside the *Star of the East*, whose crewmen, unaware of the proximity of their lost comrade, spent the rest of the day and part of the night flensing their capture. The next morning they attached lifting tackle to the stomach and hauled it on deck. There seemed to be a light, spasmodic movement from within. The sailors, expecting a large fish or perhaps a shark, slit open the paunch and discovered James Bartley: unconscious, his face, neck and hands bleached white by the gastric fluids, but still alive. For two weeks he was in a delirious condition, then began to recover. In due course he was returned to normal health, except that the acids had removed all the pigmentation from his exposed skin. He remained an albino until the day he died.

M. de Parville, scientific editor of the *Journal des Débats*, examined the case in 1914 and concluded that the account given by captain and crew was 'worthy of belief'. Modern scientists tell us that Bartley could not have survived more than a few minutes in the whale's belly, let alone the half-day or more it took the unwitting sailors on the mother ship to release this modern Jonah. But do we believe modern scientists, none of whom has actually been inside a whale's belly? Surely we can make compromise with professional scepticism by suggesting air pockets (do whales suffer from wind like everyone else?) or stomach juices whose efficacy was hindered by some cetacean ailment.

And if you are a scientist, or infected by gastric doubt, look at it this way. Many people (including me) believe the myth of Bartley, just as millions have believed the myth of Jonah. You may not credit it, but what has happened is that the story has been retold, adjusted, updated; it has shuffled nearer. For Jonah now read Bartley. And one day there will be a case, one which even you will believe, of a sailor lost in a whale's mouth and recovered from its belly; maybe not after half a day, perhaps after only half an hour. And then people will believe the myth of Bartley, which was begotten by the myth of Jonah. For the point is this: not that myth refers us back to some original event which has been fancifully transcribed as it passed through the collective memory; but that it refers us forward to something that will happen, that must happen. Myth will become reality, however sceptical we might be.

III

At 8 p.m. on Saturday, 13th May 1939, the liner *St Louis* left its home port of Hamburg. It was a cruise ship, and most of the 937 passengers booked on its transatlantic voyage carried visas confirming that they were 'tourists, travelling for pleasure'. The words were an evasion, however, as was the purpose of their voyage. All but a few of them were Jews, refugees from a Nazi state which intended to dispossess, transport and exterminate them. Many, indeed, had already been dispossessed, since emigrants from Germany were permitted to take with them no more than a nominal ten Reichsmarks. This enforced poverty made them easier targets for propaganda: if they left with no more than their allowance, they could be portrayed as shabby *Untermenschen* scuttling away like rats; if they managed to outwit the system, then they were economic criminals fleeing with stolen goods. All this was normal.

The *St Louis* was flying the swastika flag, which was normal; its crew included half-a-dozen Gestapo agents, which was also normal. The shipping line had instructed the captain to lay in cheaper cuts of meat for this voyage, to remove luxury goods from the shops and free postcards from the public rooms; but the captain largely circumvented such orders, decreeing that this journey should resemble other cruises by the *St Louis* and be, as far as possible, normal. So when the Jews arrived on board from a mainland where they had been despised, systematically humiliated and imprisoned, they discovered that although this ship was legally still part of Germany, flew the swastika and had large portraits of Hitler in its public rooms, the Germans with whom they had dealings were courteous, attentive and even obedient. This was abnormal.

None of these Jews – half of whom were women and children – had any intention of revisiting Germany in the near future. Nevertheless, in accordance with the regulations of the shipping company, they had all been obliged to buy return tickets. This payment, they were told, was designed to cover 'unforeseen eventualities'. When the refugees landed in Havana, they would be given by the Hamburg-Amerika line a receipt for the unused part of the fare. The money itself had been lodged in a special account in Germany: if ever they returned there, they could collect it. Even Jews who had been released from concentration camps on strict condition that they left the Fatherland immediately were obliged to pay for the round trip.

Along with their tickets the refugees had bought landing permits from the Cuban director of immigration, who had given a personal guarantee that they would face no difficulties entering his country. It was he who had classed them as 'tourists, travelling for pleasure'; and in the course of the voyage some passengers, particularly the younger ones, were able to make the remarkable transition from despised *Untermensch* to pleasure-seeking tourist. Perhaps their escape from Germany felt as miraculous as that of Jonah from the whale. Every day there was food, drink, and dancing. Despite a warning to crew members from the Gestapo cell about contravention of the law for the Protection of German Blood and Honour, sexual activity continued as normal on a cruise. Towards the end of the Atlantic crossing, the traditional costume ball took place. The band played Glenn Miller; Jews appeared as pirates, sailors and Hawaiian dancers. Some high-spirited girls came as harem women, with Arab dress made from bedsheets – a transformation which struck the more orthodox on board as unseemly.

On Saturday 27th May the *St Louis* anchored in Havana Harbour. At 4 a.m. the klaxon for reveille sounded, and half an hour later the breakfast gong. Small boats came out to the liner, some bearing vendors of coconuts and bananas, others containing friends and relatives who shouted up names to the rail. The ship was flying a quarantine flag, which was normal. The captain had to certify to the Port of Havana medical officer that no one on board was 'an idiot, or insane, or suffering from a loathsome or contagious disease'. When this had been done, immigration officers began to process the passengers, examining their papers and indicating whereabouts on the pier to expect their luggage. The first fifty refugees gathered at the top of the ladder, waiting for the boat to take them ashore.

Immigration, like emigration, is a process in which money is no less important than principles or laws, and often sounder than either of them. Money reassures the host country – or, in the case of Cuba, the transit country – that the new arrivals will not be a charge on the state. Money also serves to bribe the officials who have to take this decision. The Cuban director of immigration had made a great deal of money from previous boatloads of Jews; the President of Cuba had not made enough money from them.

The President had therefore issued a decree on 6th May revoking the validity of tourist visas when the true purpose of travel was immigration. Did this decree apply to those on board the *St Louis* or not? The ship had sailed from Hamburg after the law had been promulgated; on the other hand, the landing permits had been issued earlier. It was a question on which much argument and money could be spent. The number of the presidential decree was 937, which the superstitious might have noticed was also the number of passengers on board when the *St Louis* left Europe.

A delay developed. Nineteen Cubans and Spaniards were allowed to disembark, plus three passengers with authentic visas; the remaining 900 or so Jews waited for news of the negotiations which involved, variously, the Cuban President, his director of immigration, the shipping line, the local relief committee, the ship's captain and a lawyer flown in from the New York headquarters of the Joint Distribution Committee. These talks lasted several days. Factors to be considered were money, pride, political ambition and Cuban public opinion. The captain of the *St Louis*, while distrustful of both local politicians and his own shipping line, was convinced at least of one thing: that if Cuba proved inaccessible, the United States, to which most of his passengers had the right of eventual entry, would surely accept them earlier than promised.

Some of the marooned passengers were less confident, and became unnerved by the uncertainties, the delay, the heat. They had spent so long reaching a place of safety, and were now so near. Friends and relatives continued to circle the liner in small boats; a fox terrier, sent on ahead from Germany, was rowed out each day and held up towards the rail and its distant owners. A passengers' committee had been formed, to whom the shipping company gave free cabling facilities; appeals for intercession were despatched to influential people, including the wife of the Cuban president. It was during this time that two passengers attempted suicide, one with a syringe and tranquillizers, another by slashing his wrists and jumping into the sea; both survived. Thereafter, to prevent further suicide attempts, there were security patrols at night; the lifeboats were always ready, and the ship was lit up by floodlights. These measures reminded some Jews of the concentration camps they had recently left.

The *St Louis* was not meant to leave Havana empty after dropping its 937 emigrants. Some 250 passengers were booked on the return trip to Hamburg via Lisbon. One suggestion was that 250 of the Jews could at least be disembarked to make room for those on shore. But how would you choose the 250 who were to be allowed off the Ark? Who would separate the clean from the unclean? Was it to be done by casting lots?

The predicament of the *St Louis* was not a disregarded, local issue. The voyage was being logged by the German, British and American press. *Der Stürmer* commented that if the Jews chose to take up their return passages to Germany, they should be accommodated at Dachau and Buchenwald. Meanwhile, in Havana harbour, American reporters managed to get on board what they nicknamed, perhaps too easily, 'the ship that shamed the world'. Such publicity does not necessarily help refugees. If the shame belongs to the whole world, then why should one particular country – which had already accepted many Jewish refugees – be so frequently expected to bear it? The world, apparently, did not feel its shame so strongly that it moved its hand to its wallet. The Cuban government accordingly voted to exclude the immigrants and ordered the *St Louis* to leave the island's territorial waters. This did not mean, the President added, that he had closed the door on negotiations; merely that he would not consider further offers until the ship had left harbour.

How much are refugees? It depends how desperate they are, how rich their patrons, how greedy their hosts. In the world of entry permits and panic it is always a seller's market. Prices are arbitrary, speculative, evanescent. The lawyer from the Joint Distribution Committee put forward an opening offer of $50,000 for the safe landing of the Jews, and was told that the sum might usefully be trebled. But if trebled, why not trebled again? The director of immigration – who had already received $150 a head for the landing permits which had not been honoured – suggested to the shipping line a fee of $250,000 to help get decree number 937 rescinded. A purported intermediary of the President seemed to think that the Jews could be landed for $1,000,000. In the end, the Cuban government was to fix on a bond of $500 for each Jew. This price had a certain logic, being the amount of surety which each official immigrant into the country had to post. So the 907 passengers on board, who had already paid their outward and return fares, who had bought their permits and then been reduced to an official ten Deutschmarks each, would cost $453,500.

As the liner started its engines, a group of women charged the accommodation ladder; they were repelled by Cuban police with pistols. During its six days in Havana harbour the *St Louis* had become a tourist attraction, and its departure was watched by an estimated crowd of 100,000. The captain had been given permission by his superiors in Hamburg to sail for any port which would accept his passengers. At first he steamed idly in ever-widening circles, waiting to be recalled to Havana; then headed north for Miami. When the ship reached the American coast it was greeted by a US coastguard cutter. But this apparent welcome was a rebuff: the cutter was there to see that the *St Louis* did not enter territorial waters. The State Department had already decided that if the Jews were turned down by Cuba, they would not be granted entry into the United States. Money was a less direct factor here: high unemployment and reliable xenophobia were sufficient justifications.

The Dominican Republic offered to accept the refugees for the standardized market price of $500 a head; but this merely duplicated the Cuban tariff. Venezuela, Ecuador, Chile, Colombia, Paraguay and Argentina were all approached; each declined to bear the world's shame single-handed. In Miami the immigration inspector announced that the *St Louis* would not be allowed to dock in any US port.

The liner, denied entry to the whole American continent, continued steaming northwards. Those on board were aware that they were approaching the point at which it would have to swing east and head inevitably back to Europe. Then, at 4.50 on the afternoon of Sunday, 4th June, a news flash was picked up. The President of Cuba had apparently given permission for the Jews to be landed on the Isle of Pines, a former penal colony. The captain turned the *St Louis* round and headed south again. Passengers brought their luggage up on deck. That evening, over dinner, the spirits of the gala evening returned.

The next morning, three hours' sailing away from the Isle of Pines, the ship received a cable: permission to disembark had not yet been confirmed. The passenger committee, who throughout the crisis had been sending telegrams to prominent Americans asking them to intercede, could think of no one else to contact. Someone suggested the Mayor of St Louis, Missouri, thinking that the consonance of names might perhaps evoke sympathy. A cable was duly despatched.

The Cuban President had asked for a $500 surety per refugee, plus a subsidiary guarantee to cover food and lodging during the period of transit on the Isle of Pines. The American lawyer had offered (according to the Cuban government) a total of $443,000, but further stipulated that this sum was to cover not just the refugees on the *St Louis* but also 150 Jews on two other ships. The Cuban government found itself unable to accept this counter-proposal and withdrew its own offer. The lawyer for the Joint Committee responded by agreeing in full to the original Cuban demand. The government in return regretted that its offer had already been terminated and could not now be revived. The *St Louis* turned round and headed north for a second time.

As the ship began its return voyage to Europe, the British and French governments were informally sounded out to see if their countries might take the Jews. The British answer was that they would prefer to view the present difficulty in the wider context of the general European refugee situation, but that they might be prepared to consider possible subsequent entry of the Jews to Britain after their return to Germany.

There had been unconfirmed or impracticable offers from the President of Honduras, from an American philanthropist, even from a quarantine station in the Panama Canal Zone; the ship steamed on. The passenger committee addressed its appeals to political and religious leaders throughout Europe; though its messages now had to be shorter, since the shipping line had withdrawn free cabling facilities. One suggestion made at this time was that the strongest swimmers among the Jews should jump overboard at intervals, thus forcing the *St Louis* to stop and turn round. This would slow its progress towards Europe and allow more time for negotiations. The idea was not taken up.

German radio announced that since no country would agree to accept the boat-load of Jews, the Fatherland would be obliged to take them back and support them. It was not difficult to guess where they might be supported. What's more, if the *St Louis* was forced to unload its cargo of degenerates and criminals back in Hamburg, this would prove that the world's supposed concern was mere hypocrisy. Nobody wanted the shabby Jews, and nobody therefore had any right to criticize whatever welcome the Fatherland might extend to the filthy parasites on their return.

It was at this time that a group of younger Jews attempted to hijack the ship. They invaded the bridge, but were dissuaded

342 A HISTORY OF THE WORLD IN 10½ CHAPTERS

from further action by the captain. For his part, he conceived a plan of setting fire to the *St Louis* off Beachy Head, which would compel the rescuing nation to take his passengers in. This desperate scheme might even have been tried. Finally, when many had given up hope and the liner was nearing Europe, the Belgian government announced that it would admit 200 of the passengers. In the days that followed, Holland agreed to take 194, Britain 350, and France 250.

After a voyage of 10,000 miles, the *St Louis* docked at Antwerp, 300 miles from its port of departure. Relief workers from the four countries involved had already met to decide the distribution of the Jews. Most of those on board possessed the right of eventual entry into the United States, and had therefore been ascribed a number on the US quota list. It was observed that the relief workers competed for passengers with low numbers, since these refugees would leave their countries of transit the soonest.

In Antwerp a pro-Nazi youth organization had distributed handbills bearing the slogan: 'We too want to help the Jews. If they call at our offices each will receive gratis a length of rope and a long nail.' The passengers were disembarked. Those admitted to Belgium were put on a train whose doors were locked and windows nailed shut; they were told that such measures were necessary for their own protection. Those admitted to Holland were immediately transferred to a camp surrounded by barbed wire and guard dogs.

On Wednesday, 21st June the British contingent from the *St Louis* docked at Southampton. They were able to reflect that their wanderings at sea had lasted precisely forty days and forty nights.

On 1st September the Second World War began, and the passengers from the *St Louis* shared in the fate of European Jewry. Their chances rose or fell depending upon the country to which they had been allotted. Estimates of how many survived vary.

8

UPSTREAM

c/o The Jungle

Darling –

Just time for a card – we leave in half an hour – had our last night on the Johnny Walker now it's local firewater or nothing – remember what I said on the phone and don't have it cut too short. Love you – your Circus Strongman.

My own darling –

Just spent 24 hours on a bus with the dashboard covered in St Christophers or whatever the local version hereabouts is. Wouldn't have minded if the driver had gone in for some stronger magic – the old Christianity didn't seem to be having much effect on his driving. When not thinking about puking your guts up round every hairpin bend, scenery magnificent. Great big trees, mountains – that sort of thing – I've got some postcards. Crew all a bit over-excited at the moment – if I hear another joke about 'I was going Caracas back there' I think I'll strangle someone. Still, that's normal on a job like this. Not that I've ever done a job like this before, should be great fun. It'd better be after all those needles they stuck in me so I won't get beri-beri and co.

It's a relief to get away from people recognizing you as well. You know, even with the beard and glasses they still copped the face in Caracas. At the airport, of course, but that's normal anyway. No, it was funny. Guess what they'd seen me in? Not your upmarket angst number with the Pinter script that got the Palme d'Or, none of that. No, that filthy little American soap I did for Hal Screwyouupalotodos. It's STILL playing here. Kids come up in the street and say, 'Hey Mista Rick, how ya doin'?' What about that? The poverty here is something else. Still, after India nothing will surprise me. Now what have you done about your hair? I hope you haven't gone and done anything silly to it just to get your own back for me going away. I know what you girls are like, you say you'll just have it short to see what it looks like, and then you say Pedro at the salon won't let you grow it just for the moment, and then you say you've got to look your best for some wedding or other and you can't go with it straggly and then you end up not growing it again and if I don't mention it every week you think I've learned to like it and if I do mention it every week you think I'm nagging so I don't mention it and I'm stuck with it. And it's not fair to say it's because of the beard because the beard's not my fault, they just didn't shave in the jungle in whatever century it's going to be when we get there and I *know* I grew it early but that's the way I am, I like to start thinking myself into the part as soon as possible. You know what Dirk says, how he starts with the shoes, once he gets the shoes right he knows what the rest of the character's like, well with me it's the face. Sorry if it's the first thing you see in the morning, still it's not everyone who can say they've been sleeping with a Jesuit. A very old Jesuit too. Weather very hot, laundry problems I expect. Still taking those tummy tablets. Had a word with Vic about the script and he says not to worry but they always say that at this stage, don't they? I told him what I said to you on the phone about shouldn't he be given a bit more obvious humanity because priests aren't great box-office nowadays and Vic said we'd talk about it nearer the time. Getting on well with Matt – obviously there's going to be some competition once we start work but he's not half as paranoid as I thought he'd be, a bit back-slapping, still I guess that's Yanks for you. I told him my Vanessa story and he told me his and we'd both heard them before! Got stinko paralytico together on our last night in town and ended up doing the Zorba dance in a restaurant! Matt tried plate-smashing but they said it wasn't the local custom and threw us out! Charged us for the plates, too.

You know what they call post offices out here? Our Lady of Communications. You probably have to get down on your knees for next-day delivery. Not that we've seen one of them for miles. God knows if I'll be able to post this before the jungle starts. Maybe we'll come across a friendly native with a forked stick going in the right direction and I'll give him the big-screen smile and hand it over. (Joke). Don't worry about me. Love you.

– Charlie

Darling –

If you look in your photo album for our flat-smouldering party you'll see there's something missing. Don't worry – I've got it. It's the one where you've got your chipmunk face on. You've got a bit wet out here – terrible downpour couple of days ago – but you still don't mind being kissed last thing at night. You might get a bit crumpled from here on in as we've seen our last hotel for a bit. Now it's all Boy Scout stuff and bivouacs and tents. Hope I get the sleep I need. It's so hard to work on full glow when you've only had a couple of hours kip. Anyway we're well into the Jungle now. Lots of delays. Usual stuff – you arrange that on such-and-such a day you'll turn up with so many people and so much luggage and he'll transport you to the next place and when you turn up he pretends things have changed and you didn't say fifty but fifteen and anyway the price has gone up and so on and so bloody on until he gets the backhander he wants. God, when things like that happen I just feel like shouting I Want To Work in a very loud voice. I did that one day when things got hairier than usual, went down to where some bandit was trying to rip us off and practically rubbed beards with him and shouted into his face I Want To Work For Christ's Sake Let Me Work, but Vic said that wasn't being helpful.

Later. Matt was peeing in the river when one of the sparks came up and told him it wasn't a good idea. Apparently they've got this tiny fish which is attracted by the heat or whatever and can swim up your pee as you're peeing. Didn't sound likely at first but think of salmon I suppose. Then what it does is swim straight into your dick and once it gets there it sticks out a couple of spines sideways and just stays there. Ouch in spades, to say the least of it. The sparks says you can't get it out, it's like having an umbrella opened up in there, you have to have the whole doings chopped off in hospital. Matt didn't know whether to believe him but can you risk it? No one's peeing in the river at the moment, anyway.

Later. We were puttering up river late in the afternoon and the sun was beginning to go down over these huge trees and a flight of big birds, herons or something, were taking off like pink seaplanes as someone said and the second assistant suddenly stood up and yelled out This is paradise, this is fucking paradise. Actually, feeling a bit depressed, love. Sorry to lay this on you, not fair I know as I'll probably be right as rain by the time you get this. Bloody Matt getting me down. What an ego. You'd think no one else had ever made a film except him and you can see him coming on all good mates with the crew so they'll make things easier for him when he gets in front of camera, so he looks five years younger and I get the shiny nose. Vic's not tough enough for this job, to be frank. You need one of those slave-driving old studio bosses if you ask me, not a sensitive graduate who went into movies because he liked the clouds in Antonioni and then turned himself into a nouvelle vague Deutscher all hot for Truthspiel. I ask you, forty of us slogging into the Jungle all because we bought his line about needing to work our way into the reality of a couple of deeply dead Jesuit priests. How this applies to the crew as well I don't know but I expect Vic's got some theory to cover it. Us going in on foot and then the equipment being airlifted in is about as arsy-versy as you can get. He won't even let us use the radio-telephone until after we've made the rendez-vous. The focus-puller's girlfriend is having a baby and he wanted to call headquarters in Caracas to see if there was any news but Vic said no.

Bloody weather. Bloody hot all the time. Sweating like a pig, *comme un porco*. Still worrying about the script. Think I'll have to do some rewrites on my part. No chance of getting any laundry done unless we meet some tribe of washerwomen waiting for custom outside one of those zinc shacks like we saw in that village in Provence do you remember? Bloody tin sign for Coca-Cola at a trading post this morning. I ask you, hundreds of miles from bloody anywhere and the Coke reps have been there before you and shat on the landscape. Or some chum of Matt's put it there to make him feel at home. Sorry about this.

Love Charlie

Letter 3

Hey Good Looking!

Sorry about that whingeing on at the end of the last letter. Everything much better now. For one thing we've all started peeing in the river again. We were asking Fish Sparks as we call him how he knew about the fish that swims up your pee and he said he'd seen some fat explorer fellow on the box going on about it, which sounded likely enough. But then we asked him a bit more about it and he made his fatal mistake. He said this explorer had said he'd had some special underpants made so that he could pee in the river safely. He got a cricket protector, the sparks says, and cut the front bit out and stuck a tea-strainer down it. Well I ask you. If you're telling fibs, keep them simple, that's the rule, isn't it? Never over-egg the pudding. So we all had a good laugh at the sparks and all of us unzipped our flies and peed in the river whether we wanted to or not. The only person that didn't was Fish, who had to save face and went on claiming it was true.

So that cheered us up a bit as you can imagine but what really cheered us up was making contact with the Indians. I mean, if the bandits on the way here were anything to go by ('here', if you want to look it up in your schoolgirl atlas, is somewhere near the Mocapra) why should the Indians keep their word? Matt said afterwards he'd half expected the whole thing would turn out to be a wild goose chase and I told him I thought the same. But there they were, four of them, just where they said they'd be, in a clearing on a bend in the river, naked as nature intended, standing very upright which still didn't make them very tall and looking at us without any fear. Without any curiosity either, in a funny sort of way, which was odd. You expect they'll want to prod you or something. But they just stood there as if we were the odd ones not them, which when you come to think about it is dead right. They watched us unpack everything and then we set off. Didn't offer to help carry anything which was a bit of a surprise but then I suppose they're not Sherpas are they? It's about two days march apparently to the rest of the tribe and the river we're looking for. We couldn't see the track they were following at all – amazing sense of direction they must have in the Jungle. You'd be lost here I can tell you angel, especially given you don't know how to get from Shepherd's Bush to Hammersmith without a police escort.* We marched for about two hours then stopped for the night and ate fish the Indians had caught in the river while they were waiting for us. Very tired, but quite a day. Kiss you.

*Joke (not serious)

Later. A whole day on the move. Glad I did all that training in the gym. Some of the crew puffing after only half an hour or so, which isn't surprising as the only exercise they take in the normal run of things is putting their legs under a table and aiming their snouts at the trough. Oh yes and putting their hands up to order another bottle. Matt's pretty fit from all those outdoor movies where they put olive oil on his pectorals (though not as fit as he ought to be) and the two of us gave the crew a bit of a hard time, said union rules didn't apply in the Jungle, and so on. They certainly didn't want to get left behind! Fish Sparks, who's been a bit down in the mouth since we rumbled his story, thought it was terrifically funny to start calling the Indians things like Sitting Bull and Tonto, but of course they didn't understand and anyway the rest of us sort of froze him out. It just wasn't funny, anyway. They're incredible, these Indians. Walking starkers through the forest, incredibly agile, never get tired, killed a monkey in a tree with a blowpipe. Had it for dinner, well some of us did, the squeamish ones had a tin of corned beef. I had the monkey. Tasted a bit like oxtail only much redder. A bit stringy but delicious.

Tuesday. God knows how the post system's going to work. At the moment we just give it to Rojas – he's the fourth assistant and a local and he's been appointed postman. All that means is that he puts the letters into a plastic bag so they won't get eaten by beetles or woodworm or whatever. Then when we meet up with the copter he'll take the mail out. So God knows when you'll get this.

Miss you (pause while I do my Circus Strongman howl). Today we should have met up with the rest of the tribe but we aren't as fit as we might be. I bet some of the crew thought there'd be wheels right into the Jungle and food trucks parked every few miles and they'd get burgers and chips served by girls wearing flower garlands round their necks. Fat Dick the sound man probably packed a Hawaiiiiiian shirt.

You have to hand it to Vic in a way. Smallest crew-to-budget ratio in years. Me and Matt doing our own stunts (good old Norman really screwed the dollars up for me on that clause). Not even daily rushes either – the copter's only coming in every three days because Vic thinks it'll break our concentration or something no doubt posher intellectually than that. Lab report over the radio-telephone, the rushes with the copter. And the studio went along with it all. Amazing, isn't it?

No it isn't amazing, as you well know sweetie. The studio thinks Vic's a genius and gave him as much as they could until the insurance boys dug their heels in over big-name leads falling out of a canoe and then they went down the list and found a couple of guys the industry could afford to lose.* So I've been a bad boy at times but they reckon I can't walk out on a job if

I'm in the Jungle and Matt's temperamental which means he doesn't normally work unless they give him a hamper full of white powder but he seems to have kicked it and there aren't too many dealers swinging through the trees like Tarzan out here. And we agree to Vic's conditions because we bloody need to and deep down we probably think Vic's a genius too.

*Joke. Well, sort of. No real danger, I'm sure.

Wondering if it was a mistake to have the monkey last night. It certainly slowed me down a bit today, and Matt was behind a bush a lot as well.

Later. Sorry, Wednesday. Met the tribe. The greatest day of my life. Except for meeting you, babe, of course. They were just there, suddenly, as we came over a hill and saw a river below us. The lost river and the lost people side by side – amazing. They're quite short, and you'd think they were plump except it's all muscle, and they don't have a stitch on. The girls are pretty, too (don't worry, angel – riddled with diseases). The funny thing is there don't seem to be any old folks. Or maybe they've left them behind somewhere. But we did have this idea that the whole tribe went around together. Puzzling. Also, I've run out of mosquito stuff – the really powerful one anyway. Getting bitten quite a lot. Vic says not to worry – did I think Father Firmin had insect repellent all those years ago? I said authenticity was one thing but did my devoted fans really want to see me on the big screen with spots a foot across all over my face? Vic told me I had to suffer for my art. I told Vic to fuck off. Bloody Truthspiel.

Thursday. We've set up camp now on the bank. A couple of camps actually, one for whites (most of whom are brown with red spots) and one for Indians. I said why didn't we have one big camp, for Christ's sake. Some of the crew were against this because they thought they'd get their watches stolen (I ask you) and some in favour so that they could get a closer look at the women (I ask you). Vic said he thought two camps were a good idea because there would have been two originally and it would psychologically prepare the Indians for playing their ancestors, which I said was just a rationalization of elitism. Anyway things got quite hot and eventually one of the guides was sent over to talk to the Indians and the word came back that they wouldn't share their camp with us anyway, which is quite funny I suppose.

Here comes the copter so I'll end now.

                                                    Love Charlie

Letter 4

Dear Pips,

First rendez-vous! They coptered in the genny and the rest of the equipment. Great excitement (except for the Indians who ignored it all). Food, ciggies. No mosquito stuff on board – can you believe it? Another thing – Vic wouldn't let them bring in newspapers, which pissed me off. I mean we're not kids are we? Reading a two-week-old copy of The Independent isn't likely to screw up my acting, is it? Or is it? I'm amazed Vic allowed us letters. None for Charlie. I know I told you not to write except in emergency but I didn't mean it. Hope you guessed.

Friday. Look, I know you don't want to talk about it, but I think this spell of being apart will do us lots of good. In lots of ways. Really. I'm getting too old for hellraising anyway. 'MY HELLRAISING DAYS ARE OVER' SAYS TV'S 'BAD-BOY' CHARLIE. Love you.

Pippa love, I really think it's the effect of the Indians (oh, Saturday). They're so open, so direct. There they are, not a stitch on them, they say what they mean, do what they want, eat when they're hungry, make love as if it's the most natural thing in the world,* and lie down to die when they reach the end of their lives. It's really something. I don't mean I could do it myself, not straight away, I just mean I get a great sense of comradeship with these people. I almost feel I've been sent here so they can teach me a lesson about life. Does that make sense? It's all right, sweetie, I'm not coming back with a bone through my nose, but I might come back with a bit less of a bone in my head. All that business about Linda – I know we agreed not to talk about it – but I feel such a shit out here. Hurting you. Not telling the truth. Out here, with the lost river running past my feet, learning the names of birds I don't even know the names of in English, I feel good about us.

*Not personal experience. Charlie's nose clean.

Sunday. It's not just distance lends enchantment or whatever. It's something about being *here*. You remember the American astronauts, how they went to the moon and came back totally changed by looking at the earth and seeing it like just any old planet all small and a long way away? Some of them got religious or went barmy I seem to remember, but the point is they were all different when they came back. It's a bit like that with me, except that instead of going into the technological future I had to go back in time. Actually, I don't really mean that, back in time. All the crew here think the Indians are fantastically primitive just because they don't have radios. I think they're fantastically advanced and mature because they don't have radios. They're teaching me something without knowing they're doing it. I'm beginning to see things a lot more in perspective. God I'm damn sorry about Linda.

Monday. A long time setting up, then it rained. One of the girls is teaching me the language. Don't worry, chipmunk, riddled with diseases I'm sure.* Tried to find out what they call themselves, you know, name of the tribe. Guess what, THEY DON'T HAVE A NAME FOR THEMSELVES!!! and they don't have a name for their language either. Isn't that amazing!! Incredibly mature. It's like, nationalism out of the window.

*Sort of catch-phrase with the crew. If anyone starts talking about sex or looking at the Indian women, someone always says, 'Riddled with diseases I'm sure.' Probably not so funny in London.

Tuesday. There's a really good feeling now we've started. Everyone pulling together. None of this silly bloody union rules. Everyone *contributing*. I'm sure it's the influence of the Indians. It's how things should be.

Wednesday. I think my accent's improving. There's a big white stork sort of bird called a *thkarni*. I think that's how you write it down. Anyway, I say *thkarni* when one takes off or lands on the water, and the Indians think this is jolly funny. They fall about laughing. Well they aren't any better at saying Charlie.

Thursday. Not much. Bitten by 8000000000000 mosquitoes. Matt makes stupid joke. If you look closely, he's bandy-legged, I swear.

Friday. It's amazing when you think about it. Here's this tribe of Indians, totally obscure, don't even have a name for themselves. A couple of hundred years ago two Jesuit missionaries trying to find their way back to the Orinoco stumble across them, get them to build a raft and then pole the two Godmen several hundred miles south while the said Godmen preach them the Gospel and try to get them to wear Levis. Just when they get near their destination the raft capsizes, the missionaries nearly drown and the Indians disappear. Melt into the Jungle and no one sees them again until Vic's researchers track them down a year ago. Now they're helping us do exactly the same thing a couple of hundred years on. What I'm dying to know is does the tribe remember? Do they have ballads about transporting the two white men dressed as women up to the great watery anaconda to the south, or however they might put it? Or did the white men vanish from the tribe's memory as completely as the tribe vanished for the white man? So many things to think about. And what will happen when we've gone? Will they disappear again for another two or three hundred years? Or disappear forever wiped out by some killer bug and all that will be left of them is a film in which they're playing their own ancestors? I'm not sure I can get my head round that.

My blessings on thee, daughter, sin no more.*

Love, Charlie

*Joke!!

Nothing from you Sunday or Wednesday. Hope Rojas has something tomorrow. Didn't mean you not to write whatever I said. Will send this anyway.

Letter 5

Darling –

This priest outfit must be the most uncomfortable garment ever invented for Jungle travel. Makes you sweat like a pig, *comme un porco*. How did old Father Firmin keep his dignity, I ask myself. Still I suppose you could say he suffered for his religion in the same way I suffer for my art.

Sunday. My God, guess what? Fat Dick the sound man was peeing in the river last night when one of the Indians came up to him all agitated, making lots of gestures, sign language, sort of swimming with his hands and so on. Dick doesn't follow him – in fact he thinks the bloke is trying to get off with him which is a bit of a laugh if you've seen the Indian women, until the Indian runs off and fetches Miguel who's one of the guides. Lots more gestures and explanations and Dick zips up his trousers pretty smartish. Guess what? The Indian was telling him about this little fish that lives in the river and – you can guess the rest!!! Not much chance of this particular member of this particular tribe watching British telly the same night Fish Sparks was. And not much chance of Fishy learning enough of the local lingo to set up a sting like this. So we just had to accept he was right all along! Boy did he have the last laugh.

Monday. Here's a funny thing. While the Indians appear to understand roughly what we're doing – they're happy to do retakes and don't seem at all put out by this great big eye being pointed at them – they don't seem to understand about the idea of acting. I mean sure they're acting their ancestors and they're quite willing (in exchange for some Mickey Mouse presents) to build us a raft and transport us upstream on it and be filmed doing this. But they won't do anything else. If Vic says could you stand in a different way or use the pole like this and tries to demonstrate they simply won't. Absolutely refuse. This is how we pole a raft and just because a white man is watching through his funny machine we aren't going to do it any differently. The other thing is even more incredible. They actually think that when Matt and I are dressed up as Jesuits we actually are Jesuits! They think we've gone away and these two blokes in black dresses have turned up! Father Firmin is just as real a person for them as Charlie, though I'm glad to say they like Charlie more. But you can't persuade them about what's going on. The crew think this is pretty stupid of them but I wonder if it isn't fantastically mature. The crew think they're such a primitive civilization they haven't even dis-covered acting yet. I wonder if it's the opposite and they're a sort of post-acting civilization, maybe the first one on the earth. Like, they don't need it any more, so they've forgotten about it and don't understand it any longer. Quite a thought!

Wednesday. Ought to have said more about the job. Not going badly. Script isn't what I remembered, but then it never is, usually because they've changed it. Matt isn't too bad to work with. I asked Make-Up to give him a few mosquito bites but he refused point-blank. Said he wanted to be the pretty one for a change. Quite funny that – I mean it's obvious that deep down he thinks he's jolly good-looking! I suppose I'd better not tell him that thing you said about his face looking as if it was carved out of corned beef.

Thursday. Terrible thing happened. Quite terrible. One of the Indians fell off the raft and was drowned. Just swept away. We stared at the water which was pretty choppy and waited for the Indian to surface but he never did. Naturally we said we'd stop work for the day. Guess what? The Indians wouldn't hear of it. What good old troupers they are!

Friday. Thinking about yesterday's incident. We were much more upset about it than the Indians were. I mean, he must have

been somebody's brother or husband or something, but there
wasn't any crying or anything. I half expected that when we
pitched camp for the night there'd be some sort of ceremony –
I don't know, burning a bundle of clothes or whatever. Not so.
Same old jolly camp-fire life went on as per usual. I wondered if
they hadn't liked the fellow who went overboard, but that's too
obvious. Maybe they don't distinguish between life and death in
some way. Maybe they don't think he's 'gone' as we do – or at
least not gone altogether. Gone to a nicer bit of the river. I tried
this out on Matt who said, 'Hey man I didn't know you had
hippie blood.' Matt is not exactly the most spiritual and sophisticated fellow you've ever met. Believes in making your own way
through life, walking tall, shooting straight, balling chicks as he
puts it and spitting in the eye of anyone who does you wrong.
That at any rate seems to be the sum of his wisdom. He thinks the
Indians are rather cute kids who haven't yet invented the video
recorder. I must say it's pretty funny that a chap like him ends up
playing a Jesuit priest having doctrinal disputes in the rain forest.
The fact is, he's one of those perfectly efficient American actors
whose careers are decided by their image makers. I told him
about taking six months off and doing rep in the provinces just
to get back in touch with live acting and live audiences and he
reacted as if I told him I'd had a mental breakdown. Say what
you like, I think the stage is the place you learn to act. Matt can
twitch his face in any direction and crinkle up his eyes knowing
that his jailbait fans will be sitting there wetting themselves. But
can he act with his body? Call me old-fashioned, but I think a
lot of American actors just do a sort of swagger and leave it at
that. Tried to explain all this to Vic, who said I was doing fine
and Matt was doing fine and he thought we'd gel together on
screen. Sometimes I do wish he'd LISTEN to what I say. Here
comes the post, or rather the copter. Nothing from you yet.

                                        – love, Charlie

Letter 6

Pippa love –

   Look I know we said we wouldn't talk about it and maybe it's
not fair cos I don't know what state you'll be in when you get
this, but why don't we just move to the country and have babies?
No I haven't fallen in the river or anything. You've no idea how

good it's been for me out here. I've cut out coffee after lunch and almost don't smoke at all. Well the Indians don't, do they, I say to myself. The Indians don't need to support the mighty firm of Philip Morris Inc. of Richmond Va. When things get tough they sometimes chew on a little green leaf, which I reckon is their equivalent of the occasional ciggy one takes when the director is behaving like a prize muffin. So why not cut it down like they do? And that Linda thing. I know you probably don't want to hear her name ever again and if that's what you want that's my promise, but it's all to do with London isn't it? Not really to do with *us* at all. Just bloody London with its grime and filthy streets and the booze. Well that's not really living, the way we do in cities, is it? Also I think cities make people lie to one another. Do you think that's possible? These Indians never lie, same as they don't know how to act. No pretence. Now I don't think that's primitive at all, I think it's bloody mature. And I'm sure it's because they live in the Jungle not in cities. They spend all their time surrounded by nature and the one thing nature doesn't do is lie. It just goes ahead and does its thing, as Matt would say. Walks tall and shoots straight. It may not be very nice some of the time but it doesn't tell lies. Which is why I think the country and babies is the answer. And when I say the country I don't mean one of those villages just off the motorway full of people just like us buying Australian Chardonnay from the local wine merchant and the only time you hear an ooo-aarr accent is when you're listening to the Archers in the bath. I mean the real country, somewhere hidden away – Wales maybe or Yorkshire.

Sunday. The baby thing. It's to do with the Indians in a funny sort of way. You know I said they're all fantastically healthy and yet there aren't any old folks even though we thought they travelled around together in a group? Well, I finally got Miguel to talk to them about it and it turns out the reason there aren't any old folk around is because they don't live much longer than about 35. So I was wrong when I thought they were fantastically healthy and a good advert for the Jungle. The truth is it's only the fantastically healthy ones who can get by at all. What a turnaround. But the point is, I'm now older than most of this tribe will ever be and that feels like a chill wind. And if we lived in the country then it wouldn't be me coming home every night whacked out and wanting to be looked after and having a squawking infant instead. If I only took the big parts and none of this TV crap I'd just go away to film, and then when I was around I'd really be around. See? I could make a playpen for him and buy him one of those big wooden Arks with all the animals in and I could get one of those bags you carry babies around in like the Indians have had for centuries. Then I'd go striding off across the moors to get the both of us out of your hair for a bit, what do you say? By the way, I really am sorry I hit Gavin.

Monday. Bit depressed, love. Had this ludicrous tiff with Vic about a line. Six bloody words, but I *knew* Firmin wouldn't say them. I mean, I've been *living* this guy for three weeks now and Vic starts telling me how to speak? He said OK rewrite them, so I held things up for an hour and at the end of it he said he wasn't convinced. We tried it out all the same, because I insisted, and guess what? Bloody Matt wasn't convinced either. I said he couldn't tell a line of dialogue from a line of coke and anyway his face was carved out of corned beef, and he threatened to punch me. Stupid bloody film.

Tuesday. Still boiling.

Wednesday. Amazing thing. You know I said about the Indians not understanding about acting. Well in the last 2 days Firmin and Antonio have been getting more and more hostile (which isn't hard to do given how Charlie and Matt are currently feeling about one another) and you could really sense the Indians getting involved, following it all from their part of the raft as if their lives depended on it – which in a way they did I suppose because we were arguing about whether they had the right to be baptised and have their souls saved or not. They sensed this somehow, I don't know. Anyway today we had the scene where Matt had to hit me with the paddle sort of semi-accidentally. It was best balsa wood of course, not that the Indians could know, but I duly went down poleaxed and Matt started pretending it was an accident. The Indians were supposed to look on at what was happening as if these two white men in skirts were barmy. That's what they'd been told to do. But they didn't. Lots of them came rushing over to me and started stroking my face and wetting my brow and making a sort of wailing noise, and then three of them turned on Matt looking really nasty. Incredible! What's more they might have done him an injury if he hadn't pulled off his cassock pretty smartish and turned back into Matt, which calmed them down. Amazing! It was only old Matt, and that nasty priest Antonio had gone away. Then I slowly got to my feet and they all started laughing happily as if I wasn't dead after all. The good thing was that Vic kept running so we didn't miss any of it. Now he thinks he can work it in, which I'm pleased about because if this is the way the Indians react to me and Matt then maybe that's a pointer to how the fans will go.

Thursday. Vic says the lab report on yesterday's scuffle wasn't too kosher. Bet bloody Matt's been getting at him – probably knew the camera had caught him looking shit-scared. I said let's wait and see how it prints and Vic agreed but I didn't get good vibes. So much for Truthspiel: when they get it, they don't use it.

Friday. I don't think the script's up to scratch, and the whole thing's underbudgeted, but one thing I will say for it is that it's ABOUT something. I mean, it isn't afraid of the big issues. Most films aren't about anything, are they, that's what I find more and more. 'Two Priests up the Jungle' (which is what Old Fish Sparks sings from time to time to the tune of Red Sails in the Sunset) – sure, but it's about the sort of conflict running through human life in every time and every civilization. Discipline v. permissiveness. Sticking to the letter of the law v. sticking to its spirit. Means and ends. Doing the right thing for the wrong reason v. doing the wrong thing for the right reason. How great ideas like the Church get bogged down in bureaucracy. How Christianity starts off as the religion of peace but ends up violent like other religions. You could say the same about Communism or anything else, any big idea. I think this film could be really quite subversive in Eastern Europe and not because it's about priests either. Whether they'd distribute it is another matter. I said to Fish the film has a message for the trade unions as well if they could find it and he said he'd keep looking. Pippa love, think about the baby thing, won't you?

Your Charlie

P.S. Funny thing happened today. Not serious, but makes me wonder about the Indians.
P.P.S. Can't think why you haven't written.

Letter 7

Dearest Pippa –

Bloody Jungle. It just doesn't give up. Bloody clouds of flies and biting things and humming whatsits and for the first couple of weeks you think how extraordinary, well it doesn't matter getting bitten, everyone else is, except Matt with his NASA US-Govt issue personal mosquito repellent and corned-beef face-protector. But they just go on and on and bloody on. After a while you just want the Jungle to take a day off. Go on, Jungle, it's Sunday, knock it off, you want to shout as it rattles on 24 hrs per day. I don't know. Maybe it's not the Jungle it's the film. You can feel the tension mounting. Matt and me getting edgier with one another off camera as well as on. The film's all spilling over into the rest of the time. Even the Indians don't seem so sure that I'm not Firmin all the time and Matt's Antonio. It's as if they think I'm *really* Firmin and then from time to time I just pretend to be this white man called Charlie. Really upside down.

Sunday. That thing about the Indians. To tell you the truth I was a bit miffed when I found out, but now I'm beginning to see it from their point of view. I told you I was learning the language – she's really very sweet and not a stitch on but as I said no need to worry, angel, riddled with diseases I'm sure, apart from anything else, I mean. It turns out that half the words she's been teaching me are all wrong. I mean, they're real words except they're not the right ones. The first thing I learnt more or less was *thkarni* which means – well she said it meant – this white stork we've been seeing a lot of. So when we saw one go flapping by I used to shout *thkarni* and the Indians would all laugh. Turns out – and I learned this not through Miguel but our second guide who hasn't said much most of the trip – that *thkarni* is the Indians' name – well, one of their many names, to be precise – for you-know-what. The thing up which the little fish in the river swims if you aren't careful. Same goes for about half the words I've been learning from that little minx. I've learnt about 60 I suppose overall and half of them are duds – naughty words or words for something completely different. I was majorly unpleased as you can imagine at the time but I think what it does show is that the Indians have got a terrific sense of humour. So I was determined to show them I could take a joke and the next time a big stork went over I pretended not to know what it was called and asked my girl. *Thkarni* she said with a straight face. I looked very puzzled and shook my head a lot and said No it can't be *thkarni* because *this* is *thkarni* (no I didn't pull it out or anything – just pointed). And then she knew the game was up and started giggling, and so did I to show there weren't any hard feelings.

Monday. Getting near the end now. Just the big scene to do.

Taking two days off first. I think that's a silly decision by Vic but I expect he's got the unions on his back. He says it's a good idea to recharge the batteries before the big scene. I think if you're on a roll you better go with the flow. It's all right, honey, I don't really talk like that, I do it to irritate Matt, though it usually doesn't because he's so thick-skinned and thinks everyone else talks like that anyway, so I guess I do it for my own private amusement. 'Hey, Matt,' I say to him, 'we're on a roll, let's go with the flow', and he nods like some old prophet in The Ten Commandments. Anyway the plan is today and tomorrow off, then two days rehearsal for the capsizing of the raft, then Friday the big deal. Maybe Vic is right after all, we do need to be at our best. It's not just doing it right it's covering all the angles. We've got to have ropes on us as per contract in case anything happens. Don't *worry* darling it's not really dangerous. We're doing some covering footage on a stretch of the river where there are some rapids, but the actual capsizing which is meant to happen there doesn't really. The crew have got a couple of machines which churn everything up to make white water and the chippie ran up some rocks which they anchor to the bottom of the river and look just like the real thing. So no need to worry. I'm quite looking forward to it though naturally we've had a few of the old arguments about it. What happens is that both the priests get tipped into the water, one of them hits his head on a rock and the other one rescues him. Point is, who does what? I mean, here are these two, fighting tooth and nail all the way upstream, there's this huge split of doctrine going on, one of them v. authoritarian and hardline (Me) and the other very permissive and soft on the Indians (Matt). I think it would be much more effective if the one who was meant to be the hardhat and who might be expected to let the other one drown in fact saves the other one even though he thinks his ideas about the Indians and his plan to baptise them when they get to the Orinoco are blasphemous. But no, it has to be *Matt* who saves *me*. Vic says that's what's historically the case, and Matt says that's what was in the script he read back in Dudesville North Dakota or wherever he hangs his hat and that's what he's going to play. '*Nobody* rescues Matt Smeaton,' he said. He actually said it, can you imagine? '*Nobody* rescues Matt Smeaton.' I said I'd remember that if ever I found him dangling upside down by one toe from a ski-lift cable. So it's all going to go ahead as per the script.

Tuesday. Another rest day.
Later
Later
Later

– love Charlie

Jesus Pippa. Jesus. I just couldn't go on with that last letter. Jolly bits of news from each day's shooting. Couldn't go on with it, not after what happened. But I'm fine. Really I'm fine.

Later. Poor old Matt. Shit, he was a good bloke. Sure he could get under your skin but so would St Francis of Assisi on a job like this. He'd have spent all his time looking at the bloody birds in the Jungle instead of reading his cue-cards. Sorry, love. Bad taste, I know. Just can't find the way to put things. Very low. Poor old Matt. I wonder how you'll hear the news and what you'll think.

Jesus those fucking Indians. I think I'm going to die. I can hardly hold this biro. Sweating like a pig, *comme un porco*. God I do love you, Pippa, I just hold on to that.

C

I get out your photo with the chipmunk face and kiss it. That's all that matters, you and me and having babies. Let's do it, Pippa. Your mum would be pleased, wouldn't she? I said to Fish do you have kids, he said yes they're the apple of my eye. I put my arm round him and gave him a hug just like that. It's things like that keep everything going, isn't it?

It's true what they say. Go into the Jungle and you really find out what people are like. Vic's a whinger, always knew it. Whingeing on about the sodding film. I said don't worry you can always sell your memoirs to the paper. He didn't like that.

Why did they do it? Why did they do it?

love C

P.S. Wish you'd written. Would have helped now.

Letter 10

It could have been me. It could just as easily have been me. Who decides? Does anyone decide? Hey you up there in the sky, is anyone home?

I've been having this thought all day. I said to Old Fishy do you have kids and he said yes they're the apple of my eye and we just hugged each other right there in front of everyone and ever since I've been wondering what it means. The apple of my eye. What does it mean? You say words like that and everyone knows what they mean but when you look at them you can't understand them. The film's like that, the whole trip's like that. You go along thinking you know exactly what everything is, and then you stop and look at it and it doesn't make any sense and you think maybe it only made any sense in the first place because everyone was pretending it did. Does this make any sense? I mean it's like the Indians and the fake rocks that the chippie ran up. They looked at them and looked at them and the more they did the less they understood. They started off knowing they were rocks and they ended up not knowing anything. You could see it in their faces.

I'm going to give this to Rojas now. He walked past a few minutes ago and said that's the third letter you've written today why don't you put them in the same envelope and save postage? I got up and you know I swear I turned into Firmin for a moment and I said, 'Listen, Our Lady of Communications, I shall write and you will transmit as many fucking letters per day as I happen to feel like writing.' Well Firmin wouldn't have said fuck of course, but his tone was there. Sort of austere and pissed off with anything less than perfection in the world. Oh well, better go and say sorry, otherwise he'll throw them all away.

– love C

Letter 11
Waiting for copter

Pippa love –

When we get out, I'm going to do the following things. Have the biggest fucking Scotch they can pour in Caracas. Have the biggest fucking bath they can pour in Caracas. Have the longest phone call I can have with you. I can just hear your voice answering the phone, as if I've been to the shop for some ciggies and

I'm back late. Then I'm going to the British Embassy and get a copy of the Daily Telegraph and I don't care if it's weeks old and I'm going to read something I never normally look at like the nature notes if they have them. I want to be told that the house-martins are nesting or you might see a badger if you're lucky. Ordinary things that go on all the time. I'll look at the cricket scores and pretend I'm some old member in from the shires with a striped blazer and a pink gin in his fist. Maybe I'll read the births column as well. To Emma and Nicholas, a daughter, Suzie, sister to Alexander and Bill. Good old Alexander and Bill, I'll say, now you've got little Suzie to play with. You must be gentle with her, you must protect her all your lives, she's your little sister, you must make her the apple of your eye. God I'm crying Pippa, the tears are just streaming down my face.

love C

Letter 12
Caracas 21st July

Pippa love, I don't believe it, I mean I just don't believe it. We finally reach what we laughingly call civilization, we finally reach a telephone which is capable of handling transatlantic calls, I finally get my turn in the queue, I finally get through to home, and you're out. 'Number no answer, sir.' Try again. 'Number sti no answer, sir.' Try again. 'OK sir, number sti no answer.' Where are you? I don't want to ring anyone else. I don't want to ring your mum and say look we had a spot of bother but now we're back in Caracas and Matt's dead, yes, you heard it on the news but I don't want to talk about it. I just want to talk to you, honey, and I can't.

Tried again.

Tried again.

All right, so I've got a bottle of Scotch which costs about 50 quid and if the studio doesn't pay for it I'll never work for them again, and a big pile of this flimsy hotel notepaper. The others have gone out on the town. I couldn't face it. I keep remembering the last night we were here – same hotel and all – and how Matt and I went out and got stinko-paralytico together and ended up doing the Zorba dance and got thrown out and Matt pointing at me and saying to the waiters Hey don't you recognize Mista Rick from Parkway Peninsula and they didn't and made us pay for the plates.

We'd had our rest days, just three days work left. The first morning we rehearsed in the white water, pretty gingerly I don't mind saying. Vic and the crew were on the bank, Matt and I were on the raft with about a dozen Indians paddling and poling. Just to be on the safe side we had a long rope attached to the raft and tied round a tree on the bank so that if the Indians lost control the rope would pull it to a stop. Matt and I had ropes on us as per contract. So we did a run-through in the morning which was OK, then had an afternoon in the shallows with the churning machine. I thought we didn't need another day of rehearsal but Vic insisted. So the second morning we all went out again only this time wearing radio mikes as well. Vic hadn't decided whether to dub or not. The rope was attached to the tree, the crew set up on the bank, and we got ready to do three or four runs past the camera with Matt and me so busy arguing about baptising the Indians that we couldn't see the danger behind us which the audience could see for themselves. I've thought about what happened next a million times and I still don't know the answer. It was on our third run. We got the thumbs-up, started our argument and then noticed something odd. Instead of a dozen Indians on the raft there were only two, each with just a pole at the back of the raft. I suppose we thought Vic must have said try it this way because Matt and I were already into our quarrel and it shows what a pro he was to his fingertips that he carried on as per normal. So did I for that matter. Then at the end of the scene we noticed the Indians weren't doing what they normally did which was stick their poles in to stop the raft. They were just poling away and Matt shouted 'Hey, fellers, cut' but they didn't take any notice and I remember thinking maybe they're testing the rope to see if it works, and Matt and I turned at just the same moment and saw where the Indians were heading us – straight into a pile of rocks and foaming water – and I knew the rope must have broken or something. We shouted but what with the noise of the water and not knowing their language of course it wasn't any use and then we were in the water. I thought of you as we capsized, Pippa, honest I did. Just saw your face and tried to think about you. Then I tried swimming, but what with the current and the fucking cassock – and then bang I got hit in the ribs like someone had kicked me and I thought I was a goner, it must be a rock I thought and I gave up and sort of passed out. What happened was that the rope they'd put on me suddenly pulled tight. I don't remember anything else until I was on the bank throwing up water and puking in the mud while the sound-man thumped on my back and put his fists in my stomach. My line held, Matt's line broke. That's how it was, that's my luck.

Everyone was in shock, as you can imagine. Some of the crew tried getting along the bank – you know how people are sometimes found clinging to the branches of trees overhanging the river a mile or so downstream. But it wasn't like that. That sort of thing is strictly for the movies. Matt was gone, and anyway the crew couldn't get more than 20 or 30 yards beyond where they'd set up because they don't exactly have towpaths in the Jungle. 'Why were there only two?' Vic kept saying. 'Why only two?' They looked around for the Indians who'd helped them set up but they weren't there. Then they went back to camp and the only person there was Miguel the interpreter, who'd been having a long conversation with one of the Indians and when he turned round all the other Indians had scarpered.

Then we went to see what had happened to the rope round the tree and there wasn't anything left, it had just gone. Which was pretty odd as it was fixed with one of those fancy knots which simply can't pull out. No doubt as per contract. Bloody suspicious. Then we talked to Miguel again and it turned out the Indian had started this long conversation with him before we could possibly have had the accident. So they presumably knew what was going to happen. And when we looked in the camp they'd taken everything – clothes, food, equipment. What did they take the clothes for? They don't even wear them.

It was a bloody long wait for the copter, I can tell you. The Indians had taken the radio telephones (they'd have gone off with the genny if they'd had a crane) and Caracas thought they'd just broken down again so came as per normal. Two days waiting like two bloody months. Me thinking I'd probably got some filthy fever in spite of the jabs. Apparently when they pulled me out of the river and bashed the water out of my belly the first thing I said as I came round was, 'Riddled with diseases, I'm sure' and the crew broke up in this hysterical laughter. Don't remember, but it sounds like Charlie. Thought I might be in for beri-beri and co. Ouch in spades, I thought.

Why did they do it? That's what I keep coming back to. Why?

Most of the others think they did it because they're primitive –
you know, not white men, never trust a native and so on. That's
no go. I never did think they were primitive and they always told
the truth (except when they were teaching me the language) and
were a damn sight more trustworthy than some of the white men
we had on the job. The first thing I thought of was that we'd
offended them in some way we didn't know – done a terrible
insult to their gods or something. But I simply couldn't think of
anything.

The way I'm looking at it, either there's some connection with
what happened a couple of hundred years ago or there isn't.
Perhaps it's just a chance coincidence. It so happens that the
descendants of the original Indians whose raft capsized were also
in charge of another raft that capsized at about the same point in
the river. Maybe these Indians can only take so much of poling
Jesuits upstream and just instinctively snap and turn nasty and
shove them overboard. Not very likely is it? *Or* there is some
connection between the two incidents. This is what I think anyway. It seems to me that the Indians – our Indians – knew what
had happened to Father Firmin and Father Antonio all those
years ago. It's the sort of thing that gets handed down as the
women are pounding the manioc root or whatever. Those Jesuits
were probably quite big in the Indians' history. Think of that
story getting passed down the generations, each time they handed
it on it became more colourful and exaggerated. And then we
come along, another lot of white men who've also got two chaps
in long black skirts with them, who also want to be poled up the
river to the Orinoco. Sure, there are differences, they've got this
one-eyed machine and so on, but basically it's the same thing,
and we even tell them it's going to end in the same way with the
raft capsizing. I mean, it's hard to think of an equivalent, but say
you were an inhabitant of Hastings in the year 2066 and you went
down to the beach one day and these longships were coming
towards you and lots of people in chainmail and pointy helmets
got out and said they'd come for the Battle of Hastings and would
you rustle up King Harold so they could shoot him in the eye
and here was a huge wallet full of money for you to play your
part. First of all, you might be inclined to do it, wouldn't you?
And then you'd get thinking about why *they* wanted you to do it.
And one thing you might come up with – this is just my idea,
Vic isn't so sure about it – is that they (i.e. us) have come back

to re-enact the ceremony for some reason that's tremendously important to their tribe. Perhaps the Indians thought it was a religious thing, like celebrating the 500th anniversary of a cathedral or whatever.

And there's another possibility – that the Indians were actually following the argument between the Jesuits and understanding it a lot better than we thought. They – Matt and me, that's to say – were arguing about baptising the Indians, and at the point the raft capsized it looked as if I was winning the argument. I was the senior priest, after all, and I was against baptism – at least until the Indians pulled their socks up and stopped some of their filthy practices. So maybe the Indians understood this and tipped up the raft because they were trying to kill Father Firmin (me!) so that Father Antonio would survive and baptise them. How about that? Except that the first time round the Indians saw that Firmin survived and they ran away because they were afraid, and the second time round they saw they'd killed Antonio, which was quite the wrong result for them so they ran away because it had all gone wrong.

Is that right? I just know it's more complicated than it's ever going to seem in the newspapers. I shouldn't be surprised if Hollywood sends a plane to bomb the Indians and punish them for the death of Matt. Or does a remake – yes, that'd be more bloody likely. Who gets the part of Matt? What a career opportunity. I ask you.

Seem to be stuck here for a week or so. That bloody studio and its bloody lawyers. Apparently the movie has to be officially called off in some way and that takes time.

Taking this down to Our Lady of Communications and expressing it. Makes a change to be giving it to a real postman.

all love, Charlie

Letter 13

Christ don't you do that to me, and I mean *ever*. Two days out of the fucking Jungle after nearly dying and you put the phone down on me. Look, as I was trying to explain to you, she was out here working, it was a complete coincidence. I know I've been behaving like a pig, *comme un porco*, for a bit, but please read all my letters from the Jungle and you'll see I'm a changed man. It's all over between Linda and me, I told you that before I left. And I can't control where the woman works, can I? Yes I did know she was going to be in Caracas and No I didn't tell you and Yes that was wrong but would it have been better if I'd told you? How on earth did you find out anyway? No she isn't here, as far as I know or care she's in the West Indies. For God's sake, Pippa, let's not throw away five years.

– your Charlie

P.S. Am expressing this.
P.P.S. Caracas filthy dump. Stuck here at least until the 4th.
P.P.P.S. Love you.

Telegram

PLEASE CALL CHARLIE HOTEL
INTERCONTINENTAL SOONEST STOP
LOVE CHARLIE STOP

Telegram

FOR GS SAKE CALL INTERCONTINENTAL MUST
TALK SOONEST STOP LOVE CHARLIE

Telegram

WILL CALL NOON YOUR TIME THURSDAY
MUCH TO DISCUSS STOP CHARLIE

Telegram

DAMN YOU ANSWER THE PHONE OR CALL ME
PIPPA STOP CHARLIE

Letter 14

Dear Pippa –
    As you don't seem to be responding to telegrams for reasons best known to yourself, I am writing to say that I am not coming home immediately. I need time and space not just to get over the

appalling things which have happened to me in which you do not seem to show much interest but also to think through where the two of us are at. There seems no point in saying that I love you in spite of everything because that only seems to irritate you for reasons best known to yourself and which you choose neither to explain nor comment on. I will be in touch when I know where I'm at about all this.

Charlie

P.S. I'm expressing this.
P.P.S. If any of this is anything to do with that creep Gavin I will personally break his personal fucking neck. I should have hit him a lot harder in the first place. And in case you haven't noticed, he couldn't act his way out of a paper bag. No talent. No cojones.

Letter 15
St Lucia
Some bloody day or other

Listen bitch why don't you just get out of my life, go on just get out GET OUT. You always fucked things up didn't you that was your one great talent fucking things up. My friends said she's trouble and the last thing I should have done was let her move in and I was a bloody fool not to believe them. Christ if you think I'm an egotist you should look in the mirror baby. Of course I'm drunk what do you think it's one way of getting you out of my head. Now I'm going to get stinko bloody paralytico. In vino bloody veritas.

Charlie 'the Hell-Raiser'

P.S. I'm expressing this.

Telegram

RETURNING LONDON MONDAY FIFTEENTH STOP KINDLY REMOVE SELF AND POSSESSIONS FROM FLAT BEFORE THEN STOP LEAVE KEY STOP ENDIT STOP

PARENTHESIS

LET ME TELL YOU something about her. It's that middle stretch of the night, when the curtains leak no light, the only street-noise is the grizzle of a returning Romeo, and the birds haven't begun their routine yet cheering business. She's lying on her side, turned away from me. I can't see her in the dark, but from the hushed swell of her breathing I could draw you the map of her body. When she's happy she can sleep for hours in the same position. I've watched over her in all those sewery parts of the night, and can testify that she doesn't move. It could be just down to good digestion and calm dreams, of course; but I take it as a sign of happiness.

Our nights are different. She falls asleep like someone yielding to the gentle tug of a warm tide, and floats with confidence till morning. I fall asleep more grudgingly, thrashing at the waves, either reluctant to let a good day depart or still bitching about a bad one. Different currents run through our spells of un-consciousness. Every so often I find myself catapulted out of bed with fear of time and death, panic at the approaching void; feet on the floor, head in hands, I shout a useless (and disappointingly uneloquent) 'No, no, *no*' as I wake. Then she has to stroke the horror away from me, like sluicing down a dog that's come bark-ing from a dirty river.

Less often, it's her sleep that's broken by a scream, and my turn to move across her in a sweat of protectiveness. I am starkly awake, and she delivers to me through sleepy lips the cause of her outcry. 'A *very* large beetle', she will say, as if she wouldn't have bothered me about a smaller one; or 'The steps were slip-pery'; or merely (which strikes me as cryptic to the point of tautology), 'Something nasty'. Then, having expelled this damp toad, this handful of gutter-muck from her system, she sighs and returns to a purged sleep. I lie awake, clutching a slimy amphi-bian, shifting a handful of sodden detritus from hand to hand, alarmed and admiring. (I'm not claiming grander dreams, by the way. Sleep democratizes fear. The terror of a lost shoe or a missed train are as great here as those of guerrilla attack or nuclear war.) I admire her because she's got this job of sleeping that we all have to do, every night, ceaselessly, until we die, much better worked out than I have. She handles it like a sophisticated traveller unthreatened by a new airport. Whereas I lie there in the night with an expired passport, pushing a baggage trolley with a squeaking wheel across to the wrong carousel.

Anyway . . . she's asleep, turned away from me on her side. The usual stratagems and repositionings have failed to induce narcosis in me, so I decide to settle myself against the soft zigzag of her body. As I move and start to nestle my shin against a calf whose muscles are loosened by sleep, she senses what I'm doing, and without waking reaches up with her left hand and pulls the hair off her shoulders on to the top of her head, leaving me her bare nape to nestle in. Each time she does this I feel a shudder of love at the exactness of this sleeping courtesy. My eyes prickle with tears, and I have to stop myself from waking her up to remind her of my love. At that moment, unconsciously, she's touched some secret fulcrum of my feelings for her. She doesn't know, of course; I've never told her of this tiny, precise pleasure of the night. Though I'm telling her now, I suppose . . .

You think she's really awake when she does it? I suppose it could sound like a conscious courtesy – an agreeable gesture, but hardly one denoting that love has roots below the gum of consciousness. You're right to be sceptical: we should be indulgent only to a certain point with lovers, whose vanities rival those of politicians. Still, I can offer further proof. Her hair falls, you see, to her shoulders. But a few years ago, when they promised us the summer heat would last for months, she had it cut short. Her nape was bare for kissing all day long. And in the dark, when we lay beneath a single sheet and I gave off a Calabrian sweat, when the middle stretch of the night was shorter but still hard to get through – then, as I turned towards that loose S beside me, she would, with a soft murmur, try to lift the lost hair from the back of her neck.

'I love you,' I whisper into that sleeping nape, 'I love you.' All novelists know their art proceeds by indirection. When tempted by didacticism, the writer should imagine a spruce sea-captain eyeing the storm ahead, bustling from instrument to instrument in a catherine wheel of gold braid, expelling crisp orders down the speaking tube. But there is nobody below decks; the engine-room was never installed, and the rudder broke off centuries ago. The captain may put on a very good act, convincing not just himself but even some of the passengers; though whether their floating world will come through depends not on him but on the mad winds and sullen tides, the icebergs and the sudden crusts of reef.

Still, it's natural for the novelist sometimes to fret at the obliquities of fiction. In the lower half of El Greco's 'Burial of the Count of Orgaz' in Toledo there is a line-up of angular, ruffed mourners. They gaze this way and that in stagey grief. Only one of them looks directly out of the picture, and he holds us with a gloomy, ironical eye – an unflattered eye, as well, we can't help noticing. Tradition claims that the figure is El Greco himself. I did this, he says. I painted this. I am responsible, and so I face towards you.

Poets seem to write more easily about love than prose writers. For a start, they own that flexible 'I' (when I say 'I' you will want to know within a paragraph or two whether I mean Julian Barnes or someone invented; a poet can shimmy between the two, getting credit for both deep feeling and objectivity). Then again, poets seem able to turn bad love – selfish, shitty love – into good love poetry. Prose writers lack this power of admirable, dishonest transformation. We can only turn bad love into prose about bad love. So we are envious (and slightly distrustful) when poets talk to us of love.

And they write this stuff called love poetry. It's collected into books called The Great Lovers' Valentine World Anthology of Love Poetry or whatever. Then there are love letters; these are collected into The Golden Quill Treasury of Love Letters (available by mail order). But there is no genre that answers to the name of love prose. It sounds awkward, almost self-contradictory. Love Prose: A Plodder's Handbook. Look for it in the carpentry section.

The Canadian writer Mavis Gallant put it like this: 'The mystery of what a couple *is*, exactly, is almost the only true mystery left to us, and when we have come to the end of it there will be no more need for literature – or for love, for that matter.' When I first read this, I gave it in the margin the chess marking '!?' indicating a move which, though possibly brilliant, is probably unsound. But increasingly the view convinces, and the marking is changed to '!!'

'What will survive of us is love.' This is the cautiously-approached conclusion of Philip Larkin's poem 'An Arundel Tomb'. The line surprises us, for much of the poet's work was a squeezed flannel of disenchantment. We are ready to be cheered; but we should first give a prosey scowl and ask of this poetic flourish, Is it true? Is love what will survive of us? It would be nice to think so. It would be comforting if love were an energy source which continued to glow after our deaths. Early television sets, when you turned them off, used to leave a blob of light in the middle of the screen, which slowly diminished from the size of a florin to an expiring speck. As a boy I would watch this process each evening, vaguely wanting to hold it back (and seeing it, with adolescent melancholy, as the pinpoint of human existence fading inexorably in a black universe). Is love meant to glow on like this for a while after the set has been switched off? I can't see it myself. When the survivor of a loving couple dies, love dies too. If anything survives of us it will probably be something else. What will survive of Larkin is not his love but his poetry: that's obvious. And whenever I read the end of 'An Arundel Tomb' I'm reminded of William Huskisson. He was a politician and a financier, well-known in his time; but we remember him today because on the 15th of September 1830, at the opening of the Liverpool and Manchester Railway, he became the first person to be run down and killed by a train (that's what he *became*, was turned into). And did William Huskisson love? And did his love last? We don't know. All that has survived of him is his moment of final carelessness; death froze him as an instructive cameo about the nature of progress.

'I love you.' For a start, we'd better put these words on a high shelf; in a square box behind glass which we have to break with our elbow; in the bank. We shouldn't leave them lying around the house like a tube of vitamin C. If the words come too easily to hand, we'll use them without thought; we won't be able to resist. Oh, we say we won't, but we will. We'll get drunk, or lonely, or – likeliest of all – plain damn hopeful, and there are the words gone, used up, grubbied. We think we might be in love and we're trying out the words to see if they're appropriate? How can we know what we think till we hear what we say? Come off it; that won't wash. These are grand words; we must make sure we deserve them. Listen to them again: 'I love you'. Subject, verb, object: the unadorned, impregnable sentence. The subject is a short word, implying the self-effacement of the lover. The verb is longer but unambiguous, a demonstrative moment as the tongue flicks anxiously away from the palate to release the vowel. The object, like the subject, has no consonants, and is attained by pushing the lips forward as if for a kiss. 'I love you'. How serious, how weighted, how freighted it sounds.

I imagine a phonic conspiracy between the world's languages. They make a conference decision that the phrase must always sound like something to be earned, to be striven for, to be worthy of. *Ich liebe dich*: a late-night, cigarette-voiced whisper, with that happy rhyme of subject and object. *Je t'aime*: a different procedure, with the subject and object being got out of the way first, so that the long vowel of adoration can be savoured to the full. (The grammar is also one of reassurance: with the object positioned second, the beloved isn't suddenly going to turn out to be someone different.) *Ya tebya lyublyu*: the object once more in consoling second position, but this time – despite the hinting rhyme of subject and object – an implication of difficulty, obstacles to be overcome. *Ti amo*: it sounds perhaps a bit too much like an apéritif, but is full of structural conviction with subject and verb, the doer and the deed, enclosed in the same word.

Forgive the amateur approach. I'll happily hand the project over to some philanthropic foundation devoted to expanding the sum of human knowledge. Let them commission a research team to examine the phrase in all the languages of the world, to see how it varies, to discover what its sounds denote to those who hear them, to find out if the measure of happiness changes according to the richness of the phrasing. A question from the floor: are there tribes whose lexicon lacks the words *I love you*? Or have they all died out?

We must keep these words in their box behind glass. And when we take them out we must be careful with them. Men will say 'I love you' to get women into bed with them; women will say 'I love you' to get men into marriage with them; both will say 'I love you' to keep fear at bay, to convince themselves of the deed by the word, to assure themselves that the promised condition has arrived, to deceive themselves that it hasn't yet gone away. We must beware of such uses. *I love you* shouldn't go out into the world, become a currency, a traded share, make profits for us. It will do that if we let it. But keep this biddable phrase for whispering into a nape from which the absent hair has just been swept.

I'm away from her at the moment; perhaps you guessed. The transatlantic telephone gives off a mocking, heard-it-all-before echo. 'I love you', and before she can answer I hear my metallic other self respond, 'I love you.' This isn't satisfactory; the echoing words have gone public. I try again, with the same result. *I love you I love you* – it's become some trilling song popular for a lurid month and then dismissed to the club circuit where pudgy rockers with grease in their hair and yearning in their voice will use it to unfrock the lolling front-row girls. *I love you I love you* while the lead guitar giggles and the drummer's tongue lies wetly in his opened mouth.

We must be precise with love, its language and its gestures. If it is to save us, we must look at it as clearly as we should learn to look at death. Should love be taught in school? First term: friendship; second term: tenderness; third term: passion. Why not? They teach kids how to cook and mend cars and fuck one another without getting pregnant; and the kids are, we assume, much better at all of this than we were, but what use is any of that to them if they don't know about love? They're expected to muddle through by themselves. Nature is supposed to take over, like the automatic pilot on an aeroplane. Yet Nature, on to whom we pitch responsibility for all we cannot understand, isn't very good when set to automatic. Trusting virgins drafted into marriage never found Nature had all the answers when they turned out the light. Trusting virgins were told that love was the promised land, an ark on which two might escape the Flood. It may be an ark, but one on which anthropophagy is rife; an ark skippered by some crazy greybeard who beats you round the head with his gopher-wood stave, and might pitch you overboard at any moment.

Let's start at the beginning. Love makes you happy? No. Love makes the person you love happy? No. Love makes everything all right? Indeed no. I used to believe all this, of course. Who hasn't (who doesn't still, somewhere below decks in the psyche)? It's in all our books, our films; it's the sunset of a thousand stories. What would love be *for* if it didn't solve everything? Surely we can deduce from the very strength of our aspiration that love, once achieved, eases the daily ache, works some effortless analgesia?

A couple love each other, but they aren't happy. What do we conclude? That one of them doesn't really love the other; that they love one another a certain amount but not enough? I dispute that *really*; I dispute that *enough*. I've loved twice in my life (which seems quite a lot to me), once happily, once un- happily. It was the unhappy love that taught me most about love's nature – though not at the time, not until years later. Dates and details – fill them in as you like. But I was in love, and loved, for a long time, many years. At first I was brazenly happy, bullish with solipsistic joy; yet most of the time I was puzzlingly, nag- gingly unhappy. Didn't I love her enough? I knew I did – and put off half my future for her. Didn't she love me enough? I knew she did – and gave up half her past for me. We lived side by side for many years, fretting at what was wrong with the equation we had invented. Mutual love did not add up to happiness. Stubbornly, we insisted that it did.

And later I decided what it was I believed about love. We think of it as an active force. My love *makes* her happy; her love *makes* me happy: how could this be wrong? It is wrong; it evokes a false conceptual model. It implies that love is a transforming wand, one that unlooses the ravelled knot, fills the top hat with handkerchiefs, sprays the air with doves. But the model isn't from magic but particle physics. My love does not, cannot *make* her happy; my love can only release in her the capacity to be happy. And now things seem more understandable. How come I can't make her happy, how come she can't make me happy? Simple: the atomic reaction you expect isn't taking place, the beam with which you are bombarding the particles is on the wrong wavelength.

But love isn't an atomic bomb, so let's take a homelier com- parison. I'm writing this at the home of a friend in Michigan. It's a normal American house with all the gadgets technology can dream (except a gadget for making happiness). He drove me here from Detroit airport yesterday. As we turned into the driveway he reached into the glove pocket for a remote-control device; at a masterful touch, the garage doors rolled up and away. This is the model I propose. You are arriving home – or think you are – and as you approach the garage you try to work your routine magic. Nothing happens; the doors remain closed. You do it again. Again nothing. At first puzzled, then anxious, then furious with disbelief, you sit in the driveway with the engine running;

you sit there for weeks, months, for years, waiting for the doors to open. But you are in the wrong car, in front of the wrong garage, waiting outside the wrong house. One of the troubles is this: the heart isn't heart-shaped.

'We must love one another or die', wrote W. H. Auden, bringing from E. M. Forster the declaration: 'Because he once wrote "We must love one another or die", he can command me to follow him.' Auden, however, was dissatisfied with this famous line from 'September 1, 1939'. 'That's a damned lie!' he commented, 'We must die anyway.' So when reprinting the poem he altered the line to the more logical 'We must love one another and die'. Later he suppressed it altogether.

This shift from *or* to *and* is one of poetry's most famous emendations. When I first came across it, I applauded the honest rigour with which Auden the critic revised Auden the poet. If a line sounds ringingly good but isn't true, out with it – such an approach is bracingly free of writerly self-infatuation. Now I am not so sure. *We must love one another and die* certainly has logic on its side; it's also about as interesting on the subject of the human condition, and as striking, as *We must listen to the radio and die* or *We must remember to defrost the fridge and die.* Auden was rightly suspicious of his own rhetoric; but to say that the line *We must love one another or die* is untrue because we die anyway (or because those who do not love do not instantly expire) is to take a narrow or forgetful view. There are equally logical, and more persuasive, ways of reading the *or* line. The first, obvious one is this: we must love one another because if we don't we are liable to end up killing one another. The second is: we must love one another because if we don't, if love doesn't fuel our lives, then we might as well be dead. This, surely, is no 'damned lie', to claim that those who get their deepest satisfactions from other things are living empty lives, are posturing crabs who swagger the sea-bed in borrowed shells.

This is difficult territory. We must be precise, and we mustn't become sentimental. If we are to oppose love to such wily, muscled concepts as power, money, history and death, then we mustn't retreat into self-celebration or snobby vagueness. Love's enemies profit from its unspecific claims, its grand capacity for isolationism. So where do we start? Love may or may not produce happiness; whether or not it does in the end, its primary effect is to energize. Have you ever talked so well, needed less sleep, returned to sex so eagerly, as when you were first in love? The anaemic begin to glow, while the normally healthy become intolerable. Next, it gives spine-stretching confidence. You feel you are standing up straight for the first time in your life; you can do anything while this feeling lasts, you can take on the world. (Shall we make this distinction: that love enhances the confidence, whereas sexual conquest merely develops the ego?) Then again, it gives clarity of vision: it's a windscreen wiper across the eyeball. Have you ever seen things so clearly as when you were first in love?

If we look at nature, do we see where love comes in? Not really. There are occasional species which apparently mate for life (though imagine the opportunities for adultery on all those long-distance migratory swims and night flights); but on the whole we see merely the exercise of power, dominance and sexual convenience. The feminist and the chauvinist interpret Nature differently. The feminist looks for examples of disinterested behaviour in the animal kingdom, sees the male here and there performing tasks which in human society might be characterized as 'female'. Consider the king penguin: the male is the one that incubates the egg, carrying it around on its feet and protecting it for months from the Antarctic weather with a fold of its lower belly ... Yeah, replies the chauvinist, and what about the bull elephant seal? Just lies about on the beach all day and fucks every female in sight. It does regrettably seem true that the seal's behaviour is more standard than that of the male penguin. And knowing my sex as I do, I'm inclined to doubt the latter's motivation. The male penguin might just have calculated that if you're stuck in the Antarctic for years on end then the cleverest thing to do is stay at home minding the egg while you send the female off to catch fish in the freezing waters. He might just have worked things out to his own convenience.

So where does love come in? It's not strictly necessary, is it? We can build dams, like the beaver, without love. We can organize complex societies, like the bee, without love. We can travel long distances, like the albatross, without love. We can put our head in the sand, like the ostrich, without love. We can die out as a species, like the dodo, without love.

Is it a useful mutation that helps the race survive? I can't see it. Was love implanted, for instance, so that warriors would fight harder for their lives, bearing deep inside them the candlelit memory of the domestic hearth? Hardly: the history of the world teaches us that it is the new form of arrowhead, the canny general, the full stomach and the prospect of plunder that are the decisive factors in war, rather than sentimental minds drooling about home.

Then is love some luxury that sprang up in peaceful times, like quilt-making? Something pleasant, complex, but inessential? A random development, culturally reinforced, which just happens to be love rather than something else? I sometimes think so. There was once a tribe of Indians in the far north-west of the United States (I'm not inventing them), who lived an extraordinarily easy life. They were protected from enemies by their isolation and the land they cultivated was boundlessly fertile. They only had to drop a wizened bean over their shoulders for a plant to spurt from the ground and rain pods at them. They were healthy, content, and had failed to develop any taste for internecine warfare. As a result, they had a lot of time on their hands. No doubt they excelled at things in which indolent societies specialize; no doubt their basketwork became rococo, their erotic skills more gymnastical, their use of crushed leaves to induce stupefying trances increasingly efficient. We don't know about such aspects of their lives, but we do know what was the main pursuit of their generous leisure hours. They stole from one another. That's what they liked to do, and that's what they celebrated. As they staggered out of their tepees and another faultless day came smooching in from the Pacific, they would sniff the honeyed air and ask one another what they'd got up to the previous night. The answer would be a shy confession – or smug boast – of theft. Old Redface had his blanket pilfered again by Little Grey Wolf. Well, did you ever? He's coming along, that Little Grey Wolf. And what did you get up to? Me? Oh, I just snitched the eyebrows from the top of the totem-pole. Oh, not that one again. Bo-*ring*.

Is this how we should think of love? Our love doesn't help us survive, any more than did the Indians' thieving. Yet it gives us our individuality, our purpose. Take away their joyful larcenies and those Indians would be able to define themselves less easily. So is it just a rogue mutation? We don't need it for the expansion of our race; indeed, it's inimical to orderly civilization. Sexual desire would be much easier if we didn't have to worry about love. Marriage would be more straightforward – and perhaps most lasting – if we were not itchy for love, exultant on its arrival, fearful of its departure.

If we look at the history of the world, it seems surprising that love is included. It's an excrescence, a monstrosity, some tardy addition to the agenda. It reminds me of those half-houses which according to normal criteria of map reading shouldn't exist. The other week I went to this North American address: 2041½ Yonge Street. The owner of 2041 must at some point have sold off a little plot, and this half-numbered, half-acknowledged house was put up. And yet people can live in it quite comfortably, people call it home . . . Tertullian said of Christian belief that it was true because it was impossible. Perhaps love is essential because it's unnecessary.

She is the centre of my world. The Armenians believed that Ararat was the centre of the world; but the mountain was divided between three great empires, and the Armenians ended up with none of it, so I shan't continue this comparison. *I love you.* I'm home again, and there's no mocking echo on the words. *Je t'aime. Ti amo* (with soda). And if you had no tongue, no celebrating language, you'd do this: cross your hands at the wrist with palms facing towards you; place your crossed wrists over your heart (the middle of your chest, anyway); then move your hands outwards a short distance, and open them towards the object of your love. It's just as eloquent as speech. And imagine all the tender modulations that are possible, the subtleties that can be constructed from kissing knuckles, matching palms and playful fingertips whose whorled pads bear the proof of our individuality.

But matching palms mislead. The heart isn't heart-shaped, that's one of our problems. We imagine, don't we, some neat bivalve whose shape encodes the way in which love fuses two halves, two separatenesses, into a whole? We imagine this crisp symbol scarlet with a powerful blush, scarlet also with the blood of tumescence. A medical textbook doesn't immediately disenchant us; here the heart is mapped like the London Underground. Aorta, left and right pulmonary arteries and veins, left and right subclavian arteries, left and right coronary arteries, left and right carotid arteries . . . it looks elegant, purposeful, a confident network of pumping tubes. Here the blood runs on time, you think.

Reverberent facts:

- the heart is the first organ to develop in the embryo; when we are no more than the size of a kidney bean, our heart is visible, pumping away;
- in a child, the heart is proportionately much larger than in an adult: 1/130th of total body weight, as opposed to 1/300th;
- during life the size, shape and position of the heart are subject to considerable variations;
- after death the heart assumes the shape of a pyramid.

The ox heart I bought at Corrigans weighed 2lbs 13oz and cost £2.42p. The biggest available animal specimen; but also one with human application. 'He had the heart of an ox': a phrase from the literature of Empire, of adventure, of childhood. Those pith-helmeted cavaliers who despatched rhinos with a single well-placed slug from an army pistol while the colonel's daughter cowered behind the baobab had simple natures but not, if this ox was anything to go by, simple hearts. The organ was heavy, squat, bloody, clamped tight like a violent fist. Unlike the railway map in the textbook, the real thing proved close and reluctant with its secrets.

I sliced it up with a radiologist friend. 'It hadn't got long to go, this ox,' she commented. Had the heart belonged to one of her patients, he wouldn't have pangaed his way through many more Jungles. Our own small journey was effected with a Saba-tier kitchen knife. We hacked our way into the left atrium and left ventricle, admiring the porterhouse heft of the muscles. We stroked the silky Rue de Rivoli lining, poked our fingers into exit wounds. The veins were stretch elastic, the arteries chunky squid. A post-mortal blood clot lay like a burgundy slug in the left ventricle. We frequently lost our way in this compacted meat. The two halves of the heart did not ease apart as I'd fancifully imagined, but clung desperately round one another like drown-ing lovers. We cut into the same ventricle twice, believing we'd found the other one. We admired the clever valve system, and the *chordae tendineae* which restrain each valve from opening too far: a tough little parachute harness preventing over-deployment of the canopy.

After we'd finished with it, the heart lay on a stained bed of newspaper for the rest of the day, reduced to an unpromising dinner. I went through cookbooks to see what I might do with it. I did find one recipe, for stuffed heart served with boiled rice and wedges of lemon, but it didn't sound very inviting. It certainly didn't merit the name given it by the Danes, who invented it. They call this dish Passionate Love.

Do you remember that paradox of love, of the first few weeks and months of Passionate Love (it's capitalized, like the recipe, to begin with) – the paradox about time? You are in love, at a point where pride and apprehension scuffle within you. Part of you wants time to slow down: for this, you say to yourself, is the best period of your whole life. I am in love, I want to savour it, study it, lie around in languor with it; may today last forever. This is your poetical side. However, there is also your prose side, which urges time not to slow down but hurry up. How do you know this is love, your prose side whispers like a sceptical lawyer, it's only been around for a few weeks, a few months. You won't know it's the real thing unless you (and she) still feel the same in, oh, a year or so at least; that's the only way to prove you aren't living a dragonfly mistake. Get through this bit, however much you enjoy it, as fast as possible; then you'll be able to find out whether or not you're *really* in love.

A photograph develops in a tray of liquid. Previously it's been just a blank sheet of printing paper shut up in a lightproof envelope; now it has a function, an image, a certainty. We slide the photo quickly into the tray of fixer to secure that clear, vulnerable moment, to make the image harder, unchippable, solid for at least a few years. But what if you plunge it into the fixer and the chemical doesn't work? This progress, this amorous motion you feel, might refuse to stabilize. Have you seen a picture go on relentlessly developing until its whole surface is black, its celebratory moment obliterated?

Is it normal, this state of love, or abnormal? Statistically, of course, it's abnormal. In a wedding photograph, the interesting faces are not those of the bride and groom, but of the encircling guests: the bride's younger sister (will it happen to me, the tremendous thing?), the groom's elder brother (will she let him down like that bitch did me?), the bride's mother (how it takes me back), the groom's father (if the lad knew what I know now – if only *I*'d known what I know now), the priest (strange how even the tongue-tied are moved to eloquence by these ancient

vows), the scowling adolescent (what do they want to get *married*
for?), and so on. The central couple are in a profoundly abnormal state; yet try telling them that. Their condition feels more
normal than it has ever done before. *This* is normal, they say to
one another; all that time before, which we thought was normal,
wasn't normal at all.

And such conviction of normality, such certainty that their
essence has been developed and fixed by love, and is now to be
framed forever, gives them a touching arrogance. This is definitely abnormal: when else is arrogance touching? It is here.
Look at the photo again: study, beneath the happy dentition, the
serious self-satisfaction of the moment. How can you not be
moved? Couples noisy with their love (for nobody has ever loved
before – not properly – have they?) may irritate, but can't be
mocked. Even when there's something to make an emotional
conformist smirk – some thumping disparity of age, looks, education, pretension – the couple have for this moment a lacquer
finish: laughter's bubbling spittle simply wipes off. The young
man on the older woman's arm, the frump attached to the dandy,
the hostess chained to an ascetic: they all feel profoundly normal.
And this should move us. *They* will be feeling indulgent towards
us, because we are not so evidently, so rowdily in love; yet we
should be discreetly indulgent towards them.

Don't get me wrong. I'm not recommending one form of
love over another. I don't know if prudent or reckless love is the
better, monied or penniless love the surer, heterosexual or homo-
sexual love the sexier, married or unmarried love the stronger.
I may be tempted towards didacticism, but this isn't an advice
column. I can't tell you whether or not you're in love. If you
need to ask, then you probably aren't, that's my only advice (and
even this might be wrong). I can't tell you who to love, or how
to love: those school courses would be how-not-to as much as
how-to classes (it's like creative writing – you can't teach them
how to write or what to write, only usefully point out where
they're going wrong and save them time). But I can tell you why
to love. Because the history of the world, which only stops at the
half-house of love to bulldoze it into rubble, is ridiculous without it. The history of the world becomes brutally self-important
without love. Our random mutation is essential because it is
unnecessary. Love won't change the history of the world (that
nonsense about Cleopatra's nose is strictly for sentimentalists),

but it will do something much more important: teach us to stand up to history, to ignore its chin-out strut. I don't accept your terms, love says; sorry, you don't impress, and by the way what a silly uniform you're wearing. Of course, we don't fall in love to help out with the world's ego problem; yet this is one of love's surer effects.

Love and truth, that's the vital connection, love and truth. Have you ever told so much truth as when you were first in love? Have you ever seen the world so clearly? Love makes us see the truth, makes it our duty to tell the truth. Lying in bed: listen to the undertow of warning in that phrase. *Lying in bed, we tell the truth*: it sounds like a paradoxical sentence from a first-year philosophy primer. But it's more (and less) than that: a description of moral duty. Don't roll that eyeball, give a flattering groan, fake that orgasm. Tell the truth with your body even if – especially if – that truth is not melodramatic. Bed is one of the prime places where you can lie without getting caught, where you can holler and grunt in the dark and later boast about your 'performance'. Sex isn't acting (however much we admire our own script); sex is about truth. How you cuddle in the dark governs how you see the history of the world. It's as simple as that.

We get scared by history; we allow ourselves to be bullied by dates.

> In fourteen hundred and ninety-two
> Columbus sailed the ocean blue

And then what? Everyone became wiser? People stopped building new ghettoes in which to practise the old persecutions? Stopped making the old mistakes, or new mistakes, or new versions of old mistakes? (And does history repeat itself, the first time as tragedy, the second time as farce? No, that's too grand, too considered a process. History just burps, and we taste again that raw-onion sandwich it swallowed centuries ago.)

Dates don't tell the truth. They bawl at us – left, right, left, right, pick 'em up there you miserable shower. They want to make us think we're always progressing, always going forward. But what happened after 1492?

> In fourteen hundred and ninety-three
> He sailed right back across the sea

That's the sort of date I like. Let's celebrate 1493, not 1492; the return, not the discovery. What happened in 1493? The predictable glory, of course, the royal flattery, the heraldic promotions on the Columbus scutcheon. But there was also this. Before departure a prize of 10,000 maravedis had been promised to the first man to sight the New World. An ordinary sailor had won this bounty, yet when the expedition returned Columbus claimed it for himself (the dove still elbowing the raven from history). The sailor went off in disappointment to Morocco where, they say, he became a renegade. It was an interesting year, 1493.

History isn't what happened. History is just what historians tell us. There was a pattern, a plan, a movement, expansion, the march of democracy; it is a tapestry, a flow of events, a complex narrative, connected, explicable. One good story leads to another. First it was kings and archbishops with some offstage divine tinkering, then it was the march of ideas and the movements of masses, then little local events which mean something bigger, but all the time it's connections, progress, meaning, this led to this, this happened because of this. And we, the readers of history, the sufferers from history, we scan the pattern for hopeful conclusions, for the way ahead. And we cling to history as a series of salon pictures, conversation pieces whose participants we can easily reimagine back into life, when all the time it's more like a multi-media collage, with paint applied by decorator's roller rather than camel-hair brush.

The history of the world? Just voices echoing in the dark; images that burn for a few centuries and then fade; stories, old stories that sometimes seem to overlap; strange links, impertinent connections. We lie here in our hospital bed of the present (what nice clean sheets we get nowadays) with a bubble of daily news drip-fed into our arm. We think we know who we are, though we don't quite know why we're here, or how long we shall be forced to stay. And while we fret and writhe in bandaged uncertainty – are we a voluntary patient? – we fabulate. We make up a story to cover the facts we don't know or can't accept; we keep a few true facts and spin a new story round them. Our panic and our pain are only eased by soothing fabulation; we call it history.

There's one thing I'll say for history. It's very good at finding things. We try to cover them up, but history doesn't let go. It's got time on its side, time and science. However ferociously we ink over our first thoughts, history finds a way of reading them. We bury our victims in secrecy (strangled princelings, irradiated reindeer), but history discovers what we did to them. We lost the *Titanic*, forever it seemed, in the squid-ink depths, but they turned it up. They found the wreck of the *Medusa* not long ago, off the coast of Mauretania. There wasn't any hope of treasure, they knew that; and all they salvaged after a hundred and seventy-five years were a few copper nails from the frigate's hull and a couple of cannon. But they went and found it just the same.

What else can love do? If we're selling it, we'd better point out that it's a starting-point for civic virtue. You can't love someone without imaginative sympathy, without beginning to see the world from another point of view. You can't be a good lover, a good artist or a good politician without this capacity (you can get away with it, but that's not what I mean). Show me the tyrants who have been great lovers. By which I don't mean great fuckers; we all know about power as an aphrodisiac (an auto-aphrodisiac too). Even our democratic hero Kennedy serviced women like an assembly-line worker spraying car bodies.

There is an intermittent debate, in these last dying millennia of puritanism, about the connection between sexual orthodoxy and the exercise of power. If a President can't keep his pants on, does he lose the right to rule us? If a public servant cheats on his wife does this make him more likely to cheat on the electorate? For myself, I'd rather be ruled by an adulterer, by some sexual rogue, than by a prim celibate or zipped-up spouse. As criminals tend to specialize in certain crimes, so corrupt politicians normally specialize in their corruption: the sexual blackguards stick to fucking, the bribe-takers to graft. In which case it would make more sense to elect proven adulterers instead of discouraging them from public life. I don't say we should pardon them – on the contrary, we need to fan their guilt. But by harnessing this useful emotion we restrict their sinning to the erotic sphere, and produce a countervailing integrity in their governing. That's my theory, anyway.

In Great Britain, where most of the politicians are men, there's a tradition among the Conservative Party to interview the wives of potential candidates. This is, of course, a demeaning occasion, with the wife being vetted by the local members for normality. (Is she sane? Is she steady? Is she the right colour? Does she have sound views? Is she a tart? Will she look good in photos? Can we let her out canvassing?) They ask these wives, who dutifully vie with one another in supportive dullness, many questions, and the wives solemnly swear their joint commitment to nuclear weapons and the sanctity of the family. But they don't ask them the most important question: does your husband love you? The question shouldn't be misunderstood as being merely practical (is your marriage free from scandal?) or sentimental; it's an exact enquiry about the candidate's fitness to represent other people. It's a test of his imaginative sympathy.

We must be precise about love. Ah, you want descriptions, perhaps? What are her legs like, her breasts, her lips, what colour is that hair? (Well, sorry.) No, being precise about love means attending to the heart, its pulses, its certainties, its truth, its power – and its imperfections. After death the heart becomes a pyramid (it has always been one of the wonders of the world); but even in life the heart was never heart-shaped.

Put the heart beside the brain and see the difference. The brain is neat, segmented, divided into two halves as we imagine the heart should obviously be. You can deal with the brain, you think; it is a receptive organ, one that invites comprehension. The brain looks sensible. It's complicated, to be sure, with all those wrinkles and frowns and gulleys and pockets; it resembles coral, making you wonder if it might be surreptitiously on the move all the time, quietly adding to itself without your noticing. The brain has its secrets, though when cryptanalysts, maze-builders and surgeons unite, it will surely be possible to solve those mysteries. You can deal with the brain, as I say; it looks sensible. Whereas the heart, the human heart, I'm afraid, looks a fucking mess.

Love is anti-mechanical, anti-materialist: that's why bad love is still good love. It may make us unhappy, but it insists that the mechanical and the material needn't be in charge. Religion has become either wimpishly workaday, or terminally crazy, or merely businesslike – confusing spirituality with charitable dona-tions. Art, picking up confidence from the decline of religion, announces its transcendence of the world (and it lasts, it lasts! art beats death!), but this announcement isn't accessible to all, or where accessible isn't always inspiring or welcome. So religion and art must yield to love. It gives us our humanity, and also our mysticism. There is more to us than us.

The materialist argument attacks love, of course; it attacks everything. Love boils down to pheromones, it says. This bounding of the heart, this clarity of vision, this energizing, this moral certainty, this exaltation, this civic virtue, this murmured *I love you*, are all caused by a low-level smell emitted by one partner and subconsciously nosed by the other. We are just a grander version of that beetle bashing its head in a box at the sound of a tapped pencil. Do we believe this? Well, let's believe it for the moment, because it makes love's triumph the greater. What is a violin made of? Bits of wood and bits of sheep's intestine. Does its construction demean and banalize the music? On the contrary, it exalts the music further.

And I'm not saying love will make you happy – above all, I'm not saying that. If anything, I tend to believe that it will make you unhappy: either immediately unhappy, as you are impaled by incompatibility, or unhappy later, when the woodworm has quietly been gnawing away for years and the bishop's throne collapses. But you can believe this and still insist that love is our only hope.

It's our only hope even if it fails us, although it fails us, because it fails us. Am I losing precision? What I'm searching for is the right comparison. Love and truth, yes, that's the prime connection. We all know objective truth is not obtainable, that when some event occurs we shall have a multiplicity of subjective truths which we assess and then fabulate into history, into some God-eyed version of what 'really' happened. This God-eyed version is a fake – a charming, impossible fake, like those medieval paintings which show all the stages of Christ's Passion happening simultaneously in different parts of the picture. But while we know this, we must still believe that objective truth is obtainable; or we must believe that it is 99 per cent obtainable; or if we can't believe this we must believe that 43 per cent objective truth is better than 41 per cent. We must do so, because if we don't we're lost, we fall into beguiling relativity, we value one liar's version as much as another liar's, we throw up our hands at the puzzle of it all, we admit that the victor has the right not just to the spoils but also to the truth. (Whose truth do we prefer, by the way, the victor's or the victim's? Are pride and compassion greater distorters than shame and fear?)

And so it is with love. We must believe in it, or we're lost. We may not obtain it, or we may obtain it and find it renders us unhappy; we must still believe in it. If we don't, then we merely surrender to the history of the world and to someone else's truth.

It will go wrong, this love; it probably will. That contorted organ, like the lump of ox meat, is devious and enclosed. Our current model for the universe is entropy, which at the daily level translates as: things fuck up. But when love fails us, we must still go on believing in it. Is it encoded in every molecule that things fuck up, that love will fail? Perhaps it is. Still we must believe in love, just as we must believe in free will and objective truth. And when love fails, we should blame the history of the world. If only it had left us alone, we could have been happy, we could have gone on being happy. Our love has gone, and it is the fault of the history of the world.

But that's still to come. Perhaps it will never come. In the night the world can be defied. Yes, that's right, it can be done, we can face history down. Excited, I stir and kick. She shifts and gives a subterranean, a subaqueous sigh. Don't wake her. It seems a grand truth now, though in the morning it may not seem worth disturbing her for. She gives a gentler, lesser sigh. I sense the map of her body beside me in the dark. I turn on my side, make a parallel zigzag, and wait for sleep.

9
PROJECT ARARAT

IT IS A FINE afternoon and you are driving the Outer Banks of North Carolina – the Atlantic Coast's austere rehearsal for the Florida Keys. You cross Currituck Sound from Point Harbor to Anderson, then south on the 158 and you soon reach Kitty Hawk. Across the dunes you'll find the Wright Brothers National Memorial; but maybe you take a raincheck on that, and in any case this isn't the thing you remember from Kitty Hawk. No, you remember this: on the right-hand side of the road, the west side, its high prow pointing towards the ocean, stands an ark. It's large as a barn, with slatted wooden sides, and painted brown. As you turn an amused and passing head, you realize that it is a church. Where you might normally see the ship's name and port of registration perhaps, you read instead the ark's function: WORSHIP CENTER, it says. You have been warned to expect all manner of religious excrescence in the Carolinas, and so this strikes you as a piece of fundamentalist rococo, rather cute in a way, but no, you don't stop.

Later that evening, you take the seven o'clock ferry from Hatteras to Ocracoke Island. It's chill, early spring, and you feel a little cold and lost in the darkness, on the black water, with the Plough hanging upside down above you in a blazing sky rented from Universal Pictures. The ferry feels anxious too, its huge searchlight charging the water twenty yards ahead; noisily, but without conviction, it shrugs its course between the marker lights, red, green and white. Only now, as you step out on deck and your breath turns solid, do you think back to that replica ark. It is there, of course, for a purpose, and had you stopped to think instead of merely lifting your foot from the gas pedal in a merry way, you might have felt its meaning. You had driven to the place where Man first took to the air; and you are reminded instead of an earlier, more vital occasion, when Man first took to the sea.

The ark was not yet there back in 1943 when Spike Tiggler, only a year or two out of short pants, was taken to Kitty Hawk by his father. You remember Spike Tiggler? Hell, *everybody* remembers Spike Tiggler. The guy who threw the football on the moon. The guy who threw the god-damned football on the moon? That's right. Longest pass in the history of the NFL, four hundred fifty yards into the leaping hands of a volcanic crater. Touchdown! That's what he shouted, and it came crackling back to us, down here on earth. Touchdown Tiggler, that's what the crick-necked world knew him as, least for a summer or two. Touchdown Tiggler, the guy who snuck a football into the capsule (how'd he do that?). Remember when they asked him why he did it, and he just kept that poker face on him? 'Always wanted to try out for the Redskins,' he said. 'Sure hope the fellas were watching.' The fellas had been watching, just as they watched his press conference, and they wrote Touchdown asking if they could have the football, offering to pay what strikes us even now as a decent price. But Spike had left it far away in that ashen crater – in case some running-back from Mars or Venus happened by.

Touchdown Tiggler: they called him that on the banner across the street in Wadesville, North Carolina, a little one-bank town where the gas station had to double as a liquor store to make anything half-way near a profit. WADESVILLE PROUDLY WELCOMES ITS FINEST SON, TOUCH-DOWN TIGGLER. Everyone turned out that hot morning in 1971 as Tiggler rode through in a movie star's limousine with the top down. Even Mary-Beth, who twenty years earlier had allowed Spike certain liberties and spent a week or two worrying, and who'd scarcely had a good word to say about him until he was selected for Project Apollo, turned out for the occasion, and reminded those around her – she'd already refreshed their memory a couple of times before – that there'd been a time when she and Spike were, well, real close. Even then, she professed, she could see that he would go far. How far did he go with you, Mary-Beth, asked one of the sharper young wives of the town, and Mary-Beth smiled beatifically, like a Virgin in a coloring book, knowing that either way her status could only rise.

Meanwhile, Touchdown Tiggler had reached the end of Main Street and turned by the hairdresser called Shear Pleasure, which would care for your poodle too if you took him round the back, and while the public address endlessly played 'I am just a country boy/Who's always known the love and joy/Of coming home . . .'

Spike Tiggler was welcomed three times from one direction and three times from the other. The convertible moved slowly, because after the first triumphal sweep Spike got perched up on the back so that everyone could see him, and each time the limo tortoised past the gas-station-cum-liquor-store its proprietor Buck Weinhart shouted 'Drive it or milk it!' in remembrance of Spike's habit of abusing slow drivers when the pair of them used to stir up the town all those years before. Six times Buck bellowed, 'Hey, Spike, drive it or milk it!' and Spike, a stocky, dark-haired figure, waved back with a good-ole-boy inclination of the head. Later, at a civic lunch in the Wadesville diner, which Spike had once thought very grand but which now reminded him of a funeral parlor, the returning hero, at first unfamiliar in his astronaut's crewcut and city suit which made him look like he was trying out for President Eisenhower, gave a speech about always remembering where you come from however far it is you go, which was accounted fine and dignified by those present, and one of those who spontaneously replied to his words even proposed that in honor of the achievement of their favorite son they should strike Wadesville and rename the town Moonsville, an idea which flourished for a few weeks and then quietly died, partly because of opposition from Old Jessie Wade, last surviving grand-daughter of Ruben Wade, a traveling man who way back at the start of the century had decided that pumpkins might grow well on the land hereabouts. The pumpkins failed, as it happened, but that was no reason to dishonor the man now.

Spike Tiggler had not always been as popular in Wadesville as he was that day in 1971, and it wasn't just Mary-Beth's mother who'd thought him wild and regretted that the war had ended too soon for them to ship young Tiggler out East and fight the Japs instead of fighting half the town. He was fifteen when they dropped the Hiroshima bomb, an event Mary-Beth's mother deplored for purely local reasons; but in due course Spike got his war, flying F-86s up to the Yalu River. Twenty-eight missions, two MiG-15s shot down. Reason enough for celebration in Wadesville, though Tiggler did not return at that time, or for a while afterwards. As he was to explain it in 1975, during his first appeal for funds at the Moondust Diner (a change of name approved even by Jessie Wade), the movement of a man's life, of every life, is marked by escape and return. Escape and return, escape and return, like the tides that play in Albermale Sound and up the Pasquotank River to Elizabeth City. We all go out with the tide, and then we all come back in on the tide. Some of the audience hadn't ever much left Wadesville in most of their lives, so couldn't be expected to have an opinion, and Jeff Clayton remarked afterwards that the other year when he'd driven through Fayetteville and around Fort Bragg to visit the World Golf Hall of Fame at Pinehurst and come home in time for his beer ration from Alma, it hadn't felt to him much like the tides in the Pasquotank River; still, what did Jeff Clayton know, and everyone agreed to give Spike the benefit of the doubt, since Spike had not just been out inta the world but – as old Jessie Wade herself so memorably put it – had been out outa the world as well.

Spike Tiggler dated the first ratchet-click of the escape-and-return cycle in his life to the day his father took him to Kitty Hawk, way back before the replica ark went up as a worship center. At this time, there was only the flat runway and the flat open sky above, and then, across an empty road with barely the glint of a distant truck, some flat dunes and the softly churning sea. 'Where other kids found allure in the lipstick and jazz of a brawling city, Spike found it in the calming simplicity of the land, sea and sky at Kitty Hawk. This, at any rate, was how he explained it at another of his fund-raising dinners, and they believed him, even though neither Mary-Beth nor Buck Weinhart had heard him talk like that back at the time.

Spike Tiggler's home town was strong for the Democrats and even stronger for the Baptists. The Sunday after his trip to Kitty Hawk, Spike was heard displaying a rather too disrespectful sort of enthusiasm about the Wright Brothers outside the Church of the Holy Water, and old Jessie Wade opined to the thirteen-year-old that if God had intended us to fly, he'd have given us wings. 'But God intended us to drive, didn't he?' replied young Spike, a shade too quick for courtesy, and actually pointing at the freshly-shined Packard in which his elderly detractor had ridden the two hundred yards to church; whereupon Spike's father reminded him that if it were not for the Sabbath, the Lord might very well have intended Spike to receive a whack upside the head. The exchange, rather than anything about land and sea and sky, was what the inhabitants of Wadesville recalled of Spike Tiggler's conversation, c.1943.

A couple of years passed, the bomb fell on Hiroshima too soon for Mary-Beth's mother, and Spike discovered that if God hadn't given him wheels, then at least his father would occasionally loan him some. On warm evenings he and Buck Weinhart would play their game of picking out a slow automobile on a back road and trailing up behind it until their radiator grille was almost in the other fellow's trunk. Then, as they pulled softly out and swept past, the two of them would yell in unison, 'Drive it or milk it, fella!' It was in the same car and at about this time that Spike, his eyes bulging with hope, said to Mary-Beth, 'But if God didn't intend us to use it, what did he put it there for?' – a remark which set back his cause quite a few weeks, Mary-Beth being of a more church-obedient nature than young Spike, and this courting line of his in any case not being the most persuasive ever invented. A few weeks later, however, Spike found himself in the back seat murmuring, 'I really don't think I can live without you, Mary-Beth,' and this seemed to do the trick.

Spike left Wadesville not too long afterwards, and more or less the next thing the town heard was that he was flying an F-86 Sabre jet out in Korea and stopping the Communist MiGs from crossing the Yalu River. It had taken a series of moments and emotions, not all of them logically linked, to get him there, and if Spike tried to reduce his life to a comic strip, as he sometimes did, he would first of all see himself standing on the dunes at Kitty Hawk, looking out to sea; then grabbing at Mary-Beth's breast without being rejected and thinking, 'God can't strike me dead for this, he can't'; and then driving at dusk with Buck Weinhart waiting for the early stars to come out. Love of machines was there too, of course, and patriotism, and a strong feeling that he looked pretty cute in his blue uniform; but in a way it was the earlier things he remembered the more vividly. That was what he meant, when he gave his first appeal for funds in 1975, about your life coming back to the place where it started. Wisely, no doubt, he didn't translate this general sentiment into particular memories, else he probably wouldn't have gotten a contribution out of Mary-Beth for one thing.

Along with his father's car and a resentful Mary-Beth, Spike had left his faith behind when he quit Wadesville. Though he dutifully filled in 'Baptist' on all the Navy forms, he didn't think about the Lord's commands, or the blessed grace, or being saved, not even on the bad days when one of his fellow-aviators – hell, one of his friends – bought the farm. That was a friend gone, but you didn't try to raise the Lord on the radio. Spike was a flier, a man of science, an engineer. You might acknowledge God on paper forms just as you deferred to senior officers around the base; yet the moment you were most you, when you were really Spike Tiggler, the kid who'd grown up from a borrowed car on a quiet road to a roaring fighter in an empty sky, was when you'd climbed hard and were leveling out your silver wings, high up in the clear air south of the Yalu River. Then you were wholly in charge, and you were also most alone. This was life, and the only person who could let you down was yourself. On the nose of his F-86 Spike had painted the slogan 'Drive it or Milk it!' as a warning to any MiG unlucky enough to catch Lieutenant Tiggler nearly up its ass.

After the war in Korea he transferred to the Navy's Test Pilot School at Patuxent River, Maryland. When the Russians launched their first Sputnik and Project Mercury got under way, Spike volunteered, even though something inside him – and quite a few aviators outside him – insisted that on the first flights they might as well use a chimpanzee, hell, they were *going* to use a chimpanzee. The job was just riding a rocket; you were a piece of cargo with wires sticking out, a lump of meat for the scientist to study. Part of him wasn't disappointed he didn't make the first seven to be chosen, yet part of him was; and next time around he put in again and got himself accepted. It was front-page on the *Fayetteville Observer* with a photo, which made Mary-Beth forgive him and write; but seeing as his new wife Betty was going through a jealous period he pretended he'd forgot this particular girl from Wadesville and her letter received no reply.

In the summer of 1974 Spike Tiggler stood on the surface of the moon and threw a football pass four hundred and fifty yards. Touchdown! This was during a thirty-minute period when no specific tasks had been assigned and the two fellows on the surface were allowed to follow up anything that made them curious. Well, Spike had always been curious to see how far you could throw a football up there in the thin atmosphere, and now he knew. Touchdown! The voice at Mission Control sounded indulgent, and so did fellow-astronaut Bud Stomovicz when Spike said he was going to hop on over and get his ball back. He set off across the dead landscape like a Jack rabbit with tubes. The moon looked pretty rough and beat-up to Spike, and the dust he stirred, which settled back in slow motion, was like sand from a dirty beach. His football lay beside a small crater. He kicked it gently into the arid hollow, then turned around to examine the distance he had come. The lunar module, almost out of sight, seemed tiny and precarious, a toy spider with a wheezing battery. Spike was not much given to private thinking on a mission – in any case, the work schedule was devised to discourage introspection – but it struck him that he and Bud (plus Mike still circling above in the command module) were as far as you could currently get from the rest of the human species. Yesterday they had watched the earth rise, and for all their bagful of jokes it had been an awesome sight which turned your head upside down. Now, right here, he felt at the very edge of things. If he walked another ten yards, he might just fall off the world's wingtip and spin boots over helmet into deepest space. Though he knew such an occurrence to be scientifically impossible, that was how it felt to Spike Tiggler.

At this exact moment a voice said to him, 'Find Noah's Ark.'

'Don't read you,' he replied, thinking it must be Bud.

'Didn't say a word.' This time it was Bud's voice. Spike recognized it, and in any case it came through his earphones in the usual way. The other voice had seemed to come direct, to be around him, inside him, close to him, loud yet intimate.

He'd made it a dozen or so yards back towards the LM when the voice repeated its command. 'Find Noah's Ark.' Spike carried on doing his aerated moon-hop, wondering if this was somebody's joke. But nobody could have put a recorder in his helmet – there wasn't room for it, he'd have noticed, they wouldn't have allowed it. You could drive someone nutsy with a trick like that, and though one or two of his fellow-astronauts had a pretty curveball sense of humor, it mainly stopped at hollowing out a plug in your melon slice, slipping mustard into the hole and replacing the plug. Nothing as big-league as this.

'You'll find it on Mount Ararat, in Turkey,' the voice went on. 'Find it, Spike.'

There were electrodes monitoring most of Spike's physical reactions, and he guessed they'd see the needles jumping all over the graphs when this part of the mission was reviewed. If so, it wouldn't be beyond him to dream up a cover story. For the moment, he just wanted to think about what he'd heard, what it might mean. So when he returned to the LM he made a crack about a fumble by the wide receiver, and went back to being a normal astronaut, that's to say test pilot turned chimpanzee turned national hero turned stuntman turned prospective congressman or if not that then future decorative board member of a dozen corporations. He hadn't been the first man to stand on the moon, but there were never going to be so many that he'd stop being a rarity, a cause for celebrity and reward. Spike Tiggler knew a few of the angles, and Betty a whole lot more, which had helped their marriage along on several occasions. He thought he was getting a tall, athletic girl with a good figure, who read *The Joy of Cooking* on honeymoon and kept her fear to herself when he was late returning to base; but she turned out a sight more familiar with the reproductive habits of the dollar than he was. 'You do the flying and I'll do the thinking,' she'd occasionally say to him, which sounded like a tease, or at any rate both of them mostly pretended that it was only a tease. So Spike Tiggler went back to his mission and fulfilled his work schedule and let no one suspect that anything had changed, that everything had changed.

After splashdown came the personal how-de-do from the White House, then the medical, the debriefing, the first call to Betty, the first *night* again with Betty . . . and the fame. In the throbbing cities he'd always distrusted – smug Washington, cynical New York, nutsy San Francisco – Spike Tiggler was big; in North Carolina he was huge. Tickertape was upended on his head like bowls of spaghetti; his right hand discovered the fatigue of congratulation; he was kissed, hugged, pawed, slapped, punched. Small boys would dig in his vest pocket and shamelessly beg for moondust. Most of all, people just wanted to be *with* him, beside him for a few minutes, breathe in the air that he was breathing out, wonder at the man from outer space who was also the man from the neighboring county. It was after some months of fevered coast-to-coast coddling that the North Carolina state legislature, proud of its boy and a little jealous that he seemed to have somehow become a general property of the nation, announced that they were striking a medal to be awarded at a special ceremony. What more appropriate place, everyone agreed, than at Kitty Hawk, on the flat land beneath the flat sky?

Appropriate words were pronounced that afternoon, yet Spike could only half apprehend them; Betty had on a new outfit with even a hat and needed reassurance that she was looking terrific, which she was, but she didn't get it. A large gold medal, with the

Kitty Hawk on one side and the Apollo capsule on the other, was
hung around his neck; Spike's hand was battered several dozen
more times; and all the while, as he gave out the polite smile and
the inclination of the head, he was thinking about that moment
on the drive, the moment that told him.

It had been cordial, not to say flattering, in the back of the
Governor's limousine, and Betty had been looking so good he
thought he should tell her only was shy of doing so in front of the
Governor and his wife. There was the usual conversation about
gravity and moon-hopping and earth-rise and tell me, what
about going to the bathroom, when suddenly, just as they were
nearing Kitty Hawk, he saw the Ark by the side of the road. A
huge, beached ark, high at both ends, with slatted wooden sides.
The Governor followed Spike's head indulgently as it panned
through 180 degrees, then answered his question without it
being put. 'Some kinda church,' said the Governor. 'They stuck
it up not long back. Probably got a load of animals in it.' He
laughed, and Betty joined in carefully.

'Do you believe in God?' asked Spike all of a sudden.

'Couldn't get to be Governor of North Carolina without,'
came the good-humored reply.

'No, do you believe in *God*,' Tiggler repeated, with a directness that could easily be misread for something they didn't need.

'Honey,' said Betty quietly.

'I sure do think we're nearly there,' said the Governor's wife,
straightening a box-pleat with a white-gloved hand.

In their hotel room that evening, Betty was at first inclined to
be conciliatory. It must be a strain, she thought, however dandy
it might be. *I* wouldn't like to get up on platforms and tell everyone for the fiftieth time what it was like and how proud it made
me feel, even if it did make me feel proud and I did want to talk
about it for the fiftieth time. So she mothered him a little and
asked if he was feeling tired, and tried to get him to spit out any
excuse as to why not once, not once *in the whole damn day* had he
mentioned her outfit, and didn't he know how uncertain she was
whether primrose yellow was really her color. But this failed to
work, and so Betty, who could never get to sleep unless things
were out in the open, asked him if he wanted a drink and why
had he gone all funny on them just before the ceremony, and if
he wanted her frank opinion the soonest way to foul up the future
career they'd both agreed on was for him to start asking State

Governors whether or not they believed in God, for Christ's sake. Who did he think he was?

'My life has changed,' said Spike.

'Are you trying to tell me something?' Betty was normally suspicious and couldn't help noticing how many letters a famous man is liable to receive from women who didn't know him, from the Mary-Beths and all the potential Mary-Beths of the world.

'Yes,' he replied. 'You come back to where you started from. I went 240,000 miles to see the moon – and it was the earth that was really worth looking at.'

'You *do* need a drink.' She paused, half-way across the room to the frigobar, but he hadn't spoken, or moved, or gestured. 'Heck, *I* need a drink.' She sat down beside her husband with a sour mash and waited.

'When I was a kid my Pa took me to Kitty Hawk. I was twelve, thirteen. It made me into an aviator. That's all I wanted to do from that day.'

'I know, honey.' She took his hand.

'I joined the Navy. I was a good aviator. I transferred to Pax River. I volunteered for Project Mercury. I didn't get accepted at first but I kept on and they accepted me in the end. I was listed for Project Apollo. I did all the training. I landed on the moon . . .'

'I know, honey.'

'. . . and there . . . *there*,' he went on, squeezing Betty's hand as he prepared to tell her for the first time, 'God told me to find Noah's Ark.'

'Uh-huh.'

'I'd just thrown the football. I'd just thrown the football and found it and kicked it into a little crater and was wondering if I was out of range of the camera and if they'd call a foul if they spotted it, when God speaks to me. *Find Noah's Ark.*' He looked across at his wife. 'It was like, here you are a grown man and you make it to the moon and what do you want to do? Throw footballs. Time to start putting away childish things, that's what God was telling me.'

'How you sure it was God, honey?'

Spike ignored the question. 'I didn't tell anyone. I know I'm not hallucinating, I know I've heard what I've heard, but I don't tell. Maybe I'm not quite sure, maybe I want to forget it. And what happens? The very day I go back to Kitty Hawk, where it all started all those years ago, the very day I go back I see the

God-damn Ark. *Don't forget what I said* – that's His message, isn't it? Loud and clear. That's what it means. *Go ahead and get your medal, but don't forget what I said.*'

Betty took a sip of her whiskey. 'So what you gonna do, Spike?' Normally, when discussing his career, she said *we* rather than *you*; this time he was out on his own.

'I don't know yet. I don't know yet.'

The NASA psychiatrist that Betty consulted had a good line in nodding, as if to suggest that she'd have to tell him something far more outrageous before he'd throw down his pen and admit the fellow was minus some buttons, crazier than a bedbug. He nodded, and said how he and his colleagues had been anticipating a few *adjustment problems*, after all someone who went to the moon and looked back at the earth must be a bit like the first guy who ever stood on his head and took in the view from that direction, which might affect your *behavioral pattern*, and what with the stress of the flight and the enormous publicity attending the missions, it wasn't altogether surprising that one or two *reality shifts* might have taken place, but there was no reason to believe that their effects might be either serious or long-lasting.

'You're not answering my question.'

'What is your question?' The psychiatrist was not aware that she'd asked one.

'Is my husband – I don't know what technical term you might use, doctor – is my husband a fruitcake?'

There was a lot more nodding, this time in a horizontal rather than vertical plane, and examples of *perceptual disorientation* were given, and Spike's records were examined, on every one of which he had firmly written *Baptist*, and it seemed to Betty that the psychiatrist would have been more surprised if Spike *hadn't* heard God speak to him on the moon's surface, and when she asked him 'But was Spike hallucinating?' he merely replied, 'What do you think?' which didn't seem to Betty to advance the conversation, indeed it was almost as if *she* was the crazy one for doubting her husband. One result of the meeting was that Betty went away feeling she had betrayed her husband rather than helped him; and the other was that when, three months later, Spike put in for release from the space program there wasn't much serious opposition to his request as long as the whole thing was handled low-profile, because what was clear from the psychiatrist's report was that Spike was *minus some buttons*, crazier than a bedbug, a fifty-carat fruitcake, and that he probably believed after close personal inspection that the moon was made of green cheese. So there was a move to a desk job in general media promotions, then a Navy transfer back to trainers, but within a year of hopping around in the grey ash Spike Tiggler was back in civvies and Betty was wondering what happened when you fell off the box car of the gravy train.

It was Spike's announcement that he had booked the Moondust Diner in Wadesville for the first of his fund-raising get-togethers that moved Betty to wonder if the most painless thing wouldn't be to close *The Joy of Cooking* and head for an early divorce. Spike had done nothing for nearly a year except go out one day and buy a Bible. Then he'd go missing in the course of the evening, and she'd find him on the back porch, the Scripture open on his knees and his eyes turned upward to the stars. Her friends were exhaustingly sympathetic: after all it must be tough coming back from *up there* and having to readjust to the daily grind. It was clear to Betty that the fame of Touchdown Tiggler could run for quite a few years without having to put any more gas in the tank, and it was equally clear she could count on support – since fame followed by crack-up was not just American, but almost downright patriotic – but even so she felt cheated. All those years of doing what was right by Spike's career, of being shunted around the country, never quite having a proper home, waiting, hoping for the big payout . . . and then, when it comes, when those big round dollars come cascading out of the machine, what does Spike do? Instead of holding out his hat and catching them, he hits the back porch and looks at the stars. Meet my husband, he's the one with the Bible on his knees and the torn pants and the funny look in his eye. No, he didn't get himself attacked, he just jumped off the box car of the gravy train.

When Betty asked Spike what he'd like her to wear for his first public meeting at the Moondust Diner, there was some sarcasm in her voice; and when Spike replied that he'd always been fond of that primrose-yellow outfit she'd bought for when he got his medal at Kitty Hawk, she heard once again within her a voice which certainly didn't belong to the Almighty whispering the word *divorce*. But the strange thing was, he seemed to mean it, and twice, once before they departed, and again as they turned off the interstate, he commented on how fine she was looking. This was a new development she couldn't help noticing in him.

Nowadays he always meant what he said, and just said what he meant, nothing more. He seemed to have left the fun, the teasing, the dare-devilry up in that crater along with his football (that was a dumb stunt, come to think of it, and should have set some bells ringing earlier than it did). Spike had gotten serious; he'd gotten dull. He still said he loved her, which Betty believed, though she sometimes wondered if that was enough for a girl. But he'd lost his pizzazz. If this was putting away childish things, then childish things, according to Betty, had a lot to be said for them.

The Moondust Diner was full that April evening of 1975 when Spike Tiggler launched his first appeal for funds. Most of the town was there, plus a couple of newspapermen and a photographer. Betty feared the worst. She imagined headlines like 'GOD SPOKE TO ME' CLAIMS GROUNDED ASTRONAUT and WADESVILLE MAN MINUS SOME BUTTONS. She sat nervously beside her husband as the local minister welcomed him back to the community where he had grown up. There was clapping; Spike gently took her hand and didn't release it until he was on his feet and about to speak.

'It's nice to be back,' said Spike, and looked around the room, giving hi-there inclinations of the head to those he recognized. 'You know, only the other day, I was sitting on my back porch looking up at the stars and thinking about the kid I used to be, all those years ago in Wadesville. I must have been fifteen, sixteen or so, and I guess I was a bit of a handful, and old Jessie Wade, God rest her, I expect many of you recall Jessie, she said to me, "Young man, you run along screaming and shouting like that, one of these days you'll just take off," – and I reckon old Jessie Wade knew a thing or two because many years later that's just what I did, though sadly she didn't live to see her prophecy fulfilled, God rest her soul.'

Betty could not have been more surprised. He was doing a number. He was doing a goddam number on them. He didn't use to talk with much fondness about Wadesville; she'd never even heard the story about old Jessie Wade before; yet here he was, remembering it all, playing up to the folks back home. He told them a heap of stories about his childhood, and then some more about being an astronaut, which after all was what they'd mostly come for, but the message behind it all was that without these folks old Spike wouldn't have got further than Fayetteville, that it was *these folks* who'd really put him up there on the moon not those clever guys with wires coming out of their ears at Mission Control. Just as surprising to Betty was that he did this part of his address with all the old fun and teasing she thought had gone out of him. And then he came to the bit about every man's life being a process of escape and return, escape and return like the waters in the Pasquotank River (which was when Jeff Clayton thought it wasn't like that on the way to the World Golf Hall of Fame at Pinehurst); and explained how you always came back to the things and places you'd started from. Like he'd left Wadesville years before, and now he was back; like he'd been a regular attender at the Church of the Holy Water all through his childhood, had later strayed from the path of the Lord, but had now returned to it – which was news, though hardly unexpected news, to Betty.

And so, he continued, to the serious part of the evening, to the purpose of this meeting (and Betty held her breath, thinking *nutty as a fruitcake*, how are they going to handle this bit, about God telling him to leave his football in the crater and go find the Ark instead). But again Betty had underestimated Spike. He didn't refer to lunar commands from the Almighty, not once. He invoked his faith several times, and going back to where you came from all over again, and he mentioned the difficulties that had to be surmounted in the space program; so when he finally began to explain how he'd been turning over such matters on his back porch looking up at the stars, and how it seemed to him that it was time after all these years to go looking for where we came from, and that he planned to mount an expedition to recover what could be found of Noah's Ark which as everyone knew lay on the summit of Mount Ararat near the borders of Turkey and Iran, it all seemed to make sense, to be a logical progression. Project Ararat, indeed, could be seen as the obvious next venture for NASA; and listeners might even be free to conclude that NASA was being a little selfish, a little materialistic and narrow-minded, in concentrating solely on space flight, when there were other projects, closer to the heart and soul of the tax-payer, which might more usefully receive the benefit of their sophisticated technology.

He'd done a number, he'd done a goddam number, Betty thought as her husband sat down to a roomful of noise. He hadn't even mentioned money, he'd just asked them to honor him with their presence while he shared a few ideas with them, and if they judged he was thinking straight then he'd get off his tail and start looking for people to help him. That's my Spike, Betty found herself muttering, even though it was a rather different Spike from the one she had married.

'Mrs Tiggler, how do you view your husband's project?' she was asked as they stood hand-in-hand before the photographer from the *Fayetteville Observer*.

'Oh, I'm behind him one hundred ten percent,' she replied, looking up at Spike with a bridal smile. The *Observer* reported her comment, and the journalist even managed to say how striking Mrs Tiggler looked in her mustard dress with matching hat (*mustard!* said Betty to Spike, *I suppose he eats primroses on the side with his beef*). When they got home that night Spike seemed all charged up, like she hadn't seen him for a year or so, and there wasn't any question of him tucking off with his Bible on the back porch beneath the stars; no, he fair hustled her into the bedroom, where they hadn't done much else but sleep for quite a while, and Betty, who though unprepared for this event was not at all displeased, muttered something in their private code about the bathroom, but Spike said they wouldn't be bothering over that, and Betty quite liked him being this masterful.

'I love you,' said Spike later that night.

A few inches in the *Fayetteville Observer* begat a feature in the *Greensboro News and Record* which begat a small syndicated news item. After that there was silence, but Spike remained confident and recalled the bonfires he used to watch as a kid when it looked like nothing was happening until the whole thing burst into flame; and sure enough he was right, for suddenly he blazed across the front pages of the *Washington Post* and the *New York Times*. Then the TV people arrived, which set off another round of newsmen, followed by foreign TV and foreign newsmen, and all the time Betty and Spike worked hard (they were a team again, like at the beginning) to get Project Ararat under way. Reporters were given fact-sheets itemizing the latest contributions and endorsements, whether it was fifty dollars from a neighboring congregation, or a gift of ropes and tents from a well-known store. Soon there arose on Spike and Betty's front lawn a large wooden campaign thermometer; every Monday morning Spike, paintbrush in hand, inched up the mercury.

Not surprisingly, Spike and Betty liked to compare this critical time to the launch of a rocket: the countdown is exciting, the moment of ignition a thrill, but until you see that heavy mother of a silver tube starting to shift on her haunches and shoulder her way towards the heavens you know there is always a chance that you're in for an embarrassing and very public floperoo. Whatever Betty wanted, now she had decided to back her husband one hundred ten percent, she didn't want that. Betty was not of a particularly religious nature, and in her private heart she didn't know what to make of Spike's experience on the moon; but she recognized possibilities when she saw them. After a year of moody Bible study and her friends being so damn sympathetic she could scream, it wasn't so bad that Spike Tiggler was back in the news again. After Project Apollo, Project Ararat – what could be more obvious than this progression, this tiny alphabetical step? And nobody, not one of the newspapers, had even suggested that Spike might be minus some buttons, crazier than a bedbug.

Spike handled it all pretty well, and never once mentioned how God had played President Kennedy in getting the whole thing rolling. This made it easier for Betty to interest people who might have been cautious if they'd sniffed anything nutsy in the scheme. Even the Governor of North Carolina was moved to forgive Spike's brusque curiosity about the authenticity of his faith and benevolently agreed to top-table a $100-a-plate fund-raising dinner in Charlotte. Betty wore primrose yellow on such occasions with a regularity which friends deemed unnecessary, not to say unfashionable; but Spike maintained that it was his lucky color. When talking to reporters Spike sometimes asked them to mention his wife's dress, which was mustard in color, as they no doubt had observed. Some newsmen, either lazy or color-blind, dutifully obliged, which made Spike chuckle when he read the papers.

He also guested on a number of religious TV shows. Betty would sometimes quiver with apprehension as yet another sales-man in a three-piece suit cued in from the commercial break with the welcoming announcement that God's love was like the still center of a whirlwind, and one of his guests here today had actually been inside a whirlwind and could testify to the perfect peace within it, but how this meant that Christianity was a faith which kept you moving forward all the time, since you can't stand still in a whirlwind, which brought us to his second guest, Spike Tiggler, who had in his time traveled even faster than a whirl-wind but was now looking for that still center, that perfect calm, praise the Lord. And Spike, who had gone back to his astronaut's haircut and blue suit, would keep on answering politely and never once mention – as the salesman would have loved to hear – that God had been *right there*, inside his helmet, whispering in his ear. He came across as good and simple and true, which helped the checks roll in to Project Ararat, care of Betty Tiggler, who naturally paid herself a salary.

They set up a committee: the Reverend Lance Gibson, respected or at least known through most of the state, a touch fundamentalist for some but not too left-field to scare away sensible money; Dr Jimmy Fulgood, college basketball star turned geologist and scuba-diver, who would give scientific respectability to the expedition; and Betty herself, chairperson, co-ordinator and treasurer. The Governor agreed to feature on the writing paper as Emeritus Patron; and the only glitch in the whole Ararat countdown was the failure to get the Project recognized as a charitable institution.

Some of the journalists with book-learning behind them liked to ask Spike how he could be entirely sure that the Ark was to be found on Mount Ararat. Did not the Koran say it made landfall on Mount Judi, several hundred kilometers away, near the Iraqi border? And did not Jewish tradition equally differ, placing the location somewhere in Northern Israel? At which point Spike would give a little touch on the charm throttle and reply that everyone was of course entitled to their opinion, and if an Israeli astronaut wanted to go looking in Israel that was fine by him, and if a Koranic astronaut did the same in Iraq, that was fine too. Skeptical reporters went away thinking that Tiggler might be simple, but he wasn't simple-minded.

Another question occasionally put was whether the Ark – assuming its theoretical location could be found – might not have rotted away over the last however many thousand years, or been eaten by termites. Once again, Spike would not be drawn, especially not into revealing how he knew it couldn't have rotted or been eaten by termites, because God's command to find the Ark clearly implied that there was something left of it. Instead, he referred the questioner to his Bible, which the questioner appeared to have come without, but which would reveal that the Ark was made of gopher-wood, which everyone agreed was extremely hard, and therefore probably resistant to both rot and termites; then Spike mentioned examples of various things miraculously preserved down the centuries – mammoths found in glaciers, the meat on them as fresh as the chuck steak from your local Giant; and he wound up by suggesting that if anything was going to be miraculously preserved down the centuries thanks to God's almighty will, then wasn't the Ark a pretty good candidate?

The Reverend Lance Gibson consulted church historians at Baptist universities to establish current thinking on the location of the Ark; while Jimmy Fulgood went into probable wind and tide patterns around the time of the Flood. When the two of them pooled their findings, they began to favor an area on the south-east side of the mountain a couple of kilometers from the summit. Sure, Spike agreed, that's where they'd begin looking, but what about his plan for starting right at the top and descending in spider-web circles so that the ground was systematically covered? Jimmy appreciated the thinking behind this idea, yet felt he couldn't go along with it from a mountaineering point of view, so Spike bowed to him on that one. Jimmy's counter-proposal was that Spike use his connections with NASA and the Navy to get a good set of aerial reconnaissance prints of the mountain, then they could blow them up and see if anything Ark-like showed. Spike acknowledged this was a logical approach but wondered if God had really intended them to take short-cuts. Wasn't the whole vision of the Project as a sort of Christian pilgrimage, and didn't the ancient pilgrims always rough it? While he wasn't suggesting they took anything short of the best when it came to tents and ropes and boots and wrist-watches, he did feel they should hope to feel guided by something other than modern technology once they got up there.

The Reverend Gibson's pastoral activities precluded him from making the trip to Turkey, but he would furnish spiritual back-up and constantly remind the Almighty by means of prayer that his two fellow committee-members were going about the Lord's business in a far country. Betty would stay at home and field media inquiries which were sure to be running hot. The expedi-tionary party – Spike and Jimmy – were to depart in July of that year, 1977. They declined to make predictions about how long they would be away. You did not seek to outdraw the Lord, said the Reverend Gibson, unless you wanted a slug in the gut.

Various supplies had been gifted by well-wishers, church con-gregations and survivalist stores; and as Betty opened the parcels which continued to arrive right up to the eve of departure, she wondered at how the Project was being perceived in some quarters. A few of the offerings sure seemed less than Christian. You might have deduced from a glimpse of the Tigglers' Expedition Room that Spike and Jimmy were a couple of naked refugees being sent as hired killers to exterminate most of Eastern Turkey.

They left behind a lot of old clothes, some automatic weapons, four stun grenades, a garrotte and a couple of suicide pills donated by some zealot. Their payload included lightweight camping equipment, vitamin pills, a Japanese camera with one of the new zoom lenses, credit cards, American Express travelers' checks, running shoes, a pint of bourbon, thermal socks and underwear, a large plastic bag of branflakes to keep them regular, anti-diarrhea tablets, an infra-red night-sight, water-purifying pills, freeze-dried vacuum-packed food, a lucky horseshoe, flashlights, dental tape, reserve batteries for their electric razors, a pair of scabbard knives sharp enough to cut gopher-wood or disembowel an assailant, mosquito repellent, sunburn cream and the Bible. When Jimmy secretly checked their baggage he found the folded husk of a football and a small compressed-air device for inflating it; he repacked them carefully, with an indulgent grin. When Spike secretly checked the baggage he came across a box of rubbers, which he threw away and never raised with Jimmy. The committee discussed what the expedition should take as tokens of goodwill to distribute to the peasants of Eastern Turkey. Betty thought some color postcards of Spike on the moon's surface, but Spike felt this would be hitting the wrong note, seeing as they weren't on a personal ego trip but going about the Lord's business. After further reflection they took two hundred buttons commemorating the inauguration of President Jimmy Carter and his First Lady the lovely Rosalynn, which a friend of the Reverend Gibson's had been able to let them have at way below cost, and happy to be rid of them he was.

They flew to Ankara where they had to rent tuxedos for the fine dinner offered them by the Ambassador. Spike disguised his disappointment that most of the guests wanted to talk astronautics and seemed positively reluctant to question him about Project Ararat. Later they proved unimpressed, not to say downright miserly, when Spike in his after-dinner speech made a patriotic appeal for extra funds.

The message Betty had sent to Erzerum via Interchurch Travel about hiring a jeep or Land Rover couldn't have got through, and the expedition therefore proceeded in a large Mercedes. East to Horasan, then east-south-east for Dogubayazit. The country-side was neat, kind of pale green and pale brown at the same time. They ate fresh apricots and distributed images of the smiling Carters to small children, some of whom seemed pleased, though others continued to press for dollars or, failing that, ball-points. The military were everywhere, which caused Spike to reflect on the strategic significance of the area. It came as news to Jimmy that only a hundred or so years earlier Mount Ararat, or Agri Dagi as the locals insisted on calling it, had been the meeting-point of three great empires – Russia, Persia and Turkey – with the mountain divided between the three of them.

'Doesn't seem right, the Soviets having a piece of it,' commented Jimmy.

'Guess they weren't Soviets at the time,' said Spike. 'They were Christians like us when they were just Russians.'

'Mebbe the Lord took their slice of the mountain away from them when they became Soviets.'

'Mebbe,' replied Spike, not wholly certain of when the boundaries had shifted.

'Like, not letting his holy mountain fall into the hands of infidels.'

'I read you,' said Spike, a little irritated. 'But I guess the Turks aren't exactly Christians.'

'They're not as infidel as the Soviets.' Jimmy appeared reluctant to give up his theory at the first objection.

'Check.'

On the road north from Dogubayazit Spike shouted for Jimmy to stop the car. They got out and Spike pointed to a small stream. Gently, but unarguably, the water in it was flowing uphill.

'Praise the Lord,' said Spike Tiggler, and knelt to pray. Jimmy bent his head a few degrees, but remained on his feet. After a couple of minutes Spike went back to the Merc and filled two plastic water-bottles from the stream.

'It's the land of miracles,' he announced as they set off once more.

Jimmy Fulgood, geologist and scuba-diver, let a few miles go by, then tried to explain how it was not scientifically impossible for a stream to flow uphill. It depended on a certain weight and pressure of water higher up the mountain, and on the apparently uphill stretch being a comparatively small section of an overall descent. The phenomenon had, as far as he knew, been reported on previous occasions. Spike, who was driving, kept nodding away as cheerful as they come. 'Dare say you can explain it like that,' he commented at the end. 'Point is, who made the water to flow uphill in the first place? Who put it where He did so that we should see it as we were passing on the road to Ararat? The Good Lord, that's who. It's the land of miracles,' he repeated, nodding contentedly.

Jimmy had always found Spike an optimistic kind of guy; here in Turkey he became frankly ebullient. Neither mosquitoes nor misfortune troubled him; his tipping showed a true Christian generosity; and he had the habit, whenever they passed a cow on the road, of winding down the window and shouting to its owner, or even just to the countryside in general, 'Drive it or milk it, fella!' At times this could get to bug you, but Jimmy was one hundred ten percent funded by Project Ararat, so he endured such high spirits as he would have suffered bad temper.

They drove until the road ran out and the two shapes of Great and Little Ararat rose ahead of them.

'Kinda like man and wife, ain't it?' Spike remarked.

'How d'ya mean?'

'Brother and sister, Adam and Eve. The big one there and that little neat pretty one by his side. See? *Male and femle created He them.*'

'Do you think the Lord had that in mind at the time?'

'The Lord has everything in mind,' said Spike Tiggler. 'All the time.' Jimmy Fulgood looked at the twin shapes ahead of them and kept to himself the reflection that Betty Tiggler was an inch or two taller than Spike.

They sorted their equipment before entrusting themselves to the two feet the Lord had provided them with. They left the bourbon in the trunk, sensing that it was wrong to consume alcoholic liquor on the Lord's mountain; neither had they any more need for the Carter buttons. They took their travelers' checks, lucky horseshoe and Bible. During the transfer of supplies, Jimmy caught Spike sneaking the deflated football into his backpack. Then they set off up the southern approaches to the mountain, the lanky ex-basketball star a few yards behind the exuberant astronaut, like a junior officer trailing a general. From time to time Jimmy's geological interests made him want to stop and examine the rock; but Spike always insisted that they push on.

They were alone on the mountain and found their solitude exalting. They saw lizards on the lower slopes, ibex and wild goats higher up. They climbed above the operational altitude of hawks and buzzards, up towards the snowline where the only movement was the occasional dart of a small fox. In the cold nights Jimmy wrote up the expedition journal and Spike read his Bible by the stark and hissing glare of their gas-lamp.

They began on the south-eastern slope, that area of lukewarm agreement between church and science. They probed rocky gulches and looked in barren caves. Jimmy was uncertain whether they were due to find the whole Ark, preserved intact – in which case they probably couldn't miss it – or just some significant remnant: the rudder, perhaps, or some planks still caulked with bitumen.

Their first rough survey revealed nothing, which neither surprised nor disappointed them. They crossed the snowline and headed for the summit. Towards the end of their climb the sky slowly began to change color, until by the time they reached the top it appeared bright green. This place was full of miracles. Spike knelt in prayer, and Jimmy briefly joined him. Immediately below them was a gently sloping valley of snow, which ran down to a secondary peak. This could have made a natural resting-place for the Ark. But they searched it without success.

The northern side of the mountain was split by an enormous fissure. Spike pointed to where this chasm ran out, some thousands of feet below them, and said there'd once been a monastery down there. Real monks and all. Then in 1840, he said, a terrible earthquake had gotten hold of the mountain and shaken it like a dog with a rat, and the little church had fallen down, and so had the village below it, some name beginning with an A. Everyone had been killed, apparently, and even if they hadn't they would have been a bit later. See this fissure, well, four or five days after the quake a build-up of snow and water started to move down it. Nothing could stand in its way. Like the vengeance of the Lord. Wiped the monastery and the little village off the face of the earth.

Jimmy Fulgood nodded seriously to himself as he listened to the story. All this had happened, he told himself, at a time when the Soviets had owned this slice of the mountain. Of course they were Russians then, and Christians, but it proved the Lord sure did have it in for the Soviets, even before they were Soviets.

They searched for three weeks. Jimmy wondered if the Ark

might be buried deep in the cornice of ice which encircled the mountain; and Spike agreed this might be possible but if so the Lord would surely indicate it in some way. The Lord would not send them upon the mountain and then conceal from them the very reason for sending them there: such was not the nature of the Lord. Jimmy bowed to Spike on this. They searched by eye, binocular and infra-red night-sight. Spike waited for a sign. Was he sure he would recognize the sign when it came? Perhaps they should search in whichever direction the wind blew them. They searched in the direction the wind blew them. They found nothing.

Each day, as the sun heated up the plain below them and the warm air rose, a halo of cloud formed itself around the mountain-top, shutting off their view of the lower slopes; and each night, as the air cooled, the cloud dispersed. At the end of three weeks they came down to collect more supplies from the trunk of the Mercedes. They drove to the nearest village, from where Spike sent Betty a card saying No News Is Good News, which struck Betty as less clear than it could have been. Then they returned to the mountain and searched for another three weeks. During this period there was a full moon, and Spike would gaze up at it every night, remembering how the present mission had begun up there in the shifting dust. One night Jimmy stood at his elbow and examined with him the creamy, pitted orb. 'Sure looks like a custard pie,' Jimmy concluded, with a nervous laugh. 'More like dirty beach sand when you get there,' Spike replied. He continued looking up, waiting for a sign. No sign came.

It was during their third spell on the mountain – agreed to be their last for the year – that Spike made his discovery. They were a few thousand feet below the summit and had just crossed a treacherous piece of scree when they came upon a pair of caves side by side. Just like the Lord stuck two fingers in the rock, they agreed. With the incorrigible optimism which Jimmy high-mindedly endured, the former astronaut jauntily disappeared into the first of the caves; there was silence, then an echoing howl. Jimmy thought of bears – even of the abominable snow-man – until the continuing howl modulated, almost without breath being drawn, into a series of sporting whoops.

Not far into the cavern Jimmy found Spike Tiggler kneeling in prayer. A human skeleton was laid out before him. Jimmy sank down beside Spike. Even on his knees, the former basketball star retained a height advantage over the ex-astronaut. Spike extinguished his flashlight, and Jimmy did the same. A few minutes of purest silence passed in the cold darkness, then Spike murmured, 'We found Noah.'

Jimmy didn't reply. After a while they switched their flashlights back on and the two beams reverently explored the skeleton in front of them. It lay with its feet pointing towards the mouth of the cave, and seemed intact, as far as either of them could tell. There were a few scraps of cloth – some white, some of a grayish color – hanging between the bones.

'Praise the Lord,' said Spike Tiggler.

They pitched their tent a few yards down the mountainside and then searched the other cave. Spike was secretly hoping they might find Noah's wife, or maybe the Ark's log, but there were no more discoveries. Later, as the evening darkened, there was a hiss of compressed air inside the tent and then Spike Tiggler threw his football across the rocks of Great Ararat into the hesitant arms of Jimmy Fulgood. Time after time it thumped into Jimmy's large, ex-basketball-playing hands. His own returns were often poor, but Spike was not disconcerted. He threw and he threw that evening, until the air was cold and the two figures were lit only by the rising moon. Even so, Spike's eye was flawless; Jimmy felt the football homing in to him with the nocturnal accuracy of a bat. 'Hey, Spike,' he shouted at one point, 'not using that infra-red sight, are you?' and a chuckle came back from his barely visible partner.

After they had eaten, Spike took his flashlight and returned to Noah's tomb, as by now he had christened it. Jimmy, either from tact or superstition, remained in the tent. An hour or so later Spike reported that the position of the skeleton would have allowed the dying Noah to gaze out from the cave and see the moon – the very moon on whose surface Spike Tiggler had so recently stood. 'Praise the Lord,' he repeated as he zipped up the tent for the night.

After a while it became clear that neither of them was asleep. Jimmy coughed slightly. 'Spike,' he said, with some caution, 'it's ... well ... it's my perception that we have ourselves a problem.'

'We have ourselves a problem? We have ourselves a *miracle*!' Spike replied.

'Sure we have a miracle. We also have a problem.'

'Tell me how you perceive this problem, Jimmy.' The tone

was amused, tolerant, almost patronizing; the tone of a quarterback who knew his arm could be relied on.

Jimmy went carefully, not being too sure himself what to believe. 'Well, let's say I'm just thinking aloud, Spike, and let's say I'm into negativity at this moment.'

'Fine.' Nothing could harm Spike's present mood. The mixture of fierce exhilaration and relief reminded him of splashdown.

'We're looking for the Ark, right? You were . . . *told* we'd find the Ark.'

'Sure. We will. We're bound to now, next time mebbe.'

'But we were looking for the Ark,' Jimmy persisted. 'We . . . you . . . were *told* to look for the Ark.'

'We were shooting for silver, we got gold.'

'Yup. I was just wondering . . . didn't Noah strike out somewhere after the Ark landed? I mean, he lived on a few centuries, didn't he, in the Bible?'

'Sure. Three hundred fifty. Sure. That village I told you about when we were on the top. Arghuri. That's where Noah had his first settlement. Planted his vines there. Had his first farm. Built his homestead up again.'

'That was *Noah*'s village?'

'Sure was. Down in the Soviet sector,' added Spike teasingly.

Things were getting less clear to Jimmy now. 'So God let Noah's settlement get destroyed in an earthquake?'

'Musta had a reason. Always does. Anyway, that's not the point. Point is, Noah settled down there. Maybe he moved on, maybe not. Anyway, what's more likely than he came back to Ararat to be buried? When he felt the weariness of Time upon him? Probably staked out that cave the moment he stepped down from the Ark. Decided that as a sign of gratitude and obedience to the Lord for preserving him he'd drag his old bones up the mountainside when he knew his hour was upon him. Like elephants in the Jungle.'

'Spike, those bones in the cave – don't they . . . don't they look a little, how shall I put it, well-preserved? I mean, I'm only playing devil's advocate, you understand.'

'Relax, Jimmy, you're doing fine.'

'But they do look well-preserved?'

'Jimmy, we're talking miracles and signs here. You'd *expect* them to look well-preserved, wouldn't you? Noah was a real special guy. Anyway, how old was he when he died? Nine hundred fifty years. He was greatly blessed in the Lord's eye. Now if he had bones which were strong enough to carry him around for a thousand years, you'd hardly expect them to decay at the standard rate, would you?'

'I take your point, Spike.'

'Anything else worrying you?' He seemed to welcome Jimmy's doubts, confident he could field any ball thrown to him.

'Well, what exactly are we going to do?'

'We're going to tell the world, that's what we're going to do. And the world will rejoice. And many souls will come to the faith as a result of this discovery. And there will be a church built once more upon this mountainside, a church built over Noah's tomb.' In the shape of an Ark, perhaps. Or even in the shape of an Apollo spacecraft. That would be more appropriate, that would complete the circle.

'I'm with you about the repercussions, Spike. Let me put something to you, though. You and I are men of faith.'

'Men of science, too,' said the astronaut to the geologist.

'Check. And as men of faith we naturally wish to preserve our faith from any unnecessary slanders.'

'Sure.'

'Well, maybe before announcing the news we should, as men of *science*, check out what we as men of faith have discovered.'

'Meaning?'

'Meaning I think we should shut our big bazoos until we've run some lab tests on Noah's clothing.'

There was a silence from the other half of the tent as Spike realized for the first time that not everyone on earth would necessarily put their hands together the way they'd done for the astronauts coming back from the moon. Finally, he said, 'I think you're thinking good, Jimmy. I guess you've also got me wondering if we might have ourselves a problem with the clothes.'

'How d'you mean?'

Now it was Spike's turn to play the skeptic. 'Well, I'm only just supposing. You recall the story of Noah's nakedness? How his sons covered him up? Well, we can be sure Noah's bones are something special, but does that mean his clothes are something special too?' There was a pause, then he went on. 'I don't think we should give any free lunches to the doubting Thomases. What if Noah was laid out here in his burial robes, and after a few centuries they'd all been blown to dust and ashes. Then along comes some pilgrim – maybe some pilgrim who doesn't make it back safely through the infidel tribes – and finds the body. Like coming across Noah's nakedness all over again. So the pilgrim gives Noah *his* clothes – which would explain how he never got back through the lines to spread the news. But it means we get a serious mis-read on the carbon-dating tests.'

'You're right,' said Jimmy. A long silence ensued, as if each were half-daring the other to make the next logical step. Finally, Jimmy made it. 'I wonder what the legal position is.'

'Nnn,' replied Spike, not discouragingly.

'Who do you think Noah's bones belong to? Apart', Jimmy added hastily, 'from the Almighty Lord.'

'It could take years to go through all the courts. You know what lawyers are like.'

'Sure,' said Jimmy, who had never been in a court-room yet. 'I don't think the Lord would expect us to go through the legal process. Like appealing to Caesar or something.'

Spike nodded, and lowered his voice, even though they were alone on the Lord's mountain. 'Those guys wouldn't need much, would they?'

'No. No. Not much, I guess.' Jimmy relinquished his brief dream of a Navy helicopter airlifting out the whole caboodle.

Without discussing it further, the ex-astronaut and the scuba-diving geologist returned to the cave with two trembling flash-lights and set about deciding which parts of Noah's skeleton to smuggle out of Eastern Turkey. Piety, convenience and greed were all silently present. Finally they removed a small bone belonging to the left hand plus a cervical vertebra which had fallen out of position and rolled across the right scapula. Jimmy took the section of finger and Spike the neck-bone. They agreed it would be crazy not to fly home separately.

Spike routed in through Atlanta, but the media were on to him. No, he couldn't say anything at this moment in time. Yes, Project Ararat had got off to a fine start. No, no problems. No, Dr Fulgood was on a separate flight, he'd had to finalize a few things in Istanbul before departure. What sort of things? Yes, there would be a press conference in due course, and yes, Spike Tiggler hoped to have some specific, perhaps some joyous news for them on that occasion. How do you feel (all dressed in prim-rose), Mrs Tiggler? Oh, I'm one hundred ten percent behind my husband, thrilled to have him back.

The Reverend Gibson, after hesitation and much prayer, agreed that the two portions of Noah's skeleton be subjected to scientific analysis. They sent the vertebra and the finger-end to Washington, using a trusted intermediary who claimed to have dug them up in Greece. Betty waited to see if Spike had managed to haul himself back on to the box car of the gravy train.

Washington reported that the bones sent for examination were approximately one hundred and fifty years old, plus or minus twenty years. They volunteered the information that the vertebra was almost certainly that of a woman.

A sea-mist shifts listlessly across the black water as the seven o'clock ferry makes its way from Cape Hatteras to Ocracoke Island. The searchlight charges at the water ahead. Every night the vessel has to find its way again, as if for the first time. Marker lights, white and green and red, guide the boat on its nervous course. You come out on deck, shrugging against the cold, and look upward; but this time the mist has shut off the stars, and it's impossible to tell whether or not there is meant to be a moon. You shrug again, and return to the smoky cabin.

One hundred miles to the west, in the Moondust Diner, Spike Tiggler, holding aloft a plastic bottle of water from a stream that flows uphill, is announcing the launch of the second Project Ararat.

10

THE DREAM

I DREAMT THAT I woke up. It's the oldest dream of all, and I've just had it. I dreamt that I woke up.

I was in my own bed. That seemed a bit of a surprise, but after a moment's thought it made sense. Who else's bed should I wake up in? I looked around and I said to myself, Well, well, well. Not much of a thought, I admit. Still, do we ever find the right words for the big occasions?

There was a knock on the door and a woman came in, sideways and backwards at the same time. It should have looked awkward but it didn't; no, it was all smooth and stylish. She was carrying a tray, which was why she'd come in like that. As she turned, I saw she was wearing a uniform of sorts. A nurse? No, she looked more like a stewardess on some airline you've never heard of. 'Room service,' she said with a bit of a smile, as if she wasn't used to providing it, or I wasn't used to expecting it; or both.

'Room service?' I repeated. Where I come from something like that only happens in films. I sat up in bed, and found I didn't have any clothes on. Where'd my pyjamas gone? That was a change. It was also a change that when I sat up in bed and realized she could see me bollock-naked to the waist, if you understand me, I didn't feel at all embarrassed. That was good.

'Your clothes are in the cupboard,' she said. 'Take your time. You've got all day. And,' she added with more of a smile, 'all tomorrow as well.'

I looked down at my tray. Let me tell you about that breakfast. It was the breakfast of my life and no mistake. The grapefruit, for a start. Now, you know what a grapefruit's like: the way it spurts juice down your shirt and keeps slipping out of your hand unless you hold it down with a fork or something, the way the flesh always sticks to those opaque membranes and then suddenly comes loose with half the pith attached, the way it always tastes sour yet makes you feel bad about piling sugar on the top of it. That's what a grapefruit's like, right? Now let me tell you about *this* grapefruit. Its flesh was pink for a start, not yellow, and each segment had already been carefully freed from its clinging membrane. The fruit itself was anchored to the dish by some prong or fork through its bottom, so that I didn't need to hold it down or even touch it. I looked around for the sugar, but that was just out of habit. The taste seemed to come in two parts – a sort of awakening sharpness followed quickly by a wash of sweetness; and each of those little globules (which were about the size of tadpoles) seemed to burst separately in my mouth. That was the grapefruit of my dreams, I don't mind telling you.

Like an emperor, I pushed aside the gutted hull and lifted a silver dome from a crested plate. Of course I knew what would be underneath. Three slices of grilled streaky bacon with the gristle and rind removed, the crispy fat all glowing like a bonfire. Two eggs, fried, the yolk looking milky because the fat had been properly spooned over it in the cooking, and the outer edges of the white trailing off into filigree gold braid. A grilled tomato I can only describe in terms of what it wasn't. It wasn't a collapsing cup of stalk, pips, fibre and red water, it was something compact, sliceable, cooked equally all the way through, and tasting – yes, this is the thing I remember – tasting of tomato. The sausage: again, not a tube of lukewarm horsemeat stuffed into a French letter, but dark umber and succulent ... a ... sausage, that's the only word for it. All the others, the ones I'd thought I'd enjoyed in my previous life, were merely practising to be like this; they'd been auditioning – and they wouldn't get the part, either. There was a little crescent-shaped side-plate with a crescent-shaped silver lid. I raised it: yes, there were my bacon rinds, separately grilled, waiting to be nibbled.

The toast, the marmalade – well, you can imagine those, you can dream what they were like for yourselves. But I must tell you about the teapot. The tea, of course, was the real thing, tasting as if it had been picked by some rajah's personal entourage. As for the teapot ... Once, years ago, I went to Paris on a package holiday. I wandered off from the others and walked around where the smart people live. Where they shop and eat, anyway. On a corner I passed a café. It didn't look particularly grand, and just for a minute I thought of sitting down there. But I didn't, because at one of the tables I saw a man having tea. As he poured himself a fresh cup, I spotted a little gadget which seemed to me almost a definition of luxury: attached to the teapot's spout, and dangling by three delicate silver chains, was a strainer. As the man raised the pot to its pouring angle, this strainer swung outwards to catch the leaves. I couldn't believe that serious thought had once gone into the matter of how to relieve this tea-drinking gentleman of the incredible burden of picking up a normal strainer with his free hand. I walked away from that café feeling a bit self-righteous. Now, on my tray, I had a teapot bearing the insignia of some chic Parisian café. A strainer was attached to its spout by three silver chains. Suddenly, I could see the point of it.

After breakfast, I put the tray down on my bedside table, and went to the cupboard. Here they all were, my favourite clothes. That sports jacket I still liked even after people started saying, how unusual, did you buy it secondhand, another twenty years and it'll be back in fashion. That pair of corduroy trousers my wife threw out because the seat was beyond repair; but someone had managed to repair it, and the trousers looked almost new, though not so new you weren't fond of them. My shirts held out their arms to me, and why not, as they'd never been pampered like this in their lives before – all in ranks on velvet-covered hangers. There were shoes whose deaths I'd regretted; socks now deholed again; ties I'd seen in shop windows. It wasn't a collection of clothes you'd envy, but that wasn't the point. I was reassured. I would be myself again. I would be more than myself.

By the side of the bed was a tasselled bell-pull I hadn't previously noticed. I tugged it, then felt a bit embarrassed, and climbed under the sheets again. When the nurse-stewardess came in, I slapped my stomach and said, 'You know, I could eat that all over again.'

'I'm not surprised,' she replied. 'I was half expecting you to say so.'

I didn't get up all day. I had breakfast for breakfast, breakfast for lunch, and breakfast for dinner. It seemed like a good system. I would worry about lunch tomorrow. Or rather, I wouldn't worry about lunch tomorrow. I wouldn't worry about anything tomorrow. Between my breakfast-lunch and my breakfast-dinner (I was really beginning to appreciate that strainer system – you can carry on eating a croissant with your free hand while you pour) I had a long sleep. Then I took a shower. I could have had a bath, but I seem to have spent decades in the bath, so instead I took a shower. I found a quilted dressing-gown with my initials in gilt cord on the breast pocket. It fitted well, but I thought those initials were farting higher than my arse-hole. I hadn't come here to swank around like a film star. As I was staring at these golden squiggles, they disappeared from before my eyes. I blinked and they were gone. The dressing-gown felt more comfortable with just a normal pocket.

The next day I woke up – and had another breakfast. It was as good as the previous three. Clearly the problem of breakfast had now been solved.

When Brigitta came to clear the tray, she murmured, 'Shopping?'

'Of course.' It was exactly what had been on my mind.

'Do you want to go shopping or stay shopping?'

'Go shopping,' I said, not really understanding the difference.

'Sure.'

My wife's brother once came back from ten days in Florida and said, 'When I die, I don't want to go to Heaven, I want to go shopping in America.' That second morning I began to understand what he meant.

When we got to the supermarket Brigitta asked me if I wanted to walk or drive. I said let's drive, that sounds fun – a reply which she seemed to expect. On reflection, some parts of her job must be quite boring – I mean, we probably all react in much the same way, don't we? Anyway, we drove. The shopping-carts are motorized wire-mesh trolleys that whizz around like dodgems, except that they never crash into one another because of some electric-eye device. Just when you think you're going to have a prang, you find yourself swerving round the oncoming cart. It's fun, that, trying to crash.

The system's easily mastered. You have a plastic card which you push into a slot next to the goods you want to buy, then punch in the quantity you want. After a second or two, your card is returned. Then the stuff is automatically delivered and credited.

I had a good time in my wire cart. I remember when I used to go shopping in the old days, the previous days, I'd sometimes see small kids sitting inside a trolley as if it were a cage and being pushed round by their parents; and I'd be envious. I wasn't any more. And boy, did I buy some stuff that morning! I practically cleaned them out of those pink grapefruit. That's what it felt like, anyway. I bought breakfast, I bought lunch, I bought dinner, I bought mid-morning snacks, afternoon teas, apéritif munchies, midnight feasts. I bought fruit I couldn't name, vegetables I'd never seen before, strange new cuts of meat from familiar animals, and familiar-looking cuts from animals I'd never eaten before. In the Australian section I found crocodile tail-steak, fillet of water-buffalo, *terrine de kangarou*. I bought them all. I plundered the gourmet cabinet. Freeze-dried lobster soufflé with cherry-chip topping: how could I resist something like that?

As for the drinks counter ... I had no idea so many different means of intoxification had been devised. I'm mainly a beer-and-spirits man myself, but I didn't want to seem prejudiced so I bought quite a few crates of wine and cocktails as well. The labels on the bottles were very helpful: they gave detailed instructions about how drunk the contents would make you, taking into consideration factors like sex, weight and body-fat. There was one brand of transparent alcohol with a very scruffy label. It was called Stinko-Paralytiko (made in Yugoslavia) and said on it: 'This bottle will make you drunker than you've ever been before.' Well, I had to take a case of that home, didn't I?

It was a good morning's work. It might have been the best morning's work there ever was. And don't look down your nose at me, by the way. You'd have done much the same yourself. I mean, say you didn't go shopping, what would you have done instead? Met some famous people, had sex, played golf? There aren't an infinite number of possibilities – that's one of the points to remember about it all, about this place and that place. And if I went shopping first, well, that's what people like me would do. I'm not looking down my nose if you'd have met famous people first, or had sex, or played golf. Anyway, I got round to all that in due course. As I say, we're not so very different.

When we got home I was ... not exactly tired – you don't get tired – just kind of sated. Those shopping carts were fun; I didn't think I'd ever bother to walk – in fact, come to think of it, I didn't see anyone walking at the supermarket. Then it was lunchtime, and Brigitta arrived with breakfast. Afterwards, I rook a nap. I expected to dream, because I always dream if I go to sleep in the afternoon. I didn't. I wondered why not.

Brigitta woke me with tea and the biscuits I'd chosen. They were currant biscuits especially designed for people like me. Now I don't know where you stand on this one, but all my life it's been a matter of complaint that they don't put enough currants in the currant biscuits. Obviously you don't want *too many* currants in a biscuit, otherwise you'd have just a wodge of currants rather

than a biscuit, but I've always believed that the proportion of
ingredients could be adjusted. Upwards, in favour of the currants,
naturally – say, to about fifty-fifty. And that's what these biscuits
were called, come to think of it: Fifty-Fifties. I bought three
thousand packets of them.

I opened the newspaper which Brigitta had thoughtfully
placed on the tray and almost spilt my tea. No, I did spill my
tea – only you don't worry about things like that any more.
It was front-page news. Well, it would have been, wouldn't it?
Leicester City had won the FA Cup. No kidding, Leicester City
had bloody well won the FA Cup! You wouldn't have believed it,
would you? Well, maybe *you* would, if you didn't know anything
about football. But *I* know a thing or two about football, and I've
supported Leicester City all my life, and *I* wouldn't have believed
it, that's the point. Don't get me wrong, I'm not running my
team down. They're a good team, a very good team sometimes,
yet they never seem to win the big ones. Second Division cham-
pions, as many times as you like to count, oh yes, but they've
never won the First Division. Runners-up, once, sure, no problem. And as for the Cup . . . it's a fact, an undeniable fact that in
all the time I've supported Leicester City (and for all the time
before that, too), they've never won the FA Cup. They've had a
very good post-war record in reaching the Final – and just as
good a one at not capturing the trophy. 1949, 1961, 1963, 1969,
those are the black years, and one or two of those defeats were
in my opinion particularly unlucky, indeed I'd single out . . . OK,
I can see you're not that interested in football. It doesn't matter,
as long as you grasp the central fact that Leicester City had never
won anything but peanuts before and now they had secured the
FA Cup for the first time in the club's history. The match was a
real thriller, too, according to the newspaper: City won 5–4 in
extra time after coming from behind on no fewer than four
occasions. What a performance! What a blend of skill and sheer
character! I was proud of the lads. Brigitta would get me the
video tomorrow, I was sure she could. In the meantime, I took
a little champagne with the breakfast I had for dinner.

The newspapers were great. In a way, it's the newspapers
I remember best. Leicester City won the FA Cup, as I may have
mentioned. They found a cure for cancer. My party won the
General Election every single time until everyone saw its ideas
were right and most of the opposition came over and joined us.

Little old ladies got rich on the pools every week. Sex offenders repented and were released back into society and led blameless lives. Airline pilots learned how to save planes from mid-air collisions. Everyone got rid of nuclear weapons. The England manager chose the whole Leicester City team *en bloc* to represent England in the World Cup and they came back with the Jules Rimet trophy (memorably beating Brazil 4–1 in the Final). When you read the paper, the newsprint didn't come off on your hands, and the stories didn't come off on your mind. Children were innocent creatures once more; men and women were nice to one another; nobody's teeth had to be filled; and women's tights never laddered.

What else did I do that first week? As I said, I played golf and had sex and met famous people and didn't feel bad once. Let me start with the golf. Now, I've never been much good at the game, but I used to enjoy hacking round a municipal course where the grass is like coconut matting and no one bothers to replace their divots because there are so many holes in the fairway you can't work out where your divot has come from anyway, Still, I'd seen most of the famous courses on television and I was curious to play – well, the golf of my dreams. And as soon as I felt the contact my driver made on that first tee and watched the ball howling off a couple of hundred yards, I knew I was in seventh heaven. My clubs seemed perfectly weighted to the touch; the fairways had a lush springiness and held the ball up for you like a waiter with a drinks tray; and my caddy (I'd never had a caddy before, but he treated me like Arnold Palmer) was full of useful advice, never pushy. The course seemed to have everything – streams and lakes and antique bridges, bits of seaside links like in Scotland, patches of flowering dogwood and azalea from Augusta, beechwood, pine, bracken and gorse. It was a difficult course, but one that gave you chances. I went round that sunny morning in 67, which was five under par, and twenty shots better than I'd ever done on the municipal course.

I was so pleased with my round that when I got back I asked Brigitta if she'd have sex with me. She said of course she'd love to, and found me very attractive, and though she'd only seen the top half she was pretty sure the rest would be in good working order too; there were a few slight problems like she was deeply in love with someone else, and her conditions of work stated that employees were fired for having sexual relations with new arrivals, and she had a slight heart condition which meant that any extra strain could be dangerous, but if I'd give her a couple of minutes she'd slip off and get into some sexy underwear right away. Well, I debated with myself for a while about the rights and wrongs of what I'd been proposing, and when she came back, all perfume and cleavage, I told her that on balance I thought we probably shouldn't go ahead. She was pretty disappointed and sat down opposite me and crossed her legs which was a pretty sight I can tell you, but I was adamant. It was only later – the next morning, in fact – that I realized *she* had been turning *me* down. I'd never been turned down in such a nice way before. They even make the bad things good here.

I had a magnum of champagne with my sturgeon and chips that night (you don't get hangovers here, either), and was slipping off to sleep with the memory of that crafty back-spin I'd achieved with my wedge at the sixteenth to hold the ball on the upper level of that two-tier green, when I felt the covers of the bed being lifted. At first I thought it was Brigitta and felt a bit bad what with her heart condition and losing her job and being in love with someone else, but when I put my arm around her and whispered 'Brigitta?' a voice whispered back, 'No, is not Brigitta' and the accent was different, all husky and foreign, and then other things made me realize it was not Brigitta, attractive lady in many ways though Brigitta was. What happened next – and by 'next' I do not imply a brief period of time – is, well, hard to describe. The best I can do is say that in the morning I had gone round in 67, which was five under par and twenty shots ahead of my previous best, and what followed that night was a comparable achievement. I am you understand reluctant to criticize my dear wife in this department; it's just that after some years, you know, and the kids, and being tired, well, you can't help dragging one another down. It's still nice, but you sort of do what's necessary, don't you? What I hadn't realized was that if a couple can drag one another down, another couple can drag one another up. Wow! I didn't know I could! I didn't know anyone could! Each of us seemed to know instinctively what the other one wanted. I'd never really come across that before. Not, you understand, that I wish to sound as if I'm criticizing my dear wife.

I expected to wake up feeling tired, but again it was more that sense of being pleasantly full, like after the shopping. Had

I dreamt what had happened? No: there were two long red hairs on my pillow to confirm the reality. Their colour also proved that my visitor had definitely not been Brigitta.

'Did you sleep well?' she asked with a bit of a cheeky smile as she brought my breakfast.

'It was altogether a good day,' I replied, perhaps a bit pompous, because I sort of guessed she knew. 'Except', I added quickly, 'for hearing about your heart condition. I'm really sorry about that.'

'Oh, I'll muddle through,' she said. 'The engine's good for another few thousand years.'

We went shopping (I wasn't yet so lazy I wanted to stay shopping), I read the newspaper, had lunch, played golf, tried to catch up on some reading with one of those Dickens videos, had sturgeon and chips, turned out the light and not long afterwards had sex. It was a good way to spend the day, almost perfect, it seemed to me, and I'd gone round in 67 again. If only I hadn't driven into the dogwoods on the eighteenth – I think I was just too pumped up – I could have marked a 66, or even a 65, on my card.

And so life continued, as the saying goes. For months, certainly – maybe longer; after a while you stop looking at the date on the newspaper. I realized it had been the right decision not to have sex with Brigitta. We became good friends.

'What happens', I asked her one day, 'when my wife arrives?' My dear wife, I should explain, was not with me at the time.

'I thought you might be worrying about that.'

'Oh, I'm not worrying about *that*,' I said, referring to my nightly visitor, because the whole thing was a bit like being a businessman on a foreign trip, I suppose, wasn't it? 'I meant, sort of generally.'

'There isn't any generally. It's up to you. And her.'

'Will she mind?' I asked, this time referring more definitely to my visitor.

'Will she know?'

'I think there are going to be problems,' I said, once again talking more generally.

'This is where problems are solved,' she replied.

'If you say so.' I was beginning to be convinced that it might all turn out as I hoped.

For instance, I'd always had this dream. Well, I don't mean dream exactly, I mean something I wanted a lot. A dream of being judged. No, that doesn't sound right, it sounds like I wanted to have my head chopped off by a guillotine or be whipped or something. Not like that. No, I wanted to be *judged*, do you see? It's what we all want, isn't it? I wanted, oh, some kind of summing-up, I wanted my life looked at. We don't get that, not unless we appear in court or are given the once-over by a psychiatrist, neither of which had come my way and I wasn't exactly disappointed, seeing as I wasn't a criminal or a nutter. No, I'm a normal person, and I just wanted what a lot of normal people want. I wanted my life looked at. Do you see?

I began to explain this one day to my friend Brigitta, not being sure I could put it any better than the above, but she immediately understood. She said it was a very popular request, it wouldn't be hard to fix. So a couple of days later I went along. I asked her to come with me for moral support, and she agreed.

It was just what I'd expected at first. There was a fancy old building with columns and lots of words in Latin or Greek or something carved along the top, and flunkeys in uniform, which made me glad I'd insisted on a new suit for the occasion. Inside, there was a huge staircase, one of those that divides in two and does a big circle in opposite directions and then meets itself again at the top. There was marble everywhere and freshly-polished brass and great stretches of mahogany that you knew would never get woodworm.

It wasn't a huge room, but that didn't matter. More to the point, it had the right sort of feel, formal but not too off-putting. It was almost cosy, with bits of old velvet looking rather tatty, except that serious things happened here. And he was a nice old gent, the one who did me. A bit like my dad – no, more like an uncle, I'd say. Sort of friendly eyes, looked you straight in the face; and you could tell he stood no nonsense. He'd read all my papers, he said. And there they were, at his elbow, the history of my life, everything I'd done and thought and said and felt, the whole bloody caboodle, the good bits and the bad. It made quite a pile, as you'd imagine. I wasn't sure I was allowed to address him but anyway I did. I said you're a quick reader and no mistake. He said he'd had a lot of training and we had a bit of a laugh at that. Then he took a squint at his watch – no, he did it quite politely – and asked me if I wanted my verdict. I found myself squaring my shoulders and putting my hands into fists at my side with the thumbs down the trouser seams. Then I nodded and said 'Yes, sir', and felt a bit nervous I don't mind telling you.

He said I was OK. No, I'm not kidding, that's exactly what he said: 'You're OK.' I sort of waited for him to go on but he dropped his eyes and I could see his hand moving to the top document on another file. Then he looked up, gave a little smile and said, 'No, really, you're OK.' I nodded again, and this time he really was going back to his work so I turned and left. When we got out I confessed to Brigitta I'd been a bit disappointed, and she said most people were but I wasn't to take it as any reflection on me, so I didn't.

It was about this time that I took to meeting famous people. At first I was a bit shy and only asked for film stars and sportsmen I admired. I met Steve McQueen, for instance, and Judy Garland; John Wayne, Maureen O'Sullivan, Humphrey Bogart, Gene Tierney (I always had this thing about Gene Tierney) and Bing Crosby. I met Duncan Edwards and the rest of the Man Utd players from the Munich air-crash. I met quite a few Leicester City lads from the early days, most of whose names would probably be unfamiliar to you.

After a while I realized I could meet anyone I liked. I met John F. Kennedy and Charlie Chaplin, Marilyn Monroe, President Eisenhower, Pope John XXIII, Winston Churchill, Rommel, Stalin, Mao Tse-tung, Roosevelt, General de Gaulle, Lindbergh, Shakespeare, Buddy Holly, Patsy Cline, Karl Marx, John Lennon and Queen Victoria. Most of them were very nice, on the whole, sort of natural, not at all grand or condescending. They were just like real people. I asked to meet Jesus Christ but they said they weren't sure about that so I didn't push it. I met Noah, but not surprisingly there was a bit of a language problem. Some people I just wanted to look at. Hitler, for instance, now there's a man I wouldn't shake the hand of, but they arranged that I could hide behind some bushes while he just walked past, in his nasty uniform, large as life.

Guess what happened next? I started worrying. I worried about the most ridiculous things. Like my health, for instance. Isn't that crazy? Maybe it was something to do with Brigitta telling me about her heart condition, but I suddenly began to imagine things going wrong with me. Who'd have credited it? I came over all faddy and diet-conscious; I got a rowing machine and an exercise bicycle, I worked out with weights; I kept off salt and sugar, animal fats and cream cakes; I even cut down my intake of Fifty-Fifties to half a packet a day. I also had spells of worrying about my hairline, my supermarket driving (were the trolleys that safe?), my sexual performance and my bank balance. Why was I worrying about my bank balance when I didn't even have a bank? I imagined my card not working at the supermarket, I felt guilty at the amount of credit I seemed to be given. What had I done to deserve it?

Most of the time, of course, I was fine, what with the shopping, the golf, the sex and the meeting famous people. But every so often I'd think, what if I can't make it round the 18 holes? What if I can't really afford my Fifty-Fifties? Finally, I confessed these thoughts to Brigitta. She thought it time I was passed on to other hands. Brigitta's work was done, she indicated. I felt sad, and asked what I could buy her to show my gratitude. She said she had everything she needed. I tried writing a poem, because Brigitta rhymes with sweeter, but after that I could only find neater and eat her, so I sort of gave up, and in any case I thought she'd probably been given poems like that before.

Margaret was to look after me next. She looked more serious than Brigitta, all smart suits and not a hair out of place – the sort of person who's a finalist in those Businesswomen of the Year competitions. I was a bit scared of her – I certainly couldn't imagine myself suggesting sex like I did to Brigitta – and I half expected her to disapprove of the way of life I'd been leading. But she didn't, of course. No, she just said that she assumed I was pretty familiar by now with the amenities, and that she would be there if I needed more than mere practical assistance.

'Tell me something,' I asked her on our first meeting. 'It's silly to be worrying about my health, isn't it?'

'Quite unnecessary.'

'And it's silly to worry about money?'

'Quite unnecessary,' she replied.

Something in her tone implied that if I cared to look, I could probably find things that were worth worrying about; I didn't pursue this. I had plenty of time ahead of me. Time was something I would never be short of.

Now, I'm probably not the quickest thinker in the world, and in my previous life I tended to just get on with the things I had to do, or wanted to do, and not brood too much about them. That's normal, isn't it? But give anyone enough time and they'll get somewhere with their thoughts and start asking a few of the bigger questions. For instance, who actually ran this place, and why had I seen so little of them? I'd assumed there might be a sort of entrance examination, or perhaps continual assessment; yet apart from that frankly rather disappointing bit of judging by the old codger who said I was OK, I hadn't been bothered. They let me bunk off every day and improve my golf. Was I allowed to take everything for granted? Did they expect something from me?

Then there was that Hitler business. You waited behind a bush and he strolled past, a stocky figure in a nasty uniform with a false smile on his face. Fair enough, I'd seen him now, and my curiosity was satisfied, but, well, I had to ask myself, what was he doing here in the first place? Did he order breakfast like everybody else? I'd already observed that he was allowed to wear his own clothes. Did this mean he could also play golf and have sex if he wanted to? How did this thing operate?

Then there was me worrying about my health and money and the supermarket driving. I wasn't worrying about them in themselves any more, I was worrying about the fact that I'd been worrying. What was all that about? Was it more than a routine adjustment problem as Brigitta had suggested?

I think it was the golf that finally made me turn to Margaret for some explanations. There was no doubt about it, over the months and years I played that lovely, lush course with its little tricks and temptations (how many times I put the ball in the water at the short eleventh!), my game improved no end. I said as much one day to Severiano, my regular caddy: 'My game has improved no end.' He agreed, and it was not until later, between dinner and sex, that I began to reflect on what I'd said. I had opened up on the course with a 67, and gradually my score was coming down. A while ago I was shooting a regular 59, and now, under cloudless skies, I was inching down to the low 50s. I could drive 350 yards without trouble, my pitching was transformed, my putts rattled into the hole as if drawn by a magnet. I could see my target score coming down through the 40s, then – a key psychological moment this – breaking the barrier of 36, that's to say two strokes a hole average, then coming down through the 20s. *My game has improved no end*, I thought, and repeated the words *no end* to myself. But that's, of course, exactly what it couldn't do: there had to be an end to my improvement. One day I would play a round of golf in 18 shots, I'd buy Severiano a couple of drinks, celebrate later with sturgeon and chips and sex

– and then what? Had anyone, even here, ever played a golf course in 17 shots?

Margaret didn't answer a tasselled bell-pull like the blonde Brigitta; in fact, you had to apply by videophone for an interview.

'I'm worried about the golf,' I began.

'That's not really my speciality.'

'No. You see, when I first arrived I shot a 67. Now I'm down to the low 50s.'

'That doesn't sound like a problem.'

'And I'm going to go on getting better.'

'Congratulations.'

'And then one day I'll finally do the course in 18 shots.'

'Your ambition is admirable.' She sounded as if she was making fun of me.

'But then what do I do?'

She paused. 'Try going round every time in 18 shots?'

'It doesn't work like that.'

'Why not?'

'It just doesn't.'

'I'm sure there are many other courses . . .'

'Same problem,' I said, interrupting her, a bit rudely I suppose.

'Well, you could switch to another sport, couldn't you? Then come back to golf when you're tired of the other one?'

'But the problem's the same. I'd have done the course in 18 shots. Golf would be used up.'

'There are lots of other sports.'

'They'd get used up too.'

'What do you have for breakfast every morning?' I'm sure she knew the answer already from the way she nodded when I told her. 'You see. You have the same every morning. You don't get tired of breakfast.'

'No.'

'Well, think about golf as you do about breakfast. Perhaps you'll never get tired of going round in 18 shots.'

'Perhaps,' I said dubiously. 'It sounds to me as if you haven't ever played golf. And anyway, that's another thing.'

'What is?'

'The getting tired. You don't get tired here.'

'Is that a complaint?'

'I don't know.'

'Tiredness can be arranged.'

'Sure,' I replied. 'But I bet it'd be a sort of pleasant tiredness. Not one of those knackering tirednesses which just make you want to die.'

'Don't you think you're being perverse?' She was crisp, almost impatient. 'What did you want? What did you hope for?'

I nodded to myself, and we called it a day. My life continued. That was another phrase that made me grin a bit. My life continued, and my golf improved no end. I did all sorts of other things:

- I went on several cruises;
- I learned canoeing, mountaineering, ballooning;
- I got into all sorts of danger and escaped;
- I explored the Jungle;
- I watched a court case (didn't agree with the verdict);
- I tried being a painter (not as bad as I thought!) and a surgeon;
- I fell in love, of course, lots of times;
- I pretended I was the last person on earth (and the first).

None of this meant that I stopped doing what I'd always done since I got here. I had sex with an increasing number of women, sometimes simultaneously; I ate rarer and stranger foods; I met famous people all the way to the edges of my memory. For instance, I met every footballer there ever was. I started with the famous ones, then the ones I admired but weren't particularly famous, then the average ones, then the ones whose names I remembered without remembering what they looked like or played like; finally I asked for the only ones I hadn't met, the nasty, boring, violent players that I didn't admire at all. I didn't enjoy meeting them – they were just as nasty, boring and violent off the pitch as on – but I didn't want to run out of footballers. Then I ran out of footballers. I asked to see Margaret again.

'I've met all the footballers,' I said.

'I'm afraid I don't know much about football, either.'

'And I don't have any dreams,' I added, in a tone of complaint.

'What would they be for,' she replied. 'What *would* they be for?'

I sensed that in a way she was testing me, seeing how serious I was. Did it all add up to more than a mere adjustment problem?

'I think I'm owed an explanation,' I announced – a little pompously, I have to admit.

'Ask anything you like.' She settled back in her office chair.

'Look, I want to get things straight.'

'An admirable ambition.' She talked a bit posh, like that.

I thought I'd better start at the beginning. 'Look, this is Heaven, isn't it?'

'Oh yes.'

'Well, what about Sundays?'

'I don't follow you.'

'On Sundays,' I said, 'as far as I can work out, because I don't follow the days too closely any more, I play golf, go shopping, eat dinner, have sex and don't feel bad.'

'Isn't that . . . perfect?'

'I don't want to sound ungrateful,' I said cautiously, 'but where's God?'

'God. Do you want God? Is that what you want?'

'Is it a question of what I want?'

'That's exactly what it's a question of. Do you want God?'

'I suppose I thought it wasn't that way round. I suppose I thought either there would be one or there wouldn't be one. I'd find out what the case was. I didn't think it depended on me in any way.'

'Of course it does.'

'Oh.'

'Heaven is democratic these days,' she said. Then added, 'Or at least, it is if you want it to be.'

'What do you mean, democratic?'

'We don't impose Heaven on people any more,' she said. 'We listen to their needs. If they want it, they can have it; if not, not. And then of course they get the sort of Heaven they want.'

'And what sort do they want on the whole?'

'Well, they want a continuation of life, that's what we find. But . . . better, needless to say.'

'Sex, golf, shopping, dinner, meeting famous people and not feeling bad?' I asked, a bit defensively.

'It varies. But if I were being honest, I'd say that it doesn't vary all that much.'

'Not like the old days.'

'Ah, the old days.' She smiled. 'That was before my time, of course, but yes, dreams of Heaven used to be a lot more ambitious.'

'And Hell?' I asked.

'What about it?'

'Is there Hell?'

'Oh no,' she replied. 'That was just necessary propaganda.'

'I was wondering, you see. Because I met Hitler.'

'Lots of people do. He's a sort of . . . tourist site, really. What did you make of him?'

'Oh, I didn't *meet* him,' I said firmly. 'He's a man I wouldn't shake the hand of. I watched him go by from behind the bushes.'

'Ah, yes. Quite a lot of people prefer to do it that way.'

'So I thought, if he's here, there can't be Hell.'

'A reasonable deduction.'

'Just out of interest,' I said, 'what does *he* do all day?' I imagined him going to the 1936 Berlin Olympics every afternoon, watching the Germans win everything while Jesse Owens fell over, then back for some sauerkraut, Wagner and a romp with a busty blonde of pure Aryan blood.

'I'm afraid we do respect people's confidentiality.'

'Naturally.' That was right. I wouldn't want everyone knowing what I got up to, come to think of it.

'So there isn't any Hell?'

'Well, there's something we *call* Hell. But it's more like a theme park. You know, skeletons popping out and frightening you, branches in your face, stink bombs, that sort of thing. Just to give you a good scare.'

'A good scare,' I remarked, 'as opposed to a bad scare?'

'Exactly. We find that's all people want nowadays.'

'Do you know about Heaven in the old days?'

'What, Old Heaven? Yes, we know about Old Heaven. It's in the records.'

'What happened to it?'

'Oh, it sort of closed down. People didn't want it any more. People didn't need it any more.'

'But I knew a few people who went to church, had their babies christened, didn't use rude words. What about them?'

'Oh, we get those,' she said. 'They're catered for. They pray and give thanks rather as you play golf and have sex. They seem to enjoy themselves, to have got what they wanted. We've built them some very nice churches.'

'Does God exist for them?' I asked.

'Oh, surely.'

'But not for me?'

'It doesn't seem so. Unless you want to change your requirements of Heaven. I can't deal with that myself. I could refer you.'

'I've probably got enough to think about for the moment.'

'Fine. Well, until the next time.'

I slept badly that night. My mind wasn't on the sex, even though they all did their very best. Was it indigestion? Had I bolted my sturgeon? There I was, worrying about my health again.

The next morning I shot a 67 on the golf course. My caddy Severiano reacted as if it was the best round he'd seen me play, as if he didn't know I could do 20 shots better. Afterwards, I asked for certain directions, and drove towards the only visible patch of bad weather. As I'd expected, Hell was a great disappointment: the thunderstorm in the car-park was probably the best bit. There were out-of-work actors prodding other out-of-work actors with long forks, pushing them into vats labelled 'Boiling Oil'. Phoney animals with strap-on plastic beaks pecked at foam-rubber corpses. I saw Hitler riding on the Ghost Train with his arm round a Mädchen with pigtails. There were bats and creaking coffin lids and a smell of rotting floorboards. Is that what people wanted?

'Tell me about Old Heaven,' I said to Margaret the following week.

'It was much like your accounts of it. I mean, that's the principle of Heaven, that you get what you want, what you expect. I know some people imagine it's different, that you get what you deserve, but that's never been the case. We have to disabuse them.'

'Are they annoyed?'

'Mostly not. People prefer to get what they want rather than what they deserve. Though some of them did get a little irritated that others weren't sufficiently maltreated. Part of their expectation of Heaven seemed to be that other people would go to Hell. Not very Christian.'

'And were they . . . disembodied? Was it all spirit life and so on?'

'Yes indeed. That's what they wanted. Or at any rate, in certain epochs. There has been a lot of fluctuation over the centuries about decorporealization. At the moment, for instance, there's quite an emphasis on retaining your own body and your own personality. This may just prove a phase, like any other.'

'What are you smiling for?' I asked. I was rather surprised.

I thought Margaret was there just to give information, like Brigitta. Yet she obviously had her own opinions, and didn't mind telling you them.

'Only because it sometimes seems odd how tenaciously people want to stick with their own bodies. Of course, they occasionally ask for minor surgery. But it's as if, say, a different nose or a tuck in the cheek or a handful of silicone is all that stands between them and their perfect idea of themselves.'

'What happened to Old Heaven?'

'Oh, it survived for a while, after the new Heavens were built. But there was increasingly little call for it. People seemed keener on the new Heavens. It wasn't all that surprising. We take the long view here.'

'What happened to the Old Heaveners?'

Margaret shrugged, rather complacently, like some corporate planner whose predictions had been borne out to the tiniest decimal point. 'They died off.'

'Just like that? You mean, you closed down their Heaven and so they died off?'

'No, not at all, on the contrary. That's not how it works. Constitutionally, there would have been an Old Heaven for as long as the Old Heaveners wanted it.'

'Are there any Old Heaveners around?'

'I think there are a few left.'

'Can I meet one?'

'They don't take visits, I'm afraid. They used to. But the New Heaveners tended to behave as if they were at a freak-show, kept pointing and asking silly questions. So the Old Heaveners declined to meet them any more. They gave up speaking to anyone but other Old Heaveners. Then they began to die off. Now there aren't many left. We have them tagged, of course.'

'Are they disembodied?'

'Some of them are, some of them aren't. It depends on the sect. Of course the ones that are disembodied don't have much trouble avoiding the New Heaveners.'

Well, that made sense. In fact, it all made sense except for the main thing. 'And what do you mean, the others died off?'

'Everyone has the option to die off if they want to.'

'I never knew that.'

'No. There are bound to be a few surprises. Did you really want to be able to predict it all?'

'And how do they die? Do they kill themselves? Do you kill them?'

Margaret looked a bit shocked at the crassness of my idea. 'Goodness, no. As I said, it's democratic nowadays. If you want to die off, you do. You just have to want to for long enough and that's it, it happens. Death isn't a matter of hazard or gloomy inevitability, the way it is the first time round. We've got free will sorted out here, as you may have noticed.'

I wasn't sure I was taking all this in. I'd have to go away and think about it. 'Tell me,' I said, 'these problems I've been having with the golf and the worrying. Do other people react like that?'

'Oh yes. We often get people asking for bad weather, for instance, or for something to go wrong. They miss things going wrong. Some of them ask for pain.'

'For pain?'

'Certainly. Well, you were complaining the other day about not feeling so tired that – as I think you put it – you just want to die. I thought that was an interesting phrase. People ask for pain, it's not so extraordinary. We've had them requesting operations, as well. I mean, not just cosmetic ones, real ones.'

'Do they get them?'

'Only if they really insist. We try to suggest that wanting an operation is really a sign of something else. Normally they agree with us.'

'And what percentage of people take up the option to die off?'

She looked at me levelly, her glance telling me to be calm. 'Oh, a hundred per cent, of course. Over many thousands of years, calculated by old time, of course. But yes, everyone takes the option, sooner or later.'

'So it's just like the first time round? You always die in the end?'

'Yes, except don't forget the quality of life here is much better. People die when they decide they've had enough, not before. The second time round it's altogether more satisfying because it's willed.' She paused, then added, 'As I say, we cater for what people want.'

I hadn't been blaming her. I'm not that sort. I just wanted to find out how the system worked. 'So . . . even people, religious people, who come here to worship God throughout eternity . . . they end up throwing in the towel after a few years, hundred years, thousand years?'

'Certainly. As I said, there are still a few Old Heaveners around, but their numbers are diminishing all the time.'

'And who asks for death soonest?'

'I think *ask* is the wrong word. It's something you want. There aren't any mistakes here. If you want it enough, you die, that's always been the ruling principle.'

'So?'

'So. Well, I'm afraid – to answer your question – that the people who ask for death earliest are a bit like you. People who want an eternity of sex, beer, drugs, fast cars – that sort of thing. They can't believe their good luck at first, and then, a few hundred years later, they can't believe their bad luck. That's the sort of people they are, they realize. They're stuck with being themselves. Millennia after millennia of being themselves. They tend to die off soonest.'

'I never take drugs,' I said firmly. I was rather miffed. 'And I've only got seven cars. That's not very many around here. And I don't even drive them fast.'

'No, of course not. I was just thinking in general categories of gratification, you understand.'

'And who lasts longest?'

'Well, some of those Old Heaveners were fairly tenacious customers. Worship kept them going for ages and ages. Nowadays ... lawyers last quite well. They love going over their old cases, and then going over everybody else's. That can take for ever. Metaphorically speaking,' she added quickly. 'And scholarly people, they tend to last as long as anyone. They like sitting around reading all the books there are. And then they love arguing about them. Some of those arguments' – she cast an eye to the heavens – 'go on for millennium after millennium. It just seems to keep them young, for some reason, arguing about books.'

'What about the people who write the books?'

'Oh, they don't last half as long as the people who argue about them. It's the same with painters and composers. They somehow know when they've done their best work, and then they sort of fade away.'

I thought I should be feeling depressed, but I wasn't. 'Shouldn't I be feeling depressed?'

'Of course not. You're here to enjoy yourself. You've got what you wanted.'

'Yes, I suppose so. Maybe I can't get used to the idea that at some point I'll want to die.'

'Give it time,' she said, brisk but friendly. 'Give it time.'

'By the way, one last question' – I could see her fiddling with her pencils, straightening them into a row – 'Who exactly are you?'

'Us? Oh, we're remarkably like you. We could be you, in fact. Perhaps we are you.'

'I'll come back again if I may,' I said.

For the next few centuries – it may have been longer, I stopped counting in old time – I worked seriously on my golf. After a while I was going round in 18 shots every time and my caddy's astonishment became routine. I gave up golf and took up tennis. Pretty soon I'd beaten all the greats from the Hall of Fame on shale, clay, grass, wood, concrete, carpet – any surface they chose. I gave up tennis. I played for Leicester City in the Cup Final and came away with a winner's medal (my third goal, a power header from twelve yards out, clinched the match). I flattened Rocky Marciano in the fourth round at Madison Square Garden (and I carried him a bit the last round or two), got the marathon record down to 28 minutes, won the world darts; my innings of 750 runs in the one-day international against Australia at Lords won't be surpassed for some time. After a while, Olympic gold medals began to feel like small change. I gave up sport.

I went shopping seriously. I ate more creatures than had ever sailed on Noah's Ark. I drank every beer in the world and then some, became a wine connoisseur and despatched the finest vintages ever harvested; they ran out too soon. I met loads of famous people. I had sex with an increasing variety of partners in an increasing variety of ways, but there are only so many part-ners and so many ways. Don't get me wrong, incidentally: I'm not complaining. I enjoyed every bloody minute of it. All I'm saying is, I knew what I was doing while I was doing it. I was looking for a way out.

I tried combining pleasures and started having sex with famous people (no, I won't tell you who – they asked me to respect their privacy). I even took up reading. I remembered what Margaret said and tried – oh, for a few centuries or so – arguing about books with other people who'd read the same books. But it seemed a pretty arid life, at least compared to life itself, and not one worth prolonging. I even tried joining the people who sang and prayed in church, but that wasn't really my thing. I only did it because I wanted to cover all the angles before I had what I knew would be my final talk with Margaret. She looked much as she had done several millennia earlier when we'd first met; but then, so did I.

'I've had an idea,' I said. Well, you're bound to come up with something after all that time, aren't you? 'Listen, if you get what you want in Heaven, then what about wanting to be someone who never gets tired of eternity?' I sat back, feeling a touch smug. To my surprise she nodded, almost encouragingly.

'You're welcome to have a go,' she said. 'I could get you the transfer.'

'But . . . ?' I asked, knowing that there would be a *but*.

'I'll get you the transfer,' she repeated. 'It's just a formality.'

'Tell me the *but* first.' I didn't want to sound rude. On the other hand I didn't want to spend several millennia pissing about if I could be saved the time.

'People have tried it already,' Margaret said, in a clearly sympathetic tone, as if she really didn't want to hurt me.

'And what's the problem? What's the *but*?'

'Well, there seems to be a logical difficulty. You can't become someone else without stopping being who you are. Nobody can bear that. It's what we find, anyway,' she added, half implying that I might be the first person to crack this problem. 'Someone – someone who must have been keen on sports, like you, said that it was changing from being a runner to being a perpetual motion machine. After a while you simply want to run again. Does that make sense?'

I nodded. 'And everyone who's tried it has asked for a transfer back?'

'Yes.'

'And afterwards they all took the option to die off?'

'They did. And sooner rather than later. There might still be a few of them around. I could call them in if you want to ask them about it.'

'I'll take your word for it. I thought there must be a snag in my idea.'

'Sorry.'

'No, please don't apologize.' I certainly couldn't complain about the way I'd been treated. Everyone had been level with me from the start. I took a deep breath. 'It seems to me,' I went on, 'that Heaven's a very good idea, it's a perfect idea you could say, but not for us. Not given the way we are.'

'We don't like to influence conclusions,' she said. 'However, I can certainly see your point of view.'

'So what's it all for? Why do we have Heaven? Why do we have these dreams of Heaven?' She didn't seem willing to answer, perhaps she was being professional; but I pressed her. 'Go on, give me some ideas.'

'Perhaps because you need them,' she suggested. 'Because you can't get by without the dream. It's nothing to be ashamed of. It seems quite normal to me. Though I suppose if you knew about Heaven beforehand, you might not ask for it.'

'Oh, I don't know about that.' It had all been very pleasant: the shopping, the golf, the sex, the meeting famous people, the not feeling bad, the not being dead.

'After a while, getting what you want all the time is very close to not getting what you want all the time.'

The next day, for old times' sake, I played another round of golf. I wasn't at all rusty: eighteen holes, eighteen strokes. I hadn't lost my touch. Then I had breakfast for lunch and breakfast for dinner. I watched my video of Leicester City's 5–4 victory in the Cup Final, though it wasn't the same, knowing what happened. I had a cup of hot chocolate with Brigitta, who kindly looked in to see me; later I had sex, though only with one woman. Afterwards, I sighed and rolled over, knowing that the next morning I would begin to make my decision.

I dreamt that I woke up. It's the oldest dream of all, and I've just had it.

Author's Note

Chapter 3 is based on legal procedures and actual cases described in *The Criminal Prosecution and Capital Punishment of Animals* by E. P. Evans (1906). The first part of Chapter 5 draws its facts and language from the 1818 London translation of Savigny and Corréard's *Narrative of a Voyage to Senegal*; the second part relies heavily on Lorenz Eitner's exemplary *Géricault: His Life and Work* (Orbis, 1982). The third part of Chapter 7 takes its facts from *The Voyage of the Damned* by Gordon Thomas and Max Morgan-Witts (Hodder, 1974). I am grateful to Rebecca John for much help with research; to Anita Brookner and Howard Hodgkin for vetting my art history; to Rick Chiles and Jay McInerney for inspecting my American; to Dr Jacky Davis for surgical assistance; to Alan Howard, Galen Strawson and Redmond O'Hanlon; and to Hermione Lee.

J. B.

ABOUT THE INTRODUCER

SARAH CHURCHWELL is Professor of American Literature and Public Understanding of the Humanities at the University of East Anglia. She is the author of *The Many Lives of Marilyn Monroe*, and her new book, *Careless People* (about Scott Fitzgerald and *The Great Gatsby*), will appear in 2013. She writes regularly for the *New Statesman*, the *Guardian*, the *TLS*, and other newspapers.

CHINUA ACHEBE
The African Trilogy
Things Fall Apart

AESCHYLUS
The Oresteia

ISABEL ALLENDE
The House of the Spirits

ISAAC ASIMOV
Foundation
Foundation and Empire
Second Foundation
(in 1 vol.)

MARGARET ATWOOD
The Handmaid's Tale

JOHN JAMES AUDUBON
The Audubon Reader

AUGUSTINE
The Confessions

JANE AUSTEN
Emma
Mansfield Park
Northanger Abbey
Persuasion
Pride and Prejudice
Sanditon and Other Stories
Sense and Sensibility

HONORÉ DE BALZAC
Cousin Bette
Eugénie Grandet
Old Goriot

JULIAN BARNES
Flaubert's Parrot
A History of the World in
10½ Chapters (in 1 vol.)

GIORGIO BASSANI
The Garden of the Finzi-Continis

SIMONE DE BEAUVOIR
The Second Sex

SAMUEL BECKETT
Molloy, Malone Dies,
The Unnamable
(US only)

SAUL BELLOW
The Adventures of Augie March

HECTOR BERLIOZ
The Memoirs of Hector Berlioz

THE BIBLE
(King James Version)
The Old Testament
The New Testament

WILLIAM BLAKE
Poems and Prophecies

GIOVANNI BOCCACCIO
Decameron

JORGE LUIS BORGES
Ficciones

JAMES BOSWELL
The Life of Samuel Johnson
The Journal of a Tour to
the Hebrides

RAY BRADBURY
The Stories of Ray Bradbury

JEAN ANTHELME
BRILLAT-SAVARIN
The Physiology of Taste

ANNE BRONTË
Agnes Grey and The Tenant of
Wildfell Hall

CHARLOTTE BRONTË
Jane Eyre
Villette
Shirley and The Professor

EMILY BRONTË
Wuthering Heights

MIKHAIL BULGAKOV
The Master and Margarita

SAMUEL BUTLER
The Way of all Flesh

JAMES M. CAIN
The Postman Always Rings Twice
Double Indemnity
Mildred Pierce
Selected Stories
(in 1 vol. US only)

ITALO CALVINO
If on a winter's night a traveler

ALBERT CAMUS
The Outsider (UK)
The Stranger (US)
The Plague, The Fall,
Exile and the Kingdom,
and Selected Essays (in 1 vol.)

ANTHONY TROLLOPE
Barchester Towers
Can You Forgive Her?
Doctor Thorne
The Eustace Diamonds
Framley Parsonage
The Last Chronicle of Barset
Phineas Finn
The Small House at Allington
The Warden

IVAN TURGENEV
Fathers and Children
First Love and Other Stories
A Sportsman's Notebook

MARK TWAIN
Tom Sawyer
and Huckleberry Finn

JOHN UPDIKE
The Complete Henry Bech
Rabbit Angstrom

GIORGIO VASARI
Lives of the Painters, Sculptors and
Architects (in 2 vols)

VIRGIL
The Aeneid

VOLTAIRE
Candide and Other Stories

EVELYN WAUGH
(US only)
Black Mischief, Scoop, The Loved
One, The Ordeal of Gilbert
Pinfold (in 1 vol.)
Brideshead Revisited
Decline and Fall
A Handful of Dust
The Sword of Honour Trilogy
Waugh Abroad: Collected Travel
Writing
(UK & US)
The Complete Short Stories

H. G. WELLS
The Time Machine,
The Invisible Man,
The War of the Worlds
(in 1 vol., US only)

EDITH WHARTON
The Age of Innocence
The Custom of the Country
Ethan Frome, Summer,
Bunner Sisters
(in 1 vol.)
The House of Mirth
The Reef

PATRICK WHITE
Voss

OSCAR WILDE
Plays, Prose Writings and Poems

P. G. WODEHOUSE
The Best of Wodehouse

MARY WOLLSTONECRAFT
A Vindication of the Rights of
Woman

VIRGINIA WOOLF
To the Lighthouse
Mrs Dalloway

WILLIAM WORDSWORTH
Selected Poems (UK only)

RICHARD YATES
Revolutionary Road
The Easter Parade
Eleven Kinds of Loneliness
(in 1 vol.)

W. B. YEATS
The Poems (UK only)

ÉMILE ZOLA
Germinal

This book is set in BEMBO which was cut
by the punch-cutter Francesco Griffo
for the Venetian printer-publisher
Aldus Manutius in early 1495
and first used in a pamphlet
by a young scholar
named Pietro
Bembo.